Praise for the novels of
#1 *New York Times* bestselling author
Debbie Macomber

"Prolific Macomber is known for her portrayals of ordinary women in small-town America. [She is] an icon of the genre."

—*Publishers Weekly*

"It's clear that Debbie Macomber cares deeply about her fully realized characters and their families, friends and loves, along with their hopes and dreams. She also makes her readers care about them."

—*Bookreporter.com*

"Readers won't be able to get enough of Macomber's gentle storytelling."

—*RT Book Reviews*

"Debbie Macomber tells women's stories in a way no one else does."

—*BookPage*

"Debbie Macomber is one of the most reliable, versatile romance writers around."

—*Milwaukee Journal Sentinel*

"Debbie Macomber writes characters who are as warm and funny as your best friends."

—*New York Times* bestselling author Susan Wiggs

DEBBIE MACOMBER

Orchard Valley Brides

mira

mira

ISBN-13: 978-0-7783-3021-9

Recycling programs
for this product may
not exist in your area.

Orchard Valley Brides

Copyright © 2010 by Harlequin Books S.A.

The publisher acknowledges the copyright holder of the
individual works as follows:

Norah
Copyright © 1992 by Debbie Macomber

Lone Star Lovin'
Copyright © 1993 by Debbie Macomber

For questions and comments about the quality of this book, please contact us at
CustomerService@Harlequin.com.

www.Harlequin.com

Printed in U.S.A.

Also by Debbie Macomber

Blossom Street

The Shop on Blossom Street
A Good Yarn
Susannah's Garden
Back on Blossom Street
Twenty Wishes
Summer on Blossom Street
Hannah's List
The Knitting Diaries
  "The Twenty-First Wish"
A Turn in the Road

Cedar Cove

16 Lighthouse Road
204 Rosewood Lane
311 Pelican Court
44 Cranberry Point
50 Harbor Street
6 Rainier Drive
74 Seaside Avenue
8 Sandpiper Way
92 Pacific Boulevard
1022 Evergreen Place
Christmas in Cedar Cove
  (*5-B Poppy Lane* and
  A Cedar Cove Christmas)
1105 Yakima Street
1225 Christmas Tree Lane

The Dakota Series

Dakota Born
Dakota Home
Always Dakota
Buffalo Valley

The Manning Family

The Manning Sisters
  (*The Cowboy's Lady* and
  The Sheriff Takes a Wife)

The Manning Brides
  (*Marriage of Inconvenience* and
  Stand-In Wife)
The Manning Grooms
  (*Bride on the Loose* and
  Same Time, Next Year)

Christmas Books

A Gift to Last
On a Snowy Night
Home for the Holidays
Glad Tidings
Christmas Wishes
Small Town Christmas
When Christmas Comes
  (now retitled *Trading
  Christmas*)
*There's Something About
  Christmas*
Christmas Letters
The Perfect Christmas
Choir of Angels
  (*Shirley, Goodness and Mercy*,
  Those Christmas Angels and
  Where Angels Go)
Call Me Mrs. Miracle

Heart of Texas

VOLUME 1
  (*Lonesome Cowboy* and
  Texas Two-Step)
VOLUME 2
  (*Caroline's Child* and
  Dr. Texas)
VOLUME 3
  (*Nell's Cowboy* and
  Lone Star Baby)
Promise, Texas
Return to Promise

Midnight Sons

Alaska Skies
  (*Brides for Brothers* and
  The Marriage Risk)
Alaska Nights
  (*Daddy's Little Helper* and
  Because of the Baby)
Alaska Home
  (*Falling for Him,*
  Ending in Marriage and
  Midnight Sons and Daughters)

This Matter of Marriage
Montana
Thursdays at Eight
Between Friends
Changing Habits
Married in Seattle
  (*First Comes Marriage* and
  Wanted: Perfect Partner)
Right Next Door
  (*Father's Day* and
  The Courtship of Carol Sommars)
Wyoming Brides
  (*Denim and Diamonds* and
  The Wyoming Kid)
Fairy Tale Weddings
  (*Cindy and the Prince* and
  Some Kind of Wonderful)
The Man You'll Marry
  (*The First Man You Meet* and
  The Man You'll Marry)
Orchard Valley Grooms
  (*Valerie* and *Stephanie*)
Orchard Valley Brides
  (*Norah* and *Lone Star Lovin'*)
The Sooner the Better
An Engagement in Seattle
  (*Groom Wanted* and
  Bride Wanted)
Out of the Rain
  (*Marriage Wanted* and
  Laughter in the Rain)
Learning to Love
  (*Sugar and Spice* and *Love by Degree*)

You...Again
  (*Baby Blessed* and
  Yesterday Once More)
The Unexpected Husband
  (*Jury of His Peers* and
  Any Sunday)
Three Brides, No Groom
Love in Plain Sight
  (*Love 'n' Marriage* and
  Almost an Angel)
I Left My Heart
  (*A Friend or Two* and
  No Competition)
Marriage Between Friends
  (*White Lace and Promises* and
  Friends—And Then Some)
A Man's Heart
  (*The Way to a Man's Heart*
  and *Hasty Wedding*)
North to Alaska
  (*That Wintry Feeling* and
  Borrowed Dreams)
On a Clear Day
  (*Starlight* and
  Promise Me Forever)
To Love and Protect
  (*Shadow Chasing* and
  For All My Tomorrows)
Home in Seattle
  (*The Playboy and the Widow*
  and *Fallen Angel*)
Together Again
  (*The Trouble with Caasi* and
  Reflections of Yesterday)
The Reluctant Groom
  (*All Things Considered*
  and *Almost Paradise*)
A Real Prince
  (*The Bachelor Prince*
  and *Yesterday's Hero*)
Private Paradise
  (in *That Summer Place*)

Debbie Macomber's
  Cedar Cove Cookbook
Debbie Macomber's
  Christmas Cookbook

CONTENTS

NORAH   9

LONE STAR LOVIN'   195

NORAH

To my three precious granddaughters,
Jazmine, Bailey and Maddy.

One

This cowboy was too young to die!

Norah Bloomfield stared down at the unconscious face of the man in Orchard Valley Hospital's emergency room. He was suffering from shock, internal injuries and a compound fracture of the right fibula. Yet he was probably the luckiest man she'd ever known. He'd survived.

The team of doctors worked vigorously over him, doing everything possible to keep him alive. Although she was busy performing her own role in this drama, Norah was curious. It wasn't every day a man literally fell out of the sky into their backyard. Whoever he was, he'd been involved in a plane accident. From what she heard when they'd rushed him in, he'd made a gallant effort to land the single-engine Cessna in a wheatfield, but the plane's wingtip had caught the ground, catapulting it into a series of cartwheels. That he'd managed to crawl out of the wreckage was a miracle all its own.

She tightened the blood-pressure cuff around his arm and called out the latest reading. Dr. Adamson, the surgeon in attendance, briskly instructed her to administer a shot.

Their patient was young, in his early thirties. And handsome in a rugged sort of way. Dark hair, chiseled jaw, stubborn as a mule from the looks of him. His clothes, at least what was left of them, told her he was probably a cowboy. She suspected he rode in the rodeo circuit—successfully, too, if he was flying his own plane.

She glanced down at his left hand. He wasn't wearing a wedding ring and that eased her mind somewhat. Norah hated the thought of a young wife pacing the floor, anxiously waiting his arrival home. Of course, that didn't mean he wasn't married. A lot of men didn't wear wedding rings, particularly if they worked with their hands. Too dangerous.

His leg was badly broken, and once he was stabilized, he'd be sent into surgery. She didn't have a lot of experience with compound fractures, but her guess was that he'd need to be in traction for the next few weeks. A break as complex as this would take months, possibly years, to heal properly.

Norah wasn't scheduled to work tonight, but had been called in unexpectedly. She should've been home, had *planned* to be home, preparing for her oldest sister Valerie's wedding. Half of Orchard Valley would be in attendance—it was widely considered the event of the year. And five weeks after that, her second sister, Steffie, would be marrying Charles Tomaselli, in a much less formal ceremony.

There was definitely something in the air this summer, Norah mused, with both her sisters planning to get married.

Love was what floated in the air, but it had apparently evaded Norah. There wasn't a single man in Orchard Valley who stirred her heart. Not one.

She was thrilled for her sisters, but at the same time she couldn't help feeling a bit envious. If any of the three could be described as "the marrying type," it was Norah. She was by far the most domestic and traditional. Ever since she was a teenager, Norah had assumed she'd be the first of the three sisters to marry, although she was the youngest. Valerie had hardly dated even in college, and Steffie was so impulsive and unpredictable that she'd never stood still long enough to get serious about anyone. Or so it had seemed....

Now both her sisters were marrying. And this had all happened within two short months. Only weeks ago Norah would have been shocked had anyone told her Valerie would become a wife. Her oldest sister was the dedicated career woman, working her way up the corporate ladder with CHIPS, a Texas-based computer software corporation. At any rate, that was what Valerie *had* been doing—until she flew home when their father suffered a heart attack. Before Norah was aware of it, Valerie had fallen head over heels in love with Dr. Colby Winston.

Try as she might, she couldn't picture her sister as a wife. Valerie, who was so much like their father, was a dynamic businesswoman. She'd accepted the sales job with CHIPS and in less than four years had moved into upper management. She was energetic, spirited and strong-willed. If her sister was going to fall in love, Norah didn't understand how it could be with Dr. Winston. He was just as dedicated to his work, just as headstrong. To Norah's way of thinking, they had little in common—except their love for each other. In fact, watching them together had taught Norah a few things about love and commitment. They were both determined to make their marriage work, both willing to make compromises, to change and to mediate their differences.

If Valerie was going to get married at all, Norah had always assumed she'd choose someone like Rowdy Cassidy, the owner of CHIPS. For months, Valerie's phone calls and e-mails had been full of details about the maverick software developer. He'd taken Wall Street by storm with his innovative ideas, and his company had very soon become one of a very few to dominate the field. Valerie greatly admired him. But she'd given up her position with CHIPS without so much as a second's regret. There were other jobs, she'd said, but only one Colby Winston. And if she had to choose, as Cassidy had forced her to do, then that choice was clear. But then Norah had never seen anyone more in love—unless it was Steffie.

Her second sister had arrived after a long, difficult trip to be with their father and almost the same thing had happened. Suddenly, she and Charles Tomaselli, the *Orchard Valley Clarion*'s editor and now its publisher, had clashed. They'd been constantly at odds, but gradually that had changed. Not until much later did Norah learn that Charles was the reason Steffie had decided to study in Italy—both to escape him and because, thanks to him, she'd become fascinated with Italian art and culture. Steffie had been wildly in love with Charles, and Norah wasn't sure what had gone wrong, but whatever it was had sent Steffie fleeing. She guessed there'd been some sort of disagreement between them—not that it mattered. What *was* important was that Steffie and Charles had patched things up and admitted their true feelings for each other.

In typical Steffie fashion, her sister was planning a thoroughly untraditional wedding. The exchange of vows was to take place in the apple orchard, between the rows of trees with their weight of reddening apples. The reception would be held on the groomed front lawn; there would be musicians playing chamber music in the background. The wedding cake was to be a huge chocolate concoction.

So, within a few weeks of each other, her two sisters would be married. Unlike Valerie, Norah hadn't recently met a new and wonderful man. And unlike Steffie, she didn't have a secret love, someone she'd felt passionate about for years. Unless she counted Clive Owen. Norah figured she'd seen every movie he starred in ten times over. But it wasn't likely that a dashing actor was going to show up in Orchard Valley and fall passionately in love with her. A pity, really.

An hour later, Norah was washing up, preparing to head home. The cowboy, although listed in critical condition, had stabilized. He might not feel like it now, but he was lucky to be alive. The surgery on the right fibula would follow, but she wasn't sure exactly when.

Eager to leave the hospital, Norah was on her way out the door when she heard someone mention the cowboy's name.

She stopped abruptly, nearly tripping in her astonishment. "*Who* did you say he is?" she demanded, turning back to her friends.

"According to the identification he carried, his name is Rowdy Cassidy."

"Rowdy!" Susan Parsons, another nurse, laughed. "It's a perfect name for him, isn't it? He looks rowdy. Personally, I don't want to be around when he wakes up. I'm betting he's going to have all the charm of an angry hornet."

Rowdy Cassidy. Norah took a deep breath. The man was Valerie's employer. Former employer, she amended. He must've been flying in for the wedding when the accident occurred.

Norah wasn't sure what she could do with the information. Valerie, who was cool as a watermelon on ice when it came to business dealings, was a nervous wreck over this wedding.

Love had taken Valerie Bloomfield by surprise and she hadn't recovered yet. Mentioning Rowdy's accident to her sister now didn't seem right; Valerie had enough on her mind without the additional worry. Yet it didn't seem fair to keep the truth from her, either.

Who should she tell, then, Norah wondered as she walked to the staff parking lot. Surely someone should know....

It was late, past midnight, when she entered the house. Although there were several lights on, she didn't see anyone around. The wedding was at noon, less than twelve hours away.

Secretly Norah had hoped her father might still be up, but she didn't really expect it. He went to bed early these days and slept late, his body regaining its strength after the physical ordeal of a heart attack and the subsequent life-saving surgery.

"Hi," Steffie said cheerfully. She hurried downstairs, cinching her robe at the waist as she walked. Her long dark hair was damp and fell arrow-straight to the middle of her back. "I wondered what time you'd be home."

Norah stared up at her, frowning in concentration. She'd discuss this with Steffie, she decided, see what her sister had to say.

"What happened?" Steffie asked, her voice urgent.

"There was a single-engine-plane crash." Norah hesitated. "Fortunately only one man was aboard."

"Did he survive?"

Norah nodded and worried her lower lip. "Is Valerie asleep?"

Steffie sighed. "Who knows? I'd never have believed Valerie would be this nervous before her wedding. Good grief, she's arranged multimillion-dollar business deals."

"Come in the kitchen with me," Norah said, looking quickly up the staircase. She didn't want Valerie hearing this.

"What is it?" Steffie asked as she followed her into the other room. Valerie's room was directly above, but there was little chance she'd overhear the conversation.

"The man who was involved in the plane accident..."

"Yes?" Steffie prodded in a whisper.

"Is Rowdy Cassidy."

"What?" Steffie pulled out a stool at the counter and sank down on it. "You're sure?"

"Positive. Apparently he was flying in for the wedding."

"More likely he intended to stop it," Steffie said sharply.

"Stop it? What do you mean?"

Steffie's expression was intense. "Well, you know that when Valerie talked to him about opening a branch on the West Coast, he was in favor of the idea, but he wanted someone else to head it up. He refused to give her the job and said she'd have to stay in Texas if she wanted to stay with CHIPS. In other words, unless she chooses Rowdy Cassidy and her career over Colby and marriage. In fact, he seems to think he can persuade her to do just that."

"What a rotten way to act!"

Steffie agreed. "Valerie was furious. She'd hoped to continue working for CHIPS after she's married. But Rowdy was so unreasonable, she didn't have any alternative except to resign. When she announced she was marrying Colby, Rowdy didn't seem to believe her— still doesn't. Apparently he thinks it was some ploy to get him to declare his love."

"I take it Mr. Cassidy doesn't know Valerie very well." Her sister was nothing if not direct, Norah mused with a small smile. Valerie would never stoop to orchestrating such a scene, or exploiting a man's feelings for her.

When Valerie first flew home after their father's heart attack, Norah had suspected her sister might've been attracted to her employer. In retrospect, she realized Valerie greatly admired and liked Rowdy, but wasn't in love with him. Her reactions to Colby made that abundantly clear.

"But why do you think he wanted to stop the wedding?" Norah asked. If Rowdy did love her sister, he'd certainly waited until the last minute to do something about it.

"He phoned two days ago…. I took the call," Steffie said, a guilty expression crossing her face. "I didn't tell Valerie, but then—how could I?"

"Tell her what exactly?"

"That Rowdy asked her not to do anything…hasty until he'd had a chance to talk to her."

"Hasty?" Norah repeated. "Like what?"

"Like go through with the wedding."

"He had to be joking."

"I don't think so," Steffie said grimly. "He was dead serious. He claimed he had something important to say to her and that she should put everything on hold until he got here."

"And you didn't tell Valerie?"

"No," Steffie returned, her gaze avoiding Norah's. "I guess I should have, but when I told Dad—"

"Dad knows?"

"He didn't seem the least bit surprised, either." Steffie folded her arms around her middle and slowly shook her head. "He just smiled and then he said the oddest thing."

"When hasn't he?" Norah muttered.

Steffie agreed with a smile.

"What was it this time?"

Steffie didn't answer right away. She stared down at the counter for a moment. Finally she glanced up, giving a baffled shrug. "That Rowdy was arriving right on schedule."

Norah found the statement equally puzzling. "Do you think Rowdy might have called earlier and spoken to Dad?"

Once again Steffie shrugged. "Who knows?"

"But Dad seemed to feel you shouldn't say anything to Valerie about Rowdy's call?" Norah pressed.

Steffie nodded. "Yeah. He says she's got enough to worry about. I couldn't agree more. As far as I'm concerned, Cassidy had his chance. He accepted her resignation, which worked out fine since it gave Valerie more time to get everything organized for the wedding. From what she said recently, I think she might start doing some consulting. You know, help companies upgrade their computer systems."

"That's a great idea," Norah murmured.

"It isn't the wedding arrangements that have unsettled Val." Steffie spoke with the authority of one who knew. "It's being in love."

"Love," Norah repeated wistfully.

"Valerie's never been in love before, that's what threw her. Not the wedding plans or all the organizing or even the job situation."

"What surprises me the most," Norah said, recalling the past few weeks, "is how she immediately becomes composed whenever Colby's around."

"He's her emotional anchor," Steffie said knowingly. "Like Charles is mine. And—"

"Should I say anything to Val about Rowdy Cassidy?" Norah broke in.

"Sure," Steffie told her, "but my advice is to wait until after the ceremony."

Norah concurred, frowning a little.

"How badly was he injured?" Steffie asked.

"He's in critical condition and is scheduled for surgery on his leg. I think he'll be in traction for some time. He suffered some internal injuries, too, but they don't appear to be as serious as we first assumed."

"So he'll be pretty well out of it until after the wedding, anyway?"

"Oh, yes. He's not expected to fully regain consciousness until sometime tomorrow afternoon—if then."

"Then I suggest we let sleeping dogs lie," Steffie said. "It's not like a visit from Valerie would do him any good—at least, not now."

"Are you sure we're doing the right thing?" Norah wasn't nearly as confident as her sister. Valerie had a right to know about her friend's accident.

"No," Steffie admitted after a moment. "I'm not at all sure. But I just can't see upsetting Valerie now, so close to the wedding. Especially when Cassidy isn't likely to know if she goes to see him, anyway."

Norah had no idea what to do. Apparently Rowdy Cassidy cared enough for her sister to call her and even come to Orchard Valley. Perhaps he loved her. If that was the case, though, his love was too late.

Just before noon the next day, Norah was standing in the vestibule of the church with the other members of the bride's party. Everyone—except Valerie—was giggling and jittery with nerves. Valerie no longer seemed nervous; now that the day she'd worried over and waited for had finally arrived, she was completely calm. Serene.

But Norah's head was spinning. This wasn't her first wedding by any means. She'd been a bridesmaid three times before. Yet she'd never been more…excited. That was the word for it. Excited and truly happy for these two people she loved so much.

Although she'd never said anything to Valerie and certainly never to Colby, she'd been interested in the good doctor herself. Who wouldn't be? He was compassionate and gentle, but he also possessed a rugged appeal. He wasn't one to walk away from a challenge. Loving Valerie had proved as much.

Norah's oldest sister had worked hard on her wedding preparations, and all her careful planning had paid off. The church was lovely. Large bunches of white gardenias decorated the end of each pew. The sanctuary was filled with arrangements of white candles and a profusion of flowers—more gardenias, white and yellow roses, pink apple blossoms.

The bridesmaids' dresses were in different pastels and they carried flowers that complemented their color. Norah's own pale rose gown was set off by a small bouquet of apple blossoms while Steffie, wearing a soft green gown, carried lemony rosebuds.

The fragrance of the flowers mingled and wafted through the crowded church, carried by a warm breeze that drifted through the open doors.

It was all so beautiful. The flowers, the ceremony, the love between Valerie and Colby as they exchanged their vows. Several times, Norah felt the tears gather in her eyes. She hated being so sentimental, so maudlin, but she couldn't help herself. It was the most touching, most *beautiful,* wedding she'd ever attended.

Valerie was radiant. No other word could describe the kind of beauty that shone from her sister's face as she smiled up at her husband.

The reception, dinner and dance were to follow immediately afterward at the Orchard Valley Country Club. But first they were subjected to a series of photographs that seemed to take forever. Norah didn't know why she felt so impatient, why she seemed to be in such a hurry. It wasn't like her.

After that was finally over, her father took her by the arm as they headed for the limousines, which were lined up outside the church, ready to drive them to the club.

"I heard about Cassidy," he said in a low voice. "How is he?"

"I phoned the hospital this morning," Norah told him. The man had been on her mind most of the night. She hadn't gotten much sleep, which left her with plenty of time to think about Rowdy Cassidy. She'd attributed her restlessness to night-before-the-wedding jitters. She hadn't intended to call the hospital until much later; there was plenty to occupy her before the wedding. Valerie had regimented their morning like a drill sergeant, but she'd found a spare moment to make a quick call.

"Carol Franklin was on duty and she told me Rowdy had just come out of surgery."

"And?"

"And he's doing as well as can be expected."

"I thought it might be a good idea if one of us checked up on him later," David Bloomfield said under

his breath. "I'll tell Valerie and Colby about the accident myself, after the reception. I'm sure they'll want
to see him, too."

"I'll check on him," Norah offered with an eagerness
she didn't fully understand.

Her father nodded and pressed a car key into the
palm of her gloved hand. "Steal away when you can. If
anyone asks where you are, I'll make up some excuse."

He moved off before Norah could question him. Her
father seemed to assume she'd want to leave the social
event of the year, her own sister's wedding, to visit a
stranger at the hospital.

And he was right! Without knowing it, she'd been
looking for an excuse, a means of doing exactly what
her father had suggested. It was the reason she found
herself so impatient, so restless; she realized that now.
Something inside her was calling her back to the hospital. Back to Rowdy Cassidy's bedside.

There was a small break in the wedding festivities
between the dinner and the dance. The staff was clearing off the tables and the musicians were tuning up.
There should be just enough time for her to leave without anyone noticing.

Her father caught her eye, and he seemed to be thinking the same thing because he nodded in her direction.

Driving was an exercise in patience with all the lay-
ers of taffeta, but Norah managed, although she was
sure she made quite a sight.

The hospital was quiet and peaceful when she arrived. If people thought it unusual that she was strolling inside wearing a floor-length rose gown, long white

gloves and a broad-brimmed straw hat with a band of ribbon cascading down her back, they said nothing.

"What room did they put Rowdy Cassidy in?" she asked at the information desk.

"Two fifteen," Janice Wilson told her, after glancing at her computer screen. It was obvious that Janice wanted to ask a few questions about Valerie and the wedding, but Norah skillfully sidestepped them and hurried down the main hospital corridor.

When she got to his floor, she went directly into his room. Standing in the doorway, Norah let her eyes adjust to the dim light.

Rowdy's right leg was suspended in the air with a pulley. His face was turned toward the wall. Norah walked farther into the room and reached for his medical chart, which was attached to the foot of his bed. She was reading over the notations when she sensed that he was awake. He hadn't made the slightest noise or done anything to indicate he was conscious.

Yet she knew.

Norah moved to the side of his bed, careful not to startle him.

"Hello," she said softly.

His eyes fluttered open.

"Would you like a sip of water?" she asked.

"Please."

She picked up the glass and straw, positioning it at the corner of his mouth. He drank thirstily, and when he finished, raised his eyes to her.

"Am I dead?"

"No," she answered, with a reassuring smile. Obviously the medication was continuing to block out the pain, otherwise he'd know exactly how alive he was.

"Should be," he whispered, as though speaking demanded a real effort.

"You're a very lucky man, Mr. Cassidy."

He attempted a grin but didn't quite succeed. "Who are you, my fairy godmother?"

"Not quite. I'm Norah Bloomfield, Valerie's sister. And I'm a nurse. I was on call when they brought you in last night."

"Unusual uniform."

Once again Norah found herself smiling. "I was in my sister's wedding this afternoon."

If she hadn't captured his full attention earlier, she did now.

"So Valerie decided to go through with it, after all, did she?"

"Yes."

Silence filled the room.

"Damn fool woman," he muttered after a moment. He turned his head away from her and as he did, Norah noticed that his mouth had tightened with pain. His dark eyes were dulled by it.

Norah was left to speculate as to its source, physical or emotional.

Two

"In twenty years I've never worked with a more disagreeable patient," Karen Johnson was saying when Norah walked into the nurses' lounge early Monday morning. "First, he refuses the painkiller even though the doctor ordered it, then he throws a temper tantrum—and his breakfast tray ends up on the other side of the room!"

"I hope you're talking about a patient in pediatrics," Norah said, sitting down next to her friend.

"Nope. Rowdy Cassidy, the guy they brought in from that plane crash. One thing about him—he's certainly earned his name. By the way, he asked for you. At least I think it was you. He said he wanted to talk to the Bloomfield sister who wore fancy dresses. Since we both know Steffie's more likely to wear jeans and Valerie's on her honeymoon, he must mean you."

Norah smiled to herself, recalling her brief visit with Rowdy the afternoon of Valerie's wedding. So he remembered.

"Don't feel any obligation to go see him," Karen advised. "In my opinion, the man's been catered to once too often. It'd do him a world of good to acquire a little self-restraint."

From the beginning, Norah had suspected that Rowdy would be a difficult patient. He was an energetic, decisive man, accustomed to quick action. And he was probably furious about missing Valerie's wedding. He'd been thwarted at every turn, which no doubt added to his frustration.

Although Norah didn't really know Valerie's former boss, she had the distinct impression that he wasn't often foiled. Try as she might, she couldn't help feeling sorry for him. He'd gambled for Valerie's affections and lost. He'd seemed to honestly believe that her sister would have a change of heart and cancel her wedding plans if he came to Orchard Valley.

Norah waited until eleven-thirty to visit Rowdy, since that was when she took her lunch break.

He was lying in bed. His right leg, encased in plaster, was held at an angle. The blinds were drawn, casting the room into shadow. When he saw her, he levered himself into a sitting position, using a small triangular bar to pull himself upright.

"I heard you wanted to talk to me," she said, standing just inside the private room.

He didn't say anything for a moment. "So you were real."

Norah hid a grin and nodded.

"You *are* a nurse, or is this another costume?"

"I'm a nurse."

"Valerie went through with the wedding, didn't she?"

Norah raised her eyebrows. "Of course."

His frown darkened.

"What's this I hear about you throwing your breakfast tray?" she asked, stepping farther into the room.

"Who are you, my mother?" he demanded sarcastically.

"No, but when you behave like a child, you can expect to be treated like one." She walked to the window and twisted open the blinds. Sunlight spilled into the room.

Rowdy shielded his eyes. "The thing with the tray was an accident. Now kindly close those blinds," he barked.

"You're certainly in a black mood. My advice to you is to lighten up. Literally."

"I didn't ask for your advice."

"Then I'll give it to you without charge. It wouldn't be a bad idea if you took those pain shots, either. You're not afraid of a needle, are you?"

He scowled fiercely. "Close those blinds! I need my sleep."

"You aren't going to sleep unless you've got something to help you deal with the pain. Taking a painkiller isn't a sign of weakness, you know. It's common sense."

"I don't believe in drugs."

"I wish we'd known that when you were brought into the emergency room," she said with light sarcasm. "Or when you went into surgery, for that matter. It would've made for an interesting operation, don't you think? What would you've suggested we do? Have you bite into a bullet?"

"I'm beginning to detect a family resemblance here,"

he muttered. "You don't look anything like Valerie, but you're starting to talk just like her."

"I'll accept that as a compliment."

He was clearly growing weaker; levering himself upward must have depleted his strength. Norah was surprised by his ability to move at all.

She approached his bed and rearranged the pillows. He slumped back against them and sighed. "Is she happy?"

Norah didn't need Rowdy to explain who he meant by *she*. "I've never seen a more radiant bride," she told him quietly. "They've left for a two-week honeymoon. She and Colby stopped by to check on you before they went, but apparently you were still out of it."

Pain flashed in Rowdy's eyes, and once again Norah had to wonder if it was from physical discomfort or knowing that he'd truly lost Valerie.

What Rowdy didn't understand, and what Norah couldn't tell him, was that he'd never had a chance with her sister. Valerie's fate had been sealed the minute she met Colby Winston. Nothing Rowdy said or did from that point forward would've made any difference.

"Where are you going?" Rowdy revived himself enough to demand when she started to leave the room.

"I'll be back," she promised.

True to her word, she returned a couple of minutes later with Karen Johnson following her. Karen's right hand was conspicuously hidden behind her back.

"Get her out of here," he said, pointing at Karen.

"Not just yet," Norah countered smoothly.

Karen hesitated, looking at Norah, who nodded.

"What's that?" he roared when Karen brought her

arm forward to reveal the needle. She raised it to the light and squeezed gently until a drop of clear liquid appeared at the tip.

"You, Mr. Cassidy, are about to receive an injection," Norah informed him.

"No, I'm not!"

Norah thought Rowdy's protest could probably be heard from one end of the hospital to the other, but it didn't deter her or Karen. Norah held Rowdy's arm immobile while Karen swiftly administered the pain medication.

Karen fled the room at the first opportunity. Not Norah, who dragged a chair to his bedside and sat down. Rowdy was furious and made no attempt to hide his displeasure.

Norah checked her watch and calmly waited. His tirade lasted all of three minutes before he slowed down, slurring his words. His dark eyes glared back at her accusingly.

"Have you finished?" she asked politely, when his voice had dwindled to a mere whisper of outrage.

"Not quite. I'll…both…fired…out of…hospital… for this…"

"I'll give you the name of the hospital administrator, if you like," Norah said helpfully. "It's James Bolton."

He muttered under his breath. She could tell that he was fighting off the effects of the medication. His eyes drifted shut and he forced them open, scowling at her, only to have his lids close again.

"I want you to know I don't appreciate this," he said, surprising her with a rally of strength.

"I know, but it'll help you sleep and that's what you need."

He was growing more tranquil by the moment. "I thought I'd died," he mumbled.

It was a miracle he'd survived the plane crash. Norah felt thankful he had, for a number of important reasons.

"You're very much alive, Mr. Cassidy."

"An angel came to see me," he told her, his voice fading. "Dressed in pink. So beautiful...almost made me wish I *was* dead."

"Sleep now," she urged, her heart constricting at his words. He remembered her visit; he'd mentioned it when he first saw her today, and now, under the influence of the medication, he was talking about it again.

She backed away. Although his eyes were closed, he reached out for her. "Don't go," he mumbled. "Stay...a bit longer. Please."

She gave him her hand and was astonished by the vigor of his grip. Touching him had a curious effect on her. He wasn't in pain now, she knew; the tension had left his face. Norah wasn't sure why she felt compelled to brush the hair from his forehead. She was rewarded with a drowsy smile.

"An angel," he mumbled once more. Within seconds he was completely asleep. His grip on her hand relaxed, but it was a long time before Norah left his side.

Norah's father was sitting on the front porch of their large colonial home when she got home late that afternoon. He still tired easily from his recent surgery and often sat in the warmth of a summer afternoon, gazing out at his apple orchards.

"How's the patient?" he asked as Norah climbed the porch steps.

"Physically Mr. Cassidy's improving. Unfortunately I can't say the same about his disposition."

David chuckled. "I should give that boy a few pointers."

Norah grinned. Her father's own stay at the hospital had been a test of his patience—and the staff's. David hadn't been the most agreeable invalid, especially once he was on the mend. In his eagerness to return home, he'd often been irritable and demanding. Colby had said wryly that David wanted to make sure the hospital staff was just as enthusiastic about his return home as he was himself.

Norah sat on the top step, relaxing for a few minutes. Her day, much of it spent in the emergency room, had been long and tiring. "Dad," she said carefully, supporting her back against one of the white columns, "what did you mean when you told Steffie that Rowdy Cassidy had arrived right on schedule?"

Her father rocked in his chair for a moment before answering. "I said that?"

Norah grinned. "According to Steffie you did."

He shrugged. "Then I must have."

Shaking her head, she got up. As she entered the house, she could hear her father's soft chuckle and wondered what he found so amusing.

Ever since his open-heart surgery, David Bloomfield had been spouting romantic "predictions" regarding Norah's two older sisters. She hoped he wasn't intending to do that with her, too.

Valerie and Colby had been the first to fit into his

intrigue. Anyone with a nickel's worth of sense could see what was happening between those two. It didn't take a private detective to see that they were falling in love. Naturally there were a few problems, but that was to be expected in any relationship.

When their father awoke from his surgery, however, he claimed he'd visited the afterlife and talked with Grace, the girls' mother, who'd died several years earlier. He also claimed he'd looked into the future and that he knew exactly who his three daughters would marry. Colby and Valerie inadvertently lent credibility to his "vision." Their marriage made perfect sense to everyone. Certainly no one at the hospital was surprised when Colby gave Valerie Bloomfield an engagement ring. Their father, however, had crowed for a week over the happy announcement.

To complicate matters, a short time later, Steffie and Charles had fallen in love, just as her father had predicted. That case, too, was perfectly logical. Steffie had been in love with Charles for years. Charles had felt the same way about her.

Norah hadn't been privy to that information, but soon after Steffie came home it was obvious to all of them that she and Charles were meant to be together. It was only logical that they'd patch up their differences. Especially since their love had been strong enough to endure a three-year separation.

When Steffie and Charles announced *their* engagement, David had all but shouted with glee. Everything was happening just the way he'd said it would, after his near-death experience. The man had been gloating ever since. He'd gone so far as to insist that he knew when the grandchildren would begin to arrive. Valerie's would be the first, he said; she'd have identical twin sons nine months and three weeks—to the day—after her marriage.

He said it was just as well that Rowdy had rejected Valerie as manager of the Pacific Northwest branch, considering that she was going to be a mother of twins.

No one had known what to say to that, although Valerie had privately assured her sisters that she and Colby had no intention of starting their family quite so soon.

They'd all decided it was best to let their father think what he wanted. He wasn't hurting anyone, and all his talk about the future seemed to give him pleasure.

Although these proclamations from their father unsettled the Bloomfield sisters, Colby had assured them that he'd had other patients who claimed to have experienced near-death encounters. It would all pass in time, he'd said with utter confidence.

Norah couldn't help noticing, however, that her father hadn't said anything to *her* about the man in her life. He'd made some cryptic comment while he was coming out of the anesthetic. He'd smiled up at Norah and mumbled something about six children. Later she realized he was telling her she would someday be the mother of six.

The idea was ludicrous. But he hadn't said a word about it since, which was a relief. She was a medical professional and refused to take his outlandish claims seriously. Neither did she wish to be drawn into a discussion concerning them. Besides, anyone who knew the two couples would know they would've gotten married with or without David Bloomfield's dream.

"Rowdy Cassidy's a good man, Norah," her father said from behind her. "Be patient with him."

Pausing, her hand on the screen door, Norah shook her head, trying to force the cowboy—as she still thought of him—from her mind. Rowdy was ill-tempered and arrogant, and she wanted as little to do with him as possible. Norah had no intention of becoming personally involved with such a spoiled, egocentric man. *"Be patient with him."* Norah scoffed silently. If anyone needed to learn patience, it was Mr. Rowdy Cassidy.

"Norah! Thank goodness you're here," Karen Johnson said as she barreled through the double doors that led to the emergency room. Her face was red and she was panting slightly, as if she'd run all the way from the second floor.

"What's wrong?"

"It's Mr. Cassidy again. He wants to talk to you as soon as possible."

"That's unfortunate, since I'm on duty."

Karen blinked, apparently not sure what to do next. "I don't think Orchard Valley is ready for a man like Mr. Cassidy."

"What's he done *now?*"

"He had a laptop computer brought in so he could communicate with his company in Texas. Some man showed up with it yesterday."

Norah rolled her eyes.

"Cassidy can barely sit up and already he's conducting business as if he were in some plush office," Karen went on. "I can't figure out how it happened, but we all seem to be at his beck and call."

"What's he want with me?"

"How am I supposed to know?" Karen snapped. "It isn't my place to question. My job is to obey."

Norah couldn't keep from laughing. "Karen, he's only a man. You've dealt with others just like him a hundred times."

Karen shook her head. "I've never met anyone like Rowdy Cassidy. Are you coming or not?"

"Not."

Her friend ran a hand through her disheveled hair. "I was afraid you were going to say that. Would you consider doing it as a personal favor to me?"

"Karen!"

"I mean it."

Still Norah hesitated. She wasn't a servant to be summoned at Mr. High-and-Mighty's command. Even if he'd whipped the other members of the hospital staff into shape—the shape of *his* choice—she had no intention of following suit.

"I'll stop in later," she said reluctantly.

"How much later?"

"I'll wait until I'm on break."

Karen's smile revealed her appreciation. "Thanks, Norah. I owe you one."

Norah wouldn't have believed it if she hadn't seen it herself. A few days earlier, Karen would've given up her retirement to have Rowdy Cassidy removed from her floor. A mere twenty-four hours later, she was running errands for him like an eager cabin boy wanting to keep his pirate captain content.

* * *

"You can leave my lunch tray there," Rowdy instructed the young volunteer, pointing to his bedside table.

Norah watched the teenager hang back as though terrified of crossing the threshold into Rowdy's room. Considering the earlier incident with a meal tray, Norah didn't blame her.

"Come on, now," Rowdy returned impatiently. "I'm not going to bite you."

"I wouldn't believe him, if I were you," Norah said, taking the tray out of the girl's hands.

Rowdy scowled. "It's about time you got here."

"You're lucky I came at all." She didn't like what was happening. Rowdy had manipulated the staff, bullied them into getting his own way, but such methods wouldn't work with her.

"It's been three days. Where have you been?" he demanded, frowning fiercely.

"I didn't know I was obligated to visit you."

"Obligated, no, but you must feel a certain moral responsibility."

She set down the tray, and crossed her arms. "I can't say I do."

He scowled again. "Where was it you said Valerie and her...husband were honeymooning?"

"I didn't."

"Hawaii? Carlton probably hasn't got an imaginative bone in his body. Which hotel?"

"Carlton?"

"Whoever Valerie married. I'm right, aren't I? They're in Hawaii. Now tell me the name of the hotel."

"You must be joking, Mr. Cassidy. You don't think I'd be so foolish as to give you the name of the hotel so you could pester my sister on her honeymoon, do you?"

"Aha! So it *is* Hawaii."

Norah winced.

"I just wanted to send a flower arrangement," he went on, his voice a model of sincerity. "And I thought a bottle of champagne would be in order. I'd like to congratulate them, since I missed their wedding."

"A flower arrangement? Champagne? I'll just bet," Norah muttered under her breath.

Rowdy went still for a moment. "You don't know me very well, do you, Ms. Bloomfield? Or you'd appreciate that I'm not the kind of man who'd begrudge others their happiness. Now that Valerie's married Carlton, I—"

"Colby," she interrupted.

"Colby," he repeated, bowing his head slightly. "Well, I'd like to offer them both my most heartfelt congratulations."

Norah shrugged. "Sorry, I don't have the name of their hotel."

Rowdy's gaze hardened briefly. "Then I have no choice but to wait until the happy couple returns from their honeymoon."

"That's an excellent idea." Norah clasped her hands behind her back; she hadn't been completely honest with Rowdy. "Valerie didn't know about your accident until after the wedding," she told him, not quite meeting his eyes.

Rowdy said nothing for several minutes. "I didn't think she knew," he murmured, giving the impression that had she been aware of his injuries, she'd never have gone through with the wedding.

"It wouldn't have made any difference," Norah told him, unable to hide her irritation. "Anyway, she had enough on her mind without having to worry about you. So we decided not to tell her until later."

"You kept it from her?" he stormed.

"That's right, we did," she replied calmly.

He was furious; in fact, Norah had never seen a tantrum to equal his. But she ignored his outburst and went about setting up his lunch tray. She removed the domed cover from the meal, then folded the napkin and laid it across his chest.

When he paused to breathe, Norah asked, "Do you want your lunch now, or would you prefer to wait until you've calmed down?"

Rowdy's mouth snapped shut.

"Is Dr. Silverman aware you've had a computer brought in for business use?" She pointed at the laptop beside him on the bed. "Furthermore, is he aware that you're attempting to work out of this room?"

"No. Are you going to tell him?" he asked, eyeing her skeptically.

"I might."

"It doesn't matter. I'm getting out of this hick town as soon as I can arrange it."

"I'm sure the staff will do everything possible to speed the process. You've made quite a name for yourself in the past few days, Mr. Cassidy."

Before Rowdy could respond, Karen appeared in the doorway, looking frazzled. She glanced at Norah, obviously relieved that her friend was close at hand.

"It's time for your injection, Mr. Cassidy," she said.

"I don't want it."

"I'm sure Mr. Cassidy doesn't mean that, Karen," Norah said cheerfully. "He'll be more than happy to take his shot—isn't that right?"

Rowdy glared at her. "Wrong, Ms. Bloomfield."

"Fine, then. I'll hold him for you, Karen, I only hope I don't bump against his leg, since that would be terribly painful. Of course, if he passes out from the agony, it'll make giving him the injection that much simpler."

"If I take the shot I won't be able to work," Rowdy growled.

"Might I remind you that you're in the hospital to rest, not to conduct your business affairs?"

Norah took one step toward him, staring at his right leg.

"All right, all right," he grumbled, "but I want you to know I'm doing it under protest. You don't play fair—either one of you."

Karen threw Norah a triumphant look. Rowdy turned his head while she administered the pain medication. In only minutes the drug began to take effect.

Rowdy's eyes drifted shut.

"Thanks, Norah," Karen whispered.

"What's going on here?" Norah asked. She'd never known Karen or any of the others to allow a patient to run roughshod over them.

"I wish I knew." Karen sighed. "The only one he's civil to is you. The whole floor's been a madhouse since he arrived. I've never known anyone who can order people around the way he does. Even Dr. Silverman seems intimidated."

"Harry?" Norah could hardly believe it.

"I've never looked forward more to a patient's release. The crazy part is that no one's supposed to know he's here. Especially the press. His friend—the CHIPS attorney—read us the riot act about talking to anyone from the media. They're worried about what'll happen to the stocks."

Norah walked out of Rowdy's room with Karen. Now she understood why the plane crash had received only a brief mention in the news and why Rowdy's name had been omitted. "When will he be able to travel?" she asked.

Karen gave a frustrated shrug. "I don't know, but my guess is it won't be soon. His leg's going to take a long time to heal and the less he moves it now, the better his chances for a complete recovery later. He may end up walking with a cane as it is."

Norah couldn't imagine the proud and mighty Rowdy Cassidy forced to rely on a cane. For his sake, she hoped it wouldn't come to that.

At home that afternoon, Norah was still bothered by the thought of a vital man like Rowdy hobbling along with a cane. But she didn't want to think about him. He wasn't her patient and really, other than the fact that her sister had once worked for him, there was no connection between them.

She'd managed to stay away from him for three days, despite the way she felt drawn to his presence. She shook her head, bemused that he'd succeeded in causing so much turmoil. The hospital had become a whirlwind of activity and it all seemed to focus on one man. Rowdy Cassidy.

"Hi," Steffie said, breaking into Norah's thoughts.

Norah, who'd been making a salad for their dinner, realized her hands were idle. She was thinking about the hospital eleven miles down the road, instead of her task.

"I didn't know if you'd be back for dinner or not," she said, hoping her voice didn't betray the path her mind had taken.

"I wasn't sure, either," Steffie admitted, automatically heading for the silverware drawer. She counted out cutlery and began to set the kitchen table.

Norah continued with the salad, glancing up now and then to watch Steffie. Her sister looked lovelier than ever and her calm, efficient movements revealed a new contentment. A new self-acceptance.

So this was what love did. Her sisters seemed to glow with the love they felt—and the love they received. In both of them, natural beauty was enhanced by happiness.

For most of her life, Norah had been referred to as the most attractive of the three Bloomfield girls. She was blonde, blue-eyed, petite. But lately, Norah felt plain and dowdy compared to Valerie and Stephanie.

"How's everything at the hospital?" Steffie asked absentmindedly.

"I take it you're asking about Rowdy Cassidy?"

Steffie laughed. "I guess I am. You know, I can't help feeling a bit guilty about not giving Valerie his message."

"You weren't the only one."

"You didn't give her his message, either? You mean he called more than once? Oh, dear."

"I didn't talk to him," Norah countered swiftly. "But Dad did." Rowdy had never actually said so, but he'd implied that he'd phoned Valerie several times. If Steffie had answered one call and Norah none, that left only their dear, meddling father.

She was about to explain that when the phone rang. Norah reached for the receiver; two minutes later she was so furious she could barely breathe.

Slamming the phone down, she whirled on her sister. "I don't believe this. Of all the high-handed, arrogant—it's outrageous!"

"Norah, what's wrong?"

Three

"Rowdy Cassidy has had me transferred out of the emergency room!" Norah shouted, clenching her fists. "The nerve of the man!"

"But why?" Steffie wanted to know.

"So I could be there to wait on him hand and foot like everyone else." Norah stalked angrily to the other side of the kitchen. "I don't believe it! Of all the—"

"Nerve," Steffie supplied.

"Precisely."

"Surely you've got some say in this," Steffie said, as she resumed setting the table. Norah glared at her sister, wondering how Steffie could think about dinner at a time like this.

"Apparently I *don't* have a choice in the matter," Norah fumed. "I've been asked to report to Karen Johnson at seven tomorrow morning."

"Oh, dear."

"I'm so furious I could scream!"

"What's this yelling all about?" her father asked, strolling into the bright, cheery kitchen.

"It's Rowdy Cassidy again," Steffie said before Norah had the chance.

David rubbed one hand along his jaw. "I don't think you need to worry—he'll be gone soon."

His words were of little comfort to Norah. "Unfortunately, it won't be soon enough to suit me."

Her father chuckled softly and left the kitchen.

Norah arrived on the second floor early the following morning.

Karen Johnson was at the nurses' station making entries on a patient's chart. "So you heard," she said.

Norah gave her friend a grumpy smile. "I'm not happy about this."

"I didn't think you would be, but what else can we do when His Imperial Highness issues a decree?"

"Is he awake?"

Karen nodded. "Apparently he's been up for hours. He wants to see you the minute you get here," Karen said, and made a sweeping motion with her arm.

Although Norah was furious with Rowdy, her friend's courtly gesture produced a laugh. "How's he doing?"

"Better physically. Unfortunately, not so well emotionally. Being stuck in a hick-town hospital, as he so graciously describes Orchard Valley General, hasn't improved his disposition. But then, he'd find something to complain about in paradise. He wants out, and there isn't a man or woman on this floor who wouldn't grant him his wish if it was possible."

Norah pushed up the sleeves of her white cardigan sweater as she walked into Rowdy's room, prepared to do battle. He smiled boyishly when he saw her, which disarmed and confused her. She hadn't expected him to be in a good mood.

"Morning," he greeted her cheerfully.

"I want you to know I don't appreciate the fact that you've adjusted my life to suit your own purposes."

"What?" he demanded. "Asking the administrator to assign you to this floor? You were the one who gave me his name, weren't you? Aren't you being a bit selfish?"

"Me? If *I'm* selfish, what does that make you?"

"Lonely. You're the only person I know in this entire town."

"Your acquaintance is with my sister, not me," she reminded him forcefully.

"In this case, it's any port in the storm. I trust you, Norah, although I'm not sure why. You've already admitted Valerie didn't know about my accident because you didn't tell her until after the wedding. I can only assume you wanted me for yourself."

If he was hoping she'd rise to his bait, he had a long wait coming. She folded her arms and expelled a deep sigh. "I'll be bringing your breakfast in a couple of minutes," she said, turning her back on him.

When she came back, carrying the tray, Rowdy was sitting up in bed. "I need your help," he announced.

"You look perfectly capable of feeding yourself."

"I'm bored out of my mind."

"Do what everyone else does. Watch television," she said tartly. Whether he was lonely or not, she refused to pander to his moods. He'd pulled a dirty trick on her and she wasn't going to reward his behavior.

Rowdy glanced up at the blank television screen. "Please don't be annoyed with me, Norah. I'm serious."

"So am I." But she could feel herself weakening. When Rowdy turned on the charm, Norah suspected few could deny him. Karen Johnson, for instance... Well, Norah had no intention of ending up the same way.

"When will you be back?" he asked, grimacing as he examined his meal. The toast was cold. Norah could tell by the way the butter sat hard and flat on top. The eggs were runny and the oatmeal looked like paste. Norah didn't envy him.

"Someone else will be by to pick up your tray in a little while," she told him, not answering his question.

"You might as well take it now."

"Try to eat something," she suggested sympathetically.

"What? The half-cooked eggs or the lumpy oatmeal? No, thanks, I'd rather go without."

"Lunch will be more appetizing," Norah promised.

His brows arched cynically. "Wanna bet?"

Norah left his room, but she came back a few minutes later with two homemade blueberry muffins. Rowdy's eyes lit up when she set them on his breakfast tray. "I can't believe I'm doing this," she muttered.

"Where'd you get those?" As if he feared she'd change her mind, he snatched one off the tray.

"I baked last night and brought them in for the staff at coffee break this morning. Enjoy."

"I intend to." Already he was peeling away the paper. The first muffin disappeared in three bites. "These are wonderful," he said, licking the crumbs from his fingers. "Ever thought about selling the recipe?"

Norah laughed. The recipe had been her mother's and Norah guessed it had originally come from a magazine. "Not lately."

"Well, if you ever do, let me know." He was ready to dig into the second one. "By the way, Kincade's stopping by this afternoon, so hold off on those pain shots, will you?"

"Kincade?"

"My corporate attorney. Kincade and I spoke yesterday and he's hand-carrying some papers that have to be signed, so I'm going to need a clear head. Got that?"

"Yes, Your Highness."

Rowdy frowned, but said nothing. Norah shrugged, then gathered up the tray and left.

The morning passed quickly and she didn't talk to Rowdy again until near the end of her shift, at three. He was tired and out of sorts. His attorney friend had spent two hours with him, and an exhausted Rowdy had slept fitfully afterward.

"He's much calmer when you're around," Karen commented as they prepared to leave.

Norah didn't believe for a second that she'd made the slightest difference to Rowdy's behavior. If Karen wanted to thank anyone, it should be Kincade, who'd kept him occupied; at least when he was busy he didn't have time to make everyone else miserable.

On impulse she decided to check on him before she left for home. He was sitting up, listlessly flipping through channels on the television. Apparently nothing appealed to him.

"I didn't know daytime television was in such desperate straits," he muttered when he saw her. He pushed another button and the screen went blank. "I was hoping you'd stop by before you went home."

"How are you feeling?" she asked, trying to gauge his mood. He seemed somewhat revived from the nap.

"Lousy."

Norah was surprised he'd admit it. "Do you want a pain shot?"

He shook his head. "But I wouldn't mind a distraction. Can you sit down and talk for a few minutes?"

Norah made a show of glancing at her watch, although in reality she didn't have a single reason to hurry home. "I can stay for a short while, I guess." She certainly wasn't being gracious about it, but that didn't seem to bother Rowdy.

"Good."

Norah was met with the full force of his smile, and for a moment she basked in its warmth. Little wonder he inspired such loyalty and confidence in his employees. He definitely had the charisma of true leadership. Valerie had worked with him for nearly four years, dedicating her time and talent to his corporation until she had practically no life of her own. She'd done it voluntarily, too, inspired by Rowdy's own commitment to CHIPS.

"How'd the meeting with your friend go?" Norah asked conversationally.

He paused as though he'd never considered Kincade his friend. "Fine. Actually, it went very well. We've been able to keep the news of my accident from leaking to the press."

"What would be so terrible about anyone finding out

you're in the hospital?" Norah shrugged. "Karen mentioned something about the stocks."

Rowdy cast her an odd look. "You honestly don't know?" He shook his head again. "If the stockholders discovered I was incapacitated, they'd lose confidence in CHIPS and the stock could drop by several points."

"Would that really be so disastrous?"

"Yes," he returned without hesitation. "If the value declines by even a single point, that's equivalent to losing millions of dollars. Any greater loss and it becomes catastrophic, with a ripple effect that could rock the entire industry."

Either the man had an elevated sense of his own worth, or he was pessimistic by nature. Though perhaps she was being unnecessarily harsh, Norah mused. She knew next to nothing about business and finance. Nor did she care. She was content to leave the world's financial affairs in the capable hands of people like Rowdy Cassidy and her sister. She stood abruptly and walked toward the door.

"Do you have to go so soon?" Rowdy asked, disappointment in his dark eyes.

"I'll be right back," she promised.

It took her several minutes to find what she was looking for.

Rowdy brightened when she returned. "What's that?" he asked, nodding toward the rather battered box she was carrying.

"You do play games, don't you?"

"Often, but I seldom need a board."

Norah laughed. "Then I promise you this is right up your alley. It's a game of power, intrigue and skill." She set the box on the foot of his bed and slowly, dramatically, lifted the lid. She had Rowdy's full attention now.

"Checkers?" he asked with more than a hint of disbelief.

"Checkers." She drew the bedside table closer, moved his laptop and some flowers and placed the board on it. Then she pulled up a chair. "You want red or black?"

"Black to match my evil temperament." Rowdy gave an exaggerated leer, twirling an imaginary mustache.

Norah grinned. "I'm not going to argue with you."

They set up the board together. "Generally when I play a game there's something riding on the outcome," he said in a relaxed, offhand manner.

"Like what?" Norah pushed a red checker one space forward.

"Usually the stakes are big. It makes the game more... interesting."

"So what do you think we should wager on this game?" she asked. She'd forgotten how competitive men could be.

"Something small—this time," he said, studying the board.

"Give me an example." It'd been a while since she'd played checkers and she wasn't all that sure of her skills. She'd never taken games, any game, too seriously.

"I don't know..." Rowdy paused, apparently mulling it over. "How about dinner?"

"Dinner? You mean after you're discharged from the hospital?"

"No, I mean tonight."

Norah snickered. "What are you planning to do?

Order up a second tray from the kitchen? If that's the case, I'm afraid I'll have to decline."

"I won't need to order you another dinner tray," he said calmly, making his first jump and capturing one of her checkers. "I intend to win."

Rowdy did exactly that, and his winning streak continued, even when they decided the wager was two games out of three. After her second loss, Rowdy leaned back against the pillows, folded his arms and threw her a self-satisfied smile. "I'd like rare roast beef, a baked potato with sour cream, green beans and three-layer chocolate cake for dessert, preferably with coconut frosting. Homemade would be nice. Do you have a recipe for good chocolate cake?"

Stepping away from his bed, Norah propped her fists on her hips. "Is this your usual diet? Good grief, you're a prime candidate for a heart attack. I'll bet you don't exercise, either."

"Not recently." He looked pointedly at his leg. "Are you going to honor your end of the bargain or not?"

"I'm not sure yet. I'll bring your dinner, but don't hold your breath waiting for rare roast beef."

"I'm a Texan," he challenged. "I was weaned on prime rib."

"Then it's high time you started checking your cholesterol, cowboy. My father just went through open-heart surgery and it wasn't any picnic. My advice to you is to make a change in your eating habits now."

"All right, all right," Rowdy grumbled. "I'll settle for pizza and to show you how reasonable I can be, go ahead and order it with those little fish. That's healthy, right?"

"Anchovies? Do you know how high in sodium anchovies are?"

"There's no satisfying you, is there?" Rowdy chuckled. "If it isn't my cholesterol level you're fussing about, it's sodium count or something. Before you leave, you'll have me on a diet of bread and water, which is basically all I've been eating since I got in here, anyway."

Norah found herself laughing again. "I'll see to my dad's dinner and be back later with your pizza," she promised on her way out the door.

"Bring that checkerboard," he told her. "There're a few other wagers I'd like to make."

Norah had a few of her own. If everything went according to her plans, Rowdy would be as docile as a sleepy cat before he left Orchard Valley Hospital.

"You're later than usual," her father commented when she walked into the house. "Problems at the hospital?"

"Not really." She wasn't sure how much she should tell him about her time with Rowdy. Her own confusion didn't help. The man was in love with her sister, for heaven's sake! And he annoyed her no end with his tactics. The fact that she was attracted to him didn't make any sense. None whatsoever.

"I have to go back to the hospital," she said on her way upstairs, deciding not to offer any further explanation. She wanted a long bath, a short nap and a change of clothes, in that order.

"Don't worry about dinner," David called up after her. "I can take care of it. Plenty of leftovers in the fridge. Besides, I had a big lunch, so I don't have too much of an appetite."

Norah hesitated at the top of the stairs. Her father was right; he was now fully capable of looking after himself. The last thing he needed was her fussing over him. It came as something of a shock to realize that. Then she smiled. It came as a relief, too.

The hospital was quiet when Norah returned a couple of hours later. The head floor nurse smiled when she saw her carrying a boxed pizza. "I wondered what you promised him," LaVern joked. "He's been as good as gold all evening."

Opening the door with a flourish, Norah marched into Rowdy's room, balancing the pizza on the palm of one hand. "Ta da!"

Rowdy reached for the triangular bar dangling above his head and pulled himself upright. "I was beginning to think you were going to renege on our bet."

"A Bloomfield? Never!" She set the pizza box on the table and wheeled it to his side. "However I must warn you this pizza is healthy for you."

"Oh, great, you've ordered granola and broccoli toppings."

"Close. Mushroom, green pepper, onion. I had them put anchovies on your half. Personally I think you should appreciate my thoughtfulness. I can't stand those slimy little fish things—they're disgusting."

"Don't worry. I won't force you to eat any."

"Good."

Rowdy helped himself to a napkin and lifted the first slice from the box. He raised it slowly to his mouth, then closed his eyes as if in ecstasy as he chewed. "This is excellent, just excellent."

"I demand a rematch," Norah said, dragging her chair to his bedside. "When we're finished eating. Winning is a matter of personal pride now."

"Sore loser," he mumbled through a mouthful of pizza.

"What!" Norah felt the annoyance rise up inside her. Rowdy must have noticed it, too, because he grinned.

"I was teasing," he assured her. "Believe me, I don't want to bite the hand that feeds me."

"You ready for another challenge, then?" Norah asked, eager to clear away the remains of the pizza and set up the board.

"Anytime you want, sweetheart."

Norah didn't think he meant the term as one of affection and decided to ignore it. At least that was her intention....

But more than once, her concentration drifted away from the game. Before she could stop herself, she wondered what it would feel like to be Rowdy Cassidy's "sweetheart." He was opinionated and headstrong, but he could charm the birds out of the trees, as her mother used to say. He was also a man who usually got what he wanted—Valerie Bloomfield being one of the few exceptions. Norah felt oddly deflated, suddenly, as she recalled his feelings for her sister.

Almost without being aware of it, she'd lost two games in a row. Not until she made a silly mistake that cost her the second game did she realize they hadn't set their wager.

"What are you going to want next?" she muttered, irritated with herself for losing so easily. "I could bring you another blueberry muffin tomorrow morning."

Rowdy's smile was downright smug.

"How about three games out of five?" she asked hopefully.

"A deal's a deal."

"Now that's profound," Norah said in a sarcastic aside. "Fine." She spread both hands in a gesture of defeat. "You won. I'm not sure how fair or square it was, but you won."

"My, my, are you getting testy?"

She couldn't very well admit why she'd been so distracted. She stared down at the board as she rapidly gathered up the checkers. When she'd finished, he reached for her hands, holding them between his own, drawing her closer to his side. She knew she should protest, or make some effort to pull away from him. But she found it difficult to move, to speak, to do anything but gaze into his eyes.

"I'm going to kiss you, Norah Bloomfield," he said in a quiet, dispassionate voice. "I want that even more than I wanted the pizza." He gave her hands a tug and then she was sitting on the edge of the bed. Her heart was pounding hard against her ribs, her breath coming in short, painful bursts.

His mouth settled over hers, his hands in her hair, pressing her against him. Norah was shocked by the powerful sensuality she experienced. Her eyes closed slowly as excitement overtook common sense.

She didn't doubt for an instant that if she'd made the slightest protest Rowdy would have released her. But his mouth was warm, hard, compelling...

When the kiss ended, she automatically rose to her

feet and backed away. She blinked, feeling confused. "Th-that was…unfair," she stammered.

"Unfair? In what way?" he demanded.

"We didn't set the terms of the wager—I wasn't prepared for it!"

"You needed a warning?"

She brought the tips of her fingers to her lips, at a loss to explain herself. "I'm…not sure. Yes, I think so." She still felt dazed and it made her furious.

"Norah, what's wrong?"

"I don't think playing checkers was such a good idea, after all," she said coldly, recovering as well as she could. Her hands trembled as she hurriedly finished putting away the game. It wasn't until she felt a tear roll down the side of her face that she realized she was crying, and that only humiliated her more.

"I didn't mean to offend you," Rowdy said, his voice regretful.

"Then why'd you do it? Why couldn't we just be friends? Why does everything have to boil down to… to that?"

"You're making a bigger deal out of this than necessary," he said softly. "I'm sorry if I upset you. It won't happen again."

Suddenly Norah wasn't sure she wanted that reassurance. She wasn't sure *what* she wanted; that was the problem. As much as she hated to admit it, she'd enjoyed the kiss.

"We heard from Valerie and Colby," she said abruptly.

He frowned. "Are they having a good time?"

She didn't meet his eyes. "Wonderful."

"Valerie's going to be bored out of her mind within a month, you know that, don't you?"

Norah shook her head.

"I told her when she handed me her resignation." His frown deepened. "She knows it, too."

"Valerie will find something else."

"In Orchard Valley? Don't count on it. Not with her qualifications. What's she going to do? Run the school lunch program?" Rowdy was growing more animated by the minute. "Ridiculous woman, letting her emotions dictate her life. I expected better of her."

"My sister made her choice, Mr. Cassidy. If anyone was being ridiculous, it's you."

His mouth tightened at her words and Norah marveled that they could be wrapped in each other's arms one moment and sniping at each other the next.

"She and this Carlton fellow will be very happy, I'm sure," Rowdy said stiffly. He leaned back against the pillows and grimaced in obvious pain.

"It's Colby."

"Whoever," he snapped irritably.

Norah knew it was the discomfort speaking now, and relaxed. "I'll ask LaVern to bring you some pain meds."

"I don't need anything," he growled.

"Perhaps not, but as a favor to me, please take it."

"I don't owe you any favors."

Norah was offended by the sharpness of his tone. He glared at her as if he couldn't wait for her to be gone, reminding her once again that it was Valerie he was interested in—not her.

"All right," he said curtly. "I'll take the pills. Just stop looking at me like I've done something terrible.

It was only a kiss! You'd think no one had ever kissed you before."

At his words, Norah understood. That was *exactly* the way she felt, as if Rowdy Cassidy had been the first man to hold her. The first man to kiss her. It was as if she'd waited all her life for this moment, this man.

She turned and rushed from the room.

Norah dreaded the next morning, since she was scheduled to report to Rowdy's floor again. She avoided seeing him as long as possible—an entire fifteen minutes into her shift.

"Good morning," she greeted him with a bright smile.

"Sounds like you're in better spirits than you were the last time I saw you," he said, watching her closely.

"Having one's ego destroyed in a game of checkers will do that," Norah said with false cheerfulness, carrying his breakfast tray to the bedside table.

"Was it the checkers…or the kiss?"

"It looks like lumpy oatmeal and soft-boiled eggs this morning," she said, ignoring his words.

"Norah." His hand covered hers, preventing her from leaving.

"The checkers," she said dryly. "You flatter yourself if you think a kiss would unsettle me like that. I'm a big girl, Mr. Cassidy."

"Then perhaps we should try again."

"Don't be absurd."

Rowdy's hand tightened over hers. "It isn't as preposterous as you make it seem. You're very sweet, Norah

Bloomfield. A man could get accustomed to having you around."

Norah hesitated, not knowing if she should take his words as a compliment or an insult. "I'm not a plaything for your personal amusement. Now, if you'll excuse me, I've got work to do."

"Will you stop by later?"

"If I have the time." Her back was to him; she was eager to make her escape.

"If you bring the checkers game I'll give you another chance to redeem yourself. I might even let you win just so I can give you what *you* want."

"Ah, but that's where we differ," she said as breezily as she could. "You see, Mr. Cassidy, you don't have anything I want."

"Ouch," he said and as she left the room she glanced over her shoulder to see him clutching at an imaginary wound. She didn't want to laugh, but she couldn't help it.

Three hours had passed when Karen Johnson sought her out. "Check on the cowboy, would you, Norah? Something's wrong."

"Why me?" Norah protested.

"You're the only one who can go near him without getting your head ripped off."

"Did he ask for me?"

Karen frowned slightly. "Yes, but don't feel too complimented. He's throwing out plenty of names, including the governor's and a couple of congressmen. It wouldn't surprise me if they rushed to his side, either."

Karen hadn't exaggerated. By the time Norah arrived from the far end of the corridor, she could hear Rowdy ranting. His words, however, were indistinguishable, which in Norah's opinion was probably for the best.

"Rowdy," she said, standing in the doorway, hands on her hips. "What's going on in here?"

He looked up at her, placing his hand on the telephone's mouthpiece. "Word leaked out that I was in a plane crash." He sighed heavily. "CHIPS stock has already dropped two points. We're in one hell of a mess here."

Four

"Do you know of a decent secretarial service?" Rowdy demanded as soon as Norah walked in the door the next morning. He might have been sitting behind a mahogany desk preparing to command his empire. His dark eyes were sharp and alert, his jaw tense.

"Uh... I don't think so."

"What I need is a phone book."

Taken aback, Norah turned and pointed behind her. "There's one at the end of the hall."

"Get it," he said, then added, "Please."

Still Norah hesitated. "Rowdy, you seem to have forgotten you're in a hospital and not a hotel."

"I wouldn't care if I was in the morgue. I'm not about to watch the business I built—ten years of blood and sweat—go down the tubes because of a stupid broken leg."

"Your leg's far more than—"

"The telephone book," he reminded her crisply.

Norah threw her hands in the air and retrieved the phone book from the nurses' station.

"This is it?" Rowdy's eyes widened incredulously when she handed it to him. "I've read short stories longer than this."

"There's always Portland, but to be honest I don't know where I'd find a Portland directory."

"Kincade and Robbins are flying in. They'll be here by noon. I hate to ask my assistant, Ms. Emerich, to travel, but I may not have any choice. Advise the administration here that I'll be holding a press conference this afternoon." He rubbed the side of his jaw, his expression thoughtful. "While you're at it, would you arrange to have a barber drop by sometime this morning? I'm going to need a decent haircut and a shave."

"Rowdy, this is a *hospital*."

"Not anymore," he told her flatly.

"I don't have time to be running errands for you. In case you've forgotten, you're not the only patient on this floor. I can't allow you to disrupt the entire wing with camera crews and the like."

"The excitement will do them good," he told her, leafing through the Orchard Valley directory. "It'll give your patients something to tell their families during visiting hours."

Norah was beginning to get irritated. "You're not listening to me."

He went on as if she hadn't spoken, his eyes narrowed and resolute. "I'm going to hold a press conference and if I can't do it from here, I'll find someplace I can."

"You can't be moved."

"Don't bet on it."

Norah didn't, not for an instant. Rowdy would have

his way, simply because he made it impossible to oppose him and win.

Norah left him and reported what he'd told her to Karen Johnson. She was never quite sure what happened next. But before the morning ended, the hospital administrator, James Bolton, had visited Rowdy's room. Norah had no way of knowing what was discussed, but she learned a little later that a number of reporters and two camera crews would be brought into Rowdy's room early that same afternoon. Just as he'd predicted.

Orchard Valley General Hospital had never seen anything like it. Charles Tomaselli, Steffie's fiancé, showed up, and cornered Norah to ask if she could get him into the press conference.

Norah shrugged. "I'll try." She did and when she came back with a *yes,* was rewarded with a thumbs-up from Charles.

By two that afternoon, the ward looked more like a media carnival than a hospital.

"Did you ever dream it'd come to this?" Karen asked her, leaning against the counter at the nurses' station as she viewed the proceedings.

Norah shook her head. She didn't know if Rowdy had the physical stamina to withstand a lengthy interview. The news conference had been going on for nearly an hour, with no sign of ending anytime soon.

Reporters were crammed inside his hospital room, spilling out into the hallway and jostling one another. Cameras flashed as microphones were thrust in Rowdy's direction.

Patients from the other rooms stood in their doorways, gawking, trying to find out what they could. Rumors washed like floods through the hospital corridors.

At one point Norah heard the president was visiting. Someone else claimed royalty had arrived. Two other people were convinced they'd seen Elvis.

From the corner of her eye, Norah saw Kincade, Rowdy's corporate attorney. He seemed to be searching through the crowd, looking for someone. Intuitively, she realized what was happening. Rowdy had worn himself out.

"Excuse me," Norah said, thinking and acting quickly. Carrying a tray in one hand and a syringe in the other, she edged her way through the reporters and camera crews. The news staff reluctantly parted to make a path for her. She moved into the room, then held up one hand to shade her eyes from the blinding light. In an instant she saw that Kincade's concerns were well-founded. Rowdy was pale and definitely growing weaker, although he struggled to disguise it.

"You'll have to excuse me," she said in her most businesslike voice. "This will just take a couple of minutes. It's time for Mr. Cassidy's enema."

The room cleared within seconds.

Rowdy waited until the last reporter had left, then burst out laughing. Kincade and the other man Rowdy had referred to as Robbins were the only two who remained.

"Very clever," Kincade said with a smile.

"She isn't any good at checkers, but she's one heck of a nurse," Rowdy said. He lowered himself onto the pillows and closed his eyes in exhaustion. "You'll arrange everything for me, Robbins?" he asked hoarsely.

"Right away," the other man assured him.

Briefly, Norah wondered if Rowdy even knew the first names of his staff members. It was Kincade and Robbins. But he'd always referred to her sister as Valerie. He knew *her* first name.

She was about to comment, then noticed that Rowdy was already asleep. Without another word, she ushered the two men out of the room.

"Thanks," Kincade whispered gratefully.

She nodded. It was her job to look out for the welfare of her patients. She hadn't done anything extraordinary. Her means might have been a little unorthodox, but effective.

Robbins was tall and wiry and young, and Kincade was short, stocky and middle-aged. Both men were dressed in identical dark suits—the CHIPS uniforms, Norah thought wryly. She remembered her sister wearing the female version of that business suit. Though, strangely, Norah couldn't imagine Rowdy in anything but jeans and cowboy boots.

"I understand you're Valerie's sister," Robbins said in a conversational tone.

"That's right." She'd forgotten that the two men had probably worked with Valerie.

"We all miss her."

But not as much as Rowdy does, Norah mused and was surprised by a sharp, fleeting pain at the thought.

"Rowdy's transferring me to Portland to head up the expansion project," Robbins said, eyeing Norah as if she had information to give. "I was hoping that once I got settled, Valerie would consider working with me."

"I don't know," Norah told him. "You'll have to talk to her."

Robbins glanced nervously toward Rowdy's room. "Don't say anything to Rowdy. Valerie was by far the more logical choice, but I don't think those two parted on amicable terms. He accepted her resignation and then gave me the assignment that same day. Personally, I'd rather stay in Texas."

It went without saying that Robbins would move simply because Rowdy had asked it of him. Oregon. Alaska. Anywhere. Whatever other talents Rowdy possessed, and Norah didn't doubt there were many, he inspired loyalty among his employees.

"Valerie and her husband are on their honeymoon. She should be back from Hawaii sometime this week. You might have the opportunity to tell her all this yourself," Norah said, then turned away.

"Ms.—Bloomfield."

This time it was Kincade, the corporate attorney, who addressed her. "Thanks again," he said.

"No problem. I was happy to be of help."

"This isn't easy for him," the attorney added. "Rowdy's a physical man and being tied down to his bed, literally, is driving him to distraction. If it wasn't for you, I don't know what he would've done."

"Wasn't for me?" Norah hadn't done much of anything. She'd provided a little entertainment with the checkers, a little nourishment with the pizza and muffins, and she'd fallen in with his schemes, like everyone else in the hospital. But that was it.

"He's mentioned you several times. All of us at

CHIPS want you to know we appreciate everything you've done for him."

Norah nodded, accepting his gratitude, but she felt uncomfortably like a fraud. Rowdy must have greatly exaggerated the small things she'd done.

Later that afternoon, just before she was scheduled to be relieved from her shift, the office equipment began to arrive. First came a fax machine, followed by a second computer, a desktop model, complete with printer. Then two men carrying a desk with an inverted chair balanced on top passed her in the corridor.

"What's going on *now?*" Karen asked, rubbing her eyes as if she were seeing things.

"I have the feeling," Norah muttered, "that Rowdy Cassidy is about to set up office—in a *big* way."

Norah followed the desk and chair to Rowdy's room and stood staring in amazement at the transformation. He'd done exactly what she'd suspected. This wasn't a hospital room any longer, but a communications center. A man from the telephone company was busy installing a multiline phone. Heaven only knew how many lines Rowdy had ordered.

"I hate to intrude," she said sarcastically, "knowing how busy you are and all—but *what* is going on in here?"

"What does it look like?" Rowdy returned curtly. "I'm getting back to work."

"Here?"

"I don't have much choice. Robbins will be in bright and early tomorrow with my assistant, Ms. Emerich. I'll be handling as many of my own affairs as I can."

"I only hope Dr. Silverman and the rest of the hospital staff don't get in your way."

Rowdy didn't hear the sarcasm in her voice, or if he did, he ignored it. Norah sighed.

"Rowdy, this is a hospital. You're here to recover so you can go back to your life. You can't conduct business as usual. I'm sorry, I really am, but—"

"Either I conduct my business or there won't be one to go back to," he announced starkly.

"You're exaggerating."

"All four lines are connected and working," the telephone installer said, setting the phone on the bedside table.

"Thank you," Rowdy said as the man walked out the door. "Listen, Norah, you're a good nurse," he continued, "but you don't know…checkers about managing a corporation. Now loosen up before I tell everyone what a poor sport you are."

Norah felt the warmth invade her cheeks.

"This all right over here?" one of the men who'd hauled in the desk asked.

"Perfect," Rowdy answered, barely glancing in that direction. "Thank you for your trouble."

The two men left, closing the door behind them. As soon as he was alone with her, Rowdy reached for Norah's hand. "Have you recovered?" he asked, his eyes holding hers.

"I'm not the one who's sick."

"I meant from the kiss."

His comment intensified the heat in her face. "I—I don't know what you're talking about."

"Yes, you do. You've been thinking about it every minute since." He added in a whisper, "So have I."

"Uh…" What bothered Norah most was how accurate he was. She'd spent a lot of time reflecting on their kiss, despite all her efforts to push it from her mind. She'd dreaded being alone with Rowdy again, fearing he'd know how confused and flustered his touch had left her.

"You're a beautiful woman, Norah." He pressed her palm to his lips. The feel of his tongue against her skin sent hot sensation shooting up her arm.

Norah trembled and closed her eyes. He was drawing her closer to his side and like an obedient lamb she went to him. He reached for her and, finally, somewhere deep inside, she found the strength to resist.

"No…no, Rowdy. I'm Norah, not Valerie. I don't think you've figured out the difference yet." She backed away from him and hurried out of the room. He called for her once, his voice sharp with impatience, but Norah ignored him.

The afternoon was overcast and gloomy; rain threatened. Norah found her father sitting in his favorite chair beside the fireplace in his den, reading.

"I understand there was quite a commotion at the hospital this afternoon," he said, glancing up from his novel.

"You heard? Already?"

"Charles stopped in and gave Steffie and me a run-down of what happened. Sounds like a three-ring circus."

"It was ridiculous."

Her father chuckled. "I also heard how you broke up the news conference. I always knew you were a clever child, I just don't think I fully appreciated *how* clever."

"Rowdy Cassidy's impossible."

"Oh?" Although the question appeared casual, Norah wasn't fooled. Her father was doing his best to gauge how the relationship between her and Rowdy was developing. The situation with Rowdy was very like his own thirty years earlier, when he'd met Grace, who'd been a nurse, and married her. Theirs had been a hospital romance. Although her father hadn't said much, Norah knew he was hoping history would repeat itself.

In a way it troubled Norah that he hadn't questioned her more about her relationship with Valerie's former employer. She should've been relieved. He'd barely asked about Rowdy, barely revealed any interest. Nor had he mentioned his near-death dream lately, other than that one cryptic remark about Rowdy's arriving right on schedule. She certainly didn't believe her father's dream—in which he'd supposedly had a conversation, complete with predictions about all three sisters. But it had sustained him and delighted him for so long that she actually found his silence disturbing.

Norah drifted up the stairs to her room. She wished now that she'd let Rowdy kiss her. And yet it angered her that she should be feeling anything—especially when she knew how deeply Rowdy cared for Valerie.

Norah changed out of her uniform and walked slowly down the back stairs that led to the spacious kitchen. Halfway there, she could hear Steffie and Charles. They were speaking in low tones, and their words were followed by silences. Lovers exchanging promises, no doubt.

Not wanting to embarrass them, or herself, Norah made sure they heard her approach. She burst onto the scene with a smile to find her sister sitting in Charles's lap. A wooden spoon coated in spaghetti sauce was poised in front of his mouth.

With obvious reluctance, Charles dragged his gaze away from Steffie. "Thanks for getting me into that press conference this afternoon, Norah. I appreciate it."

"You're welcome." She opened the refrigerator and took out a pitcher of lemonade. Her back to the happy couple, she heard Steffie whisper something, then giggle softly.

"What time's dinner?" Norah asked, refusing to look in their direction. She got a tall glass and added ice before pouring the lemonade.

"Another hour or so."

She couldn't face Steffie and Charles just now. Seeing how happy they were, how much in love, was almost painful. "Do you need any help with dinner?"

"No, thanks," Charles answered for Steffie. "We've got everything under control here."

Norah was sure they had.

It wasn't until she was in her bedroom with the door closed that she realized how tense and rigidly controlled she'd been.

Steffie and Charles's wedding was only a few weeks away, and she was excited and happy for them both. They hadn't wanted the elaborate affair Valerie and Colby had had. Just as well, since Orchard Valley had yet to recover from the first Bloomfield wedding.

Norah was happy for her sisters. Really happy. They both deserved the love they'd found.

Love.

It had changed Valerie, turned her life upside down. Her oldest sister had never been one to reveal her emotions, but from the moment Valerie had accepted Colby's engagement ring, she'd changed. She'd become exuberant, animated. Right before Norah's eyes, love had transformed her sister into someone she hardly recognized. Valerie, who'd always been so serious, so business-minded, had become giddy with love.

It had the opposite effect on Steffie. Her middle sister had always been the emotional one, and she'd never had any qualms about expressing her opinions, no matter how outrageous they might be.

These days Steffie was calm and peaceful. When she was with Charles, she seemed to be a different woman, Norah thought. Her sister had always been in a hurry; there were people to meet, places to go, experiences to live. But no longer. She'd relaxed, slowed down.

Both her sisters were marrying men who balanced them. Men whose personalities complemented and completed theirs.

And then there was Norah.

Expelling her breath, Norah stretched out on her bed and stared at the ceiling. She dated often, but none of the men she was currently seeing affected her the way Colby and Charles had affected her sisters. Still, after watching what had happened to them, she wasn't sure what to expect in her own life. Should she expect her personality to be moderated, too? And in what way?

She'd never been as serious as Valerie or as vivacious as Steffie. She was just plain Norah.

The phone rang, but the first ring was abruptly cut off. A moment later, Steffie came pounding up the stairs, yelling, "Norah! Phone!"

Norah rolled over and picked up the phone on her bedside table. "Hello," she mumbled.

"Do you feel up to a game of checkers?"

"Rowdy?" Her heart quickened at the sound of his voice.

He chuckled. "You mean you've been playing games with other men? I'm shocked."

"I…" She didn't know what to say. Instinct told her to say yes, to agree to another game immediately. But common sense intervened. "No," she told him firmly.

"I promise no more tricks," he said as a means of inducement.

"I'm sorry. I don't think so."

There was a long silence before he spoke again. "I had another reason for calling. I wanted to thank you for everything you did this afternoon."

"It wasn't that much."

"But it helped, and I'm grateful. I've caused quite a ruckus in the orderly world of this hospital, haven't I?"

"Indeed you have," she said with a soft laugh. She had a sneaking suspicion it was the same wherever he went—Orchard Valley, Houston or New York City.

Rowdy chuckled, too, and then asked her a couple of questions, about the hospital and the town; she answered and asked him a few of her own. The conversation continued in a casual vein.

After what seemed like only minutes, Norah heard

Steffie calling her down for dinner. Norah glanced at her watch, surprised to discover that she'd been talking to Rowdy for nearly half an hour.

"I have to go."

"Well, thanks again… Norah." He said her name with an odd, breathless catch. "I always seem to be thanking you."

Running down the stairs toward the kitchen, Norah realized she felt completely revived.

It seemed as though everyone—her father, Charles and Steffie—turned to stare at her when she walked into the room. "Is something wrong?" she asked, glancing down to be sure her blouse wasn't incorrectly buttoned.

"Not a thing," her father said, reaching for the green salad. "Nope, not a thing." But Norah saw him raise his eyes to Steffie and grin from ear to ear.

Rowdy's room had been transformed into a command post. Men and women were walking briskly in and out as Norah arrived early the next morning.

She brought Rowdy his breakfast tray and found Robbins on the phone, switching from one line to another. An elegant middle-aged woman with her dark hair in a chignon sat behind the desk, working at the computer. No one seemed to notice Norah—least of all Rowdy, who was issuing orders like a general from his headquarters.

"I hope I'm not interrupting anything," Norah said, not bothering to restrain the sarcasm as she set down his tray.

"Norah." Rowdy's eyes lit up and he laid aside the file he was scanning. Horn-rimmed reading glasses were perched at the end of his nose; they only made him look more attractive.

"I brought your breakfast."

"I don't suppose you have any more of those blue-berry muffins, do you?"

"I might."

"But it's going to cost me, right?"

"Not exactly." She'd read over the notes the night staff had left regarding Rowdy and learned he'd been on the phone until all hours of the night. He'd called her, of course, but that had been much earlier in the evening.

She took the thermometer from its slot and stuck it under his tongue.

"I haven't got a fever! Why do you insist on taking my temperature so many times?" he fussed when she was through.

She made the notation and then took his wrist. "You were on the phone for nearly eight hours straight."

"Jealous?" He wiggled his eyebrows.

"I might be." She was far more concerned about his apparent lack of concern for his health.

"There were people I needed to talk to, people I had to reassure. By the way, did you see we got coverage on CNN? My plane crash put Orchard Valley on the map."

"I'm sure the mayor is thrilled."

"He offered me the keys to the city."

"Uncle Jack? He didn't!" Norah couldn't believe it.

Rowdy laughed boisterously. "No, he didn't, but he should have."

Norah finished taking his pulse and recorded the information.

"Now do I get those blueberry muffins or are you going to make me beg?"

Norah removed two wrapped muffins from her sweater pockets. "Count your blessings, Cassidy. This is the last of the batch. My dad sent them to you with his best wishes."

"Bless him." Rowdy ignored the breakfast tray and unwrapped the muffins instead. "Meet Ms. Amelia Emerich, my executive assistant. You remember Robbins, don't you?"

Norah smiled at both of Rowdy's employees.

"I know your sister Valerie," Ms. Emerich said. "A wonderful young woman. We all miss her terribly. Say hello for me, won't you?"

Norah nodded, carefully watching Rowdy. She wondered how he'd react to the mention of her sister's name. He didn't, at least not outwardly.

"Mr. Cassidy will need an hour later this morning," Norah told Robbins and Ms. Emerich. "Dr. Silverman's scheduled to—"

"What time?" Rowdy broke in.

"The schedule says ten."

"He'll have to change it. I've got an interview with *Time* magazine at ten."

"Rowdy, you can't ask Dr. Silverman to rearrange his day because you're meeting with a magazine reporter!"

"Why not? He'll understand. I'm sure he won't mind waiting. He might even want to talk to the guy from *Time* himself. I'll try to arrange it if I can."

"Kincade's calling you at eleven," Ms. Emerich told Rowdy.

"That's right. Listen," he said, directing his attention

back to Norah. "Maybe it'd be best if you had Dr. Silverman check with Ms. Emerich before he does whatever it is he needs to do."

Norah was too stunned for a moment to react. "Dr. Silverman will be here at ten," she said firmly. "If the reporter from *Time* magazine is here, then he'll need to wait outside the room like everyone else. May I remind you once again that this is a *hospital,* Mr. Cassidy? You've managed to sweet-talk other people around here, but it won't work with me. Is that understood?"

A shocked silence fell after her words. Ms. Emerich and Robbins both stood with their mouths open, as though they'd never heard anyone speak to their boss like this.

Rowdy's eyes went from dark to darker. "All right," he finally said, his voice sullen.

Norah whirled around and marched out of the room.

The results of Dr. Silverman's examination revealed signs of improvement. If his leg continued to mend, Rowdy could be discharged within two weeks. No one was more relieved than Norah.

The sooner Rowdy left, the better for her. Once he was gone, Norah felt confident her life would return to normal. Once Rowdy had left Orchard Valley, her heart could forget him.

They'd only kissed once, but it was enough—more than enough. She knew this was a dangerous man. Dangerous to her emotional well-being. More important, he was in love with her sister.

Three days later, on a Monday afternoon, Norah stopped in to find Rowdy resting. The room was silent, which was rare. Norah guessed that Ms. Emerich and Robbins were out to lunch.

"I've got your medication," she said, spilling two capsules into the palm of his hand and giving him a small paper cup filled with water.

Rowdy swallowed the pills.

He looked exhausted. Norah was furious that he insisted on working so hard, especially now when he needed to rest. He ran everyone around him ragged, yet he demanded twice as much of himself. She shook off her thoughts as she realized he was speaking to her.

"Did anyone ever tell you how much you look like an angel?" he asked.

"Just you."

"You're very beautiful, Norah Bloomfield."

"And you're very tired."

"I must be," he said on the tail end of a yawn. "I wasn't going to say anything until later."

"Say what?" she prompted.

"About your angel face. You don't look a thing like Valerie."

Her sister's name went through her like an icy chill. The sister she loved and admired. The sister she'd always looked up to and idolized. Now, Norah could barely tolerate the sound of her own sister's name.

"Rest," she advised softly.

"Will you be here when I wake up?"

"I'm not sure." The ward was full, and she didn't have time to stay at his bedside, although it was exactly what she wanted to do. "I'll be back later, when I'm finished my shift."

"Promise?" His eyelids were drifting shut even as he spoke.

"I promise." Impulsively she brushed the hair from his temple, letting her hand linger on his face. He was growing more important to her every moment, which terrified her. She dreaded the day he'd be released and in the same heartbeat willed it to hurry.

When Robbins and Ms. Emerich returned half an hour later, Norah suggested they take the remainder of the afternoon off. Rowdy would be furious, but she'd deal with him later. He was pushing himself too hard; he needed the rest.

Norah's shift had ended at five, and she was sitting at his bedside when he awoke. He must have sensed she was there because he moved his head toward her and slowly smiled. "What time is it?"

"Five-thirty."

His eyes widened. "That late? But what about—"

"I gave them the afternoon off."

"Norah," he groaned. "I wish you hadn't. I was expecting several calls." He struggled to a half-sitting position and his gaze shot to the phone. She stood and picked up the plug, dangling it from her fingers.

"You unplugged the phone?"

"As I explained earlier, you needed the rest."

Rowdy's mouth snapped shut and anger leaped into his eyes.

"And as I've explained before, this is a hospital, Mr. Cassidy, not Grand Central Station. If the call was that important they'll try again tomorrow."

Rowdy pinched his lips closed. Norah suspected it

was to prevent himself from unleashing some blistering invective.

"I do have one small piece of information for you, however," she said matter-of-factly.

Rowdy's eyes met hers, his expression inquiring.

"Valerie and Colby got home this afternoon."

Rowdy reached for the bar and sat upright, his face eager. His eyes sharpened the way they did whenever he felt strongly about something—or in this case, someone. "I need to see her right away," he said. "See what you can do to arrange it, would you?"

Five

"Valerie is just home from her honeymoon," Norah felt obliged to remind Rowdy. "You don't really expect me to drag her up here, do you?"

Rowdy seemed surprised by her question. "Of course I do. Valerie and I have unfinished business."

Norah's stomach tightened into hard knots. She'd been a fool, standing guard over Rowdy all afternoon, protecting him the way she had. Hurrying to his side the moment her shift ended... That had been her first mistake. She was determined not to make a second one. It wasn't Norah he wanted doting on him, it was Valerie.

"Valerie's married, Rowdy. Nothing's going to change that."

Pain flashed into his eyes and there was no mistaking the reason. Now, more than ever, Norah realized what a calamity it would be to risk her heart on a man in love with someone else. Especially when that someone was her own sister.

Suddenly the mist cleared in Norah's mind. Rowdy had had her transferred to his floor, not out of any desire to be near her but to have a source of information about Valerie. Even the kiss, the one she'd treasured, had been nothing but a ploy.

With her heart aching, Norah walked around to the other side of his bed, being careful to avoid the office equipment positioned in every available space.

"I never asked what you expected to accomplish when you flew into Orchard Valley. I assume you were hoping to do more than celebrate Valerie and Colby's happiness."

"Oh, yes," Rowdy admitted with an abrupt laugh, "I had to be sure Valerie knew what she was doing."

"You *couldn't* have believed Valerie would cancel the wedding!"

"That was something I had to find out. Everyone has their price."

His words stunned Norah. "You really think that, don't you?"

"Why shouldn't I? It works. I didn't want to lose Valerie, but at the same time I wasn't willing to give her what she wanted. So I gambled. She took me at face value, unfortunately, and I lost, but I might not have—except for the plane crash."

Norah shook her head. "What do you mean, you weren't willing to give Valerie what she wanted? What was that?"

"Marriage."

If she'd been shocked before, Norah was completely astounded now. She needed to sit down before her legs gave out. She sank, speechless, into the bedside chair. The man was insane. He apparently believed Valerie had contrived her engagement to Colby with the intention of prompting Rowdy into a wedding proposal.

"I'm not the marrying kind, Norah. Valerie must have known that. I can't say we ever actually talked about it, but I figure anyone who's worked with me knows I don't have time for a wife or family. Don't need 'em."

"I'm sure that's true," Norah said tightly.

Rowdy studied her closely. "Are you upset about something?"

"No. Yes!" She jumped to her feet. "Let me see if I understand you correctly. You want me to bring my sister to you, but as far as I can tell, your reasons for wanting to see her are entirely self-serving. You don't care about Valerie and Colby. The only person you care about is yourself."

He hesitated and his brows knit together as he mulled over her words. "I'm not going to tell you about the nature of my business with your sister, if that's what you're asking."

"You don't have to," she said coldly, ignoring the intense pain she felt. "I know everything I need to. If you want to talk to Valerie, I suggest you draft someone else to arrange it."

Valerie, tanned and relaxed after her honeymoon, was potting red geraniums on the sun-washed patio outside her house—the house she and Colby had bought on the outskirts of Orchard Valley. Norah was sipping iced tea under the shade of a large umbrella, watching her sister work. The pungent scent of freshly squeezed lemons drifted on the breeze. The afternoon was growing hot and humid, but neither Norah nor Valerie seemed to notice.

"What happened between you and Rowdy Cassidy when you flew back to Texas?" Norah asked.

Valerie paused, her hands deep in the potting soil. "We didn't part on good terms. I'm afraid it was my fault."

Norah said nothing, but her expression must have revealed her skepticism.

"I'm serious," Valerie insisted.

"I was sorry you had to hear about Rowdy's accident on your wedding day," Norah said. "Dad and Steffie and I weren't sure what to do. We didn't tell you because you had so much on your mind."

"Don't worry. Dad already talked to me about it. You did the right thing."

Norah's hands closed around the tea glass. She gazed into the distance for a moment, then said in a small voice, "He's in love with you."

Valerie tipped her large straw hat farther back on her head and laughed. "Rowdy might think he is, but believe me, Norah, he isn't. However, offering him my letter of resignation didn't help the situation."

She pressed the moist potting soil carefully around a geranium. "I underestimated Rowdy's ego," she explained. "He's a man who doesn't like to lose. He hasn't had much practice at it, and that's the problem. He's so wealthy he can buy anything he wants, and to complicate matters, he can charm the worm right out of an apple when he puts his mind to it."

"I—I know it isn't any of my business," Norah said,

feeling as though she was invading her sister's privacy, "but what happened when you told him about Colby?"

Valerie straightened, shaking the earth from her hands. "I didn't immediately mention I was engaged, which was a mistake. The first thing I brought up was my feasibility study on expanding CHIPS into the Pacific Northwest. I was eager to show Rowdy all my research. I presented the project in a favorable light, and I convinced him now was the time to do it.

"Before Rowdy knew I was engaged to Colby," Valerie continued, "he committed himself to the project. That thrilled me, of course, because I wanted to be the one to head it up."

"He's very savvy when it comes to business, isn't he? I mean, he's even working from his hospital bed."

"Rowdy's very talented," Valerie agreed. "But he's stubborn and he likes to have his own way."

"I've noticed," Norah said, grinning.

Valerie laughed. "I'll bet you have."

"Anyway, get back to your story."

"Well, I pushed the project, and he gave it the go-ahead—until I told him I wanted to run it myself. Rowdy said he'd rather I stayed in Texas and worked with him. He reached for my hands then and I had the feeling he was about to say something...romantic. I'm only grateful he saw my engagement ring. And that's when I told him about Colby."

Norah's heart went out to Rowdy. "He must have been shocked."

"He was, and angry, too." Valerie's face tightened at the memory. "He told me he thought I was too smart to let myself fall for that love-and-marriage stuff. He said that marrying Colby would be a disaster for my career." Valerie's gaze skidded self-consciously away from Norah. "I—I don't know if I ever said anything to you about Rowdy, but I was…attracted to him before I met Colby. When I first got home, just before Dad's surgery, I'd started to believe he might feel the same way about me."

"He does."

Valerie laughed and shook her head. "I hope I'm around to watch what happens when Rowdy actually does fall in love. It's going to knock that poor cowboy for one heck of a wallop."

"Go on," Norah encouraged.

"Where was I…oh, yes. When Rowdy discovered I was definitely engaged to Colby, he tried to talk me out of it. He even claimed it was his duty as my friend and employer to do whatever he could to keep me from making such a terrible mistake."

"He doesn't lack confidence, does he?"

"Not in the least," Valerie said with a grin. "He felt that in view of my recent poor judgment, Oregon was the worst place for me to be, so he offered the expansion project to Earl Robbins. In that case, I told him, I didn't have any choice. So I typed up my resignation and handed it to him. He seemed to think I was bluffing. He accepted the resignation, but blithely informed me that I'd recognize the error of my ways and come back to CHIPS. I won't, though, not if it means leaving Oregon."

"Did it frighten you to quit like that? You never said. All I can remember is a comment you made about taking an extended vacation until after the honeymoon."

Valerie nodded thoughtfully. "For the first while, I had the wedding plans to keep me occupied, but I soon got those under control. Colby's been wonderfully encouraging, and we've discussed a number of possibilities. I've got my application in with a couple of firms in Portland, but I don't feel a burning need to find a job right away. To be honest, I'm enjoying this time off. It feels good to plant flowers and sit in the sunshine."

"What do you think you'd like to do?" Norah asked.

"Colby and I have discussed the idea of starting a consulting business out of the house. That way I could set my own hours and work when I wanted, which appeals to me. But I'm going to do some research before I make any firm decisions. For now I'm content."

"Rowdy wants to see you," Norah said, her voice unintentionally sharp. "He's been pestering me ever since he heard you and Colby were back."

Valerie's hands stilled. "I suppose I should go visit him. I guess I owe him that."

Norah wasn't so sure.

"Did you hear?" Rowdy asked the next time Norah saw him.

"About what?"

"My stock's up two full points, and the price has remained steady all week."

To Norah's way of thinking, it must be agony to live a life controlled by the Dow Jones Industrial Average, but she didn't comment. "Congratulations."

Rowdy watched her closely. "Are you upset about our last talk?" He glanced at his two employees and kept his voice low.

"Of course not," Norah lied. "Why should I be? You want to talk to my sister, and that's perfectly understandable. As you reminded me, it isn't any of my business."

She walked around the end of his bed, removed his chart and made the necessary notations.

"I shouldn't have been so brusque."

That was only one in a long list of offenses, but Norah didn't bother to say so.

"You haven't been in to see me as often," he said.

"I've been too busy."

"Even for me?" He used a hurt little-boy tone and Norah couldn't resist smiling.

"You'll be happy to know I saw Valerie yesterday afternoon," she went on, not daring to look up, afraid of what she might read in his eyes. "I explained that you wanted to see her and she said she'd be in sometime in the next few days."

"I hope it's soon because Dr. Silverman's given the go-ahead to get me out of this rigging. I'm scheduled to be released on Friday."

Norah waited a moment, finding it difficult to identify her reactions. She was beginning to know this man, faults and all—and despite everything, she was crazy about him.

Their views often clashed, but that didn't change her feelings. And his employees, at least the ones she'd met, were deeply committed to him. It took a lot more than money to inspire such loyalty.

At the same time, Norah recognized how dangerous it was for her to be around Rowdy. He'd evoked a wide range of emotions: anger, outrage, laughter, pride and others that weren't as simple to define. It would be so easy to fall in love with him…. The mere thought terrified her.

"Aren't you going to say something?" Rowdy asked.

"We'll miss you around here." She put on a false smile. "Good grief, what'll we do for excitement now?"

"You'll think of something," he said.

"No doubt, but Orchard Valley will never be the same."

"Take a note, Ms. Emerich." Rowdy kept his gaze focused on Norah. "Small Oregon towns are no longer on my agenda. They're a risk to my health."

"I hope you understand that once you're discharged, you can't just go back to your regular work schedule," Norah pointed out.

"So I heard," Rowdy said, frowning. "I'm going to be stuck with months of physical therapy."

"Don't shortchange yourself on that, Rowdy. You need it."

He wasn't too pleased about this additional treatment, she knew. Then she sighed; he hadn't even left the hospital and already she was worrying about him. Oh, yes, she was going to miss him.

He must have seen the regret in her eyes because his own grew dark and serious. "Can you come back later?" he asked in a low voice. "Tonight. There's something I need to ask you."

Norah hesitated. "All right," she finally whispered.

"Around seven," he said briskly, "and don't eat dinner."

* * *

Norah wasn't sure what to expect that evening. She wore a sleeveless pale pink dress, the shade similar to her bridesmaid's dress. On impulse she'd worn the dangling gold earrings that had belonged to her mother. She wore them only on special occasions....

Her father didn't ask where she was going, but his complacent expression told Norah he knew. "You look absolutely beautiful," he said as she came down the stairs. "You have a wonderful evening, now."

"I'm sure I will." She half expected him to interrogate her, but he didn't ask even one question.

"I won't wait up for you."

"Have a good evening then, Dad."

"I will, sweetheart, I will," he said and then he did the oddest thing. He raised his head, eyes closed, and mumbled something she couldn't hear.

When Norah arrived at the hospital, she discovered that Rowdy had transformed his room into a romantic bower. The window shades were closed, allowing only glimmers of the evening light inside. Candles flickered from a linen-covered table, and half a dozen vases of fresh flowers were strategically placed throughout the room. The office furniture he'd had delivered was pushed as far against the wall as possible. A bottle of white wine was chilling in a silver bucket. Soft, lilting music played in the background. For an instant she wondered if she'd stepped into a dream, a fantasy.

"My goodness." The words escaped on a whisper of awe.

Rowdy wasn't wearing a hospital gown, but had dressed in a black Western shirt with string tie and a pair of jeans slit along one side to accommodate his cast. The effort he'd made touched her deeply.

"I hope you're hungry," he said, with a boyishly pleased grin.

"I'm starved," she told him, walking over to the bed. The room seemed so private, so cozy. "What's on the menu?"

"You can examine our meal for yourself. It only got here a minute ago."

Norah lifted the domed lid over the two plates and found crab-and-shrimp-stuffed sole, a wild rice pilaf and fresh broccoli with thin slivers of carrot. Two huge slices of strawberry-covered cheesecake rested next to the wineglasses.

"I had the chef check out the cholesterol, if you're interested. Plus the carb, sodium and calorie counts."

"Oh, Rowdy."

"Somehow I knew you'd swoon for cheesecake."

Norah laughed, because it was true, and because she was almost giddy with excitement—and happiness.

"Now pick up the gift that's on the edge of the table and open it."

Norah saw the small, brightly wrapped box and carried it to his bedside. She raised questioning eyes to his. "What's this?"

"You'll have to open it and see."

Norah frowned. "I didn't do anything to deserve this." She was only one of the medical professionals who'd assisted Rowdy in his recovery.

"Quit arguing with me and open it," Rowdy said. She finally nodded and carefully tore away the paper, uncovering a velvet box with the name of an expensive Portland jeweler etched in a gold flourish across the top.

She glanced at him again, still puzzled.

"Open it," he said again. "I picked it out myself."

Hardly daring to breathe, Norah lifted the lid and discovered a sapphire-and-diamond necklace, exquisite in its simplicity. She released her breath on a soft sigh of appreciation. "Oh, Rowdy… I've never seen anything so lovely."

"Then you like it?"

"Yes, but I could never accept it…."

"Nonsense. Turn around—I want to see it on you." Before she could protest further, he removed the necklace from its plush bed and opened the clasp. He held it with both hands, prepared to place it around her neck.

Norah pivoted slowly and pressed her hand to the necklace when he positioned it against her throat. She'd never been given anything so valuable or so beautiful.

"This is my way of thanking you for everything you did for me, Norah."

"But I—"

"You were my saving grace," he cut in, obviously impatient with her objections. "Arguing with you was the one thing that got me through those early days. You were generous and unselfish, even though I behaved like a spoiled brat. I'm grateful, and I want to express my gratitude."

"Well, then, I accept. And…and I thank you very much." Norah felt tears gather in the corners of her eyes. "Shall we open the wine?" she asked briskly, not wanting Rowdy to know how deeply his generosity had affected her. She lifted the wine bottle from its icy bucket and hesitated. "Are you sure you can combine alcohol with your medication?"

"I have Dr. Silverman's permission. If you don't believe me, you can call him yourself. He left his number with me in case you had any concerns."

Rowdy had thought of everything. Grinning, Norah handed him the bottle and corkscrew and watched as he deftly opened the Chablis. Norah brought over their glasses; he sampled the wine, then filled both goblets.

"We'd better eat before the fish gets cold," he said. Norah returned to the dinner table for his plate. His own place setting was neatly arranged on top of the nightstand.

"Next time we have dinner together, I'll be sitting across the table from you," he promised.

Norah sat down and spread the crisp linen napkin across her lap. In all her years of hospital work, she'd never seen anything like this. Of course, she'd never known anyone like Rowdy Cassidy, either.

"This is fabulous," Norah said after the first bite. She closed her eyes and savored the wonderful blend of seafood, sole and lightly seasoned sauce.

"Save room for dessert."

Norah eyed the huge fresh strawberries on the cheesecake. "No problem there." She felt a bit silly sitting at the table alone and after her second bite, got to her feet and carried her plate to the nightstand. "It'll do me good to stand up and eat," she told him. "I'll have more room for the cheesecake that way."

Rowdy grinned. The room was growing dark as

the sun set, a warm, intimate darkness, and the candle flames seemed to dance to the soft music.

It took Norah an instant to realize they'd both stopped eating. Slowly, his eyes holding hers, Rowdy pushed the nightstand away so there was nothing between them. His hands on her waist, he guided her to the bed.

"Sit next to me," he whispered.

She glanced at his leg, needing to gauge the effect her weight would have on the pulleys.

"I'll be fine."

Norah sat carefully on the edge of the bed. Her gaze was level with Rowdy's.

"No wonder I thought you were an angel," he whispered. The husky pitch of his voice thrilled her. "You're so beautiful…."

No man had evoked such emotions in her before. She didn't *want* to feel any of these things, not with a man like Rowdy, but she couldn't stop herself.

He took her face between his hands and rubbed the side of his thumb across her moist mouth. She sensed a barely restrained urgency in him, and still he didn't kiss her. Excitement raced through her veins.

"Rowdy." His name became a whispered plea.

She didn't completely understand what she wanted from him; he seemed to understand it better than she did herself. He reached for her and drew her unceremoniously into his arms. His mouth claimed hers, and whatever defenses she'd erected against him in the past two weeks, whatever doubts she'd harbored, were banished under the onslaught of his kiss.

Just when Norah thought she might faint with the exhilaration of his touch, Rowdy trailed his mouth across her cheek to the hollow of her throat. She sighed and sagged against him, weak and without will.

"I've wanted to do that from the first time I saw you," he whispered huskily. "When you stood there in that long pink dress—like an angel." He groaned and shook his head. "I've tried to be patient, tried to wait until I was out of this cast, but I couldn't. Not another moment."

Norah buried her hands in his thick, dark hair and placed eager kisses on his face. She'd wanted him, too. Badly. So badly that she'd been afraid to admit it, even to herself.

He kissed her again, a deeper kiss this time. "I was sure I'd go crazy these past few weeks," he murmured. "I've thought about nothing except holding you again, kissing you again. You've been so close—and yet so far away from me."

Norah felt warm and weightless in his arms. He kissed her with even greater insistence, and it seemed that she'd never experienced anything this good in her entire life. Shivers of excitement danced over her skin and she gave a deep, deep sigh.

"Come to Texas with me." The words were low and urgent. He held her tightly against him.

It took a moment for the words to sink past the fog of longing that blurred her thoughts. "Come to Texas with you?" she repeated. Slowly she eased herself from his embrace, her eyes seeking his. Her heart went wild with expectant hope.

"As my personal nurse."

Norah wondered if she'd heard him correctly. His *nurse*. He wanted her as his nurse. For one soaring moment she'd assumed, she'd hoped, that he wanted her for herself. For always. She'd dreamed he wanted her to— A blush warmed her cheeks as she realized how wrong she'd been. He'd told her before that he wasn't interested in marriage or family life. If he hadn't been willing to marry Valerie, whom he loved, then he certainly wasn't interested in her. CHIPS was his life, his reason for being. She'd witnessed it herself, the way all his energy, all his emotion, was dedicated to the success of his company.

"I'm going to need someone to look after me," he continued, reaching for her fingers and squeezing lightly, "to make sure I don't do more than I should. Someone who'll bully me into taking care of myself. Will you fly back with me, Norah?" He raised her hand to his lips and kissed her palm. "I need you."

How she'd longed to hear those words from Rowdy, but she'd wanted them to mean something very different.

Norah didn't need more than a second to decide. "I can't leave Orchard Valley."

His eyes narrowed. "Why not?"

"It's my home. I've lived here all my life. My father's here, my job is here, my family. Everything that's important to me is here."

"You'll be back in a little while. I shouldn't need you for more than…say, a couple of months."

Norah backed away from him but her feet seemed to be weighted down with cement. The little she'd eaten of her dinner rested like a concrete block in the pit of her stomach. Rowdy had arranged everything that evening in an effort to convince her to leave with him. As his nurse. Nothing more.

An overwhelming weariness came over her.

"Reconsider," he pleaded. "I promise you it won't be for long."

Norah shook her head. As far as she was concerned there wasn't anything to reconsider.

His mouth tightened with unconcealed irritation. "I'll make it worth your while. I'll triple whatever the hospital's paying you now."

She didn't doubt it. But financial concerns weren't what held her back. "I'm…pleased that you'd ask me, but it wouldn't work, Rowdy."

"Why not?" he demanded. "I'm going to need someone and I want *you*."

"But I'm not for sale."

"I didn't mean it like that," he flared, running his hand roughly through his hair. Norah could sense the frustration in him. It might have been petty of her, but she felt a fleeting satisfaction. She wanted him to taste her own disappointment.

"I don't know what it is with you Bloomfield women," he grumbled, pushing the nightstand back into place. "There's no pleasing you, is there?" He lowered his voice. "I never met a pair of more headstrong women in my life."

"You'll do just fine without me." She was slowly recovering from the influence of his touch. Valerie was right; Rowdy Cassidy knew how to stack a deck in his favor. Knowing she was attracted to him, he'd attempted to sway her decision with wine and a luscious meal—and kisses.

Rowdy sliced his cheesecake with enough force to crack the plate. "Uncooperative woman," he burst out.

Norah couldn't help laughing, despite the dull ache in her heart. "If you want, I'll recommend a reputable agency that provides nurses for private care."

"I don't want anyone but you." He stabbed a strawberry and poised it in front of his mouth. "You still haven't forgiven me for being honest, have you?"

"About what?"

"My feelings toward Valerie. I knew when I told you I'd regret it, and I was right."

"This doesn't have anything to do with my sister."

"Then why won't you fly back to Texas with me? I've got a private jet coming in. You won't lack for luxury, Norah, and if you're worried about propriety, I'll have Ms. Emerich move in with us."

"That isn't it."

"I should've guessed you'd be this stubborn. It runs in the family, doesn't it?"

"It most certainly does."

Rowdy leaned over and flipped a switch that turned off the music. "I didn't think this…dinner would work. Ms. Emerich was the one who suggested it."

Norah walked across the room and opened the blinds. "The evening's too lovely to shut out."

Rowdy folded his arms and said something she couldn't hear.

There was a polite knock at the door.

"Come in," Rowdy barked.

The door slowly opened and Valerie Bloomfield Winston stepped inside.

Six

"I'm not interrupting anything, am I?" Valerie asked. She remained on the threshold, oddly hesitant and unsure.

"Of course you're not." Despite her embarrassment, Norah managed to speak first. She felt like a five-year-old caught with her hand in the cookie jar.

Rowdy merely closed his eyes—in resignation, Norah supposed, at the prospect of facing another Bloomfield. "You might as well come in," he said ungraciously.

"If you'd rather I stopped by another time..." Valerie suggested, glancing at them doubtfully. "It wouldn't be any problem." Her gaze met Norah's, who was convinced her cheeks had flamed a fiery red.

"Don't worry," Rowdy muttered, "you weren't interrupting a thing."

"Rowdy asked me to accompany him back to Texas... as his nurse," Norah explained, her tongue stumbling over the words. She gestured weakly toward the elaborately set table and silver wine bucket.

"Ah…" Her sister was smart enough to figure out what had happened.

"Have you decided to take the job?" Valerie asked, looking at Norah.

"No," Norah said emphatically.

Rowdy frowned—again. "I should've known she'd be as stubborn as you. Norah doesn't want the job, even at ten times what she earns here."

"I should leave," Norah said, picking up her purse. "I'm sure you two have a lot to talk about."

"Don't go," Valerie countered smoothly. "The fact is, I'd rather you stayed." She pulled the wine bottle from the silver bucket and read the label. Apparently she was impressed, because her eyebrows arched. "I see you didn't spare any expense."

"Are you here to gloat or do you want to talk?" Rowdy asked irritably.

"He gets feisty," Valerie warned Norah under her breath, "when he can't have his own way."

"Quit talking about me as if I wasn't here," Rowdy snapped. He used the triangular bar to straighten himself and shift positions. "You and I need to clear the air, Valerie Bloomfield."

"I suspect we do," Valerie agreed. "And the name's Winston now."

Norah wanted to leave, but she felt rooted to the spot. Her eyes strayed from Valerie to Rowdy, wondering how much of his feelings he'd reveal to her sister. He'd loved her enough to fly to Orchard Valley, but even now she wasn't sure what his intentions had been.

"Despite everything I told you, you went ahead and married Carlton, anyway," he said in a low voice.

"Colby," Valerie and Norah corrected simultaneously.

"Whoever," Rowdy returned irritably. "You married him!" In response, Valerie raised her left hand and wiggled her ring finger.

"You can kiss your career goodbye, but you already know that, don't you?" Rowdy said. "I've seen it happen a thousand times, brilliant careers flushed down the drain and all in the name of love. As far as I'm concerned, it's a bunch of hogwash."

Valerie didn't say anything for a long moment. "At one time, working for you and CHIPS was the most important thing in my life."

"See?" Rowdy shouted, turning to Norah and pointing at Valerie, "It's happening already! And she's only been married, what? Two weeks."

"Three," Valerie inserted.

"Three weeks and already her mind is warped."

Valerie laughed, and Norah found her amusement somehow reassuring. "Love tends to do that to a person."

"Then heaven help us all." Rowdy crossed his arms over his chest and gazed steadfastly out the window. "You were one of the best," he finally said, still not looking directly at the two women. "It's a shame to lose you."

"As I recall, you didn't leave me much choice. You wouldn't give me the job I wanted, and you knew I wouldn't stay in Texas."

He winced and Norah saw a flash of regret in his eyes, a reappearance of the pain she'd noticed whenever Valerie's name was mentioned. Norah experienced a pang of her own, knowing that the man she'd begun to love cared so deeply for her sister.

"I…may have acted a bit hastily," Rowdy said with a contriteness he didn't bother to conceal. "Robbins is a good man, don't get me wrong, but he doesn't have the gut instincts you do when it comes to making a go of this expansion project. He took the assignment because I asked him to, but truth be known, you were always the person for the job. Not Robbins."

Valerie paced the room in silence; Norah almost demanded her sister say something to ease the tension. Val had told her only a little of the confrontation between her and Rowdy, but she knew an apology when she heard one. Valerie's former employer was trying to mend fences.

"What are you saying, Rowdy? That you want me back with CHIPS for the expansion project?"

"That's exactly what I'm saying."

"I'll never be the businesswoman I was, as you've pointed out. Marriage has ruined me, you know."

Rowdy's face relaxed with the beginnings of a smile. "There might be some hope for you yet. Once you're with CHIPS again, we'll work on your attitude. Of course it'll take time, training and patience, but Robbins and I should be able to whip you into shape."

Valerie didn't say anything. Norah stared at her sister, willing her to answer Rowdy. Willing her to recognize what it had cost his pride to make that offer. If Valerie didn't appreciate how difficult it was for him to admit he'd been wrong, then Norah did. Surely Val understood what he was really saying!

"I'm flattered."

For a moment Rowdy didn't react, then he slammed one hand against the other and swore under his breath. "You're going to turn me down, aren't you? I know that obstinate look of yours. Apparently it runs in the family." He was glaring at Norah as he spoke.

"I'm not committing myself either way just yet. The project will consume every waking minute for months, and I'm not sure that's what I want," Valerie told him honestly.

"You were ready to take it on before," Rowdy argued. "What's so different?"

"I'm married. I have responsibilities to someone other than myself. I didn't fully understand what that entailed when I first talked to you, but I know now, and I'm not going to let CHIPS control my life. Not anymore."

"So what do you intend to do? Stay barefoot and pregnant the rest of your life?"

"Rowdy!" Norah chastised, offended that he'd talk to her sister that way. He ignored her, frowning combatively at Valerie.

"Colby and I do eventually want children, but I was toying with the idea of starting my own business."

"Software?" His dark eyes became sharp as steel. It went without saying that Valerie could be keen competition if she chose to be.

"No," she said with amusement. "Consulting. I'll help companies determine what they need—systems, software, whatever. I'll set my own hours, and I'll train others, so once the business expands—or I do—it won't be unmanageable." She grinned at Rowdy. "I'll be able to combine work and a family in whatever way suits me best."

He nodded. "It makes sense."

Valerie smiled cheerfully. "That wasn't so hard to admit, now was it?"

"No," he agreed. His eyes softened as he studied Valerie. He seemed to have forgotten Norah was in the room. "I was a fool to ever let you leave Texas. We might've had something good between us. Something really good."

Valerie's gaze met his, and in it Norah read so many things. Her sister greatly admired Rowdy Cassidy, but the respect she held for him could never compare to the love she shared with Colby.

"I know, I know," Rowdy said with a weak smile. "Too little, too late. Well, I want to wish you and Carlton the very best."

"Colby," Valerie and Norah reminded him, and all three burst out laughing.

"You're home earlier than I expected," David Bloomfield said when Norah walked into the house an hour later. He was standing in the doorway of his den, dressed in flannel robe and slippers. A magazine lay on the arm of his favorite chair. "I was just going to make myself a cup of hot chocolate. Care to join me?"

"Sure." She trailed her father into the kitchen. "Where's Steffie?"

"She went out to dinner with Charles. I don't think she'll be home for a while."

It didn't seem possible that Steffie and Charles would be married in two weeks' time.

"Did you enjoy yourself?" David asked in that deceptively casual way of his. Norah knew her father well enough to recognize his interest as more than idle curiosity. He was eager to hear the details. And tonight, Norah was just as eager to talk.

"I had dinner with Rowdy this evening. He had the meal catered." While she was talking, Norah took a saucepan from the cupboard and set it on the stove to heat milk for their cocoa.

Her father leaned back in his chair, assuming a relaxed pose.

"Dad," Norah said, holding the milk carton in her hand and gazing absently into space. "If you had the opportunity to travel for...a job, would you take it?"

"That depends. Where would I be traveling?"

"A long way from home—but still in this country. Texas, actually. It wouldn't be for pleasure—or not exactly. It'd be a job. Sort of." Rowdy might claim he needed her, but Norah knew better. She'd end up twiddling her thumbs ninety percent of the time. Even if she did insist that Rowdy slow down his pace, he wasn't likely to listen to her. As far as she could see, her presence would serve no useful purpose, other than entertainment. Hadn't he said he enjoyed arguing with her?

"Am I to understand Rowdy's asked you to go with him when he leaves Orchard Valley?"

"As his private nurse," Norah explained, pouring milk into the pan. "It'd only be for a few weeks."

"You're not sure what you want, are you? The temptation to go with him is there, but you don't feel good about doing it. Am I right?"

Norah was a little surprised at how easily her father

had identified her dilemma, but she merely shrugged in reply.

"You like Rowdy Cassidy, don't you?" her father asked.

Norah added cocoa to the warm milk and stirred briskly. "He's stubborn as a mule, and I swear I've never known anyone more egotistical. His arrogance is beyond explaining and he—"

"But you like him." Her father spoke again, and this time his words were a statement and not a question.

Norah's hand stilled. "I think there must be something wrong with me, Dad. Rowdy's in love with Valerie—he might as well have come right out and said it."

"You're sure about that?"

Norah wasn't sure of anything. Not now. For one thing, it just didn't make sense that Rowdy could hold her and kiss her the way he had if he was really in love with her sister.

"Valerie came to see him…while I was there. He asked her to come and work for him again." She turned back to the stove and resumed stirring. Her feelings about what had taken place between Rowdy and her sister hadn't sorted themselves out in her mind yet. What did his offer to Valerie really mean? Was he so desperate to have her back in his life that he was willing to ignore her marriage to Colby? A sharp pain cut through her at the thought.

"Are you sure you're not mistaking regret for love?" her father asked gently. "Rowdy and Valerie worked together for a heck of a long time. Her engagement came as a shock to him. My feeling about their last confrontation—when Val flew to Houston—was that they both said things they later regretted."

"Valerie didn't say no, but she did ask for time to think it over. She refused to make a commitment either way." Norah poured the steaming cocoa into mugs and carried them to the table. "But you know, I think that was exactly what Rowdy expected from her. He was angry at first, but I had the impression it was more for show than anything."

David chuckled, then sipped his hot chocolate. "My guess is that being thwarted by two of my girls in one evening came as something of a shock to the boy."

Norah paused. "How'd you know I turned him down?"

David shrugged. "I just do. I'm not sure why, but I knew you had. Are you having second thoughts now?"

"And third. Earlier I was positive I'd made the right decision—and now I'm not."

Knowing that Rowdy would be out of her life in a matter of days had given her pause. His reaction was apparently the same. He didn't need a private nurse, and if she'd accepted his generous offer, she'd only be there to provide entertainment... Norah sighed.

Her father pointed at the sapphire-and-diamond necklace. "Is that new?" he asked.

Norah's hand went to her throat and she nodded. "Rowdy gave it to me—as a bribe, I suspect. I guess I should return it to him. Actually, I'd forgotten I had it on. It's beautiful, isn't it?"

"Very. If you want my advice about the necklace, keep it. Rowdy never intended it as a bribe. He's truly grateful for everything you've done." He swallowed the last of his chocolate and stood.

"How can you be so certain?" Norah wanted to know.

Her father hesitated, frowning slightly. "I just am." With that, he turned and walked away.

When Norah arrived at the hospital late the next morning, Rowdy's bed was empty.

She walked into the room and for a moment was too stunned to move. After spending a restless night weighing the pros and cons of his offer, she felt she had to talk to him again, even if it meant visiting the hospital on her day off.

"Looking for someone?" Rowdy asked from behind her.

She whirled around to discover him sitting in a wheelchair, his leg extended and supported. "When did this happen?"

"Only a few minutes ago. Sure feels good to be out of that bed."

Norah laughed and knew immediately what she wanted to do. "I imagine it does. Wait here. I'll be right back, I promise." She checked in at the nurses' station, scanned Rowdy's chart and quickly returned to his room.

"What are you doing now?" he asked when she stepped behind the wheelchair and began to push him down the hallway. "Hey, where are we going? Not so fast," he muttered. "I'm getting dizzy... Besides, I want a chance to take in the view. All I've seen for weeks are the four same walls."

"Just be patient," Norah said, enjoying herself. Finding his bed empty had sent her into a tailspin. But once she'd seen him and decided what she should do, she'd felt an overwhelming sense of relief. She was almost giddy with it.

"Are you kidnapping me?" he joked, when she backed him into the elevator. "Sounds a bit kinky, but I could go for that."

"Hush now," she said, smiling at a visiting priest who shared the elevator with them.

"I always knew you were crazy about me," Rowdy continued. "But I never realized how much."

"Rowdy!" She rolled her eyes, then looked in the priest's direction. "You'll have to excuse him, Father. He's just spent the past few weeks tied to a bed."

"So I see." The priest glanced at Rowdy's right leg.

"There were…other complications," Norah said with an exaggerated sigh.

"Poor fellow. I'll be saying a prayer for you, young man."

"Thank you, Father," Rowdy said so seriously that it was all Norah could do not to break into giggles.

The morning was gorgeous. The sun was shining, and the scent of blooming flowers drifted past on a warm breeze. Robins, goldfinches and bluebirds flitted about, chirping exuberantly.

Following a paved pathway, Norah pushed the wheelchair toward a small knoll of rosebushes that overlooked the town. Orchard Valley lay spread out like an intricate quilt below them. Norah stepped forward to watch Rowdy's face when he saw her home.

For a long moment he said nothing. "It's a peaceful sort of place, isn't it?"

"Yes," she said quietly. "People still care about one another here." She sat on a stone bench and breathed in the fresh morning air.

"Is this the reason you won't come with me?" Rowdy asked, gazing out over the town. "Because you don't want to leave Orchard Valley?"

"No," she answered honestly. "You're the reason."

"Me?" He wore a puzzled, hurt look. "It's the necklace, isn't it? You assume that because I gave you a gift I was asking you to be more than my nurse."

"No," she told him. "That didn't even cross my mind. It's so many other things." She leaned back, resting her hands on the sun-warmed bench. "I've never been more impressed by anyone than by you, Rowdy Cassidy. Your business judgment, your decisiveness, your sheer nerve. Your kindness, too. Just when I'm convinced you're the most egotistical man I've ever met, you do something wonderful that completely baffles me."

"Like what?"

"Like offering my sister the job she wanted."

"I'd behaved badly with Valerie. We both knew it, and it was up to me to make amends. I suppose you think I'm carrying a torch for her." He paused as if he were trying to decipher her expression. "But I swear that isn't true. If you must know, I felt cheated when Valerie returned to Houston engaged. I'd missed her all those weeks, and I was looking forward to having her back. Next thing I know, she announces she's going to marry some doctor." He shook his head. "I'll tell you, it felt like a slap in the face when I heard about Colby."

A weight seemed to lift from Norah's shoulders. Impulsively, she leaned forward just enough to brush her lips against his cheek.

Perplexed, Rowdy raised his hand to his jaw. "What was that for?"

"A reward for getting Colby's name right." She smiled in relief. Rowdy's resentment toward Valerie's husband was gone and, however reluctantly, he'd accepted both the situation and the man. She also had a glimmer of insight into his feelings: his pride had taken a severe battering. Rowdy was used to being in control, and suddenly—with Valerie—he wasn't. "Sorry," she said, "I didn't mean to interrupt you."

"Don't be so hasty." He folded his arms, relaxing in the warm sun. "What will you do if I say Colby's name three times in rapid succession?"

Norah smiled. "I don't know. I might go completely wild."

Rowdy laughed outright, then grew serious. "Hey, I'm going to miss you."

Norah lowered her eyes as dread filled her. "I'm going to miss you, too," she whispered.

He reached for her hands, covering them with his own. "Come with me, Norah," he said. "I'll work out something with the hospital. I'll buy the whole building if I have to, but I want you by my side."

The temptation to be with him was so strong that Norah briefly closed her eyes against the almost physical pull she experienced. "I…can't."

"Why?" he demanded, clearly exasperated. "I don't understand it. You want to come, I know you do, and I want you with me. Is that so hard to understand?"

Norah pressed her hands against the sides of his face.

He was so dear to her. When she said goodbye to him, she was sure a small part of her would die.

"Answer me," he pleaded.

Norah felt the emotion building in her, felt tears crowd into her eyes. "You need to realize something about me, Rowdy. Right now, you know me as a competent nurse, as Valerie's little sister, but you don't really *know* me. I have lots of friends and I like to go out, but basically I'm a homebody. Oh, I enjoy traveling now and again, but home is where my heart is. I love to bake and knit. Every year I plant a huge vegetable garden."

His expression revealed how mystified he was.

"I'm nothing like Valerie. She's so talented in ways I'm not."

"Do you think I've got the two of you confused?"

"No," she said softly. "I just don't want you to think of me as her replacement."

His eyes widened and he slowly shook his head. "No. I swear to you that isn't the case."

"You don't need a nurse. You'll do fine if you use a bit of common sense. Once the cast is off, you'll require physical therapy for a while, but I won't be able to help you with that, anyway. I'm not trained for it."

"I like being with you," he said defensively. "Is that so wrong?"

"No."

"Then what *exactly* is the problem?"

"You don't know the kind of person I am…."

"That's what I'd like to find out," he argued, "if you'd give me half a chance and quit being so stubborn."

"I'm traditional and old-fashioned," she said, ignoring his outburst, "and…you're not. I'm the kind of woman who enjoys sitting by the fireplace and knitting at night. I'm not an adventurer, a risk-taker, like Valerie. I love my own familiar little world. And…and someday I want to marry and raise a family."

"I wanted to hire you as a nurse," Rowdy growled. "Next thing I know, you're talking about marriage and babies. You're right—it was a terrible idea. Forget I ever suggested it."

Norah hadn't explained herself well. He assumed she was looking for a marriage proposal, and she wasn't. Refusing his job offer was simply a form of self-protection. Because it would be so easy to lose her heart to Rowdy Cassidy and she couldn't allow that to happen.

By his own admission, he wasn't the marrying kind, despite what he'd felt for Valerie. Nothing in Rowdy's life, not a wife, not children, would ever be more important to him than CHIPS.

Rowdy was due to be discharged from the hospital the following day. Norah had been on duty since seven; at nine, the flowers started to arrive. Huge bouquets of roses and orchids, one for every staff member on the second floor. Rowdy had ordered them to show his appreciation for the excellent care he'd received. The gesture touched Norah, reminding her how thoughtful and generous he could be.

She'd braced herself for this day. Within a few hours, the infamous Rowdy Cassidy would be released from the hospital. He'd be out of Orchard Valley and out of her life.

Arrangements had been made for a limousine to pick

him up at the hospital's side entrance, to avoid the ever-curious press.

Karen Johnson had asked Norah if she wanted to be the one to wheel him out, and she'd agreed. From the hospital the limousine would drive Rowdy into Portland, where he was scheduled to hold a short news conference before boarding a Learjet for Texas.

His stay at Orchard Valley Hospital was almost over. CHIPS and the world he knew best were waiting for him. Instinctively, Norah understood that once he left Orchard Valley he'd never return.

An hour later she was wheeling an empty chair down the corridor to his room when she saw her father. She was so surprised she went completely still.

"Dad, what are you doing here?"

"Can't a man come visiting without being drilled with questions?"

"Of course, but I didn't know any of your friends were here."

"They aren't. I've come to talk to that rascal Cassidy."

"Rowdy?"

"Got any other rascal cowboys I don't know about?"

"No…it's just that he's about to be discharged." She couldn't imagine what her father planned to say. In fact, the whole family seemed to be taking a new interest in Rowdy. Karen had said that Colby had stopped in to see him the day before. Apparently the two men had hit it off and could be heard laughing. Rowdy hadn't mentioned the meeting to Norah, but then there hadn't been much of a chance to talk to him, either.

"Rowdy's driver will wait," her father said confidently. "I promise I won't keep him long."

"But, Dad…"

"Give us ten minutes, will you? And make sure we're not disturbed."

Norah's heart started to race. "You'd better tell me what you intend to say to him."

Her father stopped abruptly and placed a gentle hand on her shoulder. "I'm not going to say anything about my dream, if that's what's worrying you. It's likely to scare him so bad we'll never see hide nor hair of him again."

"Dad!"

"No, it wouldn't be a good idea, Norah. The minute he heard about those six youngsters, he'd be out of here so fast it'd make your head spin."

Rowdy, nothing. *Her* head was spinning. "Then why do you want to see him?"

"That, my darling Norah, is between me and the cowboy."

Norah possessed her mother's calm nature. She wasn't easily flustered, but her father had managed to do it in a matter of seconds. She paced outside Rowdy's door, wishing desperately that the walls weren't so thick and she could listen in on their conversation.

In less than the predicted ten minutes, which felt more like a lifetime, her father reappeared, grinning from ear to ear. Norah stopped cold when he sauntered out of the room.

"He's a decent fellow, isn't he?"

Norah was too numb to do anything more than nod. With a roguish wink, her father walked away.

It took her a moment to compose herself. When she hurried into Rowdy's room, he was sitting on the bed, fully dressed, a brand-new Stetson beside him.

"Your father was just here."

"I know," she said, doing her best to act casual. "Did he have anything important to say?"

Rowdy didn't answer immediately. "Yeah, he did," he finally said. But he didn't elaborate, and Norah was left with a long list of unanswered questions.

Robbins came in to tell him the limousine was ready. Norah brought the wheelchair and adjusted Rowdy's leg in the most comfortable position. She took her time, until she realized she was only delaying the inevitable. Sooner or later she'd have to wheel him outside.

Ms. Emerich was already sitting inside the limousine. The driver was waiting to assist Rowdy, and Robbins, too, seemed eager to do what he could. But Rowdy dismissed their offers. "In a minute," he told them.

With the help of his crutches he maneuvered his way out of the wheelchair and stood upright. It was the first time Norah had seen him standing and she was astonished by what a large man he was. She came barely to his shoulders.

"Well, angel face," he said softly, his eyes holding hers, "this is goodbye."

She nodded, but found she couldn't speak for the lump in her throat.

"I wish I could say it's been fun."

Norah laughed; she couldn't help it. "You'll be your normal self again before you know it."

"I expect I will," he agreed. He reached out and touched her face. "Take care, you hear?" Then he turned away and moved toward the car.

Seven

Rowdy Cassidy drove away without so much as a backward glance. The least he could have done was kiss her goodbye, Norah thought. The least he could've done was give her one last memory....

Norah straightened, more determined than ever to put the man out of her mind. And her heart.

She'd start immediately, she decided, marching back to the hospital with every intention of calling Ray Folsom, who worked in the X-ray department. He'd asked her out to dinner a week or so earlier, but she'd been busy with Rowdy and had declined. Norah stopped at the reception desk in X-ray, planning to leave a message for Ray. The woman on duty glanced up expectantly when Norah approached.

"Anything I can do for you?" she asked.

Sighing, Norah placed both hands on the counter and opened her mouth to speak. Then she shook her head. She wasn't ready to date anyone.

Unless, of course, it was Rowdy Cassidy.

A week passed, and Norah swore it was the longest

of her life. Fortunately, the preparations for Steffie's wedding helped fill the void left by Rowdy's absence. There was some task to occupy almost every evening and for that, at least, Norah was grateful.

She noticed how closely her family watched her, and she did her best to seem cheerful and unconcerned. It went without saying that Rowdy wouldn't call. He'd laid his best offer on the table and she'd turned him down. It was over; he'd made that clear.

"Have you heard from Rowdy?" Valerie asked while the three of them sat around the kitchen table assembling wedding favors. They filled plastic champagne glasses with foil-covered Belgian chocolates and wrapped each one in pastel-colored netting, then tied a silk apple blossom to the stem with pink ribbon.

"No," Norah said, resenting the question. She struggled to keep the disappointment out of her voice. "And I don't expect to." It was on the tip of her tongue to ask her sister the same question, but she didn't. She assumed Valerie hadn't made a decision about the job yet.

"Knowing Rowdy, he's probably waiting for you to get in touch with him," Valerie said.

"Me?" Norah asked, surprised by the suggestion. "What for?"

"To tell him you've changed your mind and want to come and work for him. It's the same game he played with me."

Norah bristled. Her sister was baiting her, questioning her resolve, and that angered Norah. "He knows better," she said stiffly, "and so do you!"

Valerie grinned, apparently pleased. "He's got a well-deserved reputation for his ability to play a waiting game."

"There's no point in trying that with me." Norah twisted the netting around the plastic glass with unnecessary vigor and handed it to Steffie, who attached the ribbon.

"Men don't seem to learn stuff like that as quickly as women," Steffie mused. "Rowdy Cassidy has a few things to figure out."

Norah didn't respond to her comment, and the discussion soon returned to more general topics.

The idea of calling Rowdy had never occurred to Norah. But suddenly it made sense that, as his nurse, she should inquire about his progress. Valerie had put the idea in her mind, and now Norah began to consider it.

"I wonder how Rowdy's doing," she said conversationally to her father that same evening. She would have thought he'd be the first to suggest she ask Rowdy about his recovery, but he hadn't.

"We would've heard something if he wasn't doing well, don't you think?" he answered grumpily. "The way those newspeople reported every detail of his life, you can bet it'd be on national television if he suffered the least little setback."

So much for that. "Ray Folsom called this morning. I—I'm going to dinner with him tomorrow evening," she told her father. Dredging up some enthusiasm for the date was going to require an effort. But after a week of moping around the house, pretending she didn't miss Rowdy, Norah was determined to enjoy herself.

Ray had seemed surprised when Norah accepted the invitation. Despite her previous refusal, she'd decided, not entirely on impulse, to go out with him. He was exactly what she needed, she told herself. Even Valerie approved when she learned that Norah was going out.

"It'll do you good," Valerie assured her.

But when the time came for Ray to pick her up, Norah was no longer so sure. He brought her flowers and she found his thoughtfulness endearing but wished he hadn't. She instantly felt guilty; although she'd agreed to dinner with him, her mind was on Rowdy Cassidy, and that seemed unfair to Ray, who was gentle and considerate.

"Oh, Ray," she said, holding the small bouquet of pink carnations to her nose to breathe in their light scent. "How lovely."

He gave her a pleased smile. "I've been hoping we could get together, Norah."

She smiled back, biting her lip. Again she wondered if she'd made the right decision.

The phone rang while she was looking for a vase. Steffie answered it on the second ring and poked her head into the kitchen where Norah was chatting with Ray and arranging the flowers.

"It's for you. Do you want me to take a message?"

"Ah…" She glanced at Ray, who was leaning against the counter.

"Go ahead," Ray said, checking his watch. "We've got plenty of time."

Norah picked up the kitchen extension. "Hello," she said distractedly.

"Hello yourself, angel face."

Norah nearly slumped to her knees, she was so shocked. "Rowdy." She was grateful her back was to

Ray. She knew the color had drained from her face, and she felt weak and shaky.

"Have you missed me?"

"I—I've been busy."

"Me, too, but that hasn't kept me from thinking about you."

Norah didn't dare admit he'd been on her mind from the moment he was discharged from the hospital. Not with Ray standing right there. It wasn't in her to be so heartless.

"Listen, angel face," Rowdy continued when she said nothing. "I'm in Portland."

"You are?" Her heart pounded with glad excitement. He was less than sixty miles away.

"I'm working out some of the details on the expansion project with Robbins—I should be done in an hour or two. I was thinking I'd send a car for you now and by the time you arrive I'll be finished and we could have dinner."

"Oh, Rowdy."

"It'll be good to see you again. I've missed you, and I'm hoping you feel the same way."

Norah felt like crying; Rowdy's timing couldn't have been worse. "I can't," she told him. "I'm sorry, but I can't."

"Why not?" he demanded impatiently. "Are you working?"

"I've already got other plans."

"Break them," he said with his usual confidence. "I probably won't be in the area again soon."

"I can't do that."

"Why not?"

"I'm going to dinner with a friend and we're leaving any minute."

A pause followed her announcement. "Male or female?"

"Male."

Norah could almost feel his anger. Rowdy seemed to believe she should drop everything the moment he called her. He obviously assumed she'd spent the past week longing for him. True, she had, but she was determined to put those feelings behind her and get on with her life. The man was impossible, she fumed. He must have known he was going to be in the area; it would've been a simple matter to arrange their meeting in advance. Instead he'd waited until the very last minute. As far as Norah was concerned, if he was angry at having his plans thwarted, he had no one to blame but himself.

She might have told him that if Ray hadn't been there.

"I see," Rowdy said after a long silence. "Enjoy yourself, then."

"I'm sure I will."

"Goodbye, Norah." Before she could say another word, the line was disconnected.

She closed her eyes, needing to compose herself. When she turned around, she discovered Ray involved in conversation with Steffie. Her sister's eyes sought hers. "That was Rowdy," she said, hoping Steffie realized she would've appreciated some warning before she'd picked up the phone.

"I wasn't sure," Steffie admitted wryly, "but I thought it might have been. Next time I'll know."

"Are you ready?" Ray asked. He seemed unaware that anything was troubling her.

Norah nodded.

She enjoyed her dinner with Ray more than she'd expected to. He was genuinely charming and Norah couldn't help responding to his carefree mood.

"You're in love with that cowboy, aren't you?" Ray asked suddenly as he drove her home. When she didn't respond immediately, he added, "I understand, Norah."

"I...don't know what I feel anymore," she told him in a troubled voice.

"Love's like that sometimes," Ray said quietly. "I like you, Norah, and I was hoping there'd be a chance for us. But—" he shrugged and reached for her hand "—everything will work out in the end," he said, squeezing her fingers. "It generally does. If you need proof of that, just look at what's happened to your sisters over the past few months."

Norah smiled shakily. Ray was a wonderful man, considerate and gracious, and he'd make some woman very happy one day. But not her.

Still holding her hand, he walked her to the porch. He kissed her cheek, then whispered, "I wish it was me you were so crazy about."

"I've been rotten company, haven't I?" Norah asked guiltily.

He shook his head. "Not at all. I just hope that cowpoke realizes how lucky he is."

Norah sincerely doubted it. "Thank you for dinner, Ray. I had a wonderful time."

He kissed her once more on the cheek. "Good luck with your cowboy."

She opened the door and stood there while Ray walked down the porch steps and got into his car. She waved goodbye, staring down the driveway until he was out of sight before she stepped into the house.

Steffie was waiting in the entry. "Thank goodness you're back!" she burst out urgently.

"Is it Dad? Did he—"

"Rowdy Cassidy's here," her sister broke in, nodding toward the den.

"Here? Now?"

"Dad's kept him occupied," Steffie informed her, "but he's been here the better part of an hour and getting more restless by the minute."

Norah's heart was hammering wildly. She forced herself to calm down before walking into the den, even managing a smile.

Her eyes immediately went to Rowdy, who stood, leaning heavily on his crutches, gazing out the window that overlooked the front porch. It was obvious that he'd witnessed Ray's kiss. It was equally obvious that he wasn't pleased. He looked tall and lean and so handsome that it was all Norah could do to stop herself from rushing into his arms.

"Rowdy," she said huskily. "This is…an unexpected surprise."

Her father got to his feet and winked at her. "I'll bring both of you a cup of coffee," he told them and conveniently exited the room, leaving Norah alone with Rowdy.

Using his crutches, Rowdy levered himself around to face her, his right leg thrust out in front of him. "I trust you had an enjoyable dinner," he said stiffly.

"Very," she returned, clasping her hands together.

"I'm glad to hear it." Although he sounded anything but glad. He was frowning as he studied her, and Norah felt uncomfortable under his close scrutiny.

"Please sit down," she said, gesturing toward the chair. "I didn't know you planned to stop by."

"Would it have mattered?"

Norah winced at the undisguised anger in his voice. "I hope Dad's been keeping you entertained," she said, avoiding his question.

"He has." Rowdy sank into her father's chair and Norah sat across from him, on the ottoman.

"Is there anything I can do for you?" she asked.

He nodded slowly. "You offered to give me the name of a reputable agency," he said gruffly. "I'm still in the market for a private nurse. I assumed I could do without one. You seemed so sure I'd be fine on my own." The last words came as an accusation.

"And you're not?"

"No," he told her angrily. "I'm having one hell of a time adjusting to these crutches."

"It'll get easier with practice. A nurse can't do that for you, Rowdy. You'll have to learn to walk with them yourself."

He muttered something she couldn't distinguish, which was just as well, judging by the disgruntled look on his face.

"I'll get the name and number of the agency for you," she told him.

"Fine."

She left the room and discovered Steffie and her father standing just outside the door. They looked star-

tled, then glanced at her guiltily. Norah glared at them
both, knowing they'd blatantly listened in on her conversation with Rowdy.

Steffie cast her an apologetic smile, then hurried up
the stairs; her father chuckled with wry amusement and
wandered toward the kitchen, mumbling about coffee.

Rowdy was massaging his right thigh when Norah
returned with a slip of paper. "Your leg still aches?"
she asked.

"It really hurts," he said in a blatant effort to gain
her sympathy.

"Are you taking the medication as prescribed?" She
handed him the paper.

"I forget," he answered brusquely. "That's another
reason I need a good nurse."

"Nurse or nursemaid?" she inquired sweetly.

"Nurse."

Norah knew exactly what Rowdy Cassidy was doing,
and she wanted it understood right now that she refused
to be manipulated. If he wanted something, he'd have
to ask for it in plain English.

"You honestly think this agency will have what I
need?" he asked, eyeing her closely.

"I'm sure of it."

"I prefer someone young," he said, then added, "and
blonde, if possible. Oh, and pretty."

Norah nearly laughed out loud. Since she hadn't immediately volunteered for the position, he was hoping
to make her jealous. "You might be wiser to request
someone competent, Rowdy."

For a moment he said nothing. "It's been one week,"
he told her, his eyes steadily holding hers. "Seven days."

"It seems longer, doesn't it?" she asked softly, looking away, not wanting him to see how miserable and lonely she'd been and how hard she'd worked at pretending otherwise.

"Much longer," he admitted grudgingly. "I didn't expect to miss you this much." He frowned at her, and it took Norah a second to realize he was waiting for her to change her mind, to accept the position.

"I've missed you, too," Norah told him, weakening. He'd played on her sympathies and that hadn't worked. But her heart was vulnerable, and he knew it.

"Ever been to Texas this time of year?" he asked, clambering to his feet. Using the crutches with surprising deftness, he worked his way closer to her until mere inches separated them. Until there was only a single step between them. One small step, and she could walk straight into his arms.

Norah didn't know where she found the strength to stand still, to resist him.

"Have you?" he asked again.

Norah shook her head.

"It's the most beautiful place on earth."

"As beautiful as Orchard Valley?"

Rowdy chuckled. "You'll have to make that judgment for yourself." He was waiting. Waiting for her to come to him, to swallow her pride and sacrifice her own needs to his.

Norah knew exactly what would happen if she took that step, if she agreed to leave with Rowdy. She'd fall so deeply in love with him that she'd give up her own hopes and plans, her own pleasures—all the things that

made her Norah. She'd be unable to refuse him anything. Already she was halfway there.

He'd made it perfectly clear that he had no intention
of marrying. Nor was he interested in raising a family.
Rowdy had admitted that even if Valerie had broken
her engagement to Colby, he wouldn't have married her.

And if he hadn't been willing to marry her sister,
he wouldn't want her, either. For that matter, Norah
wasn't sure she'd agree if he *did* propose. When she
got married, she wanted a *husband,* a man who'd be
a constant part of her life, a man who shared her need
for a settled existence, with a home and family. Not a
man like Rowdy...

Norah was too sensible and pragmatic not to recognize they'd face these issues sooner or later, even if he
hadn't raised them now. And when it did happen, she
wanted to be sure he knew where she stood. Because
she'd be so head over heels in love with him that she
wouldn't be able to think.

"If the agency here isn't able to find you a nurse..."

"Yes?" he asked eagerly.

"There are bound to be a number in Texas with excellent reputations. I could ask around for you."

His face tightened. "You're so stubborn."

"It runs in the family. As you've already pointed
out. I'm surprised you didn't butt heads with Valerie
more often."

"I'm not," he said, moving awkwardly away from
her. "We were both working toward the same goals. You
and I are working at cross-purposes." He limped toward
the phone and called for his car. "You want something
I'm not willing to give you."

"What's that?" she asked.

His eyes darkened. "You want my pride."

He was wrong, but no amount of arguing was going to convince him and Norah didn't have the strength to try.

"Good seeing you again, Norah," he said unemotionally.

"You, too, Rowdy."

"If you go out with Ralph again—"

"Ray," she corrected.

"Of course, Ray. I must have forgotten."

"There's no need to be sarcastic."

"You're right," he said in a tone so cool that it seemed to frost the air between them. "In any event, I wish you the very best. I'm sure the two of you have a lot in common."

Norah said nothing.

"I came the minute I heard." Valerie's concerned voice drifted into the kitchen from the front entry the next morning. "What did he say to her?"

"I'm not sure," Steffie said. "It seems he wanted her to reconsider and go to Texas with him as his nurse."

"Norah told him no, didn't she?"

"She must have."

Her sisters appeared in the kitchen, both wearing compassionate expressions.

"I understand Rowdy stopped by last night," Valerie said gently, as though she considered Norah emotionally fragile.

"He was here, all right." She continued to stir the batter for oatmeal-and-raisin muffins. Baking had always been a means of escape for her. Some women shopped when they felt depressed; some read or slept or went to exercise classes. Norah baked.

"And?"

"And he left."

"Do you think he'll come here again?"

Clutching the bowl against her stomach, Norah whipped the batter vigorously. "Who knows?" But she hadn't expected to hear from him at all after his discharge; his visit had come as a complete surprise. However, Norah wasn't foolish enough to believe it would happen again. Rejection was difficult for any man and harder for Rowdy than most, since he'd become so accustomed to getting his own way.

He'd come to her twice, and she'd turned him down both times. He wasn't likely to try for rejection number three.

"Rowdy's been spoiled rotten," Valerie warned her.

"Isn't every man?" Norah returned calmly.

Valerie and Steffie exchanged a glance. "She'll be fine," Steffie murmured and, smiling, Valerie agreed.

Norah wished she felt as confident.

Rowdy's name wasn't mentioned again until the following evening. Norah's father was watching the news when he called for her. "Come quick!" he shouted excitedly.

Norah raced in from the kitchen to discover her father pointing at the television. "Rowdy's on the local news."

She sank into a chair and braced herself for the sight of him. The Portland news anchor reported the expansion of the Texas-based software company CHIPS, which would soon be building in the area. He went on to comment that the final papers had been signed and that the owner of CHIPS, Rowdy Cassidy, was currently in town. The ground-breaking ceremony was due to take place in two weeks.

The camera switched from the anchor to a clip of Rowdy. Norah didn't focus on him, but on the statuesque blonde woman in a nurse's uniform who stood behind him.

Her stomach felt as if someone had kicked her.

Young and blonde, just the way he'd said. And pretty...

"Norah?" Her father's voice broke into her thoughts. "Are you all right?"

"Fine, Dad," she answered cheerfully. "Why shouldn't I be?"

The phone rang shortly afterward. Her father answered; apparently it was Valerie. Norah wandered back to the kitchen to finish preparing the evening meal. She went determinedly about her task, refusing to allow emotion to take control.

She'd made her decision.

Rowdy had made his.

"Oh, Steffie," Norah said breathlessly, gazing at her sister. "You're so beautiful."

Steffie had chosen not to wear a traditional wedding gown, but a knee-length cream-colored dress with a dropped waist. A garland of fresh baby's breath and rosebuds was woven into her glossy dark hair.

Norah couldn't stop staring at the transformation she saw in her sister. Steffie looked not only beautiful but supremely happy; she glowed with serenity and a calm, sure joy.

"Everyone's outside and waiting," Valerie announced when she walked into the bedroom. She stopped abruptly when she saw Steffie.

"Oh, Steffie," she breathed, as the tears welled in her eyes. "Mom would be so proud."

"I feel just as if she were here," Steffie whispered, reaching for her wedding bouquet. "I thought I was going to miss her so much today and the most amazing thing has happened. It's as if she's been standing right beside me. I don't think I've ever felt her presence more."

"I felt the same way the day Colby and I were married," Valerie confessed. "Her love is here," she added simply.

Norah had felt it, too, although she hadn't been able to put it into words.

"Dad's waiting," Valerie told them.

Myriad emotions swirled through Norah. She was truly happy for her sister and Charles, but her heart ached. Never had she felt more alone, set apart from those she loved. Valerie had Colby and Steffie had Charles, but there was no one for her.

She walked down the stairs with her two older sisters and paused at the top of the porch steps.

White linen-covered tables dotted the sweeping expanse of the front lawn, its grass a cool, luscious green. White wrought-iron chairs were scattered about. A number of long tables groaned with an opulent display of food. The three-tiered wedding cake sat on a table of its own, protected by a small, flower-draped canopy.

The actual ceremony would take place next to the apple orchard. The trees were heavy with fruit, and a warm summer breeze drifted through the rows, rustling the leaves. Soft music floated toward Norah and she realized the time had come for her to lead the small procession.

The side yard was filled with friends and family. Norah led the others down the center aisle to the flower-decked archway; Valerie followed and took her place beside her sister.

Steffie came next, escorted by their father. Every eye was on the bride, and Norah gazed proudly at her beautiful sister.

The loneliness she'd felt earlier unexpectedly left her. She sensed her mother's presence again, a sensation so strong that Norah was tempted to turn around, to see if Grace was actually there, somewhere behind her. The pain she'd experienced was replaced by a certainty that one day she, too, would discover the love her sisters had found that summer.

Steffie paused before Pastor Wallen, who'd married Valerie and Colby a short five weeks earlier. She kissed her father's cheek and turned, smiling, to Charles.

Norah had never seen Charles look more dashing. She noticed the private smile he exchanged with his bride, the tenderness of his expression. Their love for each other was almost tangible.

Norah stood beside Valerie. Her own dress was the pink one she'd worn to Valerie's wedding. Val's was pale lavender. A sprig of baby's breath and silk apple blossoms was tucked behind Norah's ear, and Valerie wore a pearl comb that had been their mother's. Steffie handed her bridal bouquet, of white rosebuds and pale silk apple blossoms, to Norah to hold during the ceremony.

Minutes later, Stephanie Bloomfield had pledged her love to Charles Tomaselli, and Pastor Wallen had pronounced them husband and wife.

A happy cheer rose from their guests, and Steffie and Charles fled laughing from a hail of birdseed.

Norah smiled after the happy couple, then frowned. An irregular, beating sound could be heard in the distance. She glanced about, wondering at its source.

A moment later, she realized a helicopter was approaching.

Everyone gaped as the aircraft slowly descended from the sky, landing on the driveway. Norah looked at her father, who moved forward.

Norah did, too, her heart pounding as hard and as loud as the whirling blades.

The door opened and two crutches appeared before Rowdy Cassidy levered himself out. He scanned the crowd until he found Norah. Then he grinned.

"I'm not interrupting anything, am I?" he asked.

Eight

"**A**re you *interrupting* anything?" Norah repeated, laughing incredulously. "This is Steffie and Charles's wedding!"

Using the crutches, Rowdy swung his legs forward, then came to a sudden halt. "*Another* wedding?"

Norah laughed again, so happy to see him it didn't matter that they'd parted on such bad terms a week earlier. She hurried to his side, threw her arms around his neck and hugged him.

She felt his sigh and knew he was no less delighted to be with her. The crowd started to disperse as the newlywed couple reappeared to lead everyone across the lawn to the reception area.

"If I'd known there was a wedding going on I would've avoided this place like the plague," Rowdy whispered.

"Why are you so set against marriage?" Norah asked, glancing up at him.

"Look what happened to me the last time I showed up for one of your family weddings." He moved his right leg forward for her to examine the cast, which reached halfway up his thigh.

"Good to see you again, Rowdy," Colby said, his arm securely around Valerie's waist. The two men exchanged handshakes. David stepped forward to welcome him, too, chuckling at Rowdy's tendency to make grand entrances.

"When it comes to your daughters, I certainly seem to have a bad sense of timing," Rowdy told her father.

"Not in the least," David Bloomfield told him, his gaze lighting on Norah. "In fact, it couldn't be better. Isn't that right, Norah?"

Laughing, she nodded. Earlier she'd been feeling lonely and despairing; now Rowdy's dramatic arrival was like an unexpected gift.

The others drifted back to the wedding party, leaving Norah and Rowdy alone for the first time.

"How long can you stay?" Norah asked. It went without saying that their time together would be limited.

"A few hours. The ground-breaking ceremony for CHIPS Northwest is taking place later this afternoon."

Norah brought him to a chair and helped him sit down. As he laid the crutches on the grass beside him, she glanced around. "Where is she?" she asked, referring to his blonde nurse.

Rowdy didn't pretend not to know what she was talking about. He frowned and muttered a few words under his breath.

"Pardon? I didn't quite hear that," she said sweetly.

"That's because it wasn't meant for you to hear. If I tell you, you'll gloat."

"No, I won't," she promised, doing her best to swallow a laugh.

"All right," Rowdy said with a sigh, "since you insist on knowing. She didn't work out."

"And why's that? You were so sure you needed a nurse."

"I do...that is, I did need one. Unfortunately the nurse I hired was a daughter of Attila the Hun. The problem with you blondes is that your appearance is deceptive. You *look* like you'd be all sweetness and light."

"Oh, we are."

Rowdy said nothing, but the grimace he sent her made her laugh outright.

"I still need a nurse," Rowdy argued, "but I only want you. Since you're being so blasted stubborn, I'm forced to cope on my own."

In a silent-film gesture, Norah pressed the back of her hand against her forehead and expelled a beleaguered sigh. "Life is tough, Rowdy."

He waved his index finger under her nose. "I knew you'd gloat."

"I'm sorry," she told him between giggles. "I really am, but I couldn't resist."

Rowdy took her hands in his. "I've missed you, Norah, more than—"

"What you miss is getting your own way," she interrupted tartly.

Rowdy grinned. "Tell me, have you gone out with Ralph lately?"

"It's Ray, and no, I haven't."

Rowdy hesitated. "I don't have the right to ask you not to date anyone else."

"No, you don't," Norah agreed.

"Nevertheless..." Rowdy's scowl deepened. "I don't mind admitting I was worried about that guy."

"Why?" Anyone looking at her would know in an instant how deeply she cared for Rowdy. Ray was a friend, nothing more. She hadn't intended to make Rowdy jealous.

"I guess I'm more selfish than I realized," he said grudgingly. "I want you for myself."

Norah made a conscious effort to change the subject. There was no point in pursuing this; it was too painful and she knew nothing was going to change.

"Are you hungry?" she asked, noting that the guests were helping themselves to the large array of hors d'oeuvres and other dishes prepared by the caterers.

"Starved," Rowdy answered, but when she stood to get him a plate, he caught her hand. "It isn't food I need." His dark eyes held hers and Norah could feel herself moving toward him.

"Not here," she murmured, stopping herself.

"Where, then? Norah, I need to hold you. It's been driving me crazy from the moment I left the hospital."

"Rowdy, this is my sister's wedding!"

"Aren't you allowed a few minutes alone?"

"Yes, but..."

"Norah," he said decisively, "we need to talk."

"It isn't talking that interests you, Rowdy, and we both know it."

"Ah, but what interests *you?*"

Norah sighed. "You already know," she said in a low voice.

Rowdy looked around them, picked up the crutches and got to his feet. "Lead the way."

"Rowdy... I'm not sure about this."

"We'll pretend we're getting something to eat and before anyone notices we'll casually slip away. A few minutes, Norah, that's all I'm asking."

She didn't have the heart to refuse him—or herself. Their time together was so brief, and she needed him. She needed him more than she'd ever needed anyone, she thought.

If there *were* people who saw Norah and Rowdy ease themselves away from the festive crowd assembled on the front lawn, they didn't say. She steered Rowdy toward the side yard, near the orchard, where the ceremony had taken place. It was quiet and peaceful there. A light breeze wafted through the fruit trees.

Knowing it was more comfortable for Rowdy to sit rather than stand, she guided him to the first row of chairs in front of the archway.

"I certainly hope you're not hinting at something here." He nodded toward the tall flower-filled baskets. He carefully lowered himself into the chair, and Norah sat next to him. Rowdy's arm settled over her shoulders. She rested her head on his chest and sighed, closing her eyes.

She'd dreamed of moments like this. Moments of peace, without all the tension between them.

He stroked her hair and sighed, too. "I've never known a woman quite like you." His lips grazed her temple. "I've never known a woman who played checkers quite so poorly, either."

They both laughed, and Norah leaned her head back

to look into his face. The laughter fled from his eyes. Instinctively, Norah moistened her lips, expecting his kiss.

Rowdy didn't disappoint her. He lowered his mouth to hers in a way that was both gentle and undemanding.

Norah had never experienced anything more delightful. "Oh, Rowdy," she whispered with a soft moan of pleasure. "I've missed you."

His mouth returned to hers, and this time, the kiss was long and hard. Norah was flooded with a need so powerful that she entwined her arms around his neck. When they broke apart they were breathless.

"Come with me this afternoon," he pleaded.

The offer was so tempting it was all Norah could do to refuse. "I want to, but I can't leave my family. Not on Steffie's wedding day."

Rowdy tensed and she realized he was dealing with his own disappointment. "I understand. I don't like it, but I understand."

"Tell me again," she whispered, glancing up at him, "how dreadful the blonde nurse was."

"Were you jealous?"

"Insanely."

"Enough to change your mind?" he asked hopefully.

She shook her head. "I'm impressed by how well you've adapted to the crutches, though. You're doing splendidly without me."

His eyes grew serious. "That's where you're wrong, Norah." He kissed her again with an intensity that left her clinging and dizzy.

They wandered back to the wedding party a little later. Norah brought them both plates piled high with fresh fruit and a variety of hors d'oeuvres—bacon-wrapped scallops, tiny quiches, skewered shrimp. They fed each other tidbits, shared a glass of champagne and talked and laughed for what seemed like minutes but was in reality hours.

The helicopter arrived just after Steffie and Charles had cut the wedding cake. Norah watched the aircraft approach, feeling a sense of dread, knowing it would take Rowdy away from her.

She forced herself to smile. He'd been with her for several wonderful hours, the most uninterrupted time they'd had together in weeks.

Deep in her heart, she knew it would always be like this with Rowdy. A few minutes here, an hour there, squeezed in between appointments, stolen from schedules.

She stood alone on the lawn, the guests for the reception behind her, as the helicopter lifted toward the sky. She waved, her hand high above her head, until she was certain Rowdy couldn't see her anymore.

Valerie hurried to her side. "Are you all right?"

Norah offered her sister a brave smile. "I'll be fine."

"You're sure?"

Eyes blurry with tears, she nodded.

Rowdy phoned her the next three nights, and they talked for nearly an hour each time. They spoke of nonsensical trifles, of daily details and of important things, too. She told him about Steffie and Charles's romance and why the newlyweds were honeymooning in Italy. Rowdy told her about his family or, rather, lack of one— how his parents were killed when he was young and he'd been raised in a series of foster homes.

He always called late in the evening, and with the time difference it was well past midnight in Texas when they ended their conversations. He didn't need to tell Norah that he was missing an hour's sleep in order to talk to her. She knew it.

"I'm leaving for San Francisco first thing in the morning to meet with a group of important stockholders," he told her on Tuesday night. "The meetings will probably run late. I doubt I'll get a chance to call you."

"I understand." And she truly did. CHIPS would always come first for Rowdy, because it was the family he'd never had, the security he'd grown up without. She understood his obsession with the business now, and the needs that drove him.

"It isn't what I want, Norah."

"I know." She wasn't angry, not in the least. "It's fine, Rowdy." She was still trying to resign herself to the fact that it would always come to this. His company would remain the emotional center of his life. "When will you get home?"

"Saturday afternoon at the earliest."

"I'm working this weekend," she said, more because she needed to keep talking than because she felt he'd be interested in the information. "I had to trade with a friend in order to get the weekend off for Steffie's wedding. We work on a rotating schedule at the hospital. It changes every four weeks so we can spend as much time with our families as possible."

"Why do you work?" He wasn't being facetious or sarcastic; his curiosity was genuine. It wasn't financially necessary for her to hold down a job, but she loved nursing and she *needed* to work, to occupy her time in a productive, responsible and fulfilling way. She expected Rowdy to empathize with those feelings.

"My mother was a nurse. Did you know that?"

"I must have, because it doesn't come as any surprise."

Norah smiled into the receiver. "From the time I was a little girl, I knew I'd go into the medical profession."

"Did your mother work outside the home?"

"No, she quit soon after she and Dad got married, when she was pregnant with Valerie."

"Did she miss the hospital?"

"I'm sure she did, but once we were a bit older she used her medical skills in other ways. When the migrant workers came to pick apples at our orchard and a couple of neighboring ones, Mom organized a health clinic for them. She did this for years—until she became too ill to do it any longer. Then she and Dad set up a fund so the workers and their families could afford to go to the clinic in Orchard Valley." Norah swallowed hard. "She was a very special woman, Rowdy. I wish you'd known her."

"I wish I had, too, but I already guessed she was special. She raised you, didn't she?"

That was about as romantic as Rowdy ever got with her. Norah didn't expect flowery words from him, certainly nothing more than a careless term of affection. Like "angel face"…

"It'd be a whole lot more convenient for us if you worked regular hours like everyone else," Rowdy said after a moment. "Some days you're on duty, some days you're not. Half the time you end up staying later than you're scheduled to. I'm surprised you don't burn out with those long hours."

"*Me* work long hours?" she challenged with a short laugh. "Ha! You do the same thing. Even more so. I'm surprised *you* didn't burn out years ago."

"That's different."

"It is not," she insisted, "and we both know that. Only you're too proud to admit it." She paused thoughtfully. "Rowdy," she said, "I do agree that there's a difference. My life isn't dictated by my job the way yours is."

"What's so unusual about my dedication to CHIPS?" Rowdy countered sharply. "Don't forget I started the company. CHIPS is more than a job. No one's hiring me to work eighteen hours a day—I do it by choice."

Norah was well aware of the truth of his words. With a small inward sigh, she changed the topic, asking questions instead about the San Francisco meetings.

When she'd finished the call, she wandered downstairs. Without consciously realizing where she'd been headed, she found herself standing in the doorway of her father's den.

"Would you like a cup of hot chocolate?" she asked. The offer was an excuse to talk, and she suspected her father would recognize it as such.

He did. Setting aside his book, he glanced up at her. "Sure. Would you like some help?"

Before she had a chance to answer, he stood and followed her into the kitchen. While she took out the saucepan, her father retrieved the milk from the refrigerator. Norah was gratified to see how much more energetic he'd become lately; his recovery really had been miraculous, she decided.

"How's Rowdy?" he asked almost as if he'd known exactly what she wanted to discuss.

"Good," she answered, hoping to appear nonchalant. "He's taking a business trip to San Francisco in the morning. I asked him how often he's been there, and he told me he's visited the Bay area a dozen times in the past half year."

"As I recall, Valerie took several trips there with him."

"I remember that," Norah said, "but did you know that in spite of all those times Rowdy's visited San Francisco, he's never been down to Fisherman's Wharf or walked through Chinatown or taken a cruise around the Bay? When I pressed him, he admitted he's never seen anything more than the airport and the inside of a hotel meeting room."

"Rowdy Cassidy's a busy man."

"Don't you get it?" Norah cried, surprised by the strength of her emotion. "He's working himself to death, and for what? Some software company that will pass on to a distant relative he hasn't seen in twenty years. A relative who'll probably just sell his share of the stock. To strangers!"

"It bothers you that Rowdy doesn't have any heirs?" her father asked as he brought down two earthenware mugs.

"What bothers me," she returned heatedly, "is that he's working himself to death for no real reason. He's a candidate for a heart attack—the same way you were.

He's got atrocious eating habits, doesn't exercise and works too hard."

David nodded and grinned. "You know what it sounds like to me?" he asked, and not waiting for a reply added, "Rowdy Cassidy needs a wife. Don't you agree?"

As hard as she tried to concentrate on her own duties, Norah couldn't keep her mind off Rowdy. He'd already told her he wouldn't be able to call her, since his meetings with the stockholders would last until all hours of the night. For reasons she didn't understand, Norah was restless all afternoon.

When she arrived home she found her father weeding the garden she'd planted earlier that summer. He straightened and waved when he saw her.

"Looks like we've got enough lettuce here for a decent salad."

Norah crouched down in the freshly weeded row and picked a handful of radishes. "We can add a few of these, as well."

It was good to see her father soaking up the sunshine, looking healthy and relaxed. He was working part-time, managing the orchard, which kept him occupied without overtaxing him.

"Before I forget," her father said, "an envelope was delivered for you this afternoon. I think it's from Rowdy."

Norah didn't linger outside a moment longer. She couldn't imagine what Rowdy had sent her, but she wasn't waiting to find out. When they'd spoken the night before, he hadn't mentioned anything.

The envelope was propped against a vase of roses left over from Steffie's wedding. Norah's name was inked with a lavish hand across the front. Eagerly tearing it open, she discovered a first-class airline ticket to Houston.

Norah stared at it before she slowly replaced it in the envelope, which she set back on the end table. Apparently Rowdy had forgotten she was scheduled to work that weekend.

The phone rang, and when she answered she heard Rowdy's voice. "Norah," he said, "I'm glad I caught you. Listen, I've only got a couple of minutes between meetings. I wanted to be sure the ticket was delivered. This is crazy. I'm supposed to be here negotiating an important deal, but all I can think about is how long it's going to be before I can see you again. Trust me, this is no way to run a company."

"I can't fly to Houston this weekend, Rowdy," she said without preamble. "You already know that."

"Why not?"

"I'm working, remember?"

"Forgot." He swore under his breath. "Can't you get a replacement?"

"Not easily. Weekends are precious to us all, and even more so to people who are married and have families."

He didn't hesitate for an instant. "Tell whoever will work in your place that I'll pay them ten times what they normally make in a weekend. I need to see you, Norah."

"I won't do that."

She could feel his anger. "Why not?"

"I can talk until I'm blue in the face and you still

won't understand. Just take my word for it. Your plan won't work."

"You mean to say there isn't a single nurse in Orchard Valley who'd leap at the chance to earn ten times her normal salary just for working your shift?"

Norah could see that nothing useful would result from her arguing. "That's what I'm saying."

"I don't believe it."

Norah sighed. "You're entitled to believe anything you wish, but I know the people I work with. It may come as a shock to you, but family is more important than money."

"Damn it," Rowdy said angrily. "Why do you make it so difficult?"

"Rowdy, I can't live my life to suit yours. I'm sorry, I really am, but I have a commitment to my job and to my peers. I can't rush off to Texas because you happen to want me there. Nor will I allow our relationship to become nothing more than a few hours snatched between meetings and at airports."

"You seem to be taking a good deal for granted," he said stiffly.

"How's that?"

"Who told you we had a relationship?"

Norah breathed in sharply at the pain his words inflicted. "Certainly not you," she answered calmly, belying the turmoil she felt. "You're right, of course," she said when he didn't respond. "I—I guess I'd put more stock in our friendship than you intended. I apologize, Rowdy, for taking our—*my*—feelings for granted—"

"Norah," he interrupted. "I didn't mean that."

She could hear a conversation going on behind Rowdy, but she couldn't make out the details.

"Norah, I've got to go. Everyone's waiting on me."

"I know… I'm sorry about this weekend, Rowdy, but it can't be helped. Please understand."

"I'm trying, Norah. Heaven help me, I'm trying. If I get a chance later, I'll give you a call."

"Okay." She didn't want their conversation to end on a negative note, but knew it was impossible for him to talk longer.

"Rowdy," she called, her heart pounding. "I love you."

Her words were met with the drone of a disconnected line. He hadn't heard her, and even if he had, would it have made any difference?

Norah showed up for work on Saturday morning, her thoughts bleak. She'd been reassigned to the emergency room, but her heart was in a plane somewhere over California on its way to Houston, Texas.

Refusing Rowdy's offer to spend the weekend with him had been one of the most difficult things she'd ever done. And yet she'd had no choice.

Her relationship with Rowdy—and she *did* believe they had a relationship, his harsh words to the contrary—had made it over several hurdles. They were only beginning to understand and appreciate each other. Despite the present and future problems, Norah felt a new and still shaky confidence, a sense of optimism.

She hadn't heard from Rowdy, other than that one harried phone call, since he'd left Texas. She remembered his saying that he'd be back in Houston sometime Saturday afternoon. Norah planned to leave the hospital at three and hoped to hear from Rowdy shortly after she got home.

He hadn't said he'd call, but she hoped—Norah pulled herself up short. She was doing it already. Although she'd promised herself she'd never allow a man to rule her life, she'd willingly surrendered her heart—and her freedom—to Rowdy Cassidy. There wasn't a single reason to hurry home, she reminded herself. If Rowdy phoned while she was out, she'd return his call later.

Satisfied that she'd put her thinking back on track, she went about her duties. A little after eleven, the new intern, Dr. Fullbright, came into the emergency room to tell her she had a visitor in the waiting room. She immediately assumed it was Valerie, who sometimes dropped in to visit Colby.

When she saw Rowdy standing there, she stopped cold. He looked exhausted. His eyes were sunken and his features pale, but it didn't matter to Norah. Never had she been more thrilled to see anyone.

"Rowdy?" she whispered, walking into his arms. One crutch fell to the floor as he held her against him. Norah reveled in the sensation of solid warmth and felt an unexpected urge to weep. He was pushing himself too hard, putting in too many hours.

She'd repeatedly refused his offer to become his private nurse, and for the first time she wondered if she'd made a mistake. Obviously he did need someone.

She knew from what Robbins had said that Rowdy hadn't hired a replacement for Valerie and Norah assumed he was continuing to carry both loads himself.

"What are you doing here?" she asked.

"If you wouldn't come to me, I decided I'd have to come to you." His hand tangled in her hair as he spoke. "Have you had lunch yet?"

"No. I'll check and see if I can go now. We're not too busy, but I'll need to stay on the hospital grounds."

Rowdy nodded. "Can we go someplace private?"

If there was any such place in the hospital, Norah had yet to find it. "The cafeteria shouldn't be very crowded."

Rowdy didn't look wildly enthusiastic at her suggestion, but he agreed.

Norah led the way to the elevator, smiling at the two nurses already inside and regretted that she and Rowdy couldn't be alone. If they'd had at least the brief elevator ride to themselves, she might have found the courage to repeat what she'd confessed at the end of their last telephone conversation.

Norah was right; the cafeteria wasn't crowded and they were afforded some privacy in the farthest corner. Once Rowdy was comfortably seated, his crutches leaning against the wall, he caught her hand, effectively preventing her from moving to the opposite side of the table. "Sit beside me, Norah."

Something in his voice, in the way he was looking at her, told Norah this wasn't an ordinary conversation. When he'd asked for someplace private she'd assumed it was because he wanted to kiss her.

"Yes?" she asked, taking the seat.

Rowdy glanced around, apparently checking for eavesdroppers. "All right," he said with a heavy sigh. "You win."

"I win?" she repeated, frowning.

"I knew from the first what you wanted."

"You did?"

"It's what every woman wants. A gold ring on her left hand. I told you earlier, and I meant it, I'm not the marrying kind. I don't have time for a wife and a family."

Norah was utterly confused, but she said nothing.

"I couldn't sleep last night," he went on, "until I'd figured out your game plan. Even when I had, it didn't make any difference. I love you so much I can't think clearly anymore."

Norah remained bewildered. She'd tried to tell him she loved him, but he hadn't heard her in his rush to get back to his meeting.

"I love you, too, Rowdy," she told him now, her voice soft.

His eyes gentled. "That helps. Not much, but…it helps."

Norah shook her head in confusion. "I'm afraid I've missed something here. What are you trying to say?"

His mouth fell. "You mean you don't know?"

Norah shook her head again.

"I'm asking you to marry me. I'm not happy about it, but as far as I can see it's the only way."

Nine

"You're not happy about asking me to marry you," Norah echoed, too stunned to know what she was feeling.

"I told you before that I had no intention of ever marrying."

"Then what are you doing proposing to me?" she demanded. "Did you think I was so desperate for a husband I'd leap at your offer?" The numbness was gradually wearing away, and she was furious.

Norah had always been the Bloomfield with the cool head and the even temper. But her much-practiced calm was no match for this situation. Only a man like Rowdy Cassidy would have the nerve to insult a woman and propose marriage to her in the same breath.

"You're not desperate. It's just that—"

"That's not what I heard," she interrupted. "According to this oh-so-romantic proposal, you're declaring me the winner of some great prize, which I guess is you. Well, I've got news for you, Rowdy Cassidy. I wasn't even aware I'd entered the contest!"

Rowdy clenched his jaw in an unmistakable effort to hold on to his own temper. "I don't believe that. You have me so tied up in knots, I don't know which way is which anymore. It wasn't enough that you turned down the job, but you had to torment me by dating other men!"

"One date! How was I supposed to know you'd want to see me the one and only night I'd made other arrangements? I'm not a mind reader, you know. Was I supposed to be so flattered, so—so *overwhelmed* by your summons that I'd cancel my evening with Ray?"

"Yes!" he shouted.

"I refused to do that then, and I refuse to do it now. I *will not* spend my life waiting for an opening in your absolutely ridiculous schedule."

Rowdy's hand sliced the air between them. "All right, fine. Let's just drop this thing with Ralph."

"Ray!" she shouted, attracting attention from those around her.

Both were silent for several embarrassed moments.

Finally, Rowdy exhaled sharply and said, "Shall we try this again?" He studied her through half-closed eyes before proceeding. "I'll admit there were better ways of asking you to be my wife. My only excuse is that I've had almost no sleep in the past thirty hours."

Norah mellowed somewhat. "Thirty hours?"

Rowdy nodded. "It didn't help that I was looking forward to you being there when I returned home. You might recall that you turned me down on that, as well."

"It's not as though I didn't want to be with you," she assured him. "But you knew I was scheduled to work this weekend—I'd told you so myself, remember?"

"What's more important," he said through gritted teeth, "your job or me?"

"We keep rehashing the same thing," she said, throwing her hands in the air. "You want me to be at your beck and call. You're suggesting I should spend my life in limbo, waiting for you to find time for me."

"That's not what I mean at all," he said in a dangerously quiet voice. "But if you cared about me half as much as I care about you, you'd be willing to make a few minor adjustments."

"You want far more than *minor* adjustments! You want absolute control and I refuse to give you that."

"You're not even willing to compromise," he said bitterly. "With you, it's all or nothing." He looked away from her, glaring.

"Rowdy, I *am* willing to compromise. All I'm asking for is a little advance warning, so I know what to expect. Do you realize everything we've done has been on the spur of the moment? Nothing has ever been planned."

He nodded a bit sheepishly. "That's not typical for me, you know. Falling in love with you has shot my concentration, not to mention my organizational abilities, all to hell."

"Oh, Rowdy." He could be so sweet and funny when he wanted. But he acted as if loving her was some kind of…weakness. He didn't see love as something that gave you strength, the way Norah did.

"Norah," he said. His hand reached for hers and his gaze was level with her own. "I love you. Will you do me the honor of becoming my wife?"

The tears that filled her eyes and her throat made speaking impossible. All because she loved him so much.... Norah blinked, then grabbed a napkin from the shiny chrome dispenser in the middle of the table and blew her nose.

"I didn't have time to buy a ring," he told her, "but I thought you'd rather pick one out yourself. Go to any jeweler you want and have them send me the bill. Buy a nice big diamond—money's no problem. All I'm concerned about is making you happy."

Norah froze and closed her eyes at the unexpected stab of pain. Rowdy just didn't realize. No woman wanted to pick out her wedding ring alone, but she doubted he'd understand that.

"I never meant to fall in love with you," she said when she could speak again.

"I didn't mean to fall for you, either," he admitted gruffly. "Heck, I didn't even know what love was. I liked Valerie and I missed her when she was here with you and Steffie during your father's surgery, but—" he shrugged "—love had nothing to do with it."

"What are you saying?"

"I thought I loved Valerie. I know how angry I got when I learned she was marrying Colby Winston. The fact is, I did everything I could to get her to change her mind. My ego took a beating, thanks to your sister."

Norah grinned at the memory. Rowdy wasn't accustomed to losing, and it had sorely injured his pride when Valerie defied him.

"What I realized," he continued, "was that even if Valerie had broken off the engagement, I wouldn't have offered to marry her." Norah had already known that but made no comment. Rowdy sought out her gaze. "I was never in love with your sister. I might have believed I was at one time, but I know what love is now."

"You do?"

Rowdy nodded. "I'm not the marrying sort—fact is, I never thought I'd ever want a wife, but damn it all, Norah, you've got me so confused I'd be willing to do just about anything to make things right between us. I'm offering you what I'd never offer your sister or any other woman. If nothing else, that should tell you how serious I am."

Tears ran unabashed down her cheeks.

"Say you'll marry me, Norah," he coaxed.

Norah reached for another napkin and dabbed at her cheeks. "I...felt so lonely when Valerie and Steffie fell in love. It was as if the whole world had someone, but me."

"Not anymore, Norah. We have each other."

"Do we?" she asked softly. Rowdy was making this so difficult. "You'll have me, but who will I have? Who'll be there for me?"

His eyes revealed how perplexed he was. "I will, of course."

"How can you possibly ask me to be your wife when you already have one?"

"That's ridiculous," Rowdy returned impatiently. "I've never been married in my life. You're the only woman I've ever loved. I don't know where you heard anything so outlandish, but it isn't true."

"It isn't a woman I'm talking about, Rowdy, it's CHIPS."

He shook his head and frowned at her. "What are you talking about?"

"You and I aren't speaking the same language when we say *love*. To you CHIPS is everything. It's the one thing you really love—your family, your wife, your children. Your emotional security."

"You don't know what you're saying!"

"But I do! I've seen it happen over and over again. From the moment you were admitted to the hospital. Karen and I had to practically set up roadblocks in order to give you time to convalesce. Your corporate attorney was waiting outside the hospital door practically the instant he learned about your accident. You even had your own phone installed. Remember what a panic you went into the day word leaked out that you'd been in a plane crash?"

"I'm not likely to forget it. Stock in CHIPS dropped two points."

"You acted as if the world was coming to an end."

"You would, too, if you had a hundred million dollars at stake," he argued.

"Don't you understand?" she pleaded. "You don't have *time* in your life for anything or anyone else. Not me, not a family. No one."

Rowdy tensed. "What do you want from me, Norah? Blood?"

"In a manner of speaking, I guess I do. You can't go on the way you have been, working so many hours, not taking care of yourself. Eventually you'll collapse. As far as I can see, you're a prime candidate for a heart attack a few years down the road. I know you've got a management team, because Valerie was part of it, but you don't let them manage—you do it all yourself."

"I'm a candidate for a heart attack? You're just full of warmth and cheer, aren't you?"

"I need to explain my feelings. I don't want to sound so pessimistic, but I'm worried about you."

"I wouldn't be too concerned if I were you," he muttered sarcastically. "I've got an excellent life insurance policy, and since you're so worried, I'll make sure you're listed as the beneficiary. Revise my will, too."

"Oh, Rowdy, for heaven's sake. I don't want your money, I want *you.*"

He shrugged in apparent unconcern. "You wanted to be realistic? I'm only complying with your forecast of gloom and doom. And if I'm such a poor health risk, you'd best marry me now. The sooner the better, since my time's so limited."

"How can you joke about something like this?"

"You're the one who brought it up."

He was purposely misunderstanding everything she was trying to say. "What's important in life isn't things. It's people and relationships. It's the two of us building a life together, raising our family, making time for each other."

"Family," he repeated as if he'd never heard the word before. Sighing, he sagged against the back of the chair. "I should have known you'd want children. Okay, we'll work around that. I'll say yes to a child, but we stop at one, boy or girl. Agreed?"

Norah was too dumbstruck to respond.

Rowdy glanced at his watch, scowling. As usual, he was on a tight schedule, Norah thought wryly. He needed an answer and he needed it now. The luxury of his presence would always be limited, even to her.

Norah felt as though the whole world was crashing down around her. It was going to break her heart to refuse him, and what made it all the more painful was that she doubted Rowdy would ever really understand. He'd view her as irrational, demanding, sentimental.

"I've never wanted anything more in the world," she said, trying desperately to keep the emotion from her voice. She leaned toward him and pressed her hand to his face, then gently kissed his lips.

Rowdy seemed surprised by her display of tenderness. "I'll make the arrangements with a jeweler," he said, preparing to leave. He reached for his crutches.

"Rowdy," she said quietly.

He must have heard a telltale inflection in her voice, because he looked back to her. She watched as he read the message in her eyes.

The air between them went still and heavy. "You're turning me down, aren't you?"

She slowly exhaled, closing her eyes, and nodded.

Rowdy threw his Stetson on the table in disgust. "I should've known you were going to do this," he shouted.

She sniffled and said, "Despite what you're thinking, this isn't easy for me."

"The heck it isn't." He stood and in his rush to leave, dropped one of his crutches, which frustrated him even more. Before he could prevent it, the second slammed to the floor and he slumped back down in the chair.

"I want a *husband*. It takes more than a few words said before a preacher to make a marriage."

"But you aren't going to marry me, so there's no need to belabor the point, is there?" He managed to pick up one crutch, and with it was able to retrieve the second.

He obviously wanted to get away from her as quickly as possible, moving awkwardly through the cafeteria. She followed close behind.

"You got what you wanted—what you were after in the first place. You worked everything out well in advance, didn't you?"

"Worked out what?" A sick feeling attacked Norah's stomach.

He paused to look at her, his expression cynically admiring. "I have to hand it to you, Norah Bloomfield, you're quite the actress. Am I right in guessing that you worked all this out beforehand so I'd make a fool of myself proposing and you'd have the pleasure of turning me down?"

"Rowdy, that isn't true." Shocked, she trailed him out of the cafeteria. "It's just that I'd never be content with the leftover pieces of your life, with a few minutes here and there."

"Then it's best to know that now, isn't it?"

"Yes, but—"

"You're fighting a losing battle, sweetheart. I suggest you drop it. CHIPS made me what I am today, and I'm not about to give up my company just so you can lead me around by a ring through the nose." He jammed his thumb against the button to summon the elevator.

"I don't want you to give up CHIPS," she protested, but he cut her off.

"Why is it we're discussing all *your* wants? Frankly, they're overwhelming." He held himself away from her, leaning heavily on his crutches and staring at the floor numbers above the door.

When the elevator arrived, Norah stepped back and

let Rowdy enter. With some difficulty he did so, then turned to face her. If he was surprised she hadn't followed him inside, he didn't reveal it.

"Goodbye, Rowdy."

"It *is* goodbye, Norah. Don't worry about me. I plan on having a great life without you."

The elevator doors glided shut, and she brought her hand to her mouth to hold in a cry of pain. Deliberately, she removed her hand, as if she were throwing him a farewell kiss.

"How is she?"

Valerie's voice drifted through the cubicle door. Norah could have answered for herself. She'd been emotionally devastated, but she was much better now.

Although Norah had returned to the emergency room, she wasn't in any condition to work. Not knowing what to do, her supervisor had called Colby, who was on duty.

Colby had tried to listen, but hadn't been able to understand her, she was crying so hard. Her incoherent attempts to explain had merely frustrated him. Apparently he'd phoned Valerie, and she'd rushed to the hospital.

"She should go home, but I don't think she's in any shape to drive," Norah heard Dr. Adamson tell her sister.

Everyone was making it seem far worse than it was, Norah thought grumpily. Okay, so she was a bit weepy when she got back from lunch. And it was true that she hadn't been able to speak too clearly, which made her cry even more with frustration. But everything was under control now—well, almost everything.

"Norah?" Valerie knocked on the door of the emergency-room cubicle before letting herself in.

"Hi," Norah said, raising her right hand limply. "I'm doing much better than Dr. Adamson would have you believe."

"Colby's the one who's so concerned. He's never seen you like this."

"I don't think I have, either," she said, making an effort to smile. A pile of crumpled tissues lay on the gurney beside her. "I'm sorry everyone was worried about me, but really I'm fine. Or at least I will be in a little while."

"Do you want to tell me what happened?"

Norah shrugged and reached for a fresh tissue, clenching it tightly in her fist. "There's not that much to tell. Rowdy dropped in unexpectedly and asked me to marry him. I…didn't feel I had any option but to refuse."

Valerie looked as if she suddenly needed to sit down. "Let me see if I've grasped this correctly. Rowdy— Rowdy *Cassidy*—actually proposed to you?"

Norah nodded.

"He asked you to *marry* him?" Valerie asked incredulously.

Again Norah nodded. "I don't know why—he doesn't have time for me in his life. He…he wanted me to pick out my own engagement ring."

"I don't get it," Valerie said, frowning. "I thought you were in love with him."

"I am, and I'm sure he loves me—as much as Rowdy's capable of loving anyone."

It was as though Valerie hadn't heard her as she

began to pace the tiny cubicle. "Every single person who saw you and Rowdy at Steffie's wedding was convinced your engagement would be next."

"He's already married—to CHIPS," Norah whispered sadly.

"So?"

"Don't *you* understand?" Norah cried, disappointed in her sister. She'd expected sympathy from Valerie, not censure.

"I guess I don't," Valerie admitted reluctantly. "What do you expect him to do—resign from the company, give up everything he's worked so hard to achieve all these years?"

"No...of course not." Norah felt shaken. All along she'd assumed she was right, but Valerie was forcing her to question her own actions.

"Now isn't the time to worry about it," Valerie said soothingly. "Dr. Adamson asked me to drive you home. You're much too upset to work."

"But what if—"

"Don't worry, Colby said he'd get someone to cover for you."

Norah didn't even get a chance to finish. She'd started to say *What if Rowdy calls and I'm not here?* But he wouldn't phone. Norah would have staked her career on it. He was much too angry—he'd told her their goodbye was final.

Someone must have called her father, because David was standing at the door waiting when Valerie pulled into the driveway in front of the house. He poured

Norah a stiff drink, told her to sip it slowly and then advised her to nap.

Norah did so without argument. She must have been more exhausted than she realized; she didn't awaken until late the following morning.

Valerie was speaking to her father when Norah walked down the back staircase into the kitchen. They stopped talking when she appeared. It didn't take a genius to figure out what they were discussing.

"Well," Norah said casually, "what did you two decide?"

"About what?" her father questioned.

"Me. And Rowdy."

"There isn't anything for me to decide," David said, exchanging a knowing smile with Valerie. "You've got a good head on your shoulders. You'll sort out what's best for you."

Norah wished she shared her father's confidence. Rejecting Rowdy's marriage proposal was the right thing to do—wasn't it? Good grief, he didn't even have half an hour to look for an engagement ring with her! Their marriage would be a continual battle of wills. She could fight another woman for his affections, but she was defenseless against a company he'd built from the ground up, a company that was his whole life. She had no choice but to make a stand now or be miserable later.

Ten days passed, and Norah lived with a constant sense of expectation. But she wasn't sure what she was waiting for. Rowdy had made it plain that she wouldn't be hearing from him again.

Her father, too, seemed stricken with a feeling of

hopefulness. More times than she could count, Norah saw him sitting on the porch, his gaze focused in the distance as if he was waiting for someone to come barreling down the long driveway.

"He isn't coming, Dad," Norah said one evening after dinner. She brought him a cup of coffee and sat down on the front step near him.

"You're not talking about Rowdy, are you?"

"Yes, Dad, that's exactly who I'm talking about."

"I don't expect he'll come. He's got too much pride for that. Can't say as I blame him. Poor fellow's head over heels in love, and he doesn't know what to do about it. I feel sorry for the poor chap."

"He was furious with me. He might have loved me at one point, but he doesn't now." She was sure that Rowdy had completely blotted her from his mind.

"Isn't he going to be out of his cast soon?"

Norah had to stop and think. She tasted the coffee, hoping its warmth would chase away the chill she felt whenever she thought about Rowdy. Her life seemed so lonely, so cold without him.

"If I remember right, he should've had the cast removed on Monday." She didn't envy his physical therapist. Rowdy Cassidy would be a cantankerous and difficult patient.

As they were talking, Norah noticed a thin trail of dust rising from the driveway. Her father saw it, too, and Norah watched him relax, as though a long-awaited visitor had finally arrived. But Norah didn't recognize the car—or the driver.

Not until Earl Robbins climbed out of the car did

Norah remember who he was. Rowdy's employee. The one who was heading up CHIPS Northwest.

"Hello again, Norah," he greeted her, closing his door and walking toward the porch.

"Hello," she said, trying to disguise her puzzlement. She introduced her father, and as she did so, tried to imagine what had brought Robbins to see her. A sense of panic filled her when she realized something must be wrong with Rowdy.

"Is Rowdy all right?" she asked, hoping he didn't hear the near-hysteria in her voice. "I mean, he's not ill, is he?"

Robbins glanced toward David and shook his head. "I'm here because of Rowdy, but I don't want you to worry. To the best of my knowledge, he's in fine health."

"Take the young man into my den," her father instructed. "I'll see about getting some iced tea, unless you'd prefer coffee or something stronger."

"Iced tea would be fine," Robbins said with a grateful smile.

Norah directed him into her father's den and closed the door, leaning against it with her hands behind her as she tried to compose herself.

"Valerie suggested I come and talk to you," he explained, pacing as he spoke. "To be honest, I'm not sure I'm doing the right thing. I do know that Rowdy wouldn't approve of my being here. He'd have my job if he knew I was within fifty miles of this place."

If Earl Robbins didn't feel the need to sit down, Norah did. She sank onto the ottoman and clenched her hands. "How is he?" she asked, hungry for news of him.

Robbins ceased pacing. "Physically I'd say he's on

the mend. The cast is off, and he's walking with the aid
of a cane. He's more mobile than he was, which helps—
but not much."

"You didn't come here to tell me how well his leg is
mending, did you?"

Robbins grinned wryly. "No, I didn't." He walked
over to her father's desk and turned to face her. "It isn't
any of my business what went on between you and
Rowdy. In fact, I'd rather not know.

"I realize he's in love with you. Both Kincade and
I saw it happening. We sort of enjoyed watching the
transformation. I'm certainly no expert on love. I'm not
married myself. But it seemed to me that you felt just
as strongly about Rowdy."

"I do," Norah admitted. "Oh, I do."

"From the minute he was discharged from the hospital, all he thought about was you. He drove the staff
crazy. It's a miracle that group of stockholders didn't
walk out on him in San Francisco. Ms. Emerich told
me he bolted upright in the middle of the conference,
as if he didn't know where he was, then sat down and
mumbled something no one heard."

"He was probably worried about his stock," Norah
said.

"I don't think so. My guess, and that of everyone
else who's close to him, is that it was you he was thinking about in San Francisco. The same way he has ever
since you two met."

"He isn't thinking about me anymore," Norah said.

"Don't kid yourself. I'm not here for my health,
Norah, and if Rowdy ever found out, he'd have my hide
as well as my job. He's miserable."

"I suppose he's making everyone else miserable, too."

"No, and that's what's got us worried. I've never known Rowdy to be so…nice. He's keeping his unhappiness to himself. He's polite, cordial, thoughtful. No one knows what to make of it."

"I—I'm sure it'll pass."

"Perhaps," Robbins agreed, "but I can't help thinking it might not. No one's ever seen Rowdy like this. We don't know how to help him. You've got your family, but Rowdy doesn't have anyone."

"He's got CHIPS," she said, not meeting the man's direct gaze.

A knock sounded on the door, and her father came in, bringing Robbins a glass of iced tea. David glanced from him to Norah and back again, then edged out the door.

"Thank you." Robbins took a sip of tea and set the glass aside. "I came because Valerie seemed to think it was important for you to know what's happening to Rowdy. She wants you to understand how much he misses you…how lonely and lost he is. That's all. Now I won't take up any more of your time."

"Thank you for telling me." Although Norah was aware that Valerie had encouraged him to come, she was grateful. Earl Robbins had given her a lot to think about.

He nodded. "Listen, if it wouldn't be too much to ask, I'd appreciate if you didn't say anything to Rowdy about my stopping in."

"Of course," Norah agreed.

Robbins looked significantly relieved.

It took Norah about two minutes to decide what to do with the information Robbins had given her, and two days to make the arrangements.

She kissed her father on the cheek late Thursday afternoon, picked up her suitcase and headed down the porch steps to Valerie's car. Her sister was waiting to drive her to the airport.

"You call, you hear?" her father shouted after her.

"Of course I will," Norah promised. "Although he just might throw me out on my ear."

David chuckled. "That isn't likely. That man needs you—the same way I needed your mother. Be gentle with him. The poor guy doesn't have a clue what's about to happen."

Norah found his parting words a bit odd. She didn't have a clue herself. All she could do was hope for the best.

Early Friday morning, Norah arrived at CHIPS dressed in a new suit. The seventeen-floor headquarters was an impressive piece of architecture, designed in smoky black glass and glistening steel.

The first thing that occurred to Norah was how far from Orchard Valley she'd come, but that didn't deter her from her purpose. Armed with Valerie's directions and an elevator code, Norah entered the top floor that housed Rowdy's office.

"Ms. Bloomfield," Rowdy's assistant said softly when she saw Norah. The middle-aged woman slowly stood up and beamed her a wide smile.

"Hello, Ms. Emerich," Norah said uncertainly. She was having a difficult time taking everything in. She'd had no idea CHIPS was so big.

"Oh, my heavens, I'm so glad you're here." Ms. Emerich hurried from behind the desk and hugged Norah enthusiastically. "It's what we've all been praying would happen—your coming, that is. Rowdy isn't in the office just yet... I never know when he's going to show up these days. Would you like to wait for him?"

Norah nodded and followed her into Rowdy's private office.

"I'll get you some coffee," the older woman said, hands fluttering in her eagerness. "Sit down, anywhere you like. Just make yourself at home." She turned to leave. "Oh, Norah, I'm so glad you've come. "

Perhaps it was a bit presumptuous of her, but Norah chose Rowdy's chair. She sat in the plush black leather and whirled around to face the window, with its dramatic view of Houston.

Hearing someone step into the room, she turned around again and smiled, expecting to see Rowdy's assistant. Only it wasn't Ms. Emerich who'd entered, it was Rowdy Cassidy himself. And he didn't look pleased.

"What the hell do you think you're doing in my office?" he demanded.

Ten

"Rowdy." Norah couldn't take her eyes off him. It was the first time she'd seen him stand without his crutches. He looked tall and proud—and unyielding. It didn't matter; Norah had never loved him more than she did at that moment.

"What are you doing here?" he asked again.

"I—I came to talk. Sit down, please."

He leveled the full force of his scowl at her. "You're in my chair."

"Oh...sorry." She leaped up as though propelled by a spring and hurried around to the other side of the desk.

"Unfortunately, you made an error in assuming I wished to speak to you," he informed her coldly once he was seated. "As it happens, I have several appointments this morning."

Just then Ms. Emerich appeared, carrying two steaming coffee mugs, which she set down on the desk. "Good morning, Mr. Cassidy," she said cheerfully. Winking at Norah, she continued, "Mr. Deavon called and canceled his nine o'clock appointment."

Rowdy glared at her as if he didn't believe her. "Call Kincade and have him here by nine."

"I'm sorry, sir, but Mr. Kincade phoned in sick."

"Murphy, then!"

"Mr. Murphy's out, as well," she informed him, then glanced at Norah and winked again. With that, she was out the door, closing it quietly behind her.

"Annoying woman," Rowdy said under his breath. "All right," he growled, "you wanted to talk. So talk." He looked at his wristwatch. "I'll give you exactly five minutes."

Norah picked up her large purse and deposited it in her lap. The zipper made a hissing sound as she opened it. She rummaged through, then gave up and leaned forward to sip her coffee, noticing that Rowdy hadn't touched his.

"I thought you wanted to talk," Rowdy reminded her impatiently.

"I do, but I brought a list and I want to go over it with you."

"A list?"

She nodded absently, sorting through the objects in her purse. "There are some important issues I feel we have to discuss." She still couldn't seem to locate it and ended up setting her billfold and a paperback novel on the edge of his desk. She could feel Rowdy's disapproval, but was determined not to let him distract her. "Here it is," she said triumphantly, taking the folded slip of paper from the bottom of her oversize bag.

After returning everything to her purse, she zipped it shut. "Now," she began in a businesslike voice, "the first thing has to do with the engagement ring."

Rowdy's face tightened. "You can skip that one."

"Why?" She looked up from her list.

"Because there won't be one."

"All right," she said with a meaningful sigh. "I'll go on to item number two. The vice president. You've got an excellent management team, but as I said earlier, you take on far more than necessary yourself, so I'm suggesting you appoint a vice president you could work closely with over the next few years."

"Vice president of what?"

"CHIPS," she returned shortly. "What else? The way I figure it, you're going to need two, possibly three. Valerie said she'd recommend Bill Somerset, John Murphy and/or Earl Robbins. All three are familiar with the operation of CHIPS and very good managers. Valerie also seemed to think it would be a wise move because you're probably going to lose Somerset if you don't promote him."

"In a pig's eye," Rowdy argued. "Bill's completely happy working for me."

"Perhaps now, but he'll be wooed away by some other company that'll trust him with added responsibilities. A vice presidency is a natural progression for him."

"What makes you so confident of all this?"

"I'm not," she readily admitted, "but Valerie obviously knows a lot more about it than I do. These are her recommendations."

"I gathered as much."

She moved her fingernail down the list. "Another thing. We'll need to make some kind of compromise on the issue of traveling."

"Traveling?" he repeated.

"I'm not sure how much is justified or necessary, but I'd appreciate having it held down to a minimum. I should be able to go with you on some trips, and it would be ideal if we could combine business with pleasure. Maybe two or three times a year—depending, of course, on our schedules."

Rowdy's response was a humorless laugh. "You must be joking. I take that many trips in a month."

"Exactly. That's far too much. The children won't even know they have a father if you're gone that often."

"Children?" he exploded.

"That's point number seven, but I'll address the subject now. I'd like more than one child, Rowdy. I enjoy children, and I'm looking forward to being a mother. Now, I agree six may be out of line, but—"

"Six." He leaned forward, arms rigid and hands clutching the edge of his desk.

"I know, I know," she said with a sigh. "My dad seems to have that number fixed in his mind. But don't worry, I was thinking four would be good. It'd be nice if we had two boys and two girls, but it really doesn't matter."

Rowdy eyed her as if she'd gone completely berserk.

"Item number three," Norah went on without a pause. "You probably won't ever work less than forty hours a week and more likely fifty. Valerie told me there were times you didn't even bother to go home—you just slept at the office. However, I feel that would be detrimental to your health and to our relationship. If I'm going to marry you and move to Houston, I'd appreciate if you made an effort to come home every night. I do realize you're needed here and I can live with whatever hours you deem necessary, provided the house is within easy commuting distance."

"Anything else?"

"Oh, yes, there are several smaller items. Things any couple needs to discuss before marriage."

Rowdy made a show of glancing at his watch. "You might want to hurry since you've got approximately two minutes left."

"Only two minutes?"

He nodded, his look stern and unwavering.

She folded the piece of paper. "Then I won't waste any more of your time on compromises."

"Fine."

"I'll talk about my most important reason for coming here. I made a mistake when I rejected your proposal, Rowdy. You caught me off guard—I wasn't expecting it. You were right, all I could think of was what I wanted, not what you were looking for in our relationship. So I've given you my list of possible compromises to think over."

"One minute left."

Norah stood, forgetting that her purse was in her lap. It fell unceremoniously to the floor. She stooped down to pick it up and straightened awkwardly. "Could we meet and talk again soon? Then I'll listen to whatever you have to say. Actually, I'd be interested in knowing why you want to marry me when you've always been so set against marriage."

"Which is the question I've been asking myself for the past two weeks. It's unfortunate that you don't understand business practices, Norah."

"I don't even pretend to."

"And that explains why you came here. You see, the offer was made and you rejected it."

"Yes, but as I told you, I acted in haste. I should've thought things through before I—"

"Apparently you don't understand," he said without emotion. "I've withdrawn my offer."

She blinked, and a feeling of dread overwhelmed her. "But—"

"It's too late, Norah. Two weeks too late."

A numbness took hold of her limbs and she forced herself to exhale slowly. "I see... I'm sorry. I assumed, erroneously it seems, that your proposal was genuine."

"At the time it was."

"No, Rowdy, it couldn't have been. Love isn't a business transaction, something to be offered and retracted at will. It's a *feeling* and it's a commitment. That doesn't disappear overnight."

"I'm not an impulsive man, Norah...generally," he added with some reluctance. "But I was when I proposed to you. Actually you did us both a favor by rejecting my offer."

Norah was too stunned to respond for a moment. "You don't mean that."

Rowdy said nothing, and since there didn't seem to be anything else for her to say, either, she turned away from him, barely aware of where she was going.

"Goodbye, Norah."

She didn't answer him and walked blindly out of his office. She paused and closed her eyes to compose herself before proceeding.

Ms. Emerich's voice drifted toward her. "My, that didn't take long, did it?"

"Not at all," Norah returned cordially, smiling at the older woman. She stood, as though paralyzed, in the outer office. She'd made such an idiot of herself coming to Rowdy like this!

"Are you okay?"

It took a few seconds for Ms. Emerich's question to sink in. "Ah...oh, yes, I'm fine. Thank you for asking." She nodded toward the closed door that led to Rowdy's office. "Take care of him for me, will you, Ms. Emerich? He doesn't eat right and he works far too many hours. He—he needs someone."

"I've been telling him that for the past five years, but he doesn't listen."

"He's too stubborn for his own good," Norah agreed with a weak smile.

"Won't *you* be here? I was so hoping you two could patch up your differences."

Norah slowly, sadly, shook her head. "I'm afraid I... waited too long."

Ms. Emerich's eyes revealed her dismay. "Oh dear, and I was sure everything would work out."

"So was I," Norah whispered and moved toward the elevator.

The hotel where she was booked was a short distance from CHIPS's headquarters. Norah almost wished she'd walked, but with traffic so heavy and huge semitrucks roaring up and down the streets it didn't seem prudent, so she opted for a taxi.

The first person she called when she got back to the hotel was Valerie. When she told her sister what had happened, Valerie exploded.

"The man's a fool!" her sister snapped. "He's doing the same thing with you that he tried with me. Obviously he didn't learn anything the first time. Okay, fine. We'll just have to teach him all over again."

"He didn't try to bribe me, Valerie, nor did he issue any threats."

"How could he? You're holding all the cards."

Norah didn't know what her sister meant, and frankly she felt so defeated and miserable that it didn't matter. "I've already changed my flight plans. I'll be home this afternoon."

"No, you won't," Valerie told her. "That's exactly what Rowdy expects you to do. He doesn't mean a word of it, you know."

"That's not the impression he gave me."

"Wait and see," Valerie assured her. "My advice to you is stay where you are. Take in the sights, do a little shopping, relax, vacation. The last place Rowdy will ever think of looking for you is in his own backyard."

"But, Valerie—"

"Promise me," Valerie demanded. "Not a peep out of you. I can't get over this," she fumed. "That man's certainly a slow learner! Don't you worry, though, we're going to educate him once and for all."

"He isn't going to call me."

"I'm betting you'll hear from him in twenty-four hours. Thirty, tops."

"All right," Norah agreed reluctantly, although from the look on his face, Norah couldn't imagine hearing from Rowdy in thirty *days,* let alone thirty hours.

"Trust me, Norah. I know how Rowdy Cassidy operates. The only way he can deal with emotions is by treating everything like a negotiation. A business deal."

"I did what you and I discussed. I approached him as though it *was* a business deal, and I went through my list."

"Good. That he can understand."

"But it didn't do any good."

"It will, it will. Now stay right where you are, and I'll let you know as soon as we hear from the great and mighty Rowdy Cassidy."

Norah wasn't sure she was up to playing hide-and-seek, but she trusted her sister and accepted Valerie's advice. Really, she had no other option if she intended to work out her relationship with Rowdy.

For two days she lazed around the hotel pool in the morning, shopped in the afternoon and visited museums and art galleries. In the evenings she dressed for dinner and dined by herself at the hotel. She'd never felt lonelier.

On the morning of the third day, her phone rang. Norah was still in bed, although it was almost noon. She'd stayed awake most of the night worrying, certain that she should have arranged a flight back to Orchard Valley. Hanging around a hotel room like this was crazy.

"He's here," Valerie whispered when Norah answered the phone. "Dad's talking to him now, and he's doing a masterful job of keeping a straight face. He's pretending he doesn't know where you are."

Norah scrambled into an upright position. "You mean Rowdy's there…in Orchard Valley…right this minute?"

"Yup. None too happy, either, by the looks of him."

"Aren't you going to tell him I'm in Houston?"

"I might. Then again, I might not."

"Valerie Winston, that's cruel! Put Rowdy on the phone. I insist. Do you hear me?"

"I'll make it up to him," Valerie promised with a delighted chuckle. "Colby and I have talked it over and I've decided to accept Rowdy's offer to head up CHIPS Northwest. Hold on a minute, and I'll get him for you."

A minute had never lasted longer. Although she strained to hear what was happening in the background, Norah could only catch bits and pieces of the conversation. The next instant Rowdy was on the line.

"Norah?"

"Hello, Rowdy. I—"

"Valerie says you're in Houston. Is that true?"

"Yes."

He cursed under his breath. "No doubt Valerie put you up to this. If I wasn't so grateful she's agreed to take on the Northwest assignment, I'd have her hide for this." Norah could hear her sister saying something in the background and Rowdy saying something in return.

"Listen, I'm on my way back to Houston. Will you meet me at the airport?"

"Of course. I love you, Rowdy. I kept thinking of all the things I should have said to you and didn't. It wasn't until I got back to the hotel that I realized I hadn't said the most important thing of all, and that was how much I love you."

"I love you, too. You are going to marry me, aren't you?"

"Oh, yes."

"Bring your list. There're a couple of points we need

to discuss. Oh, before I forget, Bill Somerset's my new vice president."

"Oh, Rowdy, I do love you!"

"You know," he said with a heavy sigh, "I could get used to hearing you say that. Fact is, I could even get used to being a husband—and father."

"I'll be waiting at the airport when you land," Norah promised eagerly.

She met him four hours later. Rowdy walked into the arrivals lounge and directly to Norah. They just stood there for an instant, staring at each other, before he pulled her into his embrace.

"What do women want, anyway?" he murmured, then kissed her hungrily.

"Who, me or Valerie?" she asked, wrapping her arms around his neck. He'd lifted her clear off the floor, leaving her feet dangling.

"Both of you."

"Love isn't a business deal, Rowdy. It's you and me settling our differences. I don't ever want to go through this again."

"You?" he cried, and buried his face in her neck. "I don't think my heart could take it." He laughed shakily. "Until I met you, Norah Bloomfield, I didn't even know I had a heart."

Gradually he lowered her back to the floor. His eyes, so loving and intense, continued to hold hers. "I thought I'd go insane the past couple of days," he admitted. "So did everyone around me. Ms. Emerich was so furious with me she threatened to resign."

"She really is a dear."

Rowdy chuckled. "Maybe, but I advise you not to make her angry."

Norah laughed softly and slipped her arm around his waist. "What changed your mind?"

Rowdy kissed the top of her head. "Something you said a long time back."

"Something I said?"

He nodded and kissed her cheek. "About what's really important in life. You said love and fulfillment came from people and relationships. I was sitting at my desk last night, and I realized I was working myself to death for no good reason. I was filling up all the emptiness I've felt in my life with business. What I really wanted was *you*. I wanted you to lecture me about my cholesterol. I wanted you to argue with me about what we're going to name our children and where we're going to spend our vacations. I wanted you to kiss me."

"Oh, Rowdy." Tears spilled from her eyes until his face blurred before her.

"I'm crazy about you." He drew her into his arms again. "Let's start with the kissing part," he whispered.

Norah smiled through her tears. "That's one thing I won't argue about."

Epilogue

"Oh, Rowdy, I'm so anxious to see my family," Norah breathed as she settled into the airplane beside her husband. She didn't know if she'd ever grow accustomed to flying in the small jet Rowdy kept for personal use, but it was a definite convenience since the Lear could land at the tiny Orchard Valley airport.

"I don't know why Valerie had to plan a big reunion three weeks before your due date," Rowdy said, glancing at Norah's swollen abdomen. A toddler slept in his arms, head resting on Rowdy's broad shoulder. Rowdy lovingly held his hand against his son's back.

"Don't fuss. She planned this get-together a year ago, before we knew about the baby."

"I still don't think you should be traveling."

Norah smiled reassuringly at her husband. "We couldn't be in finer company. If the baby does decide to arrive early, Colby will be there to help with the delivery. Besides, Jeff arrived a week late."

"Colby's a heart surgeon," Rowdy said.

"He knows everything there is to know about babies," Norah countered, smiling softly to herself. She never would've believed Rowdy would worry so much over her pregnancies. He was fiercely protective when it came to Norah and their family.

For the first time since they'd entered the aircraft, Rowdy grinned. "Colby certainly *should* know about babies. Even now, it's difficult for me to picture Valerie as the mother of twins."

"Valerie amazes me," Norah said with a genuine sigh of admiration. Her eldest sister continued to head CHIPS Northwest, cared for both her sons and accomplished more in one day than Norah thought about doing in a week. Her family and CHIPS were both thriving.

Rowdy's eyes softened as they met Norah's. "*You* amaze me."

"I do?"

If there'd been any surprises in her marriage, they'd come from the changes she'd seen in Rowdy. No wife could ask for a more attentive husband. He'd learned to delegate duties, and CHIPS was now served by four vice presidents. He'd promoted Valerie almost immediately after she'd accepted the Northwest position.

The most incredible thing had happened as Rowdy gradually released the tight control he held over every aspect of his company. CHIPS prospered. The stock had nearly doubled in the two and a half years since Norah and Rowdy's marriage.

"I have so much to thank you for," Rowdy said, slipping his arm around her shoulder and drawing her closer. He rested his free hand on her stomach and Norah watched his eyes widen as he felt their child kick against his palm.

"The baby moved!"

Norah laughed. "Yes, I know."

Rowdy's grin broadened. "The closer the time comes for this one to be born, the more excited I get." He kissed Jeff's blond head. "I'm still surprised by the way anyone so small could take up so much of my heart," he said solemnly.

"You're a wonderful father," Norah whispered. "And you know what else?" she asked, nestling against him despite the seat belt. "You're a wonderful husband, too."

"You make that very easy, angel face." He settled his arm around her shoulders and Norah felt him kiss the top of her head. He rested his chin there. "I was thinking the other day that if we have a girl, we should name her Grace—after your mother."

Norah smiled to herself. "I'm so happy you said that."

"Does your father think baby number two will be a boy or a girl?"

Norah sighed. "Just because he was right about Valerie and Colby having twin boys, and Steffie and Charles having a little girl, that doesn't mean what he predicted for us will come true. Having six kids is probably excessive—even for us!"

Norah felt Rowdy go still. She raised her head to look into her husband's dark eyes. "You're thinking about those children again, aren't you?" she said quietly, referring to the recent, tragic death of one of his employees, who'd left two orphaned children.

Rowdy nodded. "I know what it's like to lose your mother and father. I hate the thought of those two spending the rest of their lives being shuffled from foster home to foster home the way I was."

"You have a soft heart, Rowdy Cassidy. I have a distinct feeling we're going to end up with six children, after all."

"Would you mind?"

"I wouldn't mind in the least," she assured him.

The drone of the airplane quickly put Norah to sleep. When she awoke, it was nearly time for them to land. Steffie and Charles had volunteered to pick them up at the Orchard Valley airport and drive them to the house.

Norah stepped off the plane first and was greeted with a hug from Steffie. Marriage hadn't changed her. Steffie was as graceful as a ballerina and so beautiful that it took Norah a moment to stop looking at her.

"It's so good to see you," Steffie squealed. Charles was holding a squirming toddler against his hip. "Hello, Amy," Norah said, holding out her arms to her ten-month-old niece. "Do you remember your auntie Norah?"

"She might," Steffie teased, "but I don't think she's so sure about the tummy."

"She's far more interested in getting reacquainted with Jeff," Charles said as the two cousins eyed each other.

They began walking toward the car. "How's Dad?" Norah asked.

"Never better," Charles answered. "He's so excited about this family get-together he can hardly stand it. I swear he must've been up since the crack of dawn. Wait until you see the spread he's arranged. The front yard's all ready for the barbecue."

"Dad's turned into a professional grandpa," Steffie put in. "He's wonderful with Amy and the boys. I never

thought I'd see him down on his hands and knees giving
horsey rides. Trust me, it's a sight to behold."

Norah grinned. It seemed impossible that a few years
ago she'd been convinced they would lose him. He'd
lost the will to live and given up the struggle to regain
his health.

They talked on the phone at least once a week, and
sometimes more often. Her father loved to fill her in
on Orchard Valley news. Since Charles was the local
newspaper publisher and editor, David had an inside
track on the town's affairs. Something always seemed
to be going on. Their weekly calls had helped Norah
those first weeks, when she'd missed home so much....

David Bloomfield was standing on the front porch,
waiting for his family. When Rowdy helped Norah out
of the car, he saw his son-in-law watching her tenderly
as he carried young Jeff. Charles and Steffie and little
Amy appeared next. David saw the communication between his second daughter and her husband, saw how
proud Steffie was of him and how deeply they loved
their child.

Valerie and Colby, who'd been occupied playing with
their identical twin sons on the swing set, waved and
shouted a cheer of welcome. The two boys took off running toward the parked car, laughing, their eyes shining with joy. Hand in hand, Valerie and Colby followed
them. The children's laughter rippled through the early-
afternoon air, and David grinned. His heart swelled at
the sight of his three daughters and their families. Valerie and Colby with the twins, Steffie and Charles with

their little girl, and Norah with her son and another one due within the month.

"It's just the way you said it would be," David said hoarsely, looking to the heavens. "More than I ever dreamed it would be." He wiped a stray tear from his eye and whispered, "Thank you, Grace."

* * * * *

LONE STAR LOVIN'

To Diane DeGooyer—a friend forever

One

"You're a long way from Orchard Valley," Sherry Waterman muttered to herself as she stepped out of her PT Cruiser and onto the main street of Pepper, Texas. Heat shimmered up from the black asphalt.

Drawing a deep breath, she glanced around with an appraising eye at this town, which was to be her new home. Pepper resembled any number of small mid-Texas towns she'd driven through in the past twenty-four hours.

The sun was pounding down with a vengeance, and Sherry wiped her brow with her forearm, looking for someplace to buy a cold drink. She was a couple of weeks early; she'd actually planned it like this, hoping to get a feel for Pepper and the surrounding ranch community before she took over her assignment. In an hour or so she'd drive on to Houston, where she'd visit her friend Norah Cassidy for a couple of weeks, then double back to Pepper. Although it was considerably out of her way, she was curious about this town—and

the job she'd accepted as a physician assistant, sight un-
seen, through a medical-employment agency.

Her car didn't have air-conditioning, and she'd rolled
down both windows in an effort to create a cooling
cross-draft. It had worked well enough, but along with
the breeze had come a fine layer of dust, and a throat
as dry as the sun-baked Texas street.

Clutching her purse and a folded state map, she
headed for the Yellow Rose café directly opposite. A
red neon sign in the window promised home cooking.

After glancing both ways, she jogged across the
street and hurried into the, thankfully, air-conditioned
café. The counter was crowded with an array of cowboy
types, so she seated herself by the window and reached
for the menu tucked behind the napkin canister.

A waitress wearing a pink gingham uniform with
a matching ribbon in her hair strolled casually toward
Sherry's table. "You're new around here, aren't you?"
she asked.

"Yes," Sherry answered noncommittally, looking up
from the menu. "I'll have an iced tea with extra lemon,
please, and a cheeseburger, without the fries." No need
to clog her arteries with extra fat. The meat and cheese
were bad enough.

"Iced tea and a cheeseburger," the waitress repeated.
"You wanna try our lemon meringue pie? It's the best
this side of Abilene."

"Oh, sure, why not?" Sherry said, giving up the cholesterol and carbohydrate battle without a fight. The
waitress left and returned almost immediately with the
iced tea. Sherry drank gratefully, then spread the map
across the table and charted her progress. With luck,

she should be in Houston by midafternoon the following day. Right on schedule. Her friend Norah Cassidy wasn't expecting her before Wednesday, so Sherry could make a leisurely drive of it—although she'd enjoy the drive a whole lot more if it wasn't so hellishly hot.

The waitress brought Sherry's cheeseburger on a thick, old-fashioned ceramic plate. A mound of onion and tomato slices, plus lettuce and pickles, were neatly arranged next to the open burger.

"Don't see too many strangers coming this way," the waitress commented, plunking down containers of mustard and ketchup. "Most folks stick to the freeway."

"I prefer taking the back roads," Sherry said, popping a pickle slice into her mouth.

"You headed for San Antonio?"

"Houston. I'm a physician assistant and—"

"I don't suppose you're looking for a job?"

Sherry smiled to herself. "Not really. I already have one." She didn't add that the job was right here in Pepper.

"Oh." The eager grin faded. "The town council's been advertising with one of those employment agencies for over a year."

Apparently the waitress hadn't heard that they'd hired someone. "I'm also a nurse and a midwife," Sherry added, although she wasn't sure why she felt obliged to list her credentials for the woman. The physician assistant part was a recent qualification.

The waitress nodded. "I hear lots of women like to have their babies at home these days. Most everyone from around Pepper comes to the hospital, though."

"You have a hospital here?" This was welcome news.

The town didn't look large enough to support more than a café, a couple of taverns and a jail.

"Actually it's a clinic. But Doc's made sure we've got the best emergency-room facilities within two hundred miles. Last year one of the high-school boys lost an arm, and Doc was able to save the arm *and* the kid. Wouldn't have been able to do it without all that fancy equipment. We're right proud of that clinic."

"You should be." Sherry gazed longingly at her lunch. If the waitress didn't stop chattering, it was going to get cold.

"You have family in Houston?"

Sherry added the rest of her condiments, folded the cheeseburger closed and raised it toward her mouth as a less-than-subtle hint. "No. A good friend."

The woman's eyes brightened. "I see." She left and returned a moment later, a tall, potbellied older man in tow.

"Howdy," he said with a lazy drawl. "Welcome to Texas."

Sherry finished chewing her first bite. "Thank you. It's a wonderful state."

"What part of the country you from?"

"Oregon," she replied. "A little town called Orchard Valley."

"I hear it's real pretty up there in Or-ee-gon."

"It's beautiful," Sherry agreed, staring down at her plate. If she was lucky, this cowpoke would get the message and leave her to her lunch.

"'Course living in Texas has a lot of advantages."

"That's what I understand."

"Suppose I should introduce myself," he said, holding out his hand. "Name's Dan Bowie. I'm Pepper's duly elected mayor."

"Pleased to meet you." Sherry wiped the mustard from her fingertips and extended her hand. He shook it, his eyes gleaming, then without waiting for an invitation, pulled out the chair opposite her and made himself comfortable.

"Donna Jo here was telling me you're a physician assistant."

"That's true."

"She also said you already have a job."

"That's true, too, but— "

"It just so happens that Pepper badly needs a qualified physician assistant. Now we've finally hired one, but she's not due to get here for a coupla weeks yet. So-o-o..."

Sherry abruptly decided to discontinue her charade. "Well, she's here. It's me." She smiled brightly. "I'm early, I know, but—"

"Well, I'll be! This is great, just great. I wish you'd said something sooner. We'd've thrown a welcome party if we'd known, isn't that right, Donna Jo?"

"Actually I was on my way to Houston to visit a friend, but curiosity got the better of me," Sherry explained. "I thought I'd drive through town and get a look at Pepper."

"Well, what do you think?" He pushed back his Stetson and favored her with a wide smile. "You can stay for a while, can't you?" he asked. "Now, you finish your lunch," he said as Donna Jo set a towering piece of lemon meringue pie in front of Sherry and replenished her iced tea. "Your meal's on us," he announced grandly. "Send the tab to my office, Donna Jo."

"Thank you," Sherry began, "but—"

"Soon as you're done, Miz…"

"Waterman. Sherry Waterman."

"Soon as you're done eating, I aim to show you around town. We'll stop by the clinic, too. I want Doc Lindsey to meet you."

"Well… I suppose." Sherry hoped she didn't sound ungracious. She finished her meal quickly and in silence, acutely conscious of Mayor Bowie's rapt and unwavering gaze.

The second she put her fork down, he took hold of her elbow and practically lifted her from the chair. He'd obviously regained his voice, because he was talking enthusiastically as he guided her out the café door.

"Pepper's a sweet little town. Got its name from Jim Pepper. Don't suppose you ever heard of him up there in Or-ee-gon. He died at the Alamo, and our forefathers didn't want the world to forget what a fine man he was, so they up and named the town after him. What most folks don't know is that he was darn near blind. He couldn't have shot one of Santa Ana's men if his life depended on it, which unfortunately it did."

"I'm sure his family was proud."

They strolled down the road and turned left onto a friendly looking, tree-lined street. Sherry noticed a huge old white house with a wide porch and dark green shutters and guessed it must be the clinic.

"Doc Lindsey's going to be mighty glad to meet you," the mayor was saying as he held open the gate of the white picket fence. "He's been waiting a good long while for this. Yes, indeed. A good long while."

"I'm looking forward to meeting him, too," Sherry said politely. And it was true. She'd spent the past two years going to school part-time in order to train for this job. She was excited about beginning her new responsibilities. But not quite yet. She did want to visit Norah first.

She preceded the mayor up the porch steps to the screen door. He opened it for her, and led her inside, past a middle-aged receptionist who called out a cordial greeting.

"Doc's in, isn't he?" Dan asked over his shoulder without stopping to hear the reply.

Apparently, whether or not Doc was with a patient was of no concern to Pepper's duly elected mayor. Clasping her by the elbow, he knocked loudly on a polished oak door and let himself in.

An older white-haired man was sitting in a comfortable-looking office chair, his feet propped on the corner of a scarred desk. His mouth was wide open; his head had fallen back. A strangled sound came from his throat, and it took Sherry a moment to realize he was snoring.

"Doc," Dan said loudly. "I brought someone for you to meet." When the old man didn't respond, Dan said it again, only louder.

"I think we should let him sleep," Sherry whispered.

"Nonsense. He'll be madder'n blazes if he misses meeting you."

Whereas the shouting hadn't interrupted Don Lindsey's nap, Sherry's soft voice did. He dropped his feet and straightened, blinking at Sherry as if she were an apparition.

"Who in tarnation are you?"

"Sherry Waterman," she said. "Mayor Bowie wanted us to meet."

"What ails you?"

"I'm in perfect health."

"She's that gal we hired from Or-ee-gon."

"Why in heaven's name didn't you say so?" Doc Lindsey boomed, vaulting to his feet with the energy of a man twenty years younger. "About time you got here."

"I'm afraid there's been a misunderstanding...." Sherry began, but neither man was listening. Doc slapped the mayor on the back, reached behind the door for his fishing pole and announced he'd be back at the end of the week.

He paused on his way out of the office. "Ellie Johnson's baby is due anytime now, but you won't have any problem with that. More'n likely I'll be back long before she goes into labor. She was two weeks late with her first one."

"Don't you worry," the mayor said, following Doc out the door. "I heard Sherry tell Donna Jo she's a midwife, too."

Doc shook hands with the mayor and chortled happily. "You outdid yourself this time, Danny-boy. See you in a week."

"Dr. Lindsey!" Sherry cried, chasing after him. He was already outside and on the sidewalk. "I'm not staying! I'm on my way to Houston to meet a friend." She scrambled down the steps so fast she nearly stumbled.

Doc didn't seem to hear her. The mayor, too, had suddenly developed a hearing problem.

Doc tossed his fishing pole into the bed of his truck and climbed into the front seat.

"I can't stay!" she shouted. "I'm not supposed to start work for another two weeks. I've made other plans!"

"Seems to me you're here now," Doc said. "Might as well stay. Good to have you on the team. I'll see you…" The roar of the engine drowned out his last words.

Sherry stood on the lawn, her heart pounding as she watched him drive away. Frowning, she clenched her fists at her sides. Neither man had taken the trouble to listen to her; they just assumed she would willingly forgo her plans. But darn it, she wasn't going to be railroaded by some hick mayor and a doctor who obviously spent more time sleeping and fishing than practicing medicine.

"I can't stay," she said, as annoyed with herself as she was with the mayor. This was what she got for being so curious.

"But you *can't* leave now," Mayor Bowie insisted. "Doc won't be back for a week. Besides, he's never been real good with time—a week could turn out to be ten days or more."

She pushed a stray lock of shiny brown hair off her forehead, and her blue eyes blazed. "That's unfortunate, because I'm meeting my friend in Houston and I can't be late." That wasn't entirely true but she didn't intend to start work until the agreed-upon date. On top of that, she couldn't shake the feeling that there was something not quite right about the situation here in Pepper.

"If you could stay the week, we'd all be mighty grateful," the mayor was saying.

"I'm sorry but no," Sherry told him emphatically, heading back down the street toward her car.

The mayor dogged her heels. "I'm sure your friend wouldn't mind. Why don't you phone and ask her? The city will pay for the call."

Great, Sherry thought, there were even perks. "No, thanks," she said firmly.

The mayor continued to plead. "I feel bad about this," he said. "But a week, why, only seven days, and Doc hasn't had time off in months."

Sherry kept walking, refusing to let him work on her sympathies. He seemed to have forgotten about the possibility of Doc's absence lasting as long as ten days, too.

"You have to understand," he went on, "that with Doc away there isn't anyone within miles for medical emergencies."

Sherry stopped and turned to glare at him. "It's too bad the pair of you didn't think of that sooner. I told you when you introduced yourself that I was on my way to Houston. My contract doesn't start for two weeks."

"I know." He removed his hat and looked at her imploringly. "Surely a week isn't too much to ask."

"Excuse me, miss." A stocky police officer dressed in a tan uniform had come out of the café and strolled over to her. The town sheriff, she decided. He was chewing on a toothpick and his thumbs were tucked in his belt buckle, which hung low under his protruding belly. "I don't suppose you happen to own that cute little Cruiser just there, do you?" He pointed at her car, about twenty feet away.

"As a matter of fact, I do."

His nod was slow and deliberate. The toothpick was smoothly transferred to the other side of his mouth. "I was afraid of that. Best I can tell, it's parked illegally."

"It most certainly is not," Sherry protested as the three of them reached the car. The slot was clearly marked and she'd pulled in between two other vehicles.

"See how your left rear tire is over the yellow line?" the sheriff asked, pointing.

"I suppose that carries a heavy fine?" Good grief, she thought. Before long some cowpoke was going to suggest they get a rope and hang her from the nearest tree. In that case she'd be okay, since she hadn't seen anything but brush for the last hundred miles.

"There isn't a fine for illegally parking your car," he said, grinning lazily. "But jaywalking does carry a hefty one, and I saw you cross that street with my very own eyes."

"There wasn't a crosswalk," she said.

"Sure there is," he said, still grinning. "It's down the street a bit, but it's there. I painted it myself no more'n ten years ago."

"You're going to fine me, then," she said, reaching into her bag for her wallet. "Great. I'll pay you and be done with it." After that she was going to head straight for the freeway, and when she got to Houston, she'd reconsider this job offer.

"There isn't any fine."

"But you just said there was!" Actually, Sherry was relieved. Her cash was running low and she doubted the sheriff would accept a check.

"No fine, but the jail term—"

"Jail term!" she exploded.

"Now, Billy Bob," the mayor said, placing himself between the two of them, "you don't really intend to put our doc's helper in jail, do you?"

Billy Bob rubbed his hand across the underside of his jaw as if needing to contemplate such a monumental decision.

"You'd give Pepper a bad name," the mayor went on, "and we wouldn't want that, would we?"

"You staying in Pepper, miss?" the officer asked.

Sherry's gaze connected with Mayor Bowie's. "It appears I don't have much choice, do I?"

The minute she had access to a phone, Sherry vowed, she was going to call her friend's husband, Rowdy Cassidy. Rowdy, the owner of one of the largest computer software companies in the world, had a large legal staff. He'd be able to pull a few strings for her. By the end of the day, these folks in Pepper would be facing so many lawsuits, they'd throw a parade when she left town.

"I'll walk you back to the clinic," the mayor said, smiling as though he didn't have a care in the world. "I'm sure Mrs. Colson'll be happy to give you a tour of the place."

Sherry ground her teeth and bit back a tart reply. Until she had the legal clout she needed, there was no point in voicing any more protests.

Instead, Sheriff Billy Bob himself escorted her down the street and around the corner to the clinic. The middle-aged receptionist introduced herself as Mrs. Colson and greeted Sherry with a warm smile. "I'm so glad you decided to stay."

"You make her welcome now," the sheriff instructed.

"You know I will," Mrs. Colson told him, standing and coming around the counter. "You can go on now," she told Billy Bob and, taking him by the elbow, escorted him out the door. She turned to Sherry. "Billy Bob can outstare a polecat, but underneath that tough hide of his, he's gentle as a baby."

Sherry swallowed a retort as the receptionist went on to extol the sheriff's virtues.

"One of those multitalented folks you read so much about. Not only does he uphold the law around these parts, but he makes the best barbecue sauce in the state. Wait till you taste it. Everyone thinks he should bottle and sell it, but I doubt he will."

"How...unfortunate," was all Sherry could manage.

Her mood didn't improve as Mrs. Colson gave her the grand tour. Despite her frame of mind, Sherry was impressed with the clinic's modern equipment and pleased with the small apartment at one end of the building that would serve as her living quarters.

"Doc's sure glad to get away for a few days," Mrs. Colson said amicably, ignoring Sherry's sour mood. "I can't even remember the last time he had more than a day to himself. He talks about fishing a lot—gets a pile of those magazines and catalogs. In the twenty years I've known him, I don't believe I've seen him livelier than he was today after you arrived. Guess he was thinking he'd best skedaddle before you changed your mind. I'm sure glad you didn't."

Sherry's answering smile was weak. Between Dan Bowie, Doc Lindsey and Billy Bob, she'd been completely hog-tied.

"So Dr. Lindsey's been practicing in Pepper for

twenty years?" She wondered if, like her, he'd innocently driven into town and been snared. This could
be something straight out of that old TV series, *The
Twilight Zone.*

"Thirty years, in fact, maybe more. Most folks think
of him as a saint."

Some saint, Sherry thought. With little more than a
nod of his head, he'd abandoned Pepper and her.

Mrs. Colson led her to Doc's office. "Now make
yourself at home. Do you want a cup of coffee?"

"No, thanks," Sherry answered, walking over to the
desk. The telephone caught her eye. As soon as she had
a minute alone, she'd call Houston.

But the moment Mrs. Colson left there was a knock
at the office door. Sherry groaned. She hadn't even had
time to sit down.

"Come in," she called, thinking it must be the receptionist.

In walked a tall, rawboned cowboy with skin tanned
the color of a new penny. He wore jeans, a checkered
shirt and a pair of scarred boots. A Stetson hat hooded
his dark eyes, and somehow, with the red bandana
around his neck, he looked both rough and dangerous.

"You're not Doc Lindsey," he said accusingly.

"No," she agreed tartly, "I'm not."

"Oh, good," Mrs. Colson said, following him into
the room. "I see your one-o'clock appointment is here."

"*My* one o'clock appointment?"

"Where's Doc?" the cowboy demanded.

"He's gone fishing. Now you sit down," Mrs. Colson
directed in steely tones. "You're Miz Waterman's first

patient, and I don't want her getting a bad impression of the folks in Pepper."

"I ain't talkin' to no woman about Heather."

"Why not? A woman would be far more understanding than Doc."

The cowboy shook his head stubbornly.

Personally, Sherry agreed with him.

"Don't you argue with me, Cody Bailman," Mrs. Colson said, arms akimbo. "And don't you make trouble for Miz Waterman. She's a real sweetheart."

Cody shifted his hat farther back on his head. "It ain't gonna work."

"That's right. It ain't gonna work unless you try." The receptionist took Cody by the elbow and marched him to the chair on the other side of the desk. "Now sit. You, too, Sherry." Neither of them bothered to comply, but that didn't disturb the receptionist. "Cody's here to talk about his daughter. She's twelve and giving him plenty of grief, and he comes here for advice because… well, because his wife died about ten years back and he's having a few problems understanding what's happening to Heather now that she's becoming a young woman."

"Which means I'm not talkin' to some stranger about my personal affairs," Cody said.

"It'll do you good to get everything out," Mrs. Colson assured him. "Now sit down," she said again. "Sherry, you sit, too. If you stand, it'll make Cody nervous."

Sherry sat. "What should I do?" she whispered.

"Listen," the older women instructed. "That's all Doc ever does. It seems to help."

Doc Lindsey apparently served as Pepper's psychologist, too. Sherry had received some training along those lines, but certainly not enough to qualify as a counselor.

"I'm not talkin' to a woman," Cody said.

"Did you ever consider that's the reason you're having so many problems with Heather?" Mrs. Colson pointed out, then stalked over to the door. As she reached for the knob, her narrowed eyes moved from Cody to Sherry, and her tight features relaxed into a smile. "You let me know if Cody gives you any problems, but I doubt he will." She dropped her voice. "What Heather really needs is a mother. In my opinion, Cody should remarry."

"You volunteering for the job, Martha?" Cody said.

Mrs. Colson's cheeks reddened. "I'm old enough to be *your* mother, and you darn well know it." With that she left the room, closing the door behind her.

Cody laughed and to Sherry's surprise sat down in the chair across from her, took off his hat and relaxed. As he rested one ankle on the opposite knee and stared at Sherry, the humor drained out of his face.

She wasn't sure what to do. If she hadn't felt so intimidated by this dark-haired cowboy, she'd have sent him on his way.

"You married?" he asked suddenly.

Her mouth fell open. When she finally managed to speak, her words stumbled over one another. "No, I'm not, I…that is…" She knew she sounded breathless and inane.

"Don't look so worried. I'm not expecting you to offer your services as my wife."

"I realize that," she said with as much dignity as she could muster. Unfortunately it wasn't much.

"Then how are you supposed to know about kids?"

"I have two younger brothers and a sister," she said, wondering why she thought she had to defend herself. She *should* be sending him on his way. She sighed. The longer this day lasted, the more convinced she was that she'd somehow stepped out of the present. The man sitting across from her might have come from another century.

"So you know about girls?"

"I was one not so long ago myself," she said wryly. Resigning herself to the situation, she asked, "Why don't you tell me about Heather and I'll see if I can help?"

Cody seemed to need time to think over her suggestion. Eventually he began. "Well, first off, Heather's doing things behind my back."

"What sort of things?"

"Wearing makeup and the like. The other night I went in to check up on her and I swear she had on so much silver eye shadow her eyelids glowed in the dark."

Sherry swallowed her impulse to laugh.

"No more'n about six months ago," he continued, clearly confused by his daughter's behavior, "Heather was showing signs of being one of the best cowhands I'd ever seen, but now she doesn't want anything to do with ranching. Besides that, she's, uh, getting bigger on top."

"Have you bought her a bra?"

He flushed slightly beneath his tan. "I didn't have to—she bought her own. Ordered it right off the Internet before I even knew. From what I can see, she didn't have any idea what she was doing, because the one they sent was at least five sizes too big. Instead of admitting she doesn't know about such things, she's wearing it and as best I can tell stuffing it with something. Heaven only knows what."

"My guess is tissue." That had worked for Sherry when she was a teenager.

Cody's dark eyes narrowed in concentration. "Could be. I asked her about it, and she nearly bit my head off."

Mrs. Colson was right; the poor girl did need a mother.

"Has Heather got a boyfriend?" Maybe Cody was jealous of some boy. It sounded like a good theory anyway.

Cody frowned. "Ever since she's been wearing this bra, she's got a whole passel of boys hanging around. The thing is, she doesn't like all this attention. You have to understand that until recently Heather was a tomboy."

"Heather's growing up, Cody," Sherry told him. She leaned back and crossed her arms. "She doesn't really understand what's happening to her body. She's probably frightened by the changes. Trust me, she isn't any happier about what's taking place than you are. Give her a little time and a little space, and you'll be surprised by how well she adjusts."

Cody eyed her as if he wasn't convinced he should believe her.

"Does she have any close friends?" she asked.

"Wally and Clem, but she doesn't seem to be getting along with them as well as she used to."

"What about girlfriends?"

"She has a couple, but they live here in town and we're twenty miles away. What she really needs is to talk to someone—you know, a woman, someone older than thirteen, who knows a bit more about bras and other girl stuff. And then there was this business with the 4-H—all of a sudden my daughter wants to run my life."

"The 4-H? Your life?"

"Never mind," he said, groaning heavily.

"Would you like me to talk to her?" Sherry offered. "I... I don't know if I'd be able to accomplish anything, but I'd be willing to try."

"I'd like it a whole lot," he said, his eyes softening with gratitude. He frowned again. "She's been acting like a porcupine lately, so don't be offended if she seems a bit unfriendly." Cody looked down and sighed. "Then again, she might be overly friendly. Just don't be shocked by anything she says or does, all right?"

"I won't be," Sherry promised. "We'll get along fine." She wasn't as confident as she sounded, but she found she liked Cody Bailman. It hadn't been easy for him to discuss such private matters with a stranger, a woman, no less, yet he'd put his concern for his daughter first. She was impressed.

"I found something the other day. I'm sure Heather didn't mean for me to see it."

"What was it?"

"A book. She had it tucked between the sofa cushions. It was one of those romance novels you women like so much. I tell you right now, it worries me."

"Why?"

"Well, because I don't think it's a good idea for her to be filling her head with that sort of nonsense." He muttered something else, but Sherry didn't catch it. Presumably he didn't think highly of romance.

"I'll discuss it with her if you want," Sherry said. "Of course, I won't let her know you found the book."

Cody stood. "I appreciate this, Miz…"

"Waterman. But please, call me Sherry."

"Sherry," he repeated. He held out his hand and she took it. Was it her imagination, or did he maintain contact a moment longer than necessary? Her gaze fell to their clasped hands, and he released her fingers as if he suddenly realized what he was doing. "It's been a pleasure."

"Thank you. Do you want to bring Heather in to see me tomorrow afternoon, or would you rather I paid a visit to your ranch?"

"Could you? It'd be best if this conversation seems casual. If Heather ever found out I was talking to anyone about her, she'd be madder than a mule with a mouthful of bees."

"I'll get directions from Mrs. Colson and be there shortly after lunch—say, one o'clock?"

"Great."

Cody lingered at the door and appeared to be assessing her. "Are you thinking of sticking around Pepper?"

"I was hired last month. I wasn't scheduled to start work for another two weeks, but it seems I'm starting early."

Sherry couldn't believe she'd said that. Until Cody Bailman had walked in the door, she'd been intent on demanding her two weeks. Now, she wasn't so sure.

"I'll see you tomorrow, then," Cody said, grinning broadly.

"Tomorrow," she agreed.

Still he stayed. "Might as well come by around lunchtime. The least I can do is feed you."

With a slight nod of her head, she accepted his off-hand invitation.

The phone on the desk rang, breaking the silence—and the spell that had apparently descended on both of them. Then the ring was cut off. Mrs. Colson must have picked it up.

As Cody was just about to leave, the receptionist burst through the door, a look of panic in her eyes. "That was Luke Johnson. Ellie's having labor pains, and he's scared to death he's gonna have to deliver that baby on his own. You'd better get over there quick as you can."

"Where?" Sherry asked.

"Rattlesnake Ridge," Cody said. "Come on." He gripped her elbow. "I'll drive you. You'd never find it on your own."

Two

"Rattlesnake Ridge?" Sherry muttered under her breath as she hurried with Cody toward his pickup truck. He opened the passenger door and helped her inside. Although slender, Sherry wasn't the sort of female who generally required assistance, but her comparatively meager height—five foot five, as opposed to Cody's six-two—meant she needed help this time. The tires on his truck looked as if they belonged on a tanker trailer.

It was impossible to determine the color of the vehicle, and Sherry suspected it hadn't been washed since it'd been driven off the showroom floor. Maybe, she thought, the dirt helped the rust hold the thing together.

Once she situated herself inside the cab, Cody dashed around the front and leaped in. His door made a cranking sound when he opened and closed it. He shoved the key into the ignition and the engine roared to life. She immediately noticed all the papers clipped to the dash; it looked as if he stored most of his paperwork there. She couldn't suppress a smile at his fingertip filing system.

"I'll need some things from my car," she told him. "It's parked over by the café." Cody stopped on Main Street, directly in front of her PT Cruiser and answered her unasked question.

"It's the only car I didn't recognize," he said as he opened the door and jumped down, then came around to give her a hand.

By the time Sherry was back in the pickup and fumbling with her seat belt, they were racing out of town.

Over the past few years Norah had written her long e-mails about life in Texas. One thing she'd said was that the men here were as unique as the trucks they drove. Sherry had been amused and intrigued enough to move here herself. She was beginning to understand what Norah had meant about the men.

"I wish I'd talked to Luke myself," Cody said. He glanced at Sherry as if she was somehow to blame for his friend's discomfort. "That man's so crazy about Ellie he'd lose his head completely if anything ever happened to her."

Sherry grinned. "Isn't that how a man *should* feel about his wife?"

Cody didn't answer right away. "Some men with some women, I suppose," he said a moment later.

Not wanting to discuss what he'd said or what it might imply, Sherry changed the subject. "Are there really rattlesnakes out there on Rattlesnake Ridge?" she asked conversationally.

"In Texas we tend to call a spade a spade. We don't pretty up the truth, and the truth is there's rattlers on that ridge. You'll see it isn't named Buttercup Hill."

"I see." She swallowed hard. "Are snakes a problem around here?"

"You afraid of snakes?" His gaze left the road for a few seconds.

"Not particularly," she said, trying to make her tone light. Norah hadn't said anything about snakes. "Tell me what you know about Ellie. Doc said she'd gone two weeks beyond her due date with the first pregnancy. Do you remember the baby's birth weight?"

Cody glanced at her again, his expression puzzled.

"If I'm going to be delivering this baby, any fact you can give me is helpful," she said. "Is Ellie small and delicate?"

"I guess…"

Sherry could see that Cody wasn't going to provide much information. "What else can you tell me about her?"

"Well, she's real cute."

"Young?"

"Mid-twenties. Luke wasn't interested in marriage until Ellie came to visit her grandparents a few years back. He took one look at her and he hasn't been the same since. I swear he walked around like a sick calf from the moment he met her." Cody frowned before he continued, "Unfortunately, his condition hasn't improved. It's been a long while since I've seen a man as smitten as Luke." He said this last part as if he had little patience with love or romance. "My bet is that Ellie's the calm one now."

"Her first pregnancy was normal?"

"I think so. Don't know for sure."

"Boy or girl?"

"Girl. Christina Lynn. Cute as a bug's ear, too."

"Was she a big baby?"

"Not that I recall, but then I don't know much about that sort of thing."

"How old is Christina Lynn?"

"She must be a year or so." He paused. "Is that bad?"

"Why?" His question surprised her.

"Because you frowned."

Sherry hadn't realized she had. "No, it's just that they didn't wait long before Ellie became pregnant again."

"No, but if you want the truth, I don't think this one was planned any more than Christina Lynn was. Luke's besotted—that's the only word for it. Got his head in the clouds where Ellie's concerned."

Sherry found that all rather endearing. She liked his terminology, too. *Smitten, besotted.* Here she was in her late twenties and no man had ever felt that way about her—nor she about any man. This was one of the reasons she'd decided to move out of Orchard Valley. If she stayed, she had the sinking feeling the rest of her life would have gone on just as it had been. She'd been content, but never excited. Busy, but bored. Liked, but not loved.

She'd lived her entire life in Orchard Valley, a small town where neighbors were friends and the sense of community was strong. It was one of the reasons Sherry had accepted the position in Pepper—another small town.

Norah had made the transition from Orchard Valley to Houston without difficulty, but Sherry wasn't sure she'd have done nearly as well. She didn't have a big-city mentality. But Norah's calls and e-mails about the

Lone Star state had intrigued her, and if she was going to make a change, she couldn't see doing it by half measures. So she'd answered the agency's ad with a long letter and a detailed résumé. They phoned almost immediately, and she was hired so fast, without even a personal interview, her head spun. She did learn from Dr. Colby Winston, Norah's brother-in-law, that her references had been checked and this eased her mind.

They'd been driving for about twenty minutes when Cody braked suddenly to turn off the main road and onto a rugged dirt-and-gravel one. Sherry pitched forward, and if not for the restraint of the seat belt, would have slammed against the dash.

"You all right?"

"Sure," she said, a bit breathless. "How much farther?"

"Ten miles or so."

Sherry groaned inwardly and forced a smile. Even if they'd been driving at normal speed, the road would have been a challenge. Her body jerked one way and another, and she had to grip the seat with both hands.

When at last Cody pulled into the ranch yard, the road smoothed out. He eased to a stop in front of a two-story white house, which to Sherry looked like a desert oasis, a welcoming refuge from the heat and barrenness. The windows were decorated with bright blue shutters, and brilliant red geraniums bloomed in the boxes out front. The wraparound porch was freshly painted. Sherry watched as the door swung open and a tall, rangy cowman barreled out and down the steps.

"What took you so long?" he hollered. "Ellie's in pain."

Sherry was still fiddling with her seat belt when Cody opened the door for her. His hands fit snugly around her waist as he helped her down from the cab.

"Sherry, meet Luke," Cody said.

"Where's Doc?" Luke demanded.

"Fishing," Sherry explained, holding out her hand. "I'm Sherry Waterman and I—"

Luke's hand barely touched hers as his gaze moved accusingly to Cody, interrupting her introduction. "You brought some stranger out here for Ellie? Cody, this is my wife! You can't bring just anyone to— "

"I'm a midwife, as well as a physician assistant," Sherry supplied. "I can do just about everything Dr. Lindsey does, including prescribe medication and deliver babies. Now, where's your wife?"

"Cody?" Luke looked at his friend uncertainly.

"Do you want to deliver Ellie's baby yourself?" Cody asked him.

Luke went visibly pale and shook his head mutely.

"That's what I thought." Cody's hand cupped Sherry's elbow as he escorted her into the house. "You'll have to forgive Luke," he whispered. "As I said earlier, he's been a bit…irrational ever since he met Ellie."

The door led into the kitchen. A toddler was sitting in a high chair grinning happily and slamming a wooden spoon against the tray.

"Christina Lynn, I assume," Sherry said.

The toddler's face broke into a wide smile. At least Luke's daughter seemed pleased to see her.

"Where's Ellie?" Sherry asked Luke.

"Upstairs. Hurry, please!" Luke strode swiftly toward the staircase.

Sherry followed, taking the stairs two at a time, Cody right behind her.

When Sherry reached the hallway, Luke led the way into the master bedroom. Ellie was braced against the headboard, her eyes closed, her teeth gnawing on her lower lip. Her hand massaged her swollen abdomen as she breathed deeply in and out.

Luke fell to his knees and took her free hand, kissing her knuckles fervently. "They're here. There's nothing to worry about now."

Ellie acknowledged Sherry's and Cody's presence with an absent nod. Sherry waited until the contraction had ebbed before she asked, "How far apart are they?"

"Five minutes," Ellie said. "They started hard, right after my water broke."

"How long ago was that?"

"An hour or so."

"I'd better check you, then." Sherry set down her bag at the foot of the bed and removed a pair of surgical gloves.

"Cody?" Once again Luke pleaded for his friend's advice.

"Cody," Ellie said, "kindly keep my big oaf of a husband entertained for a while." She motioned toward the door. "Make him tend to Christina Lynn—she shouldn't be left alone. Whatever you do, keep him out of this room."

"But, Ellie, you need me!" Luke protested.

"Not right now I don't, honey. Cody, please do as I say and keep Luke out of here."

Cody virtually pushed Luke out of the room. After

the pair had left, Ellie looked at Sherry. "Whoever you are, welcome. I'm delighted to see another woman."

Sherry smiled. "Sherry Waterman. I'm new to Pepper. Doc was so excited by my arrival that he took off fishing. He said you weren't due for another couple of weeks."

"I'm not, but then we miscalculated with Christina Lynn, too."

"I'll wash my hands and be right back." By the time Sherry returned, Ellie was in the middle of another contraction. She waited until Ellie had relaxed, then adjusted her pillows to make her as comfortable as possible.

"How am I doing?" Ellie asked after the pain receded. Her brow was covered with a thin sheen of perspiration. She licked her dry lips.

"You're doing just great," Sherry murmured, wiping Ellie's face with a wet rag.

"How much longer will it take?"

"A while," Sherry said gently. "Maybe several hours."

Ellie's shoulders sagged. "I was afraid of that."

Twenty minutes later, Cody appeared after knocking lightly on the bedroom door. "How's everything going up here?"

"Fine," Sherry told him. "Ellie's an excellent patient."

"I wish I could say the same for Luke. Is there anything I can get you?"

"Pillows and a C.D. player." At his frown, she explained, "Soothing music will help Ellie relax during the contractions. I have C.D.s with me."

Cody nodded and smiled at Ellie. "Don't worry about Christina Lynn. She's in her crib and sound asleep. I phoned the ranch, and our housekeeper's staying with Heather, so everything's taken care of at my end."

"Whatever you do, make sure Luke stays out of here," Ellie said. "You'd think I was the only woman who ever had labor pains. He was a wreck when Christina Lynn was born. Doc Lindsey had to spend more time with him than with me."

"I'll keep him in line," Cody said, ducking out of the room.

Sherry remembered more than one birth where the father required full-time attention. It always touched her to see that men could be so greatly affected by the birth of their children.

A couple of minutes later, Cody brought a small C.D. player and two plump pillows. Sherry arranged the pillows behind Ellie, then put in a C.D. of soft piano music.

"That's nice," Ellie said, panting.

Sherry held her hand through a powerful contraction.

"Talk to me," Ellie requested before the next one gripped her body.

Sherry described her introduction to the good people of Pepper. She told her about meeting Mayor Bowie and Doc Lindsey and Billy Bob. Ellie laughed, then as the pain came again, she rolled onto her side and Sherry massaged the tightness from the small of her back, all the while giving encouragement.

"I'm a transplant myself." Ellie spoke when she could. "I was a college senior when I came here to visit my grandparents. They've lived in Pepper for as long as I can remember. I only intended to stay a few days, but then I met Luke. I swear he was the most pigheaded, most ill-behaved man I'd ever known. I told myself I didn't want anything to do with him. To be truthful, I had kind of a crush on Cody Bailman back then."

"Obviously your opinion of Luke changed."

"My sweet Luke. You've never seen anyone tougher on the outside and so gentle on the inside. I'll never forget the afternoon he proposed. I'd decided to drive home to Dallas—good grief, I'd spent two weeks longer than I'd originally intended. Luke didn't want me to leave, but I really didn't have any choice. I had a job waiting for me and was signed up for classes in the fall. Grandma sent me off with enough food to last a month."

Sherry chuckled and waited for Ellie to breathe her way through the next contraction.

"I was five miles out of town when I saw this man on a horse galloping after me as if catching me was a matter of life or death. It was Luke." She shook her head, remembering. "When I pulled over to the side of the road, he jumped off his horse, removed his gloves, then fell to one knee and proposed. I knew then and there I wasn't ever going to find a man who'd love me as much as Luke Johnson. Suddenly nothing mattered without him, not anymore. I know my parents were disappointed that I didn't finish college, but I'm happy and that's what counts."

"You don't mind living so far away from town?"

"At first, just a little. Now I'm happy about it."

"That's a wonderfully romantic story."

Ellie smiled. "Is there a special man in your life?"

Sherry exhaled slowly. "I've never fallen in love. Oh, I had a few crushes. I dated a doctor for a while, but both of us knew it wasn't going anywhere." Sherry smiled to herself as she recalled how difficult it'd been for Colby Winston to admit he was in love with Valerie Bloomfield.

During the next few hours, Cody came up to check on their progress twice and give a report of his own. Luke, he said, had worn a path in the living-room carpet pacing back and forth, but thus far, Cody had been able to restrain him from racing up the stairs. He doubted Luke would have much hair left before the ordeal was over; he'd jerked his hands through it so many times there were grooves in his hairline.

"He loves me," Ellie said softly.

When Sherry walked Cody to the bedroom door, he asked quietly, "Will it be much longer? Luke's a mess."

"Another couple of hours."

Cody nodded and his eyes briefly held hers. "I'm glad you're here." He turned and headed down the stairs. A surge of emotion overwhelmed her, but she wasn't sure how to read it. All she knew was that she felt *alive,* acutely sensitive to sounds and colors, and she had the impression that Cody experienced the same thing.

"I'm glad you're here, too," Ellie said from behind her.

Sherry moved back to the bed. "Doc would've done just as well."

"Perhaps, but it helps that you're a woman."

The second stage of labor arrived shortly after midnight, and Ellie arched against the bed at the strength of her contractions, panting in between. Sherry coached her as she had so many others. And then, at last, with a shout of triumph, Ellie delivered a strong, squalling son.

The baby was barely in his mother's arms when the door burst open and Luke barged into the room.

"A son, Luke," Ellie whispered. "We have a son."

Luke knelt beside the bed and stared down at the angry infant in his wife's arms. The baby was a bright shade of pink, his legs and arms kicking in protest. His eyes were closed and he was yelling for all he was worth. "He looks just like you when you get mad," Ellie told her husband.

Luke nodded and Sherry noticed that his eyes were bright with tears as he bent forward and kissed his son's wrinkled brow. Then he placed his hand over Ellie's cheek and kissed her, too. "Never again," he vowed. "Our family's complete now."

Ellie's eyes drifted shut. "That's what you said after Christina Lynn was born."

"True," Luke admitted, "but that was because I couldn't bear to see you suffer. This time it's for me. I don't think I could go through this again. And I nearly lost my best friend."

"You were a long way from that, partner," Cody said from the doorway.

"I don't care. Two children are plenty. Right, Ellie? I know you said you'd like four, but you agree with me, don't you?"

Sherry moved behind the big, rangy cattleman and looked down at Ellie. "You're exhausted. You need some sleep." Lifting the baby from her arms, Sherry placed him in a soft blanket, marveling at the tiny, perfectly formed person in her hands.

"Come on," Cody urged Luke. "It's time to celebrate. Let's break open that bottle of expensive scotch you've been saving."

"She's going to do it, you know," Luke said to no one

in particular. "That woman knows I can't refuse her a thing. Before I even figure out how it happened, we're going to have four kids running around this house."

Sherry finished her duties and found Luke and Cody in the living room each holding a shot of whiskey. "Ellie and Philip are both asleep," she assured them.

"Philip," Luke repeated slowly, and a brightness came into his eyes. "She decided to name him Philip, after all."

"A family name?" Cody asked him.

Luke shrugged. "Actually, it's mine. I never much cared for it as a kid and dropped it when I started school. I insisted everyone call me by my middle name."

"Ellie says your son looks like a Philip," Sherry put in.

A wide grin split Luke's face. "I think she's right—he does." He stared down into the amber liquid in his glass. "A son. I've got a son."

Sherry smiled, then yawned, covering her mouth with one hand. It had been a long day. She'd been up since dawn, not wanting to travel in the worst heat of the day, and now it was well past two in the morning.

"Come on," Cody said, setting down his glass, "I'd better drive you back into town."

Sherry nodded as another yawn escaped. She was weary through and through.

"Thank you," Luke said. He took her limp hand and pumped it several times to show his gratitude. He seemed to have forgiven her for being a stranger.

"I'll be in touch tomorrow," Sherry promised. "Ellie did a beautiful job with this baby."

"I know." Luke looked away as if embarrassed by his

behavior earlier. "I knew the minute I saw that woman I was going to love her. What I didn't know was how lucky I was that I convinced her to marry me."

"From what Ellie told me, she considers herself the lucky one." Luke grinned hugely at Sherry's words.

"Come on, Sherry, you're beat," Cody said. "Good night, Luke."

"Night." Luke walked them to the front door. "Ellie's mother is on her way and should be here by morning. She'll be a big help. But thanks again."

By the time Sherry was inside Cody's truck, she was dead on her feet. She dreaded the long, rough drive back to town, but there was no alternative.

"Sherry." Her name seemed to come from far away. The bottom of a well, perhaps. It was then that she realized she'd been asleep.

She'd meant to stay awake, but she was obviously more tired than she'd realized, because she'd slept through that dreadful ten-mile stretch before they hit the main road. Cody must have driven with infinite care.

To compound her sense of disorientation, she noticed that her head was neatly tucked against his shoulder. She felt warm and comfortable there and wasn't inclined to move.

"We're in town already?" she asked, slowly opening her eyes.

"No. I couldn't see taking you all the way into Pepper when you're so tired."

Sherry straightened and looked around. They were parked outside a barn beside an enormous brick house with arched windows on the main floor and four gables on the second. The place was illuminated by several outdoor lights.

"Where are we?" she asked.

"My place, the Lucky Horseshoe. I figured you could spend what's left of the night here. I'll drive you back into town first thing in the morning."

Sherry was too tired to argue, not that she wanted to. She liked and trusted this man, and when he came around to help her from the cab, she found herself almost eager to feel his hands on her waist again.

Cody swung her down, and if he was feeling any of what Sherry was, he didn't show it.

"I hope I didn't make a pest of myself falling asleep on you that way," she said.

He mumbled something she couldn't quite make out. But apparently she hadn't bothered him. He led the way into the big country kitchen, turning on lights as he went.

Without asking, he took two large glasses from a cupboard and filled them with milk from the refrigerator. "You didn't have any dinner."

Sherry had to think about it for a moment. He was right. She hadn't had anything since the cheeseburger and pie at lunchtime. To her surprise, she wasn't the least bit hungry.

"Here," he said, handing her the glass of milk. "This'll tide you over till breakfast."

"Thanks."

He pulled out a chair for her, then twisted the one across from it around and straddled it. They didn't seem to have a lot to say to each other, yet the room was charged with electricity.

"So," he ventured, "you're planning to stay in Pepper?"

Sherry nodded. She liked the gruff quality of his voice. She liked his face, too, not that he was male-model handsome. His features were too strong and masculine for that, browned by the sun and creased with experience—some of it hard, she guessed.

"You'll like it here. Pepper's a good town."

Everything about Cody Bailman fascinated her. A few strands of thick dark hair fell over his high forehead, giving him a little-boy look. It was so appealing that Sherry had to resist leaning forward and brushing the hair away.

"The guest bedroom's upstairs," Cody said abruptly. He got to his feet, drained the last of his milk in three gulps and set the empty glass in the sink.

Sherry finished her own and stood, too. She'd almost forgotten how tired she was.

"This way," Cody whispered, leading her up the gently curving stairway off the entryway.

Sherry paused and glanced around at the expensive furnishings, the antiques and works of art. "Your home is lovely."

"Thanks."

Sherry followed him to the top of the stairs and then to a room at the far end of the hallway. He opened the door and cursed under his breath.

"Is something wrong?" Sherry asked.

"The bed isn't made up. Heather had a friend stay last night and she promised to change the sheets and remake the bed herself. Looks like she forgot. Listen,

I'll sleep in here and you can use my room. Janey, our housekeeper, changed the sheets just today."

"That isn't necessary," she protested. It would only take a few minutes to assemble the bed.

"You're dead on your feet," Cody returned. "Here." He reached for her hand and guided her down to the other end of the hallway.

If she'd possessed the energy, Sherry would've continued to protest, but Cody's evaluation of her state was pretty accurate.

"Call me if you need anything, and don't argue, understand?"

Sherry nodded.

Whether it was by impulse or design, she didn't know, but before he turned away, Cody leaned down and casually brushed her lips with his.

They both seemed taken aback by the quick exchange. Neither spoke for what felt like the longest moment of Sherry's life. Her pulse was pounding wildly in her throat, and Cody pressed his fingertip to the frantic throbbing. Then, before she could encourage or dissuade him, he bent his head and brought his mouth to hers a second time.

Her moist lips quivered beneath his. He moved toward her and she toward him, and soon they were wrapped in each other's arms. The kiss took on an exploring, demanding quality, as if this moment was all they'd be granted and they'd better make the most of it.

Sherry nearly staggered when he released her. "Good night, Sherry," he said, then she watched as he strode the length of the hallway. He paused when he reached the opposite end and turned back to look at her. Even from this distance, Sherry could read the dilemma in his eyes. He didn't *want* to be attracted to her, hadn't wanted to kiss her, and now that he had, he wasn't sure what to do about it.

Sherry was experiencing many of those same feelings herself. She opened the door and stepped inside his room, angry with herself for not insisting on the guest room. Because everything about these quarters, from the basalt fireplace to the large four-poster bed, seemed to say Cody.

She pulled back the sheets and undressed. She thought she'd be asleep before her head hit the pillow, but she was wrong. She tossed and turned until dawn, the image of Cody standing at the end of the hallway burned in her brain. Finally she fell into a troubled sleep.

"Hot damn."

Sherry gingerly opened her eyes and saw a pretty girl of about twelve, dressed in jeans and a red plaid shirt, standing just inside the doorway. Dark braids dangled across her shoulders.

"Hot damn," the girl repeated, smiling as if it was Christmas morning and she'd found Santa sitting under the tree.

Sherry levered herself up on one elbow and squinted against the light. "Hello."

"Howdy," the girl said eagerly.

"What time is it?" Sherry rubbed her eyes. It seemed she'd only been asleep a matter of minutes. If it hadn't been rude to do so, she would've fallen back against the pillows and covered her face with the sheet.

"Eight-thirty. Where's Dad?"

"Uh…you're Heather?"

"So he mentioned me, did he?" she asked gleefully. The girl walked into the room and leaped onto the mattress, making it bounce.

"I think you have the wrong impression of what's going on here," Sherry felt obliged to tell her.

"You're in my dad's bed, aren't you? That tells me everything I need to know. Besides, you're the first woman I've seen him bring home. No, I think I get the picture. How'd you two meet?" She tucked her knees up under her chin and looped her arms around them, preparing herself for a lengthy explanation.

"Heather!" Cody's voice boomed from the end of the hallway.

"In here!" she shouted back with enough force to make Sherry grimace.

Cody appeared as if by magic two seconds later, his large frame filling the doorway.

"Dad," Heather said with a disappointed sigh, "you've been holding out on me."

Three

"So, Dad, when's the wedding?"

"Heather!" Cody ground out furiously. He looked like he'd dressed in a hurry. He was in jeans and barefoot, and his Western-style shirt was left open, exposing his hard chest and abdomen and an attractive smattering of dark, curly hair.

"But, Dad, you've comprom—" she faltered "—ruined your friend's reputation! Aren't you gonna make an honest woman of her?"

Sherry laughed. She wondered where the girl had acquired such an old-fashioned expression, although it was clear Cody wasn't amused by his daughter's badgering. Heather's blue eyes sparkled with mischief.

"So," the girl continued, "how long has *this* been going on?"

"You will apologize to Miz Waterman," Cody insisted, his voice hard.

"Sorry, Miz Waterman," Heather said. She didn't sound at all contrite. "I guess you're new in town?"

Sherry nodded and thrust out her hand. "Call me Sherry. I'll be working with Doc Lindsey."

"Wow. That's great."

"I was with Ellie Johnson last night," Sherry said.

"Ellie had her baby?" Heather's excited gaze shot to her father.

"A boy. They named him Philip," Cody answered.

Heather slapped her hand against the mattress. "Hot damn! Luke never said anything, but I know he was hoping for a boy. But then, Luke's so crazy about Ellie he'd have been happy with a litter of kittens."

"Quit it with the swearing." Cody rubbed his forehead. "And something else—we didn't get back to the house until after two. The guest bed wasn't made up." He looked accusingly at his daughter.

"Oops." Heather pressed her fingers against her lips. "I said I'd do that, didn't I? Sorry."

Sherry gave a discreet cough. "Uh, I'd better see about getting back to town." With Doc gone she was responsible for any medical emergency that might arise. Not that she intended to be manipulated into staying. She still planned to take the time owed to her, with or without the sheriff's approval.

"You want me to see if Slim can drive her?" Heather asked her father.

"I'll do it," Cody said casually, turning away from them. "But first we'll have breakfast."

"Breakfast," Heather repeated meaningfully. She wiggled her eyebrows before slithering off the bed. "He's going to drive you back to town himself," she added, grinning at Sherry. Her smile widened and the sparkle in her eyes grew brighter. "Yup," she said. "My dad likes you. This could be interesting. It's about time he started listening to me."

"I… We only met yesterday," Sherry explained.

"So?"

"I mean, well, isn't it a little soon to be making those kinds of judgments?"

"Nope." Heather plopped herself down on the edge of the bed again. "How do you feel about him? He's kinda handsome, don't you think?"

"Ah…"

"You'll have to be patient with him, though. Dad tends to be a little dumb when it comes to women. He's got a lot to learn, but between the two of us, we should be able to teach him, don't you think?"

Sherry had gotten the impression from talking to Cody that Heather was a timid child struggling with her identity. Ha! This girl didn't have a timid bone in her body.

"I love romance," Heather said on a long drawn-out sigh. She looked behind her to be sure no one was listening, then lowered her voice. "I've been waiting for years for Dad to come to his senses about getting married again. My mom died when I was only two, so I hardly even remember her, and—"

"Heather, your father and I've only just met," Sherry reminded her. "I'm afraid you're leaping to conclusions that could be embarrassing to both your father and me."

The girl's face fell. "You think so? It's just that I'm so anxious for Dad to find a wife. If he doesn't hurry up, I'll be, like, twenty before there're any more babies. In case you haven't guessed, I really like babies. Besides, it's not much fun being an only child." She hesitated and seemed to change her mind. "Sometimes it is, but sometimes it isn't. You know what I mean?"

Sherry would have answered, given the chance, but Heather immediately began speaking again.

"You like him, don't you?"

Sherry pushed the hair away from her face with both hands. She didn't need to look in a mirror to know her cheeks were aflame. "Your father's a very nice man, but as I said before—"

"Heather!" Cody boomed again.

"He wants me to leave you alone," Heather translated with a grimace. "But we'll have a chance to talk later, okay?"

"Uh...sure." Sherry was beginning to feel dizzy, as if she'd been caught up in a whirlwind and didn't know when she'd land—or where.

It was impossible not to like Cody's daughter. She was vibrant and refreshing and fun. And not the least bit timid.

"Great. I'll talk to you soon, then."

"Right."

Fifteen minutes later, Sherry walked down the stairs and into the kitchen. Cody and Heather were sitting at the table and a middle-aged woman with thick gray braids looped on top of her head smiled a warm welcome.

"Hello," Sherry said to the small gathering.

"Sherry, this is Janey," Cody said. "She does the cooking and housekeeping around here."

"Hi, Janey." Sherry nodded and noticed the eager look exchanged between Heather and the cook. Heather, it seemed, hadn't stopped smiling from the moment she'd discovered Sherry sleeping in her father's bed. The housekeeper looked equally pleased.

"Janey's been around forever," Heather said as she stretched one arm across the table to spear a hot pancake with her fork.

Janey chuckled in a good-natured way. "I'm a bit younger than Heather believes, but not by much. Now sit down and I'll bring you some cakes hot off the griddle."

Breakfast was delicious. Cody didn't contribute much to the conversation, not that Sherry blamed him. Anything he said would be open to speculation. A comment on the weather would no doubt send Heather into a soliloquy about summer being the perfect time of year for a wedding. The girl seemed determined to do whatever she could to arrange a marriage for her father. Sherry's presence only worsened the situation.

After they'd finished eating, Cody said he needed a few minutes to check with his men. Sherry took the opportunity to phone the Johnson ranch and see how Ellie and the baby were doing. She spoke to Luke, who said that everything was well in hand, especially since Ellie's mother had arrived that morning. Once again, he thanked Sherry for her help.

"You ready?" Cody asked when she hung up the phone.

"All set. Just let me say goodbye to Janey."

When Sherry walked into the yard a few minutes later, Cody was waiting for her. Heather had come with her, and the girl paused when she saw her father standing outside the pickup. "You aren't driving her back in that old thing, are you? Dad, that truck's disgusting."

"Yes, I am," Cody said in a voice that defied argument. It didn't stop Heather, however.

"But Sherry's *special.* Don't you want to take her in the Caddie?"

"It's fine, Heather," Sherry insisted, opening the door of the truck herself. Unfortunately she was six inches too short to boost herself into the cab. Cody's aid seemed to come grudgingly. Maybe he regretted not accepting Heather's advice about which car to drive, she thought.

Sherry waved to the girl as they pulled out of the yard. Heather, with a good deal of drama, crossed her hands over her heart and collapsed, as if struck by how very sweet romance could be. With some effort, Sherry controlled her amusement.

Cody's ranch was huge. They'd been driving silently for what seemed like miles and were still on his spread. She asked him a couple of questions about the Lucky Horseshoe, to which he responded with little more than a grunt. He was obviously a grouch when he didn't get a good night's sleep.

About ten minutes outside of town he cleared his throat as if he had something important to announce. "I hope you didn't take anything Heather said seriously."

"You mean about you making an honest woman out of me?"

He snorted. "Yes."

"No, of course I didn't."

"Good."

He sounded so relieved it was all she could do not to laugh.

"The kiss, too," he added, his forehead wrinkled in a frown.

"Kisses," she said, reminding him there'd been more than one.

Despite her restless sleep, Sherry hadn't given the matter much thought. She did so now, concluding that they'd both been exhausted and high on the emotional aftermath of the birth and the roles they'd each played in the small drama. In those circumstances, being attracted to each other was completely understandable. The kisses had been a celebration of the new life they'd helped usher into the world. There hadn't been anything sexual about them...had there?

"Let's call them a breach of good judgment," Cody suggested.

"All right." That wasn't how Sherry would've defined them, but Cody seemed comfortable with the explanation—and pleased with her understanding.

They remained silent for the rest of the trip, and Sherry considered the situation. She found she agreed with him; their evening together had been like a moment out of time. Nevertheless, disappointment spread through her—almost as though she'd been standing on the brink of a great discovery and had suddenly learned it was all a hoax.

Her entire romantic career had followed a similar sorry pattern. Just when she thought perhaps she'd connected with her life's partner in Colby Winston, she'd realized she felt no great emotion for him. Certainly nothing like what Ellie had described.

Sherry knew precious little of love. Four years earlier, she'd watched the three Bloomfield sisters back

home in Orchard Valley find love, all within the space
of one short summer. Love had seemed explosive and
chaotic. Valerie and Colby had both been caught un-
awares, fighting their attraction and each other. Sherry
had stood by and watched the man she'd once seriously
dated fall head over heels in love. She knew that this
was what she wanted for herself.

Then Valerie's sister Steffie had returned from Italy.
She and Charles were brought back together after a
three-year separation and they, too, had seemed unprepared for the strength of their feelings. They were married only a few weeks after Valerie and Colby.

But the Bloomfield sister who'd surprised Sherry
the most was Norah. They'd been schoolmates, sharing
the same interests and often the same friends. Sherry
couldn't help smiling whenever she thought of Norah
and Rowdy. The lanky Texan millionaire hadn't known
what hit him when he fell for Norah, and the funny
thing was Norah hadn't, either. All of Orchard Valley had seemed to hold its collective breath awaiting
the outcome of their romance. But Norah and Rowdy
made the ideal couple, in Sherry's opinion. Nothing,
outside of love, would have convinced Norah to leave
Orchard Valley.

In the years since Norah had left Oregon, Sherry
had been busy studying and working toward her degree, too absorbed in her goal to find time for relationships. But now she was ready. She wanted the love her
friends had found, the excitement, the thrill of meeting
that special someone. She wanted a man who felt about
her the way Luke felt about Ellie. A man who'd look at
her like Colby Winston looked at Valerie Bloomfield.

Cody brought the truck to a stop behind Sherry's car. Sherry unbuckled the seat belt and reached for her purse and medical bag.

"I really appreciate the ride," she said, holding out her hand for him to shake.

"You're welcome." He briefly took her hand, then leaped from the cab and came around to help her down. When his hands circled her waist, his eyes held hers. For the longest moment she didn't move, *couldn't* move, as if his touch had caused some strange paralysis. But when he shifted his gaze away, she placed her hands on his shoulders and allowed him to set her on the ground. As she met his eyes again, she saw surprise and a twinge of regret.

Cody eased away from her, and Sherry sensed that an invisible barrier had been erected between them. Irritation seemed to flicker through him. "I'm not going to apologize for kissing you last night," he said abruptly.

"But you regret it?"

"Yes, more now than before."

The harsh edge in his voice shocked her. "Why?" Her voice fell to a whisper.

"Because it's going to be difficult not to do it again." With that, he stalked back to the driver's side of the pickup, climbed in and roared off.

Sherry got into her car and drove the short distance to the clinic, parking in the small lot behind the building. When she walked in the front door, Mrs. Colson broke into a delighted smile. "Welcome back."

"Thanks. Ellie had a beautiful baby boy."

"So I heard. Word spreads fast around here. Ellie claims she'll never have another baby without you there.

She thinks you're the best thing that's happened to Pepper since we voted in sewers last November."

Sherry laughed. "I don't suppose you've heard from Doc Lindsey?"

"Yes. He called this morning to see if everything was working out."

Sherry was relieved. At least the physician had some sense of responsibility. "I want to talk to him when he phones in again."

"No problem. He wants to talk to you, too. Apparently there's been a misunderstanding—you weren't scheduled to begin work for another two weeks."

"That's what I've been trying to tell everyone," Sherry said emphatically. "I made the mistake of driving through town, and everyone figured that because I was here I was starting right away."

Mrs. Colson fiddled with a folder from the file drawer, pulling out a sheet of paper and glancing through its contents. "Doc's right. It's in the contract, plain as day. So, why *are* you here so early?"

"I was just passing through on my way to Houston," she explained patiently—and not for the first time. "Mayor Bowie assumed I was here to stay and so did Doc. Before I could stop him, he was out the door with his fishing pole in hand."

"You should've said something."

Sherry resisted the urge to scream. "I tried, but no one would listen."

"Well, Doc told me to tell you he'll be back in town sometime this afternoon. He says the fish don't bite this early in the season, anyway."

"I'll need to call my friends and tell them I'm going

to be late," Sherry said. She hadn't had a chance to phone Norah yesterday, thanks to the events of the afternoon and evening.

"Sure, go right ahead."

Sherry decided to wait until she'd showered and changed clothes before she contacted Norah. It was midmorning before she felt human again.

"I'm in Pepper," Sherry explained once she had Norah on the line. "It's a long story, but I won't be able to leave until later this afternoon, which will put me in Houston late tomorrow."

"That's no problem," Norah was quick to assure her. "I'm so glad you're coming! I've missed you, Sherry."

"I've missed you, too."

"How do you like Texas so far?" Norah wanted to know.

Given Sherry's circumstances, it was an unfair question. "I haven't been here long enough to really form an opinion. But the natives seem friendly, and with a little practice I think I'll be able to pick up the language."

Norah chuckled. "Oh, Sherry, I am *so* looking forward to seeing you! Don't worry, I'm going to give you a crash course on the state and the people once you arrive. You're going to love it—just the way I do."

Sherry didn't comment on that. "How's Rowdy?" she said instead.

"Busy as ever. That man runs circles around me. So many people want his time and attention, but that's all right. It's me he comes home to every night, me he sits across the dinner table from and me he loves. He's such a good father and an even better husband."

"Val and Steffie send their love. Your dad, too."

"Talking to you makes me miss them even more. Rowdy promised we'd fly to Orchard Valley this fall, but I doubt my dad's going to wait that long. I half expect him to drop by for a visit before the end of the summer."

Sherry chuckled. "Well, at least I'll be there before he is."

"It wouldn't matter," Norah said. "You're welcome anytime."

Sherry felt a lot better after talking to her friend. But Norah sounded so happy she couldn't quite squelch a feeling of envy. Norah and Rowdy had two small children and were adopting two more. Norah had always been a natural with children. Sherry never did understand why her friend, with her affinity for kids, hadn't chosen pediatrics.

In an effort to help pass the time until Doc's arrival, Sherry read several medical journals in his office. When she looked up, it was well past noon.

Mrs. Colson stuck her head in the door, "Do you want me to order you some lunch?" she asked.

"No, thanks." Her impatience for Doc to get back had destroyed her appetite.

"I'm going to order a salad for myself. The Yellow Rose is real good about running it over here. You sure I can't talk you into anything?"

"I'm sure."

Donna Jo stopped off fifteen minutes later with a chef's salad and sat down on a chair in the reception area. Mrs. Colson was behind the counter, and Sherry was sitting on another chair with her purse and suitcase, ready to go. "The Cattlemen's Association's in town for lunch," Donna Jo told the receptionist, removing her shoe and massaging her sore foot. She eyed Sherry with the same curiosity she had a day earlier. "I hear you delivered Ellie's baby last night."

Word had indeed gotten around. Sherry nodded.

"You must've spent the night out there with her and Luke, because Mayor Bowie came into the café this morning looking for you. You weren't at the clinic."

"Actually, Cody Bailman drove me over to his house."

"You stayed the night at Cody's?" Donna Jo asked, her interest piqued. Mrs. Colson studied Sherry with undisguised interest.

"It was after two by the time I finished. I was exhausted, and so was Cody." She certainly didn't want these two getting the wrong impression. "Nothing happened. I mean, nothing that was, uh…" She gave up trying to find the right words. "Cody was a perfect gentleman."

"Isn't he always?" Donna Jo winked at Mrs. Colson.

"Is there something wrong with my spending the night at Cody's?"

"Not in the least," Mrs. Colson immediately said. "Cody's a gentleman."

"As much of a gentleman as any Texan gets," Donna Jo amended. "Martha, are you going to tell her, or am I?"

"Tell me what?" Sherry said.

Donna Jo and Mrs. Colson shared a significant look.

"What?" Sherry demanded again.

"I don't think so," Mrs. Colson said thoughtfully. "She'll find out soon enough on her own."

"Yeah." Donna Jo nodded. "You're right."

"*What* will I find out on my own?" Sherry tried a third time, but again her question was ignored.

"Martha here tells me you're bent on leaving town," the waitress said conversationally. "Stop in at the café on your way out and I'll pack you a lunch to take along. You might not be hungry now, but you will be later."

"Thanks, I'll do that."

Doc showed up around two that afternoon, looking tired and disgruntled. "I've been up since before dawn," he muttered. "It didn't make sense that I wasn't reeling in any fifteen-inchers until I realized it was too early in the month."

"I'll be back in less than two weeks," Sherry promised, "and next time the fish are sure to be biting."

"I hope so," Doc grumbled. "You might've said something about arriving early, you know."

Sherry nearly had to swallow her tongue to keep from reminding him that she'd done everything but throw herself in front of his truck to keep him from leaving.

She'd almost passed the café when she remembered her promise to Donna Jo and pulled to a stop. The waitress was right; she should take something to eat, as well as several cold sodas. Already it was unmercifully hot. She grinned, remembering Donna Jo's remark that the locals who escaped to Colorado for the summer weren't real Texans. Apparently folks were supposed to stay in Texas and suffer.

The café was nearly empty. Sherry took a seat at the counter and reached for the menu.

"What'll you have?" Donna Jo asked.

"Let's see… A turkey sandwich with tomato and lettuce, a bag of chips and three diet sodas, all to go."

Donna Jo went into the kitchen to tell the chef. When she came back out her eyes brightened. "Howdy, Cody."

"Howdy." Cody slipped onto the stool next to Sherry's and ordered coffee.

"Hi," he said, edging up his Stetson with his index finger as if to get a better look at her.

"Hi." It was silly to feel shy with him, but Sherry did. A little like she had in junior high when Wayne Pierce, the boy she'd had a crush on, sat next to her in the school lunchroom. Her mouth went dry and she felt incapable of making conversation.

"I was wondering if I'd run into you this afternoon."

"Cody's in town for the local cattlemen's meeting," Donna Jo explained as she placed a beige ceramic mug full of steaming coffee in front of Cody.

"Doc's back," Sherry said, although she wasn't certain he understood the significance of that. "He said the fishing was terrible, but then, it generally is about now."

He shrugged. "You're having a rather late lunch, aren't you?"

Donna Jo set a brown paper bag on the counter along with the tab. "I was planning to eat on the road," Sherry said, thanking Donna Jo with a smile. She slipped her purse strap over her shoulder and opened the zipper to take out her wallet.

A frown appeared on Cody's face. "You're leaving?"

"For Houston."

His frown deepened. "So soon?"

"I'll be back in a couple of weeks." She slid off the stool and was surprised when Cody slapped a dollar bill and some coins on the counter and followed her to the register.

"Actually I was hoping to talk to you," he said, holding open the café door.

"Oh?" She headed for her car.

Cody continued to follow. "Yeah, it's about what I said this morning." His eyes refused to meet hers. "I was thinking about it on my way back to the ranch, and I realized I must've sounded pretty arrogant about the whole thing."

"I didn't notice," Sherry said. It was a lie, but only a small one. She found it charming that he wanted to correct the impression he'd made.

"It's just that Heather's on this marriage kick...."

"We both agreed it was a lapse in judgment," she told him. "Let's just forget it ever happened."

He jammed his fingers into his pockets as Sherry opened her car door. "I wish I could," he said so low Sherry wasn't sure she'd heard him accurately.

"Pardon?" she said, looking up at him and making a feeble attempt at a smile.

"Nothing," he said gruffly. "I didn't say anything."

"You wish you could what?" she pressed.

He glanced away, and his wide shoulders heaved with a labored sigh. "I wish I could forget!" he said forcefully. "There. Are you happy now?"

"No." She shook her head. "I'm confused."

"So am I. I like you, Sherry. I don't know why, but I do, and I don't mind telling you it scares the living daylights out of me. The last time I was this attracted to a woman I was—" he rubbed the side of his jaw "—a heck of a lot younger than I am now. And you're leaving."

"But I'll be back." The rush to get to Houston at the earliest possible moment left her. Nothing appealed to her more right now than exploring what was happening between her and Cody Bailman.

"But you won't be back for two weeks." He made it sound like an eternity. His face tightened. "By the time you're back it won't be the same."

"We don't know that."

"I do," he said with certainty.

Sherry was torn. "Are you asking me to stay?"

His nostrils flared at the question. "No," he said emphatically, and then more softly, "No." He moved a step closer. "Aw, what the hell," he muttered crossly. He reached for her, slipped his arm around her waist, pulled her toward him— and kissed her.

At last he drew back and sighed. "There," he said, his breath warm against her face. "Now go, before I make an even bigger fool of myself."

But Sherry wasn't sure she was capable of moving, let alone driving several hundred miles. She blinked and tried to catch her breath.

"Why'd you do that?" she demanded.

"Darned if I know," Cody admitted, sounding none too pleased with himself.

Sherry understood his consternation when she glanced around her. It seemed the entire town of Pepper, Texas, had stopped in midmotion to stare at them. A couple of men loitering outside the hardware store were watching them. Several curious faces filled the window at the Yellow Rose, including Donna Jo's. The waitress, in fact, looked downright excited and gave Sherry a thumbs-up.

"We've done it now," Cody said, scowling at her as if she were to blame. "Everyone's going to be talking."

"I'd like to remind you I wasn't the one who started this."

"Yeah, but you sure enjoyed it."

"Well, this is just fine, isn't it," she said, glad for an excuse to be on her way. "I'm outta here." Tossing her lunch bag onto the passenger seat, she slipped inside the car.

"Sherry, blast it, don't leave yet!"

"Why? What else have you got planned?"

"Okay, okay, I shouldn't have kissed you, I'll be the first to agree." He rubbed his hand along the back of his neck. "As I said before, I like you."

"You have a funny way of showing it."

He closed his eyes and nodded. "I've already made a mess of this, and I haven't even known you for a whole day. Listen, in two weeks Pepper's going to hold its annual picnic and dance. Will you be there?" He gave her the date and the time.

She hesitated, then nodded.

"If we still feel the same way, then we'll know this has a chance," he said. He spun on his heel and walked away.

Four

"What can I tell you about Texas?" Norah asked Sherry as they sat by the swimming pool in the yard behind her sprawling luxury home. Both three-year-old Jeff and baby Grace were napping, and Norah and Sherry were spending a leisurely afternoon soaking up the sun. "Texas is oil wells, cattle and cotton. It's grassy plains and mountains."

"And desert," Sherry added.

"That, too. Texas is chicken-fried steak, black-eyed peas and hot biscuits and gravy. Actually, I've discovered," Norah said with a grin, "that most Texans will eat just about anything. They've downed so many chili peppers over the years that they've burned out their taste buds."

"I've really come to love this state." Sherry sipped from her glass of iced tea. "Everyone's so friendly."

"It's known as the Lone Star state, but a lot of folks call it the Friendship state, too."

That didn't surprise Sherry.

"The men are hilarious," Norah continued, her eyes

dancing with silent laughter. "Oh, they don't mean to be, but I swear they've got some of the craziest ideas about…well, practically everything. To give you an example, they have this sort of unwritten code, which has to do with *real* Texans versus everyone else in the world. A real Texan would or wouldn't do any number of things."

"Such as?"

"Well, a real Texan believes in law and order, except when the law insists on a fifty-five-mile-an-hour speed limit. They consider that unreasonable. And clothes… A real Texan wouldn't dream of decorating his Stetson with feathers or anything else, with the possible exception of a snake band, but only if he'd killed the snake and tanned the skin himself. And the jeans! I swear they refuse to wash them—they wear 'em until they can stand up on their own."

Sherry laughed. She'd run into a few of those types herself on her journey across the vast state. But no one could compete with the characters she'd met in Pepper. Mayor Bowie, Donna Jo and Billy Bob. The way that man had manipulated her into staying in town!

And Cody Bailman… He kept drifting into her mind, although she'd made numerous attempts to keep him out. She'd tried hard to forget their last meeting, when he'd kissed her in broad daylight in front of half the town. But nothing helped. Cody Bailman was in her head day and night. It didn't seem possible that a man she'd known for such a short while—

"Sherry."

Sherry looked up and realized Norah was waving a hand in front of her face. "You're in another world."

"Sorry, I was just thinking about, uh, the folks back in Pepper."

"More than likely it's that cattleman you were telling me about."

Sherry lowered her gaze again, not surprised Norah had read her so easily. "I can't stop thinking about him. I thought that once I was with you, I'd be able to get some perspective on what happened between us. Not that anything really did—happen, I mean. Good heavens, I was only in town for about twenty-four hours."

"You like him, don't you?"

"That's just it," Sherry said, reaching for her drink and gripping it tightly. "I'm not sure how I feel about him. It's all messed up. I don't know Cody well enough to have an opinion, and yet…"

"And yet, you find yourself thinking about him, wishing you could be with him and missing him. All of this seems impossible because until a few days ago he wasn't even in your life."

"Yes," Sherry returned, astonished at the way Norah could clarify her thoughts. "That's *exactly* what I'm feeling."

"I thought so." Norah relaxed against the cushion on the patio chair and sighed, lifting her face to the sun. "That's how it was with me after Rowdy was released from the hospital and went home to Texas. My life felt so empty without him. He'd only been in the hospital a couple of weeks, but it seemed as if my whole world revolved around him."

"Rowdy, fortunately, felt the same way about you," Sherry said, knowing Cody was as perplexed as she was by the attraction *they* shared.

"Not at first," Norah countered. "I amused him, and being stuck in traction with that broken leg, the poor guy was desperate for some comic relief. I happened to be handy. Being Valerie's sister added to my appeal. You know, he actually came to Orchard Valley to break up her engagement to Colby! I don't think it was until much later that he fell in love with me—later than he's willing to admit now, at any rate."

"Don't be so sure." Sherry still remembered the chaos Rowdy Cassidy had brought into the tidy world of Orchard Valley General. His plane had crashed in a nearby field and he'd been taken, seriously injured, to Emergency. He'd been a terrible patient—demanding and cantankerous. Only one nurse could handle him…. Sherry had known he was in love with Norah long before he'd ever left the hospital, even if he wasn't aware of it himself. Norah's feelings had been equally clear to her. It seemed she could judge another's emotions better than her own.

"I'm sorry, in a way, that you took this position in Pepper," Norah said. "I know it's pure selfishness on my part, but I was hoping if you moved to Texas you'd settle closer to Houston."

"I don't think I realized how large this state is. Central Texas didn't look that far from Houston on the map. I found out differently when I had to drive it."

"I wish you'd taken the time to stop in San Antonio. Rowdy took me there for our first anniversary, and we fell in love all over again. Of course, it might've had something to do with the flagstone walks, the marvelous boutiques and the outdoor cafés." Norah sighed longingly at the memory.

"It sounds wonderful."

"It was," Norah said wistfully. "We rode in a river taxi down the San Antonio River and...oh, I swear it was the most romantic weekend we've ever spent."

"I'll make a point of visiting San Antonio soon," Sherry said.

"Don't go alone," Norah insisted. "It's a place for lovers."

"Okay. I'll make sure I'm crazy in love before I make any traveling plans."

"Good." Norah gave a satisfied nod.

Rowdy returned home from the office earlier than usual with wonderful news. He and Norah were hoping to adopt two small children who'd been orphaned the year before. Because of some legal difficulties, the adoption had been held up in the courts.

"Looks like we're going to be expanding our family shortly," Rowdy said, kissing Norah before taking the chair next to her and reaching for her hand.

Sherry found it almost painful to see these two people so deeply in love. It reminded her how alone she was, how isolated her life had become as more and more of her friends got married and started families. Sherry felt like someone on the outside looking in.

"Grace's new tooth broke through this afternoon," Norah told Rowdy after she'd poured him a glass of iced tea.

"This I've got to see," he said, getting up and heading toward the house.

"Rowdy," Norah called after him. "Let her sleep. She was fussy most of the afternoon."

"I thought I'd take her and Jeff swimming."

"Yes, but wait until they wake up from their naps." Norah smiled at Sherry. "Sometimes I think Rowdy's nothing more than a big kid himself. He's looking for someone to play with."

"He's wonderful. I could almost be jealous."

"There's no need," Norah said, squeezing Sherry's arm. "Your turn's coming, and I think it's going to be sooner than you expect."

"I hope so," Sherry said, but she didn't have any faith in her friend's prediction.

"Sherry," Rowdy said, turning back from the house. "I did a bit of checking on that cattleman you mentioned the other night." He removed a slip of paper from his inside pocket. "Cody James Bailman," he read, "born thirty-five years ago, married at twenty-one, widowed, one daughter named Heather. Owns a ten-thousand-acre spread outside Pepper. He was elected president of the local Cattlemen's Association three years running."

"That's it?" Norah asked.

"He raises quarter horses, as well as cattle."

That didn't tell Sherry much more than she already knew.

"He seems like a decent guy. I spoke to a man who's known Bailman for several years and he thinks highly of him. If you want my advice, I say marry the fellow and see what happens."

"Rowdy!" Norah chastised.

"That's what we did, and everything worked out, didn't it?"

"Circumstances are just a tad different, dear," Norah said, glancing apologetically toward Sherry.

"Marriage would do them both good," Rowdy continued. He turned to Sherry and nodded as if the decision had already been made. "Marry the man."

"Marry the man." As Sherry drove toward Pepper several days later, Rowdy's words clung to her mind. Cody's parting words returned to haunt her, as well. *If we still feel the same way, then we'll know this has a chance.* But what could have changed in their two weeks apart? What could they possibly have learned?

Because of a flat tire fifty miles on the other side of nowhere, followed by a long delay at a service station, Sherry was much later than she'd hoped. In fact, she was going to miss part of the scheduled festivities, including the parade. But with any luck she'd be in town before the dance started.

She'd tried phoning Cody's ranch several times on her cell, but there hadn't been any answer. No doubt everyone was enjoying the community celebration. With nothing left to do, she drove on, not stopping for lunch, until she arrived in Pepper.

The town had put on its best dress for this community event. A banner reading "Pepper Days" was stretched across Main Street. The lampposts were decorated with a profusion of wildflowers, and red, white and blue crepe paper was strung from post to post.

Several brightly painted cardboard signs directed her to the city park and the barbecue. As soon as she turned off Main and onto Spruce, Sherry smelled the enticing aroma of mesquite and roasting beef. Various signs sent participants and onlookers to the far end of the park, where a chili cook-off was in progress. Sherry was fortunate to find a parking space on a side street.

Country music blared from loudspeakers, and colorful Chinese lanterns dotted the cottonwood trees.

People were milling around the park, and Sherry didn't recognize anyone. She would've liked to freshen up before meeting Cody, but she was already late and didn't want to take the time. Besides, her calf-length denim skirt, cowboy boots and Western shirt with a white fringe were perfect for the festivities. The skirt and shirt had been a welcome-to-Texas gift from Norah.

"Sherry!"

She whirled around to see Cody's daughter waving and racing toward her. Not quite prepared for the impact as Heather flung herself at her, Sherry nearly toppled backward.

"I knew you'd come! I never doubted, not even for a second. Have you seen my dad yet?"

"No, I just got here."

"He didn't think you were going to come. Men are like that, you know. It's all a way to keep from being disappointed, don't you think?"

But Cody's attitude disappointed Sherry. "I said I'd be here."

"I know, but Dad didn't have a lot of faith that you'd show up. I did, though. Do you like my hair?" Heather looked extremely pretty with her thick dark hair loose and curling down her back. She whipped back the curls and tossed her head as if she were doing a shampoo commercial. She gazed up at Sherry, her eyes wide and guileless; she'd probably practiced the look in front of the bathroom mirror—something Sherry had done herself as a teenager. "Come on, let's go find my father," Heather said urgently.

It didn't take long for Sherry to spot Cody. He was talking to a group of men who were gathered in a circle. Their discussion seemed to be a heated one, and Sherry guessed the topic was politics. Not until she got closer did she realize they were contesting the pros and cons of adding jalapeño peppers to Billy Bob's barbecue sauce.

"They're just neighbors," Heather whispered as they approached. "Dad can talk to them anytime."

Unwilling to interrupt him, Sherry stopped the girl's progress.

"But this could go on for hours!" Heather protested, apparently loudly enough for her father to hear, because at that moment he turned and saw them.

His eyes moved from his daughter to Sherry, and he couldn't seem to believe she was really there. He excused himself to his friends and began walking toward her.

"Hello, Cody." The words seemed to stick in Sherry's throat.

"I didn't think you were going to come," he said.

"I had a flat tire on the way, and it took ages to repair. I phoned, but I guess everyone at the Lucky Horseshoe had already left for the picnic."

"Are you hungry?"

"Starved," she said.

Cody pulled a wad of bills from his pocket, peeled off several and handed them to Heather. "Bring Sherry a plate of the barbecue beef."

"But, Dad, I wanted to talk to her and—"

Cody silenced the protest with a single look.

"All right, I get it. You want to be alone with her.

How long should I stay away?" The question was posed with an elaborate sigh. "An hour? Two?"

"We'll be under the willow tree," Cody said, ignoring her questions and pointing to an enormous weeping willow about fifty feet away.

"The willow tree," Heather repeated, lowering her voice suggestively. "Good choice, Dad. I couldn't have thought of a better place myself."

Cody gave a sigh of relief as Heather trotted off. "You'll have to forgive my daughter," he said, shaking his head. Then he smiled. "She was as eager for you to return as I was."

His words and smile went a long way toward reassuring Sherry. Their separation had felt like a lifetime to her. Two weeks away from a man she'd known only briefly; it didn't make sense. And yet, she couldn't deny how she felt.

All at once Sherry felt scared. Scared of all the feelings crowding inside her. Scared of being with Cody again, of kissing him again, of making more of this attraction than he intended or wanted. Her feelings were powerful, alien. At first she'd attributed them to being with Norah and Rowdy and seeing how happy they were.

Now here she was with Cody, sitting under the shadowy arms of a weeping willow, and her confusion returned a hundredfold. This man affected her in a thousand indescribable ways, but she was worried; she wasn't sure her feelings were because of Cody himself. Maybe it was the exciting promise he represented. The happiness waiting for her just around the corner, just out of reach. She desperately wanted the joy her friends had found. She was tired of being alone, tired of walking into an empty apartment. She wanted a husband, a home and a family. Was that so much to ask?

Cody spread out a blanket for them to sit on. "How were your friends?"

"Very much in love." It wasn't what Sherry had meant to say, but the first thing that sprang to her lips. She looked away, embarrassed.

"Newlyweds?"

"No." She shook her head. "They've been married four years and have two children. In a few weeks they'll be adding two adopted kids to the family."

"They sound like a compassionate, generous couple."

His words warmed her heart like a July sun. Rowdy and Norah *were* two of the most generous people Sherry had ever known. It was as if they were so secure in their love for each other that it spilled over and flowed out to those around them.

"What's wrong?"

This man seemed to sense her thoughts and emotions so accurately that nothing less than the truth would do. "I'm scared to death of seeing you again, of feeling the way I feel about you. I don't even *know* you, and I feel... That's just it, I don't know what I feel."

He laughed. "You're not alone. I keep telling myself this whole thing is nuttier than a pecan grove. I don't really know you, either. Why you, out of all the women I've met over the years?"

"I'm not interrupting anything, am I?" Heather burst through the hanging branches and stepped onto the blanket. She crossed her legs and slowly lowered herself to the ground before handing Sherry a plate heaped high with potato salad, barbecued chicken and one of the biggest dill pickles Sherry had ever seen.

Heather tilted her head to one side. "They've run out of beef. I told Mayor Bowie this was for Sherry, and he wanted me to ask you to save a dance for him. He's been cooking all afternoon, and he says he's looking forward to seeing a pretty face, instead of a pot of Billy Bob's barbecue sauce."

"This smells heavenly," Sherry said, taking the plate and digging in.

Cody looked pointedly at his daughter, expecting her to make herself scarce, but she looked back at him just as pointedly. "So, have you come to any conclusions?" Heather asked.

"No. But then we haven't had much time *alone,* have we?"

"You've had enough."

Cody closed his eyes. "Heather, please."

"Are you going to ask Sherry to dance, or are you going to wait for Mayor Bowie to steal her away from you? Dad, you can't be so nonchalant about this business. Aren't you the one who says the early bird catches the worm? You know Mayor Bowie likes Sherry."

"The mayor's a married man."

"So?" Heather said, seeming to enjoy their exchange. "That didn't stop Russell Forester from running off with Milly You-Know-Who."

If the color in his neck was any indication, Cody's frustration level was reaching its peak. But Sherry welcomed the intrusion. She needed space and time to sort through her reactions, her feelings. Everything had become so intense so quickly. If Heather hadn't interrupted them when she had, Sherry was certain she would've been in Cody's arms—although it was too soon to cloud their feelings with sexual awareness.

"The chicken's delicious," Sherry said, licking her fingers clean of the spicy sauce. "I don't think I've ever tasted any as good as this."

"Cody Bailman, are you hiding Sherry under that tree with you?" The toes of a pair of snakeskin boots stepped on the outer edges of the blanket just under the tree's protective foliage.

Heather cast her father a righteous look and whispered heatedly, "I *told* you Mayor Bowie was going to ask her first."

Cody stood and parted the willow's hanging branches. "She's eating."

"Howdy, Mayor," Sherry said, smiling up at him, a chicken leg poised in front of her mouth. "I understand you're the chef responsible for this feed. You can cook for me anytime."

"I'm not a bad dancer, either. I thought I'd see if you wouldn't mind taking a spin with an old coot like me."

She laughed. "You're not so old."

"What'll your wife think?" Cody asked, his tone jocular, but with an underlying...what? Annoyance? Jealousy? Sherry wasn't sure.

Pepper's mayor waved his hand dismissively. "Hazel won't care. Good grief, I've been married to the woman for thirty-seven years. Besides, she's talking to her friends, and you know how that bunch loves to idle away an afternoon gossiping. I thought I'd give them something to talk about."

"Sherry?" Cody glanced at her as if he expected her to decline.

Frankly, Sherry was flattered to have two men vying for her attention, even if one of them was old enough to be her father and looked as if he'd sampled a bit too much of his own cooking over the years.

"Why, Mayor, I'd be delighted."

Cody didn't look pleased.

"I told you this was going to happen," Heather reminded him indignantly. "Your problem, Dad, is that you never listen to me. I read romance novels. I know about these things."

A laugh hovered on Sherry's lips. She hoisted herself up and accepted Mayor Bowie's hand as he led her to the dancing platform.

Cody and Heather followed close behind. Because Mayor Bowie was chatting, she couldn't quite hear the conversation between father and daughter, but it seemed to her that Heather was still chastising Cody.

Although it was early in the evening, the dance floor was crowded. Willie Nelson was crooning a melodic ballad as the mayor deftly escorted Sherry onto the large black-and-white-checkered platform. He placed one hand at her waist and held her arm out to one side, then smoothly led her across the floor.

"How're you doin', Sherry?" a woman asked.

She turned to see Donna Jo dancing with the sheriff. Sherry waved with her free hand. Doc Lindsey danced briskly by with Mrs. Colson, first in one direction and then another.

Mayor Bowie was surprisingly light on his feet, and he whirled Sherry around so many times she started to get dizzy. When the dance ended, she looked up to find Cody standing beside the mayor.

"I believe this dance is mine," he said.

"Of course." The mayor gracefully stepped aside and turned to Heather. Bowing, he asked the giggling twelve-year-old for the pleasure of the next dance.

Heather cast Sherry a proud look and responded with a dignified curtsy.

"So, we meet again," Sherry said, slipping her left arm onto Cody's shoulder.

"You should've danced with me first," he muttered.

"Why?" She wasn't sure she approved of his tone or his attitude. Mayor Bowie certainly couldn't be seen as competition!

"If you had, you would've spared me a lecture from my daughter. She seems to be doing research on romance, and apparently I've committed several blunders. According to Heather, my tactics aren't sophisticated enough." He made a wry grimace.

Sherry couldn't help noticing that they were doing little more than shuffling their feet, while other couples whirled around them. Cody seemed to notice it, too, and exhaled sharply.

"That's another thing," he said. "My own daughter suggested I take dance lessons." He snorted. "Me, as if I have time for that kind of nonsense. Listen, if you want to date a man who's good at this, you better know right now it isn't me."

Sherry had already figured that out for herself, not that it mattered. Cody sighed again.

"Is something else bothering you?" Sherry asked.

"Yes," he admitted grudgingly. "You feel good in

my arms. I'm probably breaking some romance code by telling you that. Darned if I know what a man's supposed to say and what he isn't."

Sherry closed her eyes. "That was very sweet."

Cody was silent for the next few minutes. "What about you?" he asked gruffly.

Sherry pulled back enough so he could read the question in her eyes. His own were dark and troubled.

"It'd help if you told me the same thing," he said. "That you…like being with me, too." He shook his head. "I've got to tell you, I feel silly."

"I do enjoy being with you."

He didn't seem to hear. "I feel like I'm on display for everyone to inspect."

"Why's that?"

He looked away, but not before she saw his frown. "Let me just say that kissing you in public didn't improve the situation. It was the most asinine thing I've ever done in my life. I made a fool of myself in front of the entire town."

"I wouldn't say that," she whispered, close to his ear. "I liked it."

"That's the problem," he grunted. "So did I. You know what I think? This is all Heather's doing. It started with that crazy project of hers. I swear the kid's going to ruin me."

"Heather's project?"

"Forget I said that."

"Why are you so angry? Is it because I danced with the mayor?"

"Good heavens, no. This has nothing to do with that."

"Then what *does* it have to do with?"

"You," he grumbled.

Dolly Parton's tremulous tones were coming out of the speakers now. It was a fast-paced number, not that Cody noticed. He didn't alter his footwork, but continued his laborious two-step.

"Cody, maybe we should sit down."

"We can't."

"Why not?" she asked.

"Because the minute we do, someone else is gonna ask you to dance, and I can't allow that."

She stared up at him, more confused by the moment. "Why not? Cody, you're being ridiculous."

"I don't need you to tell me that. I've been ridiculous ever since I saw you holding Ellie's baby in your arms. I've been behaving like a lovesick idiot from the first time I kissed you. I can understand what caused a normally sane, sensible man like Luke Johnson to chase after a sports car on his horse because he couldn't stand to let the woman he loved leave town. And dammit, I don't like it. Not one bit."

What had first sounded rather romantic was fast losing its appeal. "I don't like what I feel for you, either, Cody Bailman. I had a perfectly good life until you barged in."

"So did I!"

"I think we should stop while we're ahead," she murmured, pulling away from him. "Before we say something we'll regret." She dropped her arms to her sides and stared up at him.

"Great," he said. "Let's just do that."

With so many couples whirling about, Sherry found it difficult to make her way off the dance floor, but she managed. To her consternation, Cody followed close behind.

Catching sight of Ellie beneath the shade of an oak tree, Sherry hurried in that direction, determined to ignore Cody. She was halfway across the park when she heard him call after her.

"Sherry! Wait up!"

She didn't bother to turn around to see what had detained him. When she reached Ellie, the woman smiled up at her brightly.

"I see you've just tangled with the most stubborn man this side of Luke Johnson."

Five

"Cody infuriates me," Sherry announced, sinking down next to Ellie Johnson on the blanket under the tree. She wrapped her arms around her knees and sighed in frustration.

"Men have infuriated women since the dawn of time. They're totally irrational beings," Ellie said calmly while patting her infant son's back. Philip was sleeping contentedly against her shoulder.

"Irrational isn't the word for it. They're *insane*."

"That, too," Ellie agreed readily.

"No one but Cody could use a compliment to insult someone!"

"Luke did when we first started dating," Ellie told her. "He'd say things like 'You're not bad-looking for a skinny girl.'"

Despite her annoyance with Cody, Sherry laughed.

Cody had been waylaid by Luke, Sherry noticed. Luke carried Christina Lynn on his shoulders, and the toddler's arms were reaching toward the sky in an apparent effort to touch the fluffy clouds. Sherry hoped

Ellie's husband was giving Cody a few pointers about relationships.

Forcing her thoughts away from the men, Sherry sighed again and watched Ellie with her baby son. Philip had awoken and she turned him in her arms, draped a receiving blanket over her shoulder, then bared her breast.

"He's thriving," Ellie said happily. "I can't thank you enough for being with me the night he was born. Having you there made all the difference in the world."

"It wasn't me doing all the work," Sherry reminded her.

"Then let's just say we make an excellent team." Ellie stroked her son's face with her index finger as he nursed greedily. "I'm really glad you're going to live in Pepper. I feel like you're a friend already."

Sherry glanced up to see Heather marching toward them, hands on hips. Her eyes were indignant as she stopped and talked briefly to her father and Luke before flinging her arms in the air and striding over to Ellie and Sherry.

"What did he do *now?*" Cody's daughter demanded. "He said something stupid, right?" In a display of complete disgust, she slapped her sides. Then she lowered herself to the blanket. "I tried to coach him, but a lot of good that did." She eyed her father angrily. "No wonder he never remarried. The man obviously needs more help than I can give him."

Ellie and Sherry exchanged a smile. "Don't try so hard, Heather," Ellie said.

"But I want Dad to remarry so I can have a baby brother or sister. Or one of each."

"Heather," Sherry began, "your father said something about a project you were involved in, and then he immediately seemed to regret mentioning it."

"He's never gonna let me forget it, either," the girl muttered. "Neither is anyone else in town."

"You have to admit, it *was* rather amusing," Ellie added.

"Oh, sure, everyone got a big laugh out of it."

"Out of what?" Sherry wanted to know.

"My 4-H project. I've been a member for a few years and every spring we work on one project for the next twelve months. One year I raised rabbits, and another year I worked with my horse, Misty. This spring I gave the whole town a big laugh when I decided my project was going to be helping my dad find a wife."

"You weren't serious!" Sherry was mortified.

"I was at the time, but now I can see it wasn't a great idea," Heather continued. "Anyway, everyone talked about it for days. That's one of the worst things about living in a small town. Dad was furious with me, which didn't help."

"That's why you were so excited when you met me," Sherry said in a thoughtful voice.

"You're darn right, especially when I found you sleeping in Dad's bed."

Sherry shot a glance at Ellie and felt her face grow warm. "Cody slept in the guest room."

"My friend Carrie Whistler spent the night before at my place, and I was supposed to change the sheets, but I forgot," Heather explained to Ellie, then turned her attention back to Sherry. "You're just perfect for Dad, and I was hoping you might grow to, you know, love him. You'd make a terrific mother."

Sherry felt tears burn the backs of her eyes. "I don't think anyone's ever paid me a higher compliment, Heather, but love doesn't work that way. I'm sorry. I can't marry your father just because you want a baby brother or sister."

"But you like him, don't you?"

"Yes, but—"

"Until he said something stupid and ruined everything." Heather's face tensed.

"Why don't you let those two figure things out for themselves?" Ellie suggested to the girl. "Your interference will only cause problems."

"But Dad won't get anything right without me!"

"He married your mother, didn't he?" Ellie reminded her. "It seems to me he'll do perfectly well all on his own."

"I *like* Sherry, though. Better than anyone, and Dad does, too. His problem is he thinks love's a big waste of time. He told me he wanted to cut to the chase and be done with it."

"He said that?" Sherry glared over at him. Cody must have sensed it, because he looked at her and grimaced at the intensity of her expression. He said something to Luke, who turned their way, too. Luke's shoulders lifted in a shrug. Then he slapped Cody's back and the two of them headed in the direction of the cook-off area.

"He said he's too busy with the ranch to date anyone or to bother with what he calls 'hearts-and-flowers' stuff."

Sherry felt like a complete fool for having constructed this wild romantic fantasy in her mind. Cody had never been interested in her. From the very first, he'd been trying to mollify his daughter. Sherry had just appeared on the scene at a convenient moment. She felt sick to her stomach. This was what happened when she allowed herself to believe in romance, to believe in love. It seemed so easy for her friends, but it wasn't for her.

"I've had a long day," Sherry said, suddenly feeling weary. "I think I'll go unpack my bags, soak in the tub and make an early night of it."

"You can't!" Heather protested. "I signed you and Dad up for the three-legged race, the egg toss and the water-balloon toss. They have the races in the evening because it's too hot in the afternoon."

"I doubt that your father wants me as a partner."

"But he does," Heather insisted. "He's won the egg toss for years and years, and it's really important to him. It's one of those ego things."

"Unfortunately, he's already got egg on his face," Sherry muttered to Ellie, who laughed outright.

"Please stay," Heather begged. "Please, please, please. If you don't, I can't see myself ever forgiving Dad for ruining this opportunity."

Sherry was beginning to understand Cody's frustration with his daughter. "Heather, don't play matchmaker. It'll do more harm than good. If your father's genuinely interested in dating me, he'll do so without you goading him into it. Promise me you'll stay out of this."

Heather looked at the ground and her pretty blue eyes grew sad. "It's just that I like you so much and we could have lots of fun together."

"We certainly don't need your father for that."

"We don't?"

"Trust me," Ellie inserted, "a man would only get in the way."

"Would you go shopping for school clothes with me? I mean, to a real town with a mall that's got more than three stores, and spend the day with me?"

"I'd love it."

Heather lowered her eyes again, then whispered, "I need help with bras and...and other stuff."

Sherry smiled. "We'll drive into Abilene and make a day of it."

Heather's eyes lit up like sparklers. "That'd be great!"

"So, I'll leave you to partner your dad on the egg toss."

The glimmer in her eyes didn't fade. "I was thinking the same thing." She looked mischievous. "This could be the year Dad loses his title as the egg champion."

"Heather," Sherry chastised, "be nice to your father."

"Oh, I will," she promised, "especially since you and I have reached an understanding."

"Good. Then I'm heading over to the clinic now."

"You're *sure* you won't stay? There's a fireworks display tonight. It's even better than the one we had on the Fourth."

"I think Sherry's seen all the fireworks she needs for one night," Ellie put in.

"You're right, I have. We'll talk soon, Heather. Bye, Ellie." She leaned over and kissed the top of Philip's head. "Let's make a point of getting together in the next little while."

"I'd like that," Ellie said.

Sherry was halfway back to her car when Cody caught up with her. He fell into step beside her. "I didn't mean to offend you," he said.

Sherry sighed and closed her eyes. "I know."

"But you're still mad?"

"No. Discouraged, perhaps, but not mad." She arrived at her car and unlocked it. "I talked to Heather and she told me about her 4-H project. It explained a lot."

"Like what?"

"Like why you're interested in me. Why you chose to drive me to the ranch instead of town after Ellie's baby was born."

"That had nothing to do with it! We were both dog-tired, and my place was a lot closer than town."

"You don't need to worry," Sherry said, unwilling to get involved in another debate with him. She was truly weary and not in the best of moods, fighting the heat, disappointment and the effects of an undernourished romantic heart. "I had a nice chat with Heather. You've done a wonderful job raising her, Cody. She's a delightful girl. Unless you object, I'd like to be her friend. She and I have already made plans to go clothes-shopping in Abilene."

"Of course I don't object."

"Thank you." She slipped inside her car and started the engine. She would've driven away, but Cody prevented her from closing the door.

He frowned darkly. "I don't mean to be obtuse, but what does all this mean?"

"Nothing, really. I'm just…cutting to the chase," she said. "I'm explaining that it isn't necessary for you to play out this charade any longer."

"What charade?"

"Of being attracted to me."

"I *am* attracted to you."

"But you wish you weren't."

He opened and closed his mouth twice before he answered. "I should've known you'd throw that back in my face. You're right. I don't have time for courtin' and buying flowers and the like. I've got a ranch to run, and this is one of the busiest months of the year."

Sherry blinked, not sure what to make of Cody. He seemed sincere about not meaning to offend her, and yet he constantly said and did things that infuriated her.

"The problem is," Cody continued, still frowning, "if I don't stake my claim on you now, there'll be ten other ranchers all vying for your attention."

"Stake your claim?" He made her sound like an acre of water-rich land.

"You know," he said. "Let everyone in town see you're my woman."

"I'm not *any* man's woman."

"Not yet, but I'd like you to think about being mine." He removed his hat; Sherry guessed that meant he intended her to take him seriously. "If you'd be willing to run off and get married, then—"

"Then *what?*"

"Then we'd be done with it. See, like I said, I don't have the time or energy to waste on courtin' a woman."

Sherry nodded slowly, all the while chewing the inside of her cheek to keep from saying something she'd wish she hadn't. So much for romance! So much for sipping champagne and feeding each other chocolate-covered strawberries in the moonlight, a fantasy she'd had for years. Or a romantic weekend in San Antonio, the way Norah had described. No wonder Heather was frustrated with her father. The girl must feel as if she was smacking her head against a brick wall.

"Well?" Cody demanded.

Sherry stared at him. "Are you kidding me?"

"Of course not! I meant every word." He paused to take a deep breath. "I like you. You like me. What else is there? Sure, we can spend the next few months going through all those ridiculous courtin' rituals or we can use the common sense God gave us and be done with this romance nonsense."

"And do what?" Sherry asked innocently.

"Get married, of course. I haven't stopped thinking about you in two weeks. You didn't stop thinking about me, either. I saw it in your eyes no more'n an hour ago. You know what it's like when we kiss. Instead of playing games with each other, why not admit you want me as much as I want you? I never did understand why women always complicate a basic human need. A bunch of flowery words isn't going to make any difference. If you want kids, all the better."

Sherry carefully composed her response. Apparently she took longer than he thought necessary.

"Well?" he pressed.

She looked up at him, her gaze deliberately calm. "I'd rather eat fried rattlesnake than marry a man who proposed to me the way you just did."

Cody stared at her as if not sure what to make of her response, then slammed his hat back on his head. "This is exactly the problem with you women. You want everything served to you on a silver platter. And for your information, fried rattlesnake happens to be pretty good. Doesn't taste all that different from chicken."

"Well, I wouldn't eat it even if it *was* served on a silver platter," Sherry snapped. This conversation was over. He'd frustrated her before, but now she was really angry.

"That's your decision, then?"

"That's my decision," she said tightly.

"You're rejecting my proposal?"

"Yup."

"I should've guessed," Cody said. "I knew even before I opened my mouth that you were going to be pig-headed about this."

"Don't feel bad," she said with feigned amiability. "I'm sure there are plenty of women who'd leap at your offer. I just don't happen to be one of them." She reached for the handle of the still-open door, and he was obliged to move out of the way.

"Good night, Cody."

"Goodbye," he muttered and stalked away. He turned back once as if he wanted to argue with her some more, but changed his mind. Sherry threw her car into gear and drove off.

"What happened between my dad and you after we talked?" Heather asked in a whisper over the telephone. She'd called Sherry first thing the next morning.

"Heather, I'm on duty. I can't talk now."

"Who's sick?"

"No one at the moment, but—"

"If there's no one there, it won't hurt to talk to me for a couple of minutes, will it? Please?"

"Nothing happened between your dad and me." Which of course wasn't true. She'd been proposed to, if you could call it that, for the first time in her life.

"Then why is Dad acting like a wounded bear? Janey threatened to quit this morning, and she's been working for Dad since before I was born."

"Why don't you ask your father?"

"You're kidding, right? No one wants to talk to him. Even Slim's staying out of his way."

"Give him time. He'll cool down."

"If I could wait that long, I wouldn't be calling you."

"Heather," Sherry said, growing impatient, "this is between your father and me. Let's just leave it at that, shall we?"

"You don't want my help?"

"No," Sherry said emphatically. "I don't. Please, drop it, okay?"

"All right," the girl agreed reluctantly. "I won't ask any more questions about whatever it is that *didn't* happen that you don't want to talk about."

"Thank you."

"I hope you know what a sacrifice this is."

"Oh, I do."

"You might think that just because I'm a kid I don't know things. But I know more than either you or Dad realize. I—"

Sherry rolled her eyes. "I need to get off the phone."

Heather released a great gusty sigh. "All right. We're still going shopping for school clothes, aren't we? Soon, 'cause school starts in less than two weeks."

"You bet." Sherry suggested a day and a time and

reminded Heather to check with her father. "I'll make reservations at a nice hotel, and we'll spend the night."

"That'll be *great!* Oh, Sherry, I really wish you and Dad could get along, because I think you're fabulous."

"I think you're pretty fabulous, too, honey. Now listen, I have to go. I can't tie up the line."

"Next time I call, I'll ask Mrs. Colson to take a message. You can call me back later when you're not on duty."

"That sounds like a good plan."

Sherry had just finished with her first patient of the afternoon, a four-year-old with a bad ear infection, when Mrs. Colson handed her a phone message. Sherry should've suspected something when the receptionist smiled so broadly.

Sherry took the slip and stuck it in the pocket of her white uniform jacket, waiting until she was alone to read it. When she did, she sank into a chair and closed her eyes. The call was from Heather. She'd talked to her father, and apparently he had business in Abilene that same weekend and was making arrangements for the three of them to travel together. He'd call her soon, Heather said.

This was going to be difficult. Knowing Cody, he'd turn a simple shopping trip into a test of her patience and endurance. She'd have to set some ground rules.

Cody was supposed to pick her up at the clinic early Saturday morning. Sherry was standing on the porch waiting. It'd been a week since she'd last seen him, four days since their stilted conversation on the phone—and a lifetime since she'd dreaded any trip more.

Her heart sank when the white Cadillac pulled to a stop in front of the clinic.

Cody got out of the car and climbed the steps. Sherry saw Heather scramble over the front seat and into the back.

"Hello," Sherry said, tightening her grip on her overnight case.

"Hello." His voice was devoid of emotion as he reached for her bag.

"I thought we should talk before we leave," she said when he was halfway down the steps.

"Fine." He didn't sound eager.

"Let's call a truce. It shouldn't be difficult to be civil to each other, should it? There's no reason for us to discuss our differences now or ever again, for that matter."

"No," he agreed, "it shouldn't be the least bit difficult to be civil."

And surprisingly, it wasn't. The radio filled in the silences during the long drive, and when the stations faded, Heather bubbled over with eager chatter. Cody seemed to go out of his way to be amiable, and Sherry found her reserve melting as the miles slipped past.

The hotel Cody chose in Abilene was situated close to a large shopping mall. Heather was ready to head for the shops the minute they checked in to their spacious two-bedroom suite.

"Hold your horses," Cody said. He had his briefcase with him. "I probably won't be back until later this evening."

"What about dinner?" Heather wanted to know.

"I've got an appointment."

"Don't worry about us," Sherry told him. "Either we'll order something from room service or eat downstairs. If we're feeling adventurous, we'll go out, but I don't imagine we'll go far."

"What time will you be back, Dad?"

Cody paused. "I can't say. I could be late, so don't wait up for me."

"Can I watch a movie?" She stood in front of the television and read over the listings offered on the printed card.

"If Sherry doesn't object, I can't see any reason why not."

Heather hugged her father and he kissed her head. "Have fun, you two."

"We will," Sherry said.

"Spend your money wisely," he advised on his way out the door, but the look he cast Sherry assured her he trusted her to guide Heather in her decisions.

The girl waited until her father was out of the room before she hurled herself onto the beige sofa and threw out both arms. "Isn't this great? You brought your swimsuit, didn't you? I did."

Sherry had, but she wasn't sure there'd be enough time for them to use the hotel pool.

"It's almost as if we're a real family."

"Heather…"

"I know, I know," she said dejectedly. "Dad already lectured me about this. I'm not supposed to say anything that might insin…insinuate that the two of you share any romantic interest in each other." She said this last bit in a tinny voice that sounded as if it were coming from a robot.

"At least your father and I understand each other."

"That's just it. You don't. He really likes you, Sherry. A lot. He'd never admit it, though." She sighed and cocked her head. "Men have a problem with pride, don't they?"

"Women do, too," Sherry said, reaching for her purse. "Are you ready to shop till we drop, or do you want to discuss the troublesome quirks of the male psyche?"

It didn't take Heather more than a second to decide. She bolted from the sofa. "Let's shop!"

The mall close to the hotel consisted of nearly fifty stores, of which twenty sold clothing, and they made a point of visiting each and every one. When they were back in the hotel, arms laden with packages, Sherry discovered they'd bought something in more than half the stores they'd ventured into.

Heather was thrilled with her purchases. She removed the merchandise from the bags and spread the outfits over the two beds in their room, quickly running out of space. The overflow spilled onto the sofa and love seat in the living room. Two pairs of crisp jeans and several brightly colored blouses. Several T-shirts. A couple of jersey pullovers and a lovely soft cardigan. Two bras—the right size for Heather's still-developing figure—and matching panties. Sherry had talked Heather into buying a couple of dresses, too, although the girl insisted the only place she'd ever wear them was church. Their biggest extravagance had been footwear—five pairs altogether. Boots, sneakers, dress shoes—to go with her Sunday dresses—a sturdy pair for school and a pair of bedroom slippers.

Sherry wasn't immune to spending money on herself, and she'd purchased a gorgeous black crepe evening dress. Heaven only knew where she was going to wear it, but she'd been unable to resist.

"I have an idea!" Heather announced. "Let's dress up really nice for dinner. I'll wear my dress and new shoes and you can wear *your* new dress, and then we'll go down and order lobster for dinner and charge it to the room so Dad'll pay for it."

An elegant dinner to celebrate their success held a certain appeal—and gave Sherry an unexpected chance to wear her new finery—but charging it to the room didn't seem fair to Cody. "I don't know, Heather..."

"Dad won't mind," Heather said. "He's grateful you're willing to shop with me, and he'll be even happier now that I have bras that fit me. So, come on— what do you think?"

"I think dinner's a marvelous idea." They could work out the finances later.

Heather rummaged through the bags stacked on Sherry's bed until she found what she was looking for. "We should do our nails first, though, shouldn't we?"

They'd discovered the hottest shade of pink nail polish Sherry had ever seen. Heather had fallen in love with it and convinced Sherry her life wouldn't be complete without it.

"Our hair, too."

"Why not?" If they were going to dress up, there was no point in half measures. Heather was filled with such boundless enthusiasm Sherry couldn't help being infected with it, too.

Using jasmine-scented bubble bath, Sherry soaked in the tub, washed her hair and piled it high on her head, wrapping it in a white towel. Putting on a thick terry-cloth robe supplied by the hotel, she met Heather, who'd made use of the second bathroom, back in the living room.

Heather, also in a thick terry-cloth robe, eagerly set the bottle of hot-pink polish on the table.

"Only for our toes, not our fingers," Sherry instructed.

Heather was clearly disappointed, but she nodded. She balanced one foot, then the other against the edge of the coffee table, and Sherry painted the girl's toenails, then had Heather paint hers. They were halfway through this ritual, with Heather's nail polish almost dry, when the key turned in the lock. They both looked up to see Cody stroll casually into the room.

"Dad!" Heather bounded to her feet and raced over to her father. "We had a *fabulous* day. Wait'll you see what we bought."

Cody set down his briefcase and hugged his daughter. "I take it you had a fun afternoon."

"It was wild. I spent oodles of money. Sherry did, too. She bought this snazzy black dress. It wasn't on sale, but she said she had to have it. When you see her in it, you'll know why."

Cody didn't comment on that. His eyes narrowed when he saw his daughter's feet. "What have you done to your toes?"

"Isn't it great?" Heather said rhapsodically, wiggling her toes for his inspection.

"Will they make your feet glow in the dark?"

"No, silly!"

Sherry finished painting the last of her own toenails and screwed the top back on the bottle of polish. "We were going to dress up in our new outfits and go downstairs and have dinner in the dining room," she said. "That's all right, isn't it?"

"Anything you want. Dinner's on me."

"Even lobster?" Heather asked, as though she wasn't entirely sure how far his generosity would stretch.

"Even lobster. I just sold off the main part of my herd for the best price I've gotten in years."

"Congratulations." Sherry stood, with folded tissues between her toes, and tightened the belt on her robe.

"Then you're all through with your business stuff?" Heather asked.

"I'm finished."

"That's even better! You'll join us for dinner, right? You don't mind if Dad comes, do you, Sherry?"

Cody's eyes connected with Sherry's and his smile was slightly cocky, as if to suggest the ball was in her court.

"Of course I don't mind." There wasn't anything else she could say.

"You'll wear your slinky new dress," Heather said. "Dad." She turned to her father. "Your eyeballs are going to pop out of your head when you see Sherry in it."

Cody's gaze was on his daughter when he spoke. "It's too late for that. They popped out of my head the first time I saw her."

Six

Sherry wasn't sure why she felt so nervous. Maybe it had something to do with her new outfit. She suspected it was a mistake to wear that particular dress with this particular man.

She styled her glossy brown hair carefully, arranging it on top of her head with dangling wisps at her temples and neck. She wished she could tame her heart just as easily. She tried not to place any importance on this evening out, tried to convince herself it was just a meal with friends. That was all they were. Friends. The promise of more had been wiped away. Yet none of her strategies were succeeding; they hadn't even come close to succeeding. She was falling in love with this no-nonsense cattleman, despite the fact that there wasn't a romantic bone in his body.

When they'd finished dressing, the three of them met in the suite's living room. Sherry endured—and, at the same time, thrilled to—Cody's scrutiny. The dress was sleeveless with a dropped waist and a skirt that flared out at her knees in a triple layer of sleek ruffles. The high-heeled black sandals were the perfect complement.

"Doesn't she look like a million bucks?" Heather asked.

Without taking his eyes from Sherry, Cody nodded. "Very nice."

"Heather, too," Sherry said.

Cody seemed chagrined that she'd had to remind him to compliment his daughter. His eyes widened with appreciation as he gazed at Heather.

"Wow," he murmured. "Why…you seem all grown-up."

"I'm nearly thirteen, you know, and that means I'm almost a woman."

"You certainly look like one in that pretty dress." The glance he flashed at Sherry was filled with surprised gratitude. He seemed to be asking how she'd managed to convince his daughter to buy something other than jeans and cowboy boots.

Seeing Cody in a smart sports jacket with a pale blue shirt and a string tie had a curious effect on Sherry. She couldn't look at him and not be stirred. As much as she hated to admit it, he was a handsome man. When they'd first met, she'd been struck by the strength and authority she sensed in him. Those same traits were more prominent than ever now.

"Are we going to dinner, or are we going to stand around and stare at each other all evening?" Heather asked bluntly, looking from her father to Sherry and back again.

"By all means, let's eat," Cody said.

"Yes, let's." Sherry was shocked by how thin and

wavery her voice sounded. Apparently she wasn't the only one who noticed, because Heather sent her a curious look, then grinned broadly.

Dinner truly was an elegant affair. The small dining room was beautifully decorated with antique fixtures and furnishings. The tables were covered with white linen tablecloths, and the lights were muted. Both Heather and Sherry ordered the lobster-tail dinner, while Cody chose a thick T-bone steak. When a three-piece musical ensemble started to play, Heather glanced pointedly at both her father and Sherry.

"You're going to dance, aren't you?" she said.

"The music is more for mood than dancing," Sherry explained, although she wouldn't have refused if Cody had offered. But she knew he didn't much care for dancing, so an offer wasn't likely.

Their salads arrived, all Caesars with garlicky croutons. Heather gobbled hers, and when Sherry turned to her, silently suggesting she eat more slowly, the girl wiped the dressing from the corner of her mouth and shrugged. "I'm too hungry to linger over my food like you and Dad are."

Sherry's appetite was almost nil, a stark contrast to an hour earlier—before Cody had returned to the suite. She was almost sorry he was with them, because she couldn't enjoy her food. But although she was uncomfortably aware of his presence, she was still glad to be sharing this time with him and Heather.

Their entrées were served, and Sherry was grateful to Heather, who single-handedly carried the conversation. She chattered nonstop between bites of lobster, relating the details of the afternoon. Cody concentrated on his food, occasionally murmuring a brief response to his daughter's comments.

But whatever was happening between Cody and her, if indeed anything was, felt strange to Sherry. Cody seemed withdrawn from her both physically and emotionally. A sort of sultry tension suffused the air about them, as if they were waging battles against themselves, against the strong pull of the attraction they shared. Thank goodness, she thought, for Heather's easy banter.

Sherry hardly touched her meal, but nothing went to waste, because after Heather finished her own dinner, she polished off what remained of Sherry's.

When their dinner plates had been taken away and Heather was waiting for the blueberry-swirl cheesecake she'd ordered, Sherry excused herself and retreated to the ladies' room. She applied fresh lipstick, taking her time, not ready to go back to the table yet. She was uncertain of so many things. Cody had told her how much he *didn't* want to be attracted to her, and she'd found his words somewhat insulting. Now she understood. She was attracted to him, and she didn't like it, either, didn't know how to deal with it. What troubled her most was that she seemed to be weakening toward him. She'd always thought of herself as strong-willed, but now her defenses were crumbling. She was afraid that, as the evening progressed, it would become increasingly difficult to hide her feelings—and that could be disastrous.

Sherry had rejected his less-than-flattering proposal. Cody made it sound as if he was too busy rounding up cattle to go out with her or to focus on developing a relationship. But it was much more than that. He wasn't willing to make an emotional commitment to her, and Sherry would accept nothing less.

She was on her way back into the dining room when a tall, vaguely familiar-looking man approached her. His eye caught hers, and he hesitated a moment before speaking.

"Excuse me," he said, smiling apologetically, "but don't I know you?"

Sherry studied him, thinking the same thing, but unable to decide where or when she'd met him. "I'm not from this area," she said. "This is my first time in Abilene."

He frowned and introduced himself, but that didn't help. "It'll come to me," he said. "Do I look familiar to you?"

Sherry gave him her name. "You do look familiar, but I can't place you."

"Me, neither. Well... I'm sorry to have disturbed you, Sherry."

"That's okay."

When she reached the table, Cody's eyes were full of questions. "Do you know that man?"

"I'm not sure. He said his name's Jack Burnside." She paused. "He thought we'd met before. We might have, but neither of us can remember when or where. I'm generally good about remembering people. It's a little embarrassing."

Cody snickered. "Don't you know a come-on when you hear it? That guy's never met you—he was just looking for an excuse to introduce himself. His ploy's as old as the hills. I thought you were smarter than that."

"Apparently not," Sherry said lightly, refusing to allow Cody the pleasure of irritating her.

"I think you should dance with Sherry," Heather suggested a second time, pointing at the minuscule dance floor, where several other couples were swaying to the music.

"I'm sure your father would rather we—"

"As it happens, I'd be happy to give it a try." Cody's gaze seemed to hold a challenge.

Sherry blinked. Cody had managed to surprise her once again. She stood when he pulled out her chair. His hand felt warm on the small of her back as he guided her to the polished floor.

He turned her into his arms with a flair, making her skirt fan out from her knees. Then he brought her close to him, so close she was sure she could feel his heart beating.

Sherry wasn't fooled; she knew exactly what he was doing, although she doubted he'd ever admit it. He hadn't asked her to dance because of any great desire to twirl her around the floor, but to make sure Jack Burnside understood she was with him.

His attitude angered her, yet in some odd way pleased her, too. She was gratified to realize the attraction was mutual.

While Cody might have escorted her onto the dance floor to indicate that she was with *him,* Sherry thought he was as unprepared as she was for the impact of their physical closeness. Cody's hold on her gradually grew more possessive. His hand slid upward from her waist until his fingers splayed across her back. Of its own volition, her head moved closer to his until her temple rested against the lean strength of his jaw. Her eyes drifted shut, and she breathed in the scent of spicy aftershave. The music was pleasant, easy and undemanding. Romantic.

As soon as she realized what she was doing, allowing herself to be drawn into the magic of the moment, she pulled away and concentrated on the music. Cody didn't attempt anything beyond a mere shuffling of his feet, which suited Sherry just fine.

She quickly saw her mistake. With her head back, their eyes inevitably met, and neither seemed inclined to look away. They continued to stare at each other, attempting to gauge everything that remained unspoken between them. The longer they gazed at each other the more awkward it became. Seconds ripened into minutes....

Sherry was the first to look away. Cody's hand eased her head toward his, and she sighed as her temple again unerringly came to rest against his jaw. Her eyes had just drifted shut when, out of the blue, she remembered where she'd met Jack Burnside.

"College," she said abruptly, freeing herself from Cody's embrace. She glanced about the restaurant until she spotted Jack. "I do know him," she said. "We met in Seattle years ago." Taking Cody by the hand, she led him off the dance floor to a table at the far side of the restaurant, where Jack was eating alone. He stood at their approach.

"Jack," she said, slightly breathless, "you're right, we do know each other. I'm Sherry Waterman. Your sister and I were roommates in our junior year at college. You were in Seattle on business and took us both to dinner. That must've been about twelve years ago."

Jack's face broke into a wide grin. "Of course. You're Angela's friend. I was sure we'd met."

"Me, too, but I couldn't remember where."

"So, how are you?"

"Fine," Sherry replied. "I'm living in Texas now."

"As a matter of fact, so am I. Small world, isn't it?" He looked fleetingly at Cody.

"Very small," Sherry agreed.

Jack seemed especially pleased to have made the connection. "I never forget a face, especially one as pretty as yours."

Sherry blushed at the compliment. "This is Cody Bailman."

The two men exchanged brisk handshakes. "Please join me," Jack invited, gesturing toward the empty chairs at his table.

"Thanks, but no," Cody said. "My daughter's with us and she's rather shy. She'd be uncomfortable around a stranger, I'm afraid." Cody refused to meet Sherry's baffled glance. Heather *shy?*

The three of them spoke for a few more minutes, and then Sherry and Cody returned to their table and an impatient Heather.

Sherry knew that the reason she'd dragged Cody off the dance floor was more than the opportunity to prove she was right about Jack. It was a way of breaking the romantic spell they'd found themselves under. Cody had made her feel vulnerable, and she'd seized the opportunity to show him she wasn't.

"Who were you talking to?" Heather asked, craning her neck. "I didn't think you two were *ever* going to come back."

"The man who approached me earlier," Sherry said. "I remembered who he was, so we went over to speak to him. His sister and I are friends, although Jack and I only met once."

"Apparently your time with him was memorable," Cody drawled. Sherry caught the hint of sarcasm in his voice and was amused.

He paid the bill, and the three of them began to leave the dining room. Cody glanced in Jack's direction, then back at Sherry, and said stiffly, "You're welcome to stay and visit with your friend, if you like."

"I've visited enough, thanks," she said, following him and Heather to the elevators.

They weren't back in the suite thirty seconds before Heather changed out of her dress and into her pajamas and new fuzzy slippers. The girl sank down in front of the television set, studying the pay-per-view movie guide. She checked out her selection with Cody, who gave his approval.

Sherry changed out of her dress and into a comfortable pair of jeans and a cotton T-shirt, then wandered back into the living room to sit on the sofa with Heather. Her mind wasn't on the movie the girl had chosen; it was on Cody and what had happened while they were dancing.

When they'd left Pepper, the emotional distance between them had felt both wide and deep. Now she wasn't sure what to think. He was sitting at the table, with his briefcase open in front of him. He reached for the phone and ordered a pot of coffee from room service.

What made things so difficult was how strongly she was attracted to him. She realized there was little chance for a truly loving relationship between them and that saddened her. His life was ranching. He needed a woman to appease Heather—though certainly there'd be benefits. Cody would be generous with her in every way except the one that mattered. With himself.

Sherry wanted a man who cherished her, a man who was willing to do whatever he could to win her heart, even if it *was* the busiest time of the year. She wanted a husband who'd withhold none of himself from her. And Cody couldn't offer that.

"Something troubling you?" he asked, looking up from his paperwork.

The question snapped her out of her reverie. "No," she said. "What makes you ask?"

"You look like you're about to cry."

Strangely that was exactly how she felt. She managed a chuckle. "Don't be silly."

Heather fell asleep halfway through the movie. When Cody noticed that his daughter had curled up on the sofa and nestled her head in Sherry's lap, he stood, turned off the TV after a nod from Sherry, and gently lifted the girl into his arms. Heather stirred and opened her eyes as if she wanted to scold him for treating her like a little girl, but she obviously thought better of it and let him carry her to bed.

Sherry pulled back the covers, and Cody placed his daughter, who seemed to have fallen right back to sleep, on the bed. Sherry tucked her in, dropping a kiss on Heather's forehead. Silently they moved from the room, then paused as if they were suddenly aware that they were now alone.

Luckily Sherry had remembered to bring a book with her and decided to sit on the couch and bury herself in it. Although Cody sat at the table, busy with his own affairs, Sherry had never been more conscious of him. Agreeing to the suite had been a mistake. She should've insisted on two rooms—on different floors.

"Would you like some coffee?" Cody's question cut into the silence.

"No, thanks." If it wasn't so early, she'd make her excuses and go to bed too, but it would look ridiculous to turn in at nine-thirty.

Unexpectedly Cody released a beleaguered sigh. "All right," he said. "Shall we air this once and for all and be done with it?"

"Air what?" she asked, innocently.

"What's happening between us."

"I wasn't aware that anything was…now."

He closed his briefcase with a deliberate lack of haste, then stood and walked over to the sofa. He sat down on the opposite end, as far from her as he could get and still be on the same piece of furniture. "I've had more than a week to give your rejection of my proposal consideration."

Sherry spoke softly. "I shouldn't have said what I did."

He tilted his head and a hopeful expression appeared on his face. "You mean you've changed your mind and decided to marry me?"

"No." She didn't like to be so blunt, but it seemed

the only way to reach Cody. "I regret saying I'd rather eat fried rattlesnake."

"Oh." His shoulders slumped. "I should've known it wouldn't be that easy." He grabbed a pen and pad. "I'd like to know exactly what you find so objectionable about me."

"Nothing. You're honest, hardworking, trustworthy. My grandmother, if she were alive, would call you a salt-of-the-earth kind of guy, and I'd agree with her. It would be very easy to fall in love with you, Cody. Sometimes I think I already have, and that terrifies me."

"Why?" He sounded sincere.

"Because you don't love me."

His face fell. "I *like* you. I'm attracted to you. That's a lot more than many other couples start out with."

"Love frightens you, doesn't it? You lost Heather's mother, and you've guarded your heart ever since."

"Don't be ridiculous." He stood and walked to the window, shoving his hands in his pants pockets and staring out at the night. His back was to her, but that didn't prevent Sherry from hearing the pain in his voice. "Karen died ten years ago. I hardly even remember what she looked like anymore." He turned to look at her. "That's the problem with you women. You read a few magazine articles and romance novels and then think you're experts on relationships."

"You loved her, didn't you?"

"Of course I did, and I grieved when she died."

"You didn't remarry," she told him quietly, afraid of agitating him further.

"I didn't have the time, and to be truthful, my life was full enough without letting a woman dominate my time. That's why I want to set the record straight right now. I'm not about to let a wife put a collar around my neck and lead me around like a puppy."

"Karen did that?"

"No." He scowled fiercely. "But I've seen it happen to plenty of other men, including Luke."

"Ellie doesn't seem the type to do something like that."

Cody frowned. "I know—Luke put the collar around his own neck." He returned to the table, wrote on the pad and glanced at her. "I was thinking you and I might reach some sort of compromise."

"Is that possible?"

"I don't know," he answered. "But it might be if we try."

"Before we go any further, I want it understood that I have no intention of changing who you are, Cody. That's not what marriage is about."

His look told her he didn't believe her. But Sherry had no intention of arguing with him. He'd believe whatever he wanted.

"This isn't working," Cody said, thrusting his hand through his hair in frustration. "I was hoping to make a list, so I'd know what you want from me."

"For what?"

He dropped the pen he still held on the table. "So we can put an end to this foolishness and get married!"

Their conversation had taken so many twists she was no longer sure exactly what they were discussing.

"You still want to marry me?" she asked.

"Obviously. Otherwise I wouldn't risk making a fool of myself twice."

"Why?" she asked, genuinely curious.

"Damned if I know," he snapped. He took a moment to compose himself and come to grips with his temper. "Because I like the way you feel in my arms. And I like kissing you."

"That's all?" she asked.

"No. I also want to marry you because my daughter clearly adores you. On top of that, you're easy on the eyes, you're intelligent and well-read."

"Ah," Sherry said.

Her response seemed to succeed in making him angrier. "There's sparks between us—you can't deny it."

This man had the most uncanny way of insulting her with compliments. But it was impossible for her to be angry and, in fact, she was more amused than offended.

"We've only kissed twice," she reminded him.

"Only twice?" He sounded surprised. "Well, I guess you pack quite a wallop."

Sherry decided to accept that as a definite compliment, and she smiled. He was suddenly standing in front of her, his hands reaching for hers, drawing her up so that she stood before him. "I can't stop thinking about how good you taste," he whispered. His mouth was inches from her own.

Sherry knew that a kiss would muddle her reasoning, but it was already so tangled it shouldn't matter.

He pulled her closer. For one crazy moment all they did was stare at each other. Then Cody spoke. "It's been a long time since I've kissed a woman the way I want to kiss you." His words were low and heavy with need.

"I'm not afraid," Sherry said simply.

"Maybe not, but I sure am." His arms went around

her, folding her against his chest. How right this felt, Sherry thought. How perfectly their bodies fit together....

His voice was ragged and oddly breathless when he said, "You kiss me."

Sherry didn't hesitate, not for an instant. She placed her hands on either side of his head and drew it down toward hers. Their lips met in an uncomplicated kiss. Sweet, gentle, undemanding. Then it changed in intensity. What had seemed so sweet and simple a moment earlier took on a magnitude and power that left her head swimming and her lungs depleted of air.

Cody groaned and his mouth slanted hard over hers.

This wasn't the type of kiss that burned itself out, that made the gradual transformation from passionate to pleasant. This kiss was a long way from being complete before it grew too hot, too heady for either of them to handle.

Sherry wasn't sure who moved first, but they broke apart and stepped back. Space, she needed space, and from the look of him, so did Cody. Sherry's chest was heaving, her heart pounding, and her emotions threatened to fly out of control.

Cody spoke first. "I think," he said raggedly, "that it's a fair assumption to say we're sexually compatible."

Sherry nodded mutely. This brief experiment with the physical aspects of their relationship had proved to be more potent than she'd thought possible. She raised her trembling fingers to her lips.

Suddenly, standing seemed to require a great deal of energy, so Sherry moved back to the sofa and sat, hoping she seemed confident and composed. She felt neither.

Cody joined her as he had earlier—sitting on the far end of the sofa where there wasn't any possibility of accidentally touching her.

He reached over to the nearby table for the same pad and pencil. "Thus far, your main objection to marrying me is…" He hesitated, then reviewed his notes and set aside the pad.

"I want to be sure of something," Sherry said when she was reasonably certain her voice would sound even and steady. "Heather's 4-H project."

Cody's gaze shot to hers.

"Your sudden desire for a wife—does it have anything to do with that?"

His shoulders squared defensively. "Yes and no. To be honest, I hadn't given much consideration to marrying again until this past year, and Heather had a lot to do with that. She's at the age now when she needs a woman's influence. She realized it herself, I think, before I did. Otherwise she wouldn't have come up with that crazy project idea."

"I see." Sherry found the truth painful, but was glad he hadn't lied.

"That doesn't mean anything, though. I didn't meet you and immediately decide you'd be a perfect mother for Heather. I looked at you and decided you were a perfect wife for *me,* with one exception."

"What's that?"

"You want everything sugar-coated."

"Cody, it's much more than that!"

He shook his head. "I'm not the kind of guy to decorate something with a bunch of fancy words. Nor do I have the time to persuade you I'm decent enough to be your husband. If you haven't figured that out by now, flowers and candy ain't going to do it."

"Don't be so sure," she teased.

"That's what you want, is it?" He was frowning so fiercely, his lips were a tight line.

"I want a man who's willing to make an emotional commitment to me, and that includes time to come to know each other properly. I'm not willing to settle for anything less. If you're serious about marrying me, Cody, then you're going to have to prove to me you're sincere. I won't accept some…some offhand proposal."

"You're looking for *romance,* aren't you?" he asked starkly.

"If you want to call it that," she said. "I need to know I'm important to you, that this attraction isn't just a passing thing."

"I asked you to marry me, didn't I?" He sounded thoroughly disgusted. "Trust me, a man doesn't get any more serious than that."

"Perhaps not," Sherry agreed. "But a woman needs a little more than a proposal that talks about cutting to the chase and being done with it."

"You want me down on one knee with my heart on my sleeve, telling you I couldn't survive without you?"

She raised her eyebrows. "That would be a start." *If you meant it,* she added silently.

"I thought so." Cody stood and marched over to his briefcase. He threw his pen and pad inside, then slammed down the lid. "Well, you can forget it. I'm willing to compromise, but that's as far as it goes. Take it or leave it, the choice is up to you."

Sherry closed her eyes. "I believe we've both made our choices."

Seven

Sherry sat in a booth at the Yellow Rose, sipping coffee and mulling over the events of the weekend in Abilene. Doubt assailed her from all sides. Twice now, she'd rejected Cody's marriage proposal.

The irony of the situation didn't escape her. For years she'd longed for a husband and family. She'd been looking for a change in her life. This was why she'd uprooted herself and moved halfway across the country.

She'd been in Texas for less than a month, and in that time she'd been held captive by a community, helped deliver a beautiful baby boy and received a marriage proposal—twice. This was some kind of state.

Cody. She wished she could think clearly about him. The fact that she'd met a man who attracted her so powerfully came as a shock. That he should feel equally drawn to her was an unexpected bonus.

Donna Jo strolled over to the booth and refilled her coffee. "You're looking a little under the weather," the waitress commented. "How'd your weekend with Cody and Heather go?"

It was no surprise that Donna Jo knew she'd spent the weekend with the Bailmans. "We had a lot of fun."

Donna Jo set the glass pot on the table. She shifted her weight, as if what she had to say was of momentous importance. "Take my word for it, honey, that man's sweet on you."

Sherry's only response was a weak smile. "I heard about Heather's 4-H project. That's what you and Mrs. Colson wanted me to find out on my own, wasn't it?"

Donna Jo did a poor job of hiding her amusement. "I wondered how long it'd take you to learn about that. Cody's kid's got a good head on her shoulders. Heather figured that suggesting *she* find him a wife would get her father's attention and by golly she was right." Donna Jo laughed at the memory. "Cody was stunned. He's lived so long without a woman that I don't think re-marrying even entered his mind. You're sweet on him, too, aren't you?"

"He's a good man." Sherry tried to sound noncommittal.

"Cody's one of the best. He can be cantankerous, but then he wouldn't be a man if he wasn't. Now, I don't have any dog in this fight, but—"

Sherry stopped her. "You don't have a dog? They fight dogs in Texas?" she asked in horror.

"Of course not! It's an old Texan saying, meaning I don't have a stake in what happens between you and Cody. I've been married a whole lot of years myself, and personally I'd like to see Cody find himself a decent wife." Her smile widened. "Folks in the Yellow Rose been talking about you two, and everyone says Cody should marry you. Are we gonna have a fall wedding?"

"Uh…"

"Leave Doc's helper alone," the sheriff called out from his perch at the counter, "and bring that coffee over here."

"Hold your horses, Billy Bob. This is the kind of information folks come into the Yellow Rose for. Trust me, it isn't the liver-and-onion special they're after. It's gossip. And everyone wants to know what's happening with Cody and Sherry."

Every single person in the café seemed to be staring at Sherry, waiting for a response.

"I hear you and Heather traveled with him to Abilene," the sheriff said, twisting around to face her. "That sounds promising. Right promising."

"Sure does," someone else agreed.

"Here's how I see it," a second man intoned. Sherry hadn't formally met him, but she knew he was the local minister. "A man wasn't meant to be alone. A woman neither. Now, I know there're plenty of folks who'd argue with me, but it seems if you're both wanting the same thing, then you should get on with it."

With everyone looking at her so expectantly, Sherry felt obligated to say something, anything. "I… Thanks for the advice. I'll take it into consideration." She couldn't get out of the café fast enough. Everyone appeared to have either a question or some tidbit of wisdom.

By the time Sherry reached the clinic, she regretted opening her mouth. She had no idea so many people would be interested in her relationship with Cody.

Mrs. Colson looked up from her desk when Sherry came through the front door. "Good morning," the receptionist greeted her cheerfully, her eyes full of curiosity.

"Morning," Sherry said, hurrying past. Her eagerness to escape didn't go unnoticed.

"How was your weekend with Cody and Heather?" Mrs. Colson called after her.

"Great." Sherry got her jacket from behind the exam-room door and was buttoning it up when the receptionist let herself in. "I heard that Cody popped the question. I don't even think Donna Jo knows this yet. Is it true?"

Sherry's hands fumbled with the last button and her heart fell straight to her knees. "Who told you that?"

"Oh, you could say I heard it on the grapevine. And not just *any* grapevine."

"You should know by now how unreliable that can be," Sherry said as unemotionally as she could, unwilling to swallow the bait.

Mrs. Colson raised her brows. "Not this time. My source is dependable. I have my ways of learning things."

A "dependable" source? That had to be Janey the housekeeper. Or Heather...

"This town's worse than Orchard Valley," Sherry muttered. "I hardly know Cody Bailman. What makes you think he'd ask a casual acquaintance to marry him, and furthermore, what makes you assume I'd accept?"

"Casual acquaintance, is it?" Mrs. Colson asked. "Seems to me you know him well enough to dance cheek to cheek in some fancy hotel restaurant, don't you?"

"You know about that, too?" Sherry's jaw dropped.

Yes, it had to be Heather. "Is nothing sacred in this town?"

"Morning." Doc Lindsey strolled into the room; seeing Sherry, he paused and grinned broadly. "I hear you're marrying Cody Bailman. He's a damn good man. Congratulations." He patted Sherry's back and sauntered out of the room.

Sherry clenched her fists and looked up at the ceiling while she counted to ten. Apparently the folks in Pepper had nothing better to do than speculate on Cody's love life.

"Cody's waited a long time for the right woman," Mrs. Colson stated matter-of-factly on her way out the door. "I only hope his stubbornness doesn't ruin everything."

"Mrs. Colson," Sherry said, hanging the stethoscope around her neck. "I don't mean to be rude or unfriendly, but I'd rather not discuss my personal affairs with you or Donna Jo or Billy Bob or anyone else."

"The mayor's got a good ear if you change your mind."

Sherry gritted her teeth in her effort not to lose her temper. Something would have to be said, and soon; the situation was getting out of hand.

Sherry saw several patients that morning, the majority of them children having physicals before the start of the school year, which was only a week away. Rather than risk another confrontation with Donna Jo and the lunch crowd at the Yellow Rose, she ordered a chef's salad and had it delivered.

At one, Mrs. Colson ushered her into Doc's office, where a tall, regal-looking older woman in a lovely blue suit was waiting for her. The woman's hair was white, and she wore it in an elegant French roll.

"Hello," Sherry said. The older woman sat, her legs crossed, her designer purse in her lap.

"You must be Sherry. I'm Judith Bailman, Cody's mother. I've come from Dallas to meet you."

Sherry felt an overwhelming urge to sit down, too. "I'm pleased to make your acquaintance, Mrs. Bailman."

"The pleasure is mine. I understand there are several things we need to discuss."

Sherry couldn't seem to make her mouth work. She turned and pointed at the door in a futile effort to explain that she was on duty. Unfortunately, no patients were waiting at the moment.

"Mrs. Colson's arranged for us to have several minutes of privacy, so you don't need to worry we'll be interrupted."

"I...see." Sherry claimed Doc's chair, on the other side of the desk, nearly falling into it. "What can I do for you, Mrs. Bailman?"

"I understand my son's proposed to you?" She eyed Sherry speculatively.

Sherry didn't mean to sound curt, but after everything that had happened that day, she was in no mood to review her private life with anyone. "I believe that's between Cody and me."

"I quite agree. I don't want to be nosy. I hope you'll forgive me. It's just that Cody's been single all these years, so I couldn't help getting excited when Heather mentioned—"

"Heather?" Sherry interrupted. Just as she'd expected. That explained everything.

"Why, yes. My granddaughter phoned me first thing this morning." A smile tempted the edges of her mouth. "She's concerned that her father's going to ruin her best chance at having a mom and being a big sister, and knowing my son, I'm betting she's right."

"Mrs. Bailman—"

"Please, call me Judith."

"Judith," Sherry said, "don't get me wrong, I think the world of Cody and Heather. Your son did ask me to marry him—in a rather offhand way."

The woman's mouth tightened. "That sounds like Cody."

"If you must know, I turned him down. Cody makes marriage seem about as appealing as a flu shot."

Judith laughed. "I can see I'm going to like you, Sherry Waterman."

"Thank you." She wasn't accustomed to having an entire town and now the man's mother involved in one of her relationships. At least when she lived in Orchard Valley, her life was mostly her own. The minute she'd been hired to work in Pepper, her personal business was up for grabs.

"I hope you'll forgive me for being so blunt, but are you in love with Cody?"

Sherry meant to explain that she was attracted to Judith's son, then add how much she respected and liked him, but instead, she found herself nodding.

The full impact of the truth took her by storm. She closed her eyes and waited several seconds for the torrent of emotion to pass.

Judith smiled and sighed with apparent relief. "I guessed as much. I tried speaking to him about you, but he refused. Truth be known, I would've been surprised if he *had* listened," she murmured. "That boy's more stubborn than a mule."

The description was apt, and Sherry smiled.

"If he knew I was here, he'd never forgive me, so I'm going to have to ask for your discretion."

"Of course." Sherry glanced worriedly at the door.

"You needn't worry that Martha Colson will say anything. We've been friends for years." She looked past Sherry and out the window. "Be patient with him, Sherry. He's closed himself off from love, and I know he's fighting his feelings for you with the full strength of his will. Which, I might add, is formidable."

That much Sherry knew.

"Cody deserves your love," Judith went on. "Sure he has his faults, but believe me, the woman my son loves will be happy. When he falls in love again, it'll be with his whole heart and soul. It may take some time, but I promise you the wait will be worth it."

Sherry wasn't sure how to respond. "I'll... I'll remember that," she promised.

"Now—" Judith gave a deep sigh and stood "—I should be on my way. Remember, not a word to either my son or my granddaughter."

"I promise."

Judith hugged her and said again, "Be patient with Cody."

"I'll try," Sherry whispered.

Cody's mother left by the back door. When Mrs.

Colson returned, her sparkling eyes met Sherry's and she said, "This visit will be our little secret, won't it?"

"What visit?" she replied.

Friday evening, Sherry sat out on the porch in front of the clinic enjoying the coolness. She rocked peacefully on the swing and listened to the night sounds. Crickets telegraphed greetings to one another, and music from the local tavern drifted toward her.

Evenings were her favorite time. Sherry loved to sit outside and think about her day. Her life was falling into a pattern now as she adjusted to the people of Pepper. Often she read or called family and friends or sent e-mails using her laptop computer. Norah's birthday was coming up soon, and Sherry had spent the earlier part of the evening writing her a long, chatty message.

Her heart seemed to skip a beat when Cody's pickup drew to a stop by the clinic. She got up and walked over to the steps, leaning against the support beam as he climbed out of the cab and came toward her.

"Hi, Sherry," he said, his expression a bit sheepish.

"Hi, Cody."

He looked at her for several seconds as if trying to remember the purpose of his visit. Sherry decided to make it easier for him. "Would you care to sit with me?" She motioned toward the swing.

"Don't mind if I do." He'd recently shaved and the familiar scent of his aftershave floated past her as he moved to the swing.

They sat side by side, swaying gently. Neither seemed ready to talk.

"I was on my way over to a friend's place to play poker," he said at last, "when I saw you sitting here."

"I do most evenings. Nights are so beautiful here. I love stargazing. It's one of the reasons I'd never be happy in a big city. Sometimes the sky's so full I can't stop looking."

"Have you had a good week?" he asked.

"A busy one. What about you?"

"The same." His eyes met hers. "Any problems?"

"Such as?"

He shrugged and looked past her to the street. "I thought there might've been some talk about, you know, us."

"There was definitely some heavy speculation after our trip last weekend."

"Anyone pestering you?"

"Not really. What about you?"

He laughed lightly. "You mean other than Heather and Janey?"

The bench squeaked in the quiet that followed.

"I've been thinking about what you said," he finally muttered. "About romance."

"Oh?"

"To my way of thinking, it's not neooooooory."

Sherry frowned. "So you've said." Countless times, but reminding him of that would have sounded petty and argumentative. The moment was peaceful, and she didn't want to ruin it.

"Tell me what you want and I'll do it," he said decisively.

"You want a *list?*"

"That'd help. I'm no good at this sort of thing, and I'm going to need a few instructions."

Sherry turned to look at him. She pressed her hand to his cheek. "That's really very sweet, Cody. I'm touched."

"If that's the only way I can convince you to marry me, then what the heck, I'll do it. Just tell me what you want, so I don't waste a lot of time."

"I… I hate to disappoint you, but giving you instructions would defeat the purpose. It has to come from your heart, Cody." She moved her hand to his chest and held it there. "Otherwise it wouldn't be sincere."

A frown quickly snapped into place. "You want me to do a few mushy things to prove I'm sincere, but you aren't willing to tell me what they are?"

"You make it sound silly."

"As far as I'm concerned, it is. Asking you to marry me is as sincere as I can get. And if that isn't good enough—"

Their peace was about to be destroyed, and Sherry was unwilling to let it happen. So she acted impulsively and stopped him the only way she knew would work.

She kissed him.

The instant her mouth covered his, she felt his anger melt away. His kiss was both tender and fierce. His breath was warm, his lips hot and eager, and the kiss left her trembling.

Then he began kissing her neck, from her chin to her shoulder. As always happened when he touched her, Sherry felt like Dorothy caught up in the tornado, spinning out of control before landing in a magical land. When he raised his head from hers, she immediately missed him. Missed his warmth, his passion, his closeness.

Cody started to say something, then changed his mind. He raised his finger to her face and brushed it down her cheek. "I have to go."

She wanted him to stay, but wouldn't ask it of him.

"The guys are waiting for me. They're counting on me."

"It's all right, Cody."

He stood and thrust his hands in his jeans pockets, as if to stop himself from reaching for her again. That thought helped lighten the melancholy she experienced at his leaving.

"It was good to see you again," he said stiffly.

"Good to see you, too," she returned just as stiffly.

He hesitated on the top step and turned back to face her. "Uh, you're sure you don't want to give me a few tips on, uh, romance?"

"I'm confident you aren't going to need them. Follow your heart, Cody, and I promise you it'll lead directly to mine."

He smiled, and Sherry swore she'd never seen anything sexier.

She didn't hear from Cody all day Saturday, which was disappointing. She'd hoped he'd taken her words to heart and understood what she'd been trying to say.

Yes, she wanted to be courted the way women had been courted for centuries. But she also wanted to be *loved.* Cody was more afraid of love than he was of marriage.

Late that night when she was in bed reading, she

heard something or someone outside her bedroom window. At first she didn't know what to make of it. The noise was awful, loud and discordant. Several minutes passed before she realized it was someone playing a guitar, or rather, attempting to play a guitar.

She pulled open the blinds and looked out to see Cody standing on the lawn, crooning for all he was worth. Whatever he was singing—or thought he was singing—was completely unrecognizable to her.

"Cody!" she shouted, jerking up the window and poking her head out. "What on earth are you doing?"

He started to sing louder. Sherry winced. His singing was worse than his guitar-playing. Holding up the window with one hand, she covered her ear with the other.

"Cody!" she shouted again.

"You wanted romance," he called back and then repeatedly strummed the guitar in a burst of energy. "This comes straight from the heart, just like you wanted."

"Have you been drinking?"

He laughed and threw back his head, running his fingers over the guitar strings with hurried, unpracticed movements. "You don't honestly think I'd try this sober, do you?"

"Cody!"

The sound of a police siren in the background startled Sherry. It was the first time she'd heard one in Pepper. Apparently there was some kind of trouble, but Sherry didn't have time to think about that now, not with Cody serenading her, sounding like a sick bull.

"Cody!"

"What's the matter?" he shouted. "You said you wanted romance. Well, this is it. The best I can do."

"Give me a minute to get dressed and I'll be right out." She started to lower the window, then poked her head out again. "Don't go away, and quit playing that guitar!"

"Anything you want," he said, strumming even more wildly and discordantly than before.

Lowering the window didn't help. Cody knew as much about guitar-playing as she did about mustering cattle. Pulling on jeans and a light sweater, she slipped her feet into tennis shoes and hurried out the door. Fortunately the siren, too, had stopped.

As she came out onto the porch, she was gratified to realize he'd stopped playing. It wasn't until she'd reached the bottom step that she noticed the police car parked in front of the clinic.

Hurrying around to the side of the building, she encountered Cody and a sheriff's deputy, whose flashlight was zeroed in on her romantic idiot.

"Is there a problem here?" Sherry asked. She hadn't met this particular deputy, but the name tag above his shirt pocket read Steven Bean.

"No problem, isn't that right, Mr. Bailman?"

"None whatsoever," Cody said, looking almost sober. If it wasn't for the cocky smile he wore, it would've been impossible to tell he'd been drinking. "I only had a couple shots of whiskey," he explained. "I had to, or I'd never have had the guts to pull this off."

"Are you arresting Mr. Bailman?" Sherry asked.

"We've had three calls in the last five minutes," Deputy Bean said. "The first call said there was a wounded animal in town. The second caller thought there was a fight of some kind going on. And the third one came from Mayor Bowie. He said we had the authority to do whatever was necessary to put an end to that infernal racket. Those were his precise words."

"I may not be another Willie Nelson, but my singing isn't that bad," Cody protested.

"Trust me, Bailman, it's bad."

Cody turned to Sherry for vindication. Even though he was serenading her in the name of romance, even though he was suffering this embarrassment on her behalf, she couldn't bring herself to lie.

"I think it'd be better if you didn't sing again for a while," she suggested tactfully.

He sent her an injured look, then turned to the deputy. "Are you gonna take me to jail?" he demanded.

"I could, you know," Deputy Bean told him.

"On what grounds?" Sherry challenged.

"Disturbing the peace, for starters."

"I didn't know it was unlawful to play the guitar," Cody said, sounding aggrieved.

"It is the way you do it," Deputy Bean muttered.

"He won't be doing it again," Sherry promised, looking at Cody. "Right?"

"Right." Cody held up his hand.

The deputy sighed and lowered his flashlight. "In that case, why don't we just drop this? I'll let you off with a warning."

"Thank you," Sherry said.

The deputy began to leave, but Cody stopped him. "Will there be a report of this in the paper on Wednesday?"

The officer shrugged. "I suppose. The *Weekly* reports all police calls."

"I'd appreciate it if you could see that this one doesn't make the paper."

"I can't do that, Mr. Bailman."

"Why not?"

"I'm not the one who turns the calls over to Mr. Douglas. He comes in every morning and collects them himself."

"Then make sure he doesn't have anything to collect," Cody said.

The deputy shrugged again. "I'll do my best, but I'm not making any promises. We got three calls, you know."

Cody waited until the patrol car had disappeared into the night before he removed his Stetson and slammed it against his leg. He frowned at his mangled hat and tried to bend it back into shape.

"I've ruined the best hat I've ever had because of you," he grumbled.

"Me?"

"You heard me."

"Are you blaming me for this…this fiasco?"

"No!" he shouted back. "I'm blaming Luke. He was the one who said I should serenade you. He claimed it didn't matter that I couldn't play the guitar or sing. He said women go crazy for this kind of stuff. I should've known." He indignantly brushed off the Stetson before setting it back on his head, adjusting the angle.

"It was very sweet, Cody, and I do appreciate it."

"Sure you do. Women get a real kick out of seeing a grown man make a jackass out of himself in front of the whole town."

"That's not fair!"

"You know what?" Cody barked, waving his arms, "I was liked and respected in this town before you came along making unreasonable demands. All I want is a wife."

"*You're* being unreasonable."

Cody shook his head. "The way I see it, you're waiting for some prince to come along and sweep you away on his big white horse. Well, sweetheart, it isn't going to be me."

For a moment, Sherry was too shocked to respond. "I didn't ask you to serenade me. Or to sweep me away on your horse."

"Oh, no," he said, walking toward the gate. "That would've been too easy. On top of everything else, I'm supposed to be psychic or something. You won't tell me what you want. It's up to me to read your mind."

"That's not fair," she repeated.

"You said it, not me."

"Cody—" She stopped herself, not wanting to argue with him. "You're right. I'm out of line expecting a man who wants to marry me to love me too."

Cody apparently didn't hear her, or if he did, he chose to ignore her *and* her sarcasm. "Luke. That's where I made my mistake," he said. "I assumed my best friend would know all the answers, because for all his bumbling ways, he managed to marry Ellie."

"You're absolutely right," Sherry said, marching up the steps. "You could learn a lesson or two from your friend. At least he was in love with the woman he wanted to marry and wasn't just looking for someone to warm his bed and keep his daughter happy."

Cody whirled around and shook his finger at her. "You know what I think?"

"I don't know and I don't really care."

"I'm going to tell you, anyway, so listen."

She crossed her arms and heaved an exasperated sigh.

"Cancel the whole thing!" Cody shouted. "Forget I asked you to marry me!"

"Cody!" someone hollered in the distance. Sherry looked up in time to see a head protruding from the upstairs window of the house across the street. "Either you shut up or I'm calling the sheriff again."

"Don't worry," Cody hollered back. "I'm leaving."

Eight

"Is it true?" Heather asked the following morning as Sherry walked out of church. "Did you nearly get my dad arrested?"

Sherry closed her eyes wearily. "Did Cody tell you that?"

"No." Heather's eyes were huge and round. "I heard Mrs. Morgan telling Mrs. James about it. They said Dad was standing under your bedroom window singing and playing the guitar. I didn't even know Dad could play the guitar."

"He can't. I think you should ask your father about what happened last night," Sherry told her, unwilling to comment further. She couldn't. Cody would find some way of blaming her, regardless of what she said.

"He didn't come to church this morning. He had Slim drive me to town because he said his head hurt."

Served him right, thought Sherry.

"School starts the day after tomorrow," Heather announced. "Do you want to know what I'm going to wear for the first day? My new jeans, that black T-shirt and my new shoes."

"Sounds perfect," Sherry said.

"I've got to go." Heather glanced across the parking lot. "Slim's waiting for me in the pickup. When are you going to come to the house again? I was kind of hoping you would last week. I was thinking of having my hair cut and I found this really cool style in my friend Carrie's magazine. I wanted to show it to you."

"Ask your father if you can stay after school one afternoon this week, and I'll drive you home," Sherry suggested. "But tell him—" she hesitated "—I won't be able to stay. Make sure he knows that. I'll just drop you off."

"Okay," Heather said, walking backward. "That'd be great. Do you mind if Carrie comes along? She wants to meet you, too, and her place isn't that far from mine."

"Sure."

"Thanks." Heather's smile lit up her whole face. "I'll call and let you know which day is good."

Sherry waved and the girl turned and raced over to the pickup. Sighing, Sherry started toward her own car. She hadn't gone more than a few steps when she heard Ellie Johnson call her.

"Sherry," Ellie said, walking in her direction. "Have you got a minute?"

"Sure."

"I've been meaning to call you all week, but with the baby and everything, it slipped my mind. I know it's short notice, but I'd love for you to come to the house for dinner. I've got a roast in the slow cooker. Drop by in a little while and we can visit for a few hours. Luke's so busy these days I'm starved for companionship."

"I'd love to."

"That's wonderful." Ellie seemed genuinely pleased. "You won't have any problems finding your way, will you?"

Sherry told her she wouldn't. As it happened, she was eager for a bit of female companionship, too. With Ellie, Sherry could be herself. She didn't worry that she'd have to endure an inquisition or make explanations about Cody and her.

When Sherry arrived at the ranch an hour or so later, Ellie came out onto the porch to greet her. One-year-old Christina Lynn was thrilled to have company, and she tottered excitedly over to Sherry, who scooped her up and carried her into the kitchen.

After giving Ellie's daughter the proper attention, Sherry asked about Philip. "He's sleeping," she was assured. "I fed him and put him down. Christina Lynn's due for her nap, too, but I promised she could visit with you first." Sherry sat down at the kitchen table, and the toddler climbed into her lap and investigated, with small probing fingers, the jeweled pin she wore.

It had been several weeks since Sherry had spent time with Norah and her kids, and she missed being with young children. Christina Lynn seemed equally infatuated with her.

While Sherry devoted herself to the world of a small child, Ellie poured them glasses of iced tea, which she brought to the kitchen table.

"I suppose you heard what happened?" Sherry asked, needing to discuss the events of the night before. After all, there was sure to be some sort of backlash, since Cody seemed to blame Luke as much as he did her.

"There were rumors at church this morning. Is it true Cody was almost arrested?"

"Yes. For disturbing the peace."

A smile quivered at the edges of Ellie's mouth. "I'm afraid Cody Bailman has a few lessons to learn about women."

"I would've thought his wife, Karen, had taught him all this."

"I never knew her, of course," Ellie said, reaching for her glass, "but apparently Luke did. I've asked him about her."

"What did he tell you?" Sherry was more than curious. She sensed that the key to understanding Cody was rooted in his marriage, however brief.

"From what I remember, Cody met Karen while they were in college. He was away from home for the first time and feeling lonely. Luke was surprised when he married her—at least that's what he told me. She was something of a tomboy, even at twenty. In many ways I suspect she was the perfect rancher's wife. She loved riding and working with cattle. What I heard is there wasn't anything she couldn't do." Ellie hesitated and looked away as if carefully judging her words. "Luke also said Karen wasn't very interested in being a wife or mother. She resented having to stay home with the baby." She took a deep breath.

"Luke also told me they had some huge fights about it. Karen died in a car accident after one of them. She'd threatened to leave Cody and Heather, but Luke doubts that she meant it. She mentioned divorce on a regular basis, dramatically packing her bags and lugging them out to the car. No one'll ever know if she meant it that particular time or not because she took a curve too fast and ran off the road. She died instantly."

"How sad."

"I know Cody loved Karen," Ellie continued. "I admire him for picking up the pieces of his life and moving forward."

"I do, too. I didn't realize his marriage had been so traumatic."

"It wasn't always unhappy. Don't misunderstand me. Cody cared deeply for his wife, but I don't think he was ever truly comfortable with her, if you know what I mean."

Sherry wasn't sure she did, but she let it pass.

"He's at a loss when it comes to showing a woman how he feels. The only woman he ever loved was so involved in herself that she didn't have much love left for anyone else, including him or Heather."

"He's afraid," Sherry whispered. But it wasn't for any of the reasons she'd assumed. After learning he was a widower, Sherry believed he'd buried himself in his grief. Now she understood differently. Cody feared that if he loved someone again, that love would come back to him empty and shallow.

"Be patient with him," Ellie advised.

Sherry smiled. "It's funny you should say that. A few days ago someone else said the same thing."

"Cody's so much like Luke. I'd like to shake the pair of them. Luke wasn't any different when we first met. He seemed to assume that if he loved me he'd lose part of himself. He put on this rough-and-tough exterior and was so unreasonable that…suffice it to say we had our ups and downs, as well."

"What was the turning point for you and Luke?"

Ellie leaned back in her chair, her expression thoughtful. "My first inclination is to say everything changed when I decided to leave Pepper. That's when Luke raced after my car on his horse and proposed. But it really happened about a week before that." She sighed and sipped her tea. "To hear Luke tell it, we fell in love the moment we set eyes on each other. Trust me, it wasn't like that. For most of the summer we argued. He seemed to think I was his exclusive property, which infuriated me."

"What happened?"

"Oh, there wasn't any big climactic scene when we both realized we were destined for each other. In fact, it was something small that convinced me of his love for me—and eventually mine for him.

"Luke had taken me horseback riding, and I'd dared him to do something stupid. I can't even remember what it was now, but he refused, rightly so. It made me mad and I took off at a gallop. I'm not much of a horsewoman and I hadn't gone more than a few feet before I was thrown. Luckily I wasn't hurt, but my pride had taken a beating and Luke made the mistake of laughing at me.

"I was so furious I left, figuring I'd rather walk back to the ranch than ride. Naturally, it started to rain— heavily—and I was drenched in seconds. Luke, too. I was so angry with him and myself that I wouldn't speak to him. Finally Luke got down off his horse and walked behind me, leading the two mares. He wouldn't leave me, although heaven knew I deserved it. I thought about that incident for a long time afterward, and I realized this was the kind of man I wanted to spend the rest of my life with."

"But you decided to leave Pepper shortly after that."

"Yes," Ellie admitted cheerfully. "It was the only way. He seemed to think marriage was something we could discuss in three or four years."

"It's something Cody wants to discuss every three or four minutes."

Ellie laughed. "Do you love him?"

"Yes," Sherry said in a soft voice. "But that's not the problem."

"Cody's the problem. I know what you mean."

"He wants me to marry him, but he doesn't want to get emotionally involved with me. He makes the whole thing sound like a business proposition, and I'm looking for much more than a…an arrangement."

"You frighten him."

"Good, because he frightens me, too. We met that first day I arrived in town, and my life hasn't been the same since."

Ellie patted Sherry's hand. "Tell me, what's all this about you insisting on romance? I overheard Cody talking to Luke yesterday afternoon. I wish I could've recorded the conversation, because it was quite funny. Luke was advising Cody on a variety of ways to—" she made quotation marks with her fingers "—win your heart."

Sherry rolled her eyes. "That's the thing. Cody already has my heart. He just doesn't know what to do with it."

"Give him time," Ellie said. "Cody's smarter than he looks."

A little later, Sherry helped her friend with the dinner preparations. Christina Lynn awoke from her nap and gleefully "helped" Sherry arrange the silverware around the table. A few minutes before five, Luke returned home, looking hot and dusty. He kissed his wife and daughter, showered and joined them for dinner.

They sat around the big kitchen table and after the blessing, Luke handed Sherry the bowl of mashed potatoes. He said, "So Cody came to see you last night." He cast a triumphant smile at his wife. His cocky grin implied that if Sherry and Cody were married anytime soon, he'd take the credit.

"Honey," Ellie said brightly, "Cody was nearly arrested for disturbing the peace. And from what Sherry told me, he blames you."

"*Me?* I wasn't the one out there making a first-class fool of myself."

"True, but you were the one who suggested he do it."

"That shouldn't make any difference." Luke ladled gravy over his meat and potatoes before reaching for the green beans. "As long as Sherry thought it was romantic, it shouldn't matter." He glanced at Sherry and nodded as if to accept her gratitude.

"Well, yes, it was, uh—"

"Romantic," Luke supplied, looking hopeful.

"It was…romantic, yes. Sort of."

"It was ridiculous," Ellie inserted.

"A man's willing to do ridiculous things for a woman if that's what she wants."

"I don't, and I never said I did," Sherry was quick

to inform him. "It bothers me that Cody would think I wanted him to do anything so…"

"Asinine," Ellie said.

"Exactly."

Luke was grinning from ear to ear. "Isn't love grand?"

"No, it isn't," a male voice boomed from the doorway. Cody stood on the other side of the screen. He swung it open and stepped inside, eyeing Luke as if he was a traitor who ought to be dragged before a firing squad.

"Cody!" Ellie greeted him warmly. "Join us for dinner?"

"No, thanks, I just ate. I came over to have a little talk with Luke. I didn't realize you had company."

"If it makes you uncomfortable, I'll leave," Sherry offered.

"Don't," Ellie whispered.

Cody's gaze swung to Sherry and it seemed to bore into her very soul. He was angry; she could feel it.

"Come in and have a coffee at least," Ellie said, picking up the pot and pouring him a cup. Cody moved farther into the kitchen and sat down at the table grudgingly.

"I suppose you heard?" Cody's question was directed at Luke and filled with censure. "The next time I need advice about romance—or anything else—you're the last person I'm gonna see."

Sherry did her best to concentrate on her meal and ignore both men.

"I assumed because you got Ellie to marry you,"

Cody went on, "you'd know the secret of keeping a woman happy."

"He does!"

Three pairs of eyes moved to Ellie. "He loves me."

"Love." Cody spat the word as if the very sound of it was distasteful.

"That could be why a smart woman like Sherry is hesitant to marry you," Ellie said.

"I don't suppose she mentioned the fact that I've withdrawn my offer. I've decided the whole idea of marriage is a mistake. I don't need a woman to make a fool out of me."

"Not when you do such a good job of it yourself," Ellie said dryly.

Sherry's grip on her fork tightened at the flash of pain that went through her. It hurt her to think she'd come this close to love only to lose it.

"Anyway," Ellie said, "I'm sorry to hear you've changed your mind, Cody." Then she grinned. "I've got apple pan dowdy for dessert. Care for some?"

"Apple pan dowdy?" Cody's eyes lit up. "I think I could find room for a small serving."

Sherry wasn't sure how Ellie arranged it, but within a matter of minutes she was alone in the kitchen with Cody. Philip began to cry and Ellie excused herself. Then Luke made some excuse to leave, taking Christina Lynn with him.

"Would you like more coffee?" Sherry asked.

"Please."

She refilled his cup, then replaced the pot. Never had she been more conscious of Cody than at that moment.

"Heather said something about visiting you after

school one day." He was holding his mug with both hands and refusing to look at her.

"If you don't object."

"No, of course not. You're the best thing to happen to that girl in years. I never thought anyone could convince her to wear a dress."

"She just needed a little guidance." Sherry moved around the kitchen, clearing off the table and stacking dirty dishes in the sink. At last she said, "I hope that whatever happens between you and me won't affect my relationship with Heather."

"Don't see why it should. I hope you two will always be friends."

"I hope so, too."

They didn't seem to have much to say after that.

Sherry was the first to venture into conversation again. "I'm sorry about last night."

He shrugged. "I'll get over it—someday." The beginnings of a smile touched his mouth. He stood and carried his mug to the sink. "I need to get back to the ranch. Give Ellie and Luke my regards, will you?"

Sherry nodded, not wanting him to leave but unable to ask him to stay. She walked him to the door. Cody hesitated on the top step, frowning.

"It'd help a whole lot if you weren't so pretty," he muttered before moving rapidly toward his truck.

"Cody," Sherry called after him, hurrying out the door and onto the top step. When he turned back to her, she wrapped her arms around her middle and said, "Now *that* was romantic."

"It was? That's the kind of thing you want me to say?"

"Yes," she said.

"But that was simple."

She smiled. "It came from the heart."

He seemed to stiffen. "The heart," he repeated, placing his hand on his chest. He opened the door of his truck, then looked back at her. "Do you want me to say things like 'God robbed heaven of one of its loveliest angels the day you were born' and stuff like that?"

"That's very sweet, Cody, but it sounds like a line that's been used before."

"It has been," he admitted, his eyes warming with silent laughter. "But I figured it couldn't hurt, especially since it's true."

"Now that was nice."

With an easy grace he climbed into the pickup and closed the door. Propping his elbow against the open window, he looked at her once more, grinning. "Plan on staying for dinner the night you bring Heather home."

"All right, I will. Thanks for the invitation."

Sherry watched him drive away. The dust had settled long before she realized she wasn't alone.

"He's coming around," Ellie commented. "I don't think he knows it himself yet, but he's falling in love with you hook, line and sinker."

That was exactly what Sherry wanted to hear. Hope blossomed within her and she sighed in contentment.

Monday evening, Sherry was sitting on the porch swing again, contemplating the events of the weekend. She'd sent a long e-mail to her parents, telling them all about Cody and their rocky relationship.

When she saw his Cadillac turn the corner and pull

to a stop in front of the clinic, she wasn't sure what to think. Heather leaped out of the passenger side and dashed up the walkway.

"Dad needs you!"

The girl's voice was high and excited, but her smile indicated that there was no real emergency.

"It's nothing," Cody said, walking toward her. He held a box of chocolates in one hand and a bouquet of wildflowers in the other.

"The flowers are for you," Heather explained. "Dad picked them himself."

"If you don't mind, I prefer to do my own talking," Cody growled. "Here," he said, thrusting the flowers and candy at Sherry. Then he jerked up the sleeve of his shirt and started scratching his forearm.

"Both his arms are a real mess," Heather whispered.

"Heather!"

"He's in one of his moods, too."

Sherry was too flabbergasted to respond right away. "Well, thank you for the flowers. And the candy."

"That's romantic, isn't it?" his daughter prompted. "Dad asked me what I thought was romantic, and I said flowers and chocolate-covered cherries. They're my favorite, and I bet you like them, too."

"I do." She returned her gaze to Cody.

"What did you get into? Why are you so itchy?"

"This is why he needs you," Heather said in a loud whisper. A cutting look from Cody silenced her.

"Like she said, I picked the flowers myself."

"It looks like you might've tangled with something else," she said, reaching for his arm and moving him toward the light so she could get a better view. "Oh,

Cody," she whispered when she saw the redness and the swelling.

"Poison ivy," he told her.

"Let me get you some calamine for that."

"He was hoping you would," Heather said. "He's real miserable. But we can't stay long, because I have to get over to Katie Butterfield's house and pick up my math book by eight o'clock."

Sherry led Cody into the clinic and got a bottle of calamine lotion, swabbing the worst of the swelling with that. She gave him an antihistamine for the itch, as well.

Heather sat in the corner of the room, the chocolates in her lap. "Janey says you should give Dad an *A* for effort. I think so, too." This last bit was added between bites of candy.

"Heather, I didn't buy those for you," Cody said irritably.

"I know, but Sherry doesn't mind sharing them, do you?"

"Help yourself."

"She already has," Cody muttered.

Sherry put the lotion away while Cody rolled down his sleeves and snapped them closed at the wrists. "Heather, don't you have something to occupy yourself with outside?"

"No."

"Yes, you do," he said pointedly.

"I do? Oh, I get it, you want to be alone with Sherry. Gee, Dad, why didn't you just say so?"

"I want to be alone with Sherry."

"Great." Heather checked her watch. "Is fifteen minutes enough, or do you need longer? Don't forget I have to be at Katie's by eight."

Cody sighed expressively, and Sherry could tell his patience was in tatters. "Fifteen minutes will be fine. I'll meet you on the porch."

"I can take the chocolates?"

"Heather!"

"All right, all right." She threw him an injured look on her way outside. "I know when I'm not wanted."

"Not soon enough, you don't," her father said.

Now that they were alone, Cody didn't seem to know what he wanted to say. He paced the room restlessly, without speaking.

"Cody?"

"I'm thinking."

"This sounds serious," Sherry said, amused.

"It *is* serious. Sit down." He pulled out a chair, escorted her to it and sat her down, then stood facing her.

"I'm sorry about the poison ivy," Sherry ventured.

He shrugged. "My own fault. I should've noticed it, but my head was in the clouds thinking about you."

"I know it's painful. The poison ivy, I mean."

"It won't be as bad as the razzing I'm going to get when folks learn about this—on top of my behavior Saturday night."

"Oh, Cody," she whispered, feeling genuinely contrite, aware that her insistence that he be "romantic" and demonstrate his feelings had led directly to his actions. He was trying hard to give her what she wanted, yet he didn't seem to understand what that really was. Yes, she wanted the sweet endearing things a man did for a woman he was courting, but more than that, she needed him to trust her, to open up to her.

"Listen, the other day I said I was withdrawing my proposal of marriage, but we both know I wasn't serious."

Sherry hadn't known that at all, but was pleased he was willing to say so.

"I'm not sure what to do anymore, and every time I try to give you what you say you need, it turns into another disaster."

He crouched before her and took both her hands in his. She saw how callused they were, the knuckles chafed, yet to her they were the most beautiful male hands she'd ever seen.

"You wanted romance, and I swear to you, Sherry, I've given it my best shot. If it's romantic to nearly get arrested for a woman, then I should receive some kind of award."

She nodded, trying not to smile.

"I don't blame you for the poison ivy—that was my own fault. I wanted to impress you with the wildflowers. I could've bought you a bouquet of carnations and that fancy grass from the market. Les Gilles sells them for half price after seven, but I figured you'd think those wildflowers were more romantic."

"I do. They're beautiful. Thank you."

"I've done every romantic thing I can think of for you. I don't know what else you want. I've sung to you, I've brought you candy—I know Heather's the one eating it, but I'll buy you another box."

"Don't worry about it."

"I am worried, but not about the chocolates." He

stared at the floor for a moment. "I know you're concerned that Heather was the one who prompted my proposal, her wanting a brother or sister and all. In a way I suppose she did—at first. I'm asking you to marry me again, only this time it's for me."

"Five minutes." Heather's voice trilled from the other side of the clinic door.

Cody closed his eyes, stood and marched over to the door. "Heather, I asked for some time alone with Sherry, remember?"

"I'm just telling you that you've used up ten minutes, and you only have five more. I can't be late, Dad, or Katie will be gone—and so will my book."

"I remember."

"Dad, you've wasted another whole minute lecturing me."

Cody shook his head helplessly and returned to Sherry's side. "Now, where was I?"

"We were discussing your proposal."

"Right." He wiped his face. "I guess what I have to tell you is that I don't know how to be romantic. All I know is how to be me. I'm wondering if that'll ever be good enough for you."

"Stop." She raised both hands. "Go back to what you were saying before Heather interrupted you."

He looked confused.

"You said you were asking me to marry you, not for Heather's sake, but for yours."

"So?"

"So," she said, straightening in her chair, "are you trying to tell me you love me?"

He rubbed his hand along the back of his neck. "I'm

not going to lie to you, Sherry. I don't know if I love you, but I do know there hasn't been a woman in the last decade who makes me feel the things you do. I've swallowed my pride for you, nearly been arrested for you. I'm suffering a bout of poison ivy because all I think about is you."

His words sounded like the lyrics of a love song. Sherry was delighted. But before she could speak, they were interrupted.

"Dad!"

"All right, all right," Cody said impatiently. "I'm coming."

Sherry got to her feet, not wanting him to leave. "I'll be over at the ranch one afternoon this week," she volunteered hastily. "That'll give us both time to think about what we want."

Cody smiled and briefly touched her face. "I'll do what I can to keep Heather out of our hair."

"I heard that!"

Cody chuckled and, leaning forward, kissed Sherry gently on the lips. "Your kisses are sweeter than any chocolate-covered cherries."

"Hey, Dad, that was good," Heather announced on her way through the door. "I didn't help him with that, either," she told Sherry.

Nine

"I hate to impose on you," Ellie said for the third time.

"You're not imposing," Sherry insisted also for the third time. "Christina Lynn and I will get along fine, and Philip won't even know you're gone." As if to confirm her words, Christina Lynn crawled into Sherry's lap and planted a wet kiss on her cheek. "Now go," Sherry said. She stood up, with the toddler tucked against her hip, and escorted Ellie to the door. "Your husband wants to celebrate your anniversary."

"I can't believe he arranged all this without me knowing!"

Luke appeared then, dressed in a dark suit, his hair still damp beneath his hat. His arm went around Ellie's waist. "We haven't been out to dinner in months."

"I know, but..."

"Go and enjoy yourself," Sherry insisted. The more time she spent with Luke and Ellie, the more she grew to like them, individually and as a couple. Luke wasn't as easy to know as his wife, but Sherry was touched by the strength of his love for Ellie and his family. Luke had called her on Tuesday morning to ask if she'd mind staying with the children Wednesday night while he took Ellie out for a surprise dinner to celebrate their third wedding anniversary. Sherry had been honored that he'd want her to look after his kids. He then told her there wasn't anyone he'd trust more.

Later, when she arrived at the ranch and Ellie was putting the finishing touches on her makeup, Luke had proudly shown Sherry the gold necklace he'd purchased for his wife. Sherry suspected her friend would be moved to tears when she saw it and told him so. Luke had beamed with pleasure.

"If Philip wakes up," Ellie said, "there's a bottle in the fridge."

"Ellie," Luke said pointedly, edging her toward the door. "We have a dinner reservation for six."

"But—"

"Go on, Ellie," Sherry urged. "Everything will be fine."

"I know. It's just that I've never left Philip before, and it seems a bit soon to be cutting the apron strings."

Sherry laughed and bounced Christina Lynn on her hip. "We're going to have a nice quiet evening all by ourselves."

"You're sure—"

"Go," Sherry said again. She stood on the porch with Christina Lynn as Luke and Ellie drove off. The little girl waved madly.

For the first half hour, Christina Lynn was content to show Sherry her toys. She dragged them into the living room and proudly demonstrated how each one worked. Sherry oohed and ahhed at all the appropriate moments. When the toddler had finished, Sherry helped her return the toys to the chest that Luke had made for his daughter.

Having grown tired of her game, Christina Lynn lay down on the floor and started to fuss. "Mama!" she demanded as if suddenly realizing that her mother wasn't there.

"Mommy and Daddy have gone out to eat," Sherry explained patiently. Thinking Christina Lynn might be hungry, she heated her dinner and set the little girl in her high chair. But apparently Christina Lynn wasn't hungry, because the meal landed on the floor in record time.

"Mama!" Christina yelled, banging her little fists on the high-chair tray.

"Mommy's out with Daddy, sweetheart."

Christina Lynn's lower lip started to wobble.

"Don't cry, honey," Sherry pleaded but to no avail. Within seconds Christina Lynn was screaming.

Sherry lifted her from the high chair and carried her into the living room. She sat in the rocker trying to soothe her, but Christina Lynn only wept louder.

Inevitably her crying woke Philip. With Christina Lynn clinging to her leg, Sherry took the whimpering infant from his bassinet and changed his diaper. Holding him against her shoulder, she gently patted his back, hoping to urge him back to sleep.

That, however, proved difficult, especially with Christina Lynn still at full throttle. The little girl was wrapped around Sherry's leg and both she and Philip were wailing loudly enough to bring the house down. Sherry was in despair, trying to soothe both children to no avail.

That was how Cody found her.

She didn't hear him come in, so she was surprised to discover him standing in the hallway outside the children's bedroom, grinning hugely.

"Hi," he said. "Luke told me you were sitting with the kids tonight. Looks like you could use a little help."

"Christina Lynn," Sherry said gratefully. "Look—Uncle Cody's here."

Cody moved into the room and dislodged the toddler from Sherry's leg, lifting her into his arms. Christina Lynn hid her face in his shoulder and continued her tearful performance.

"What's wrong with Philip?" Cody asked over the din.

"I think he might be hungry. If you'll keep Christina Lynn occupied, I'll go heat his bottle."

They met in the living room, Sherry carrying the baby and the bottle. Cody was down on the floor, attempting to interest the toddler in a five-piece wood puzzle, but the little girl wanted none of it.

Philip apparently felt the same way about the bottle. "He's used to his mother nursing him," Sherry said. "Besides, I don't think he's all that hungry, after all. If he was, he'd accept the bottle quickly enough."

She returned it to the kitchen and sat down in the chair with Philip, rocking him until his cries abated. Christina Lynn's wails turned to soft sobs as she buried her face in the sofa cushions.

"You've got your hands full."

Sherry gave a weary sigh. "Imagine Ellie handling them both, day in and day out. The woman's a marvel."

"So are you."

"Hardly." Sherry didn't mean to discount his compliment, but she was exhausted, and Luke and Ellie hadn't been gone more than a couple of hours. "I don't know how Ellie does it."

"Or Luke," Cody added. He slumped onto the end of the sofa and lifted an unresisting Christina Lynn into his arms. She cuddled against him, and at last silence reigned.

"Come sit by me," Cody said, stretching his arm along the back of the couch.

Sherry was almost afraid to move for fear Philip would wake up, but her concern was groundless. The infant didn't so much as sigh as she tiptoed over to the couch. As soon as she was comfortable, Cody dropped his arm to her shoulder and pulled her closer. It was wonderful to be sitting with him this way, so warm and intimate.

"Ah, peace," he whispered. "Do I dare kiss you?"

Sherry smiled. "You like to live dangerously, don't you?" She raised her head and Cody's mouth brushed hers. Softly at first, then he deepened the kiss, until she was so involved in what was happening between them she nearly forgot Philip was in her arms.

She broke off the kiss and exhaled on a ragged sigh. "You're one powerful kisser."

"It isn't me, Sherry. It's *us*."

"Whoever or whatever, it's dangerous." She nestled her head against his shoulder. "I don't think we should do that again."

"Oh, I plan to do it again soon."

"Cody," she said, lifting her head so their eyes could meet, "I'm not here to, uh, make out with you."

"Shh." He pressed his finger to her lips.

She pressed her head against his shoulder again. His arm was around her. She enjoyed the feeling of being linked to him, of being close, both physically and emotionally. It was what she'd sought from the beginning, this bonding, this intimacy.

When she felt his breathing quicken, she straightened and read the hunger in his eyes, knowing it was a reflection of her own. Cody lowered his mouth to hers, claiming her with a kiss that left her weak.

She was trembling inside and out. Neither of them spoke as they kissed again and again, each kiss more potent than the last. After many minutes, Sherry pulled back, almost gasping with pleasure and excitement.

"I can't believe we're doing this," she whispered. Each held a sleeping child. They were in their friends' home and could be interrupted at any time.

"I can't believe it, either," Cody agreed. "Damn, but you're beautiful."

They didn't speak for a few minutes, just sat and savored the silence and each other.

"Sherry, listen—" Cody began.

He was interrupted by the shrill ringing of the telephone. Philip's piercing cry joined that of the phone. Christina Lynn woke, too, and after taking one look at Cody and Sherry, burst into tears and cried out for her mom.

Cody got up to answer the phone. He was back on the couch in no time. He cast Sherry a frustrated look. "That was my daughter. She heard I was over here helping you babysit Christina Lynn and Philip, and she's mad that I left her at home."

"I think," Sherry said, patting Philip's back, "she got her revenge."

Cody grinned. "It was selfish of me not to bring her, but I wanted to be alone with you."

"We aren't exactly alone," she said. She looked down at Luke and Ellie's children, who had miraculously calmed again and seemed to be drifting off.

"True, but I was counting on them both being asleep. Luke thought they'd be and—"

"Luke," Sherry broke in, pretending to be offended. "Do you mean to tell me this was all prearranged between you and Luke?"

"Well…"

"Did you?" Sherry could have sworn Cody was blushing.

"This all came about because of you and the fuss you made over wanting romance. Luke got a bit whimsical and thought he'd like to do something special for his anniversary. Then he got worried that Ellie wouldn't go because she wouldn't want to leave the children. It's hard to be romantic with a couple of kids around."

Sherry looked at Christina Lynn and Philip and smiled. "They didn't seem to deter us."

"True, but we're the exception." After a pause he said, "Put your head back on my shoulder." He slid his arm around her. "It feels good to have you this close."

"It feels good to me, too."

He kissed the crown of her head. Sherry closed her eyes, never dreaming she'd fall asleep, but she must have, because the next thing she heard was Luke and Ellie whispering.

She opened her eyes and her gaze met Ellie's. "They were a handful, weren't they?" she asked with a smile.

"Not really," Sherry whispered.

"All four of you are worn to a frazzle. Even Cody's asleep."

"I'm not now," he said, yawning loudly.

Ellie removed Philip from Sherry's arms, and Luke took his daughter from Cody's. They disappeared down the hallway to the children's room, returning soon after.

"How was your dinner?" Sherry asked.

"Fantastic." Ellie's eyes were dreamy. She sat in the rocking chair while Luke went into the kitchen. He reappeared a few minutes later carrying a tray with four mugs of coffee.

"I can't remember an evening I've enjoyed more." Ellie's hand went to her throat and the single strand of gold Luke had given her for their anniversary. "Thank you, Sherry."

"I'll be happy to watch the kids anytime."

"I don't mean for watching the kids—I... I certainly appreciate it, but there's more. Luke told me I should thank you because it was Cody talking to him about love and romance that made him realize he wanted our anniversary to be extra-special this year."

Luke stood behind the rocking chair and leaned forward to kiss his wife's cheek.

"I think it's time we left," Cody suggested, "before this turns into something, uh, private."

"You could be right," Sherry agreed.

With eyes only for each other, Ellie and Luke didn't seem to notice they were leaving until Sherry was out the front door.

"Stick around, you two," Luke protested. "You haven't finished your coffee."

"Another time," Cody answered, leading Sherry down the steps.

"Night," Sherry called to her friends.

"Night, and thanks again," Ellie said, standing in the doorway, her arm around her husband's waist, her head against his shoulder.

Cody escorted Sherry to her car, then hesitated before turning away. "I'll see you soon," he said, frowning.

She was puzzled by the frown. She watched as his gaze swung back to Luke in the doorway and then to her again. Then he sighed and stepped away.

Sherry would have given her first month's wages to know what Cody was thinking.

"Dad was furious with me," Heather said when she stopped in at the clinic the next afternoon. Doc was out doing house calls, like the old-fashioned country doctor he was.

"Hi, Heather," Sherry greeted her. "Why was he mad?"

"He told me I had the worst sense of timing of anyone he's ever known. First the night he brought you the candy and flowers, and then when you were watching Christina Lynn and Philip."

"It's all right," Sherry assured her. "Your father and I'll get everything straightened out sooner or later." But Cody hadn't said anything about marriage lately, and Sherry was beginning to wonder.

"I'm not supposed to butt into Dad's business or

yours, and I don't mean to, but I hope you decide to marry us. I don't even care about the babies so much anymore. I really like you, Sherry, and it'd be so much fun if you were always around."

"I'd enjoy that, too."

"You would?" Sherry instantly brightened. "Can I tell Dad you said that, 'cause I know he'd like it and—"

"That might not be a good idea." Sherry removed her white jacket and tossed it in the laundry hamper. She was finished for the day and eager to see Cody.

"I thought your friend Carrie was going to come by with you," she said.

"She couldn't. That's why I can't show you the way I want my hair cut."

"Oh, well. I'll see the magazine another time."

"Especially if you're going to stay around." Heather pressed her books against her as her eyes grew wistful. "I can hardly wait for you to move in with us."

"I didn't say I was moving in with you, Heather. Remember what Ellie told you at the picnic?"

Heather rolled her eyes in exasperation, as if reciting it for the hundredth time. "If I interfere with you and Dad, I could hurt more than help."

"You got it."

Before leaving the clinic, Sherry ran a brush through her hair and touched up her makeup. "You're sure Janey and your father are expecting me tonight?"

"Of course. Dad specifically said I should stop by today and invite you, but if you can't come, that's fine, too, 'cause Slim's in town and he can take me home."

The phone rang just then, and Sherry let Mrs. Colson answer it. The receptionist came back for Sherry.

"It's a nice-sounding man asking for you."

This surprised Sherry. The only "nice-sounding man" who interested her was Cody Bailman, but Mrs. Colson would have recognized his voice.

She walked into her office and picked up the receiver. "This is Sherry Waterman."

"Sherry, it's Rowdy Cassidy. I know it's short notice, but I was wondering if you could fly to Houston for dinner tonight?"

"Fly to Houston? Tonight?"

"It's Norah's birthday, and I'd love to surprise her."

"But there isn't a plane for me to catch, and it'd take you hours to fly to Pepper to get me."

"I'm here now, at the airstrip outside town."

"Here?"

"Yeah, I flew into Abilene this morning and I got to thinking on my way home that I should bring you back with me. I know it's a lot to ask, but it'd give Norah such a boost. She loves Texas, but after your visit, she got real homesick. It'd mean a lot to her if you'd come and help celebrate her birthday."

Sherry hesitated and looked at Heather, not wanting to disappoint Cody's daughter, either. "I need to be back by nine tomorrow morning."

"No problem. I can have one of my staff fly you back first thing. What do you say?"

"Uh…" Sherry wished she had more time to think this over. "Sure," she said finally. "Why not?" Norah was her best friend, and she missed her, too.

They made the arrangements to meet, and Sherry hung up. "You heard?" she asked Heather.

Heather lowered her head dejectedly.

"It's for a surprise birthday dinner. Norah's the reason I moved to Texas, and she'd do it for me. Besides, you said Slim can take you back to the ranch."

"Yeah, I know."

"How about if you stop by after school tomorrow?" Sherry asked, hating to disappoint Heather. "It'd be even better, wouldn't it, because Carrie might be able to come."

Heather nodded, but not with a lot of enthusiasm. "You're right. It's just that I was really looking forward to having you out at the ranch again. I think Dad was, too."

"There'll be plenty of other times, I promise. You'll explain to your father, won't you?"

Heather nodded. Sherry dropped her off at the feed store, where Slim's pickup was parked. She stayed long enough to be sure the older man was available to drive Heather to the ranch.

From there she drove to the landing strip. Rowdy was waiting for her, and after greetings and hugs, Sherry boarded his company jet and settled back in the cushioned seat.

"So how's Pepper been treating you?" Rowdy asked.

"Very well. I love Texas."

"Any progress with that cattleman?"

She smiled. "Some."

"Norah's going to be glad to hear that." He grinned with satisfaction. "She's going to be very surprised to see you, but even more surprised to see her father. He arrived earlier this afternoon. My driver picked him up at the airport and is giving him a quick tour of Houston and Galveston Island. If everything goes according to schedule, we should get to the house at about the same time."

"You thought all this up on your own?"

"Yep." He looked extremely proud of himself. "I talked to Norah's father a couple months back about flying out, but as I said, having you join us was a spur-of-the-moment idea. Norah's going to be thrilled."

To say that Norah was thrilled—or surprised—was putting it mildly. As Rowdy had predicted, David Bloomfield arrived within minutes of her and Rowdy. They'd waited in the driveway for him, and the three of them walked into the house together.

Rowdy stood in the entryway and, his eyes twinkling, called, "Norah, I'm home!"

Norah appeared and Rowdy threw open his arms. "Happy birthday!" he shouted and stepped aside to reveal David Bloomfield and Sherry, standing directly behind him.

"Daddy!" Norah cried, enthusiastically hugging her father first. "Sherry!" Norah wrapped both arms around her, eyes bright with tears.

"You thought I forgot your birthday, didn't you?" Rowdy crowed.

Norah wiped the tears from her face and nodded. "I really did. I had the most miserable day. The kids were both fussy, and I felt like I'd moved to the ends of the earth and *everyone* had forgotten me."

"This is a long way from Orchard Valley," her father said, putting his arm around his youngest daughter, "but it isn't the end of the earth—although I think I can see it from here."

Norah chuckled. "Oh, Dad, that's an old joke."

"You laughed, didn't you?"

"Come on in and make yourselves comfortable," Rowdy invited, ushering them into the living room. "I certainly hope you didn't go to any trouble for dinner," he said to Norah.

"No. I was feeling sorry for myself and thought we'd order pizza. It's been that kind of day."

"Good—" Rowdy paused and looked at his watch "—because the caterer should get here in about ten minutes."

Norah was floored. "Is there anything else I should know about?"

"This?" He removed a little velvet box from his pocket, then put it back. "Think I'll save that for later when we're alone."

David laughed and glanced around. "Now, where are those precious grandchildren of mine?"

"Sleeping. They're both exhausted. But if you promise to be quiet, I'll take you upstairs for a peek. How long are you staying? A week, I hope."

David and Sherry followed Norah upstairs and tiptoed into the children's rooms. Sherry was fond of David Bloomfield and loved watching his reaction as he looked at his grandchildren. Sherry remembered several years back, when David had suffered a heart attack and almost died. His recovery had been nothing short of miraculous.

By the time they came back downstairs, the caterer was there and the table had been set for an elegant dinner. The candles were lit, the appetizers served and champagne poured.

"Rowdy did this once before," Norah said, reaching for her husband's hand. Rowdy brought her fingers to his mouth and brushed his lips over them. "He wanted something from me then. Dinner was all part of a bribe to get me to leave Orchard Valley and be his private nurse."

Rowdy laughed. "It didn't work. Norah didn't believe I loved her, and I can't say I blame her, since I didn't know it myself. All I knew was that I couldn't imagine my life without her. You led me on quite a merry chase—but I wouldn't have had it any different."

"Are you trying to bribe my daughter this time?" David asked.

Rowdy shook his head. "Nope. I have everything I need."

The shrimp appetizer was followed by a heart-of-palm salad. Norah turned to Sherry. "How's everything going with you and Cody?"

Sherry shrugged, unsure how much she should say. "Better, I guess."

"I have to tell you, I got a kick out of your last e-mail. He actually proposed to you by saying he wanted to cut to the chase?"

"Sounds like a man who knows what he wants," Rowdy commented.

"Cody's come a long way since then. He's trying to understand what I want, but I don't think he's quite figured it out." She lowered her gaze and sighed. "Currently he's suffering from the effects of poison ivy. He ran into a patch of it while picking wildflowers for me."

"Well, as you say, he's certainly trying hard."

"I wish now I'd been more specific," Sherry said, smoothing her napkin. "I love Cody and I want romance, yes, but more than that, I want him to share himself with me, his thoughts and ideas, his dreams for the future. What worries him most is the fear that if he loves me he'll lose his identity. He says he isn't willing to let any woman put a collar around his neck."

"Sounds reasonable," David said.

"He's really a darling." Sherry wanted to be sure everyone understood her feelings.

"You love him?"

Sherry nodded. "I did almost from the first."

"Let me talk to him," Rowdy offered.

"It wouldn't do any good," Sherry said. "His best friend, who's happily married, already tried, and Cody just thinks Luke's lost his marbles."

"He'll feel differently once he's married himself."

"Didn't you tell me Cody has a twelve-year-old daughter?" Norah asked.

Sherry nodded. "I don't know a lot about his marriage, just enough to know they were both pretty immature. His wife was killed in a car accident years ago."

"And he's never thought about marrying again until now?" David inquired.

"Heather had a lot to do with his proposal, but—" She stopped, remembering how Cody had told her that the first time he'd asked her to marry him had been for Heather's sake, but now it was for his own. "With time, I believe he'll understand it isn't flowers that interest me or serenading me in the dead of night—it's trusting and sharing. It's a sense of belonging to each other."

"It's sitting up together with a sick baby," Norah murmured.

"And loving your partner enough to allow him to be himself," Rowdy continued. "And vice versa."

"And looking back over the years you were together, knowing they were the best ones of your life," David added thoughtfully.

Sherry hoped that eventually Cody would understand all of this. His mother had asked her to be patient, and Ellie had given her the same advice. It was difficult at times, but she held on to the promise of a future together.

Sherry left early the next morning. Norah walked out to the car with her, dressed in her robe, her eyes sleepy. "I wish you could stay longer."

"I do, too."

"If you ever want to get away for a weekend, let me know, and I'll have Rowdy send a plane for you."

"I will. And thank you."

The flight back to Pepper seemed to take only half the time the trip into Houston had. She glanced at her watch as she walked to her car, pleased to see she had plenty of time before she went on duty at the clinic.

Driving down Main Street, Sherry was struck once more by the welcome she felt in Pepper. It was as if this was her home and always would be. The sight of Cody's pickup in front of the clinic came as a surprise. She pulled around to the back of the building, parking in her appointed slot, and hurried inside.

Cody wasn't anywhere in sight. "Mrs. Colson," she asked, walking out to the reception area. "Have you seen Cody?"

"No, I was wondering that myself. His truck's here, but he doesn't seem to be around."

Stepping onto the porch, Sherry glanced around. A movement, ever so slight, from Cody's truck caught her eye. She ran down the walkway to discover Cody fast asleep in the cab.

"Cody," she called softly through the open window, not wanting to startle him. "What are you doing here?"

"Sherry?" He bolted upright, banging his head on the steering wheel. "Damn!" he muttered, rubbing the injured spot. He opened the door and nearly fell onto the street in his eagerness.

"Have you been drinking?" she demanded.

"No," he returned angrily. "Where the hell have you been all night?"

"With my friend in Houston," she told him, "although where I was or who I was with is none of your business."

"Some hotshot with a Learjet, from what I heard."

"Yes. As I understand it, Rowdy's a legend in the corporate world."

"I see." Cody slammed his hat onto his head. "What are you trying to do? Make me jealous?"

"Oh, for crying out loud, that's the stupidest thing you've ever said to me, Cody Bailman, and you've said some real doozies. Rowdy's married."

"So you're flying off with married men now?"

"Rowdy's married to my best friend, Norah. It was her birthday yesterday, and on his way home from Abilene, he decided to surprise Norah by bringing me back with him."

Cody frowned as if he didn't believe her. "That's not the story Heather gave me. She said I had to do something quick, because you were seeing another man."

Cody paced the sidewalk in front of her. "This is it, Sherry. I'm not willing to play any more games with you. I've done everything I can to prove to you I'm sincere, so if you want to run off with a married man at this point—"

"I didn't run off with a married man!" she said hotly. "For you to even suggest it is ridiculous."

"I spent the entire night sleeping in my pickup, waiting for you to get back, so if I happen to be a bit short-tempered, you can figure out why."

"Then maybe you should just go home and think this through before you start throwing accusations at me."

"Maybe I should," he growled.

Sherry was mortified to find out that they had an audience. Mrs. Colson was standing on the porch, enthralled with their conversation. The woman across the street, who'd been watering her roses, had long since lost interest in them and was inadvertently hosing down the sidewalk. Another couple rocking on their porch seemed to be enjoying the show, as well.

"I'm serious, Sherry. This is the last time I'm going to ask." Cody jerked open the truck door and leaped inside. "Are you going to marry me or not? Because I've had it."

"That proposal's about as romantic as the first one."

"Well, you know what I think of romance." He started the engine and ground the gears.

He'd just pulled away from the curb when she slammed her foot down on the pavement. "Yes, you idiot!" she screamed after him. "I'll marry you!"

Ten

"I don't think he heard you, dear," the lady watering the roses called out to her.

"I don't think he did, either," the older man on the porch agreed, standing up and walking to his gate to get a better look at Sherry.

"I can't believe he drove away," Mrs. Colson said. "That man's beside himself for want of you. Cody may be stubborn, but he isn't stupid. Mark my words, he'll come to his senses soon."

Sherry wasn't sure she wanted him to. He was too infuriating. Imagine—suggesting she was seeing a married man behind his back!

"Do you want me to phone Cody for you, dear, and explain?" Mrs. Colson suggested as Sherry marched up the steps and in the front door.

Sherry turned and glared angrily at the receptionist.

"It was only a suggestion," Mrs. Colson muttered.

"I can do my own talking."

"Of course," Mrs. Colson said pleasantly, clearly not offended by the reprimand. "I'm positive everything will work out between you and Cody. Don't give a moment's heed to what he said earlier. Everyone knows how stubborn he can be."

"I'm not the least bit positive about *anything* having to do with that man," Sherry returned. Cody had been telling her for weeks that this was her last opportunity to marry him, that he wasn't going to ask her again.

A half hour later, when Sherry came out of her office reading a file Doc Lindsey had left for her to review, she heard Mrs. Colson speaking quietly into the phone.

"I swear you've never seen anyone so angry in all your life as Cody Bailman was this morning," she said. "He just peeled out of here, and all because he's so crazy about—"

"Mrs. Colson," Sherry said.

The receptionist placed her hand over the receiver, but didn't even glance upward. "I'll be with you in a minute." She put the receiver to her ear again and continued, "And dear, dear Sherry. Why, she's so overwrought she can hardly—"

Suddenly Mrs. Colson froze, swallowed once, and then looked at Sherry. "Is there anything I can do for you?" she managed, her face flushing crimson.

"Yes," Sherry said. "You can stop gossiping about me."

"Oh, I was afraid of that. You've got the wrong impression. I never gossip—ask anyone. I *have* been known to pass on information, but I don't consider that gossiping." Abruptly she replaced the receiver.

Sherry scowled at the phone, wondering what the person on the other end was thinking.

"I was only trying to help," Mrs. Colson insisted. "Donna Jo's known Cody all his life and—"

"You were speaking to Donna Jo?" Sherry wondered how anyone got any work done in this town.

"Why, yes. Donna Jo's friends with Cody's mother, same as I am. She has a vested interest in what happens between you two. So do Mayor Bowie and the sheriff, and we both know those two spend a lot of time over at the Yellow Rose."

"What's my schedule like this morning?" Sherry asked wearily.

Mrs. Colson flipped through the pages of the appointment book. "Mrs. O'Leary's due at ten, but she's been coming to see Doc for the past three years for the same thing."

"What's her problem?"

Mrs. Colson sighed heavily. "Mrs. O'Leary's over seventy and, well, she wants a nose job. She's convinced she lost Earl Burrows because her nose was too big, and that was more'n fifty years ago."

"Didn't marry someone else?"

"Oh, yes. She married Larry O'Leary, but I don't think it was a happy union, although she bore him eight sons. Doc says it's the most ridiculous thing he's ever heard of, a woman getting her nose done at the age of seventy. When she comes in, he asks her to think about it for another six months. She's been coming back faithfully every six months for three years."

"If she sees me, I'll give her a referral. If she's that set on a new nose, then she should have it."

"I told Doris you'd feel that way—that's why I set the appointment up with you," Mrs. Colson said. She looked pleased with herself. "If you want, I can save Doris the trouble of coming in and give her the name of the referral."

"All right. I'll make a few calls and get back to you in a couple of minutes. Am I scheduled to see anyone else?"

"Not until this afternoon." The receptionist seemed almost gleeful at the news. "You're free to go for a long drive, if you like." She looked both ways, then added, "No one would blame you for slipping out for a few hours...."

Sherry wasn't sure if she was slipping out or flipping out. She made a couple of calls, gave Mrs. Colson the names of three plastic surgeons to pass on to her first patient of the day, then reached for her purse.

She was halfway to the door when it burst open and Donna Jo rushed in. "I'm so glad I caught you!" she said excitedly. "You poor, poor girl, you must be near crazy with worry."

"Worry?"

"About losing Cody. Now, you listen here, I've got some advice for you." She paused, inhaled deeply and pressed her hand to her generous bosom. "Sherry Waterman, fight for your man. You love him—folks in town have known that for weeks—and we're willing to forgive you for leaving in that fancy jet with that handsome cowboy. By the way, who *was* that?"

"Rowdy Cassidy, and before you say another word, I didn't leave with him like you're implying."

"We know that, dear."

"Rowdy Cassidy?" Martha Colson whispered. "Not *the* Rowdy Cassidy?"

"That's who she said," Donna Jo muttered irritably. "Now let her talk."

"There's nothing more to say." Sherry didn't want to spend what free time she had talking about her excursion of the night before, although both women were eager for details. "I'm going to do as you suggest and take a long drive this morning."

"Now you be sure to stop in at the café and let me know what happens once you're through talking to Cody," Donna Jo instructed.

"Who said I was going to talk to Cody?"

"You *are* going to him, aren't you?" Donna Jo said. "You have to. That poor boy's all thumbs when it comes to love and romance. Personally, I thought you did a smart thing, asking for a little romance first, but everyone agrees that it's time for you to put Cody out of his misery."

"He's suffered enough," Mrs. Colson added.

"Who would've believed Cody Bailman would be like this with a woman. I will say it took a mighty special one," Donna Jo concluded, winking at Sherry.

With half the town awaiting the outcome of her trip to Cody's ranch, Sherry hopped in her car and drove to the Lucky Horseshoe. Odds were he'd be out on the range somewhere, so she didn't know what good her visit would do. Nevertheless, she had to try.

She saw Cody almost immediately. He was working with a gelding in the corral when she arrived, leading him around the enclosed area. Several other men stood nearby, watching and talking among themselves.

Climbing out of her car, Sherry walked over to the fence and stood there for a few minutes, waiting for

Cody to notice her. He seemed preoccupied with his task, putting the gelding through his paces. Sherry was sure he knew she was there, and she was willing to be ignored for only so long.

Five of the slowest minutes of her life passed before she stepped onto the bottom rung of the fence and braced her arms on the top one.

"Cody!"

He turned to face her, his eyes blank.

This was much harder than Sherry had expected. On the drive out to his ranch, she'd envisioned Cody's eyes lighting up with pleasure at the sight of her. She'd imagined him hugging her, lifting her from the ground and swinging her around, his eyes filled with love and promises.

"Yes?" he said at last.

"When you drove away this morning, I... I didn't think you heard me," she said weakly.

Cody led the gelding over to one of his hands, removed his hat long enough to wipe his forehead, then strolled toward her as if he had all the time in the world.

Sherry found it impossible to sense what he thought, what he felt. He revealed no emotion.

"I...guess you're not ready to talk yet," Sherry said.

"You were the one who told me to go home."

"I know, but I was hoping you'd have thought things out by now and realized I'd never fool around with my best friend's husband." Or anyone else when she was so desperately in love with Cody. It seemed as if their evening with Christina Lynn and Philip had been forgotten.

"It was Rowdy Cassidy you left with, wasn't it?"

Sherry nodded.

"You certainly have friends in high places."

"It's Norah I know, not Rowdy."

"So you left on a moment's notice with a man who's virtually a stranger?"

Sherry closed her eyes and prayed for patience. "Would you stop being so stubborn! If you honestly believe I'm the type of woman who'd run around with a married man, then you don't know me at all!"

"*I'm* stubborn!" he exploded. "Do you realize what I've gone through because of you? I've been the butt of everyone's jokes for weeks. My reputation with the other ranchers is in shambles—and I'm still scratching." He removed his glove, rolled up a sleeve and scraped his fingernails across his forearm. "I've done everything I can to earn your love, and I'm done."

"That's the problem. You want my love, but you aren't willing to give me yours. It wasn't really romance I was looking for, Cody, it was *love.* I wanted you to care about me, enough that you'd be willing to do whatever it took to win my heart." She said the words seriously, earnestly. "You never understood that. From the very first, you've been looking for a shortcut, because you didn't want to be bothered. Well, guess what? No woman wants to be considered an annoyance."

"So that's what you think."

"What am I supposed to think with the things you've been saying?"

"That's just fine."

He turned away as if this was the end of their conversation, as if everything that needed to be said had been said. Sherry knew a brush-off when she saw one. Anything else she might say would fall on deaf ears.

She walked over to her car, climbed in and started the engine. She'd shifted into gear and begun to drive away when she changed her mind. Easing the car into Reverse, she pulled alongside the corral fence and stuck her head out the open window, intending to shout at him—but no words came.

She drove out of the yard, tires screeching. It'd been a mistake to try to reason with Cody. Her better judgment insisted she wait several days and let him cool down before she attempted to reopen communications. She should've listened to her own heart instead of Mrs. Colson's and Donna Jo's eagerly offered advice.

Sherry wasn't sure what made her look in her rearview mirror, but when she did, her breath jammed in her throat. Cody was riding bareback, chasing after her on the gelding he'd been working with minutes earlier. The horse was in full gallop, and Sherry was astonished that he managed to stay on.

She came to a stop, and so did the gelding. Cody slid off his back and jerked open her car door.

"Are you going to marry me or not?" he demanded. He was panting hard.

Sherry eyed him calmly. "Do you love me?"

"After everything I've been through, how can you ask me a question like that!" he snapped. "Yes, I love you. What does it take to convince you I mean it? Blood?"

"No," she whispered, biting her lower lip.

"I love you, Sherry Waterman," he said. "Would you do me the honor of becoming my wife?"

She nodded through her tears.

"Hot damn!" he shouted, then hauled Sherry into his

arms so fast her breath fled her lungs. A second later, his mouth was on hers.

His kiss left her trembling. "Cody..." she said, breaking away from him. "You maniac! You chased after my car on a horse just the way Luke came after Ellie, and you always said that was such a stupid thing to do."

He opened his mouth as though to deny it, but didn't say a word. He blinked, then smiled sheepishly. "So I did. Guess this is what love does to a man."

"Do you really love me?"

"Love you?" he cried. "Yes, Sherry, I love you."

"But you—"

"Don't even say it." He kissed her again, this kiss far less urgent, more...loving. After a few minutes he released her and said, "Let's go."

"Where?" she asked.

"Where else? A preacher. I'm not giving you the opportunity to change your mind."

She threw her arms around his neck again. "I'm not going to, not ever." It was Sherry who initiated the kissing this time, and when they finished, Cody was leaning against the side of her car. His eyes were closed and his breathing was labored. Then he reached for her again and swung her off the ground.

"Put me down," Sherry said. "I'm too heavy."

"No, you're not," Cody declared. "I'm calling the preacher right now and we'll get the license this afternoon."

"Cody," she said, "put me down!"

He finally did, then looked at her firmly. "I've waited ten long years for you, and I'm not putting this wedding off another day. If you want one of those big fancy shindigs, then…" He paused.

"A small ceremony is fine." She grinned.

"With a reception big enough to fill the state of Texas, if that's what you want."

"I want my family here."

"I'll have airplane tickets for them by noon."

"Cody, are we crazy?"

"Yes, for each other, and that's just how it's supposed to be. Luke told me that, and I didn't understand it until I met you." He grimaced comically. "Sherry Waterman, what took you so long?"

She stared at him and felt the laughter bubble up inside her. Flinging her arms around his neck, she kissed him soundly. "For the life of me I don't know."

Sherry returned to the office sometime later to find both Mrs. Colson and Donna Jo standing on the porch waiting for her.

Sherry greeted them as she strolled past.

"How'd it go with Cody?" Donna Jo asked urgently. The pair followed her into the clinic.

"Everything went fine," Sherry said. She couldn't help it; she enjoyed keeping them guessing.

"Fine?" Mrs. Colson repeated. She looked at Donna Jo. "What does *fine* tell us?"

"Nothing," the waitress responded. "I learned a long time ago not to listen to the words, but to study the expression. *Fine,* the way Sherry just said it, tells me there's going to be a wedding in Pepper soon."

"Isn't the lunch crowd at the café by now?" Sherry asked.

"Ellen can handle it," Donna Jo said, sitting in the closest chair.

"She's not wearing a diamond," Martha Colson pointed out.

"No diamond?" Donna Jo looked incredulous. "I was sure you'd come back sporting the biggest rock this side of Mexico."

"You mean one like this?" Sherry dug into her purse and pulled out the ring Cody had given her. She slipped it on her finger, feeling heady with joy and excitement. Mrs. Colson and Donna Jo screamed delightedly and Sherry hugged them both.

"When's the wedding?"

"Soon, just like you said," Sherry told them, her heart warming. She and Cody had called Sherry's family and made what arrangements they could over the phone. Afterward, Cody had given her the ring, one he'd been patiently carrying with him for weeks.

Sherry wasn't able to explain more. The door opened, and Heather let out a cry and vaulted into her arms.

"Who told you?" Sherry asked when she caught her breath. Cody had planned to pick up his daughter after school and bring her over to the clinic so they could tell her together.

"Dad," Heather explained. "He came by the school. Men are so funny—they can't keep a secret at all."

Cody walked into the clinic behind her, looking sheepish. "You don't mind, do you?"

"Of course not." Sherry hugged her soon-to-be daughter.

"Hey, I need a hug, too," Cody said, wrapping his arms around Sherry and holding her against him.

"Now *that's* romantic," Mrs. Colson sighed.

"I could just cry," Sherry heard Donna Jo say.

"How soon do you think it'll be before Sherry has a baby?" Heather whispered.

"A year," Mrs. Colson whispered back.

"A year?" Cody lifted his head. He smiled down at Sherry and winked. "I don't think it'll take nearly that long."

* * * * *

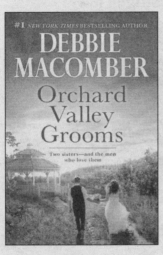

Join #1 *New York Times* bestselling author

DEBBIE MACOMBER

for the *Midnight Sons* series, where three
brothers head a campaign to bring women
to their small Alaskan town!

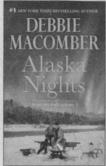

Collect them all!

"Debbie Macomber's *Midnight Sons* is a delightful
romantic saga. Each book is a powerful, engaging
story in its own right. Unforgettable!"
—#1 *New York Times* bestselling author
Linda Lael Miller

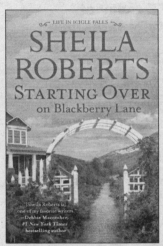

Get 2 Free Books,
Plus 2 Free Gifts -
just for trying the Reader Service!

DEBBIE MACOMBER

33019	ALASKA HOME	___ $7.99 U.S.	___ $9.99 CAN.
33018	ALASKA NIGHTS	___ $7.99 U.S.	___ $9.99 CAN.
33017	ALASKA SKIES	___ $7.99 U.S.	___ $9.99 CAN.
32988	OUT OF THE RAIN	___ $7.99 U.S.	___ $9.99 CAN.
32918	AN ENGAGEMENT IN SEATTLE	___ $7.99 U.S.	___ $9.99 CAN.
32798	ORCHARD VALLEY GROOMS	___ $7.99 U.S.	___ $9.99 CAN.
31894	ALWAYS DAKOTA	___ $7.99 U.S.	___ $9.99 CAN.
31888	DAKOTA HOME	___ $7.99 U.S.	___ $9.99 CAN.
31883	DAKOTA BORN	___ $7.99 U.S.	___ $9.99 CAN.
31838	THE MANNING SISTERS	___ $7.99 U.S.	___ $9.99 CAN.
31678	HOME IN SEATTLE	___ $7.99 U.S.	___ $8.99 CAN.
31645	TO LOVE AND PROTECT	___ $7.99 U.S.	___ $8.99 CAN.
31624	ON A CLEAR DAY	___ $7.99 U.S.	___ $8.99 CAN.
31598	NORTH TO ALASKA	___ $7.99 U.S.	___ $8.99 CAN.
31587	A MAN'S HEART	___ $7.99 U.S.	___ $8.99 CAN.
31580	MARRIAGE BETWEEN FRIENDS	___ $7.99 U.S.	___ $8.99 CAN.
31551	A REAL PRINCE	___ $7.99 U.S.	___ $8.99 CAN.
31457	HEART OF TEXAS VOLUME 3	___ $7.99 U.S.	___ $8.99 CAN.
31441	HEART OF TEXAS VOLUME 2	___ $7.99 U.S.	___ $8.99 CAN.
31426	HEART OF TEXAS VOLUME 1	___ $7.99 U.S.	___ $8.99 CAN.
31413	LOVE IN PLAIN SIGHT	___ $7.99 U.S.	___ $9.99 CAN.
31395	GLAD TIDINGS	___ $7.99 U.S.	___ $9.99 CAN.
31357	I LEFT MY HEART	___ $7.99 U.S.	___ $9.99 CAN.
31325	A TURN IN THE ROAD	___ $7.99 U.S.	___ $9.99 CAN.

(limited quantities available)

TOTAL AMOUNT	$ _____
POSTAGE & HANDLING	$ _____
($1.00 for 1 book, 50¢ for each additional)	
APPLICABLE TAXES*	$ _____
TOTAL PAYABLE	$ _____

(check or money order—please do not send cash)

To order, complete this form and send it, along with a check or money order for the total above, payable to MIRA Books, to: **In the U.S.:** 3010 Walden Avenue, P.O. Box 9077, Buffalo, NY 14269-9077; **In Canada:** P.O. Box 636, Fort Erie, Ontario, L2A 5X3.

Name: _____

Address: _____ City: _____

State/Prov.: _____ Zip/Postal Code: _____

Account Number (if applicable): _____

075 CSAS

*New York residents remit applicable sales taxes.
*Canadian residents remit applicable GST and provincial taxes.

MIRA®

MDM0517BL